The Stranger

KATE RIORDAN

PENGUIN BOOKS

PENGUIN BOOKS

UK | USA | Canada | Ireland | Australia
India | New Zealand | South Africa

Penguin Books is part of the Penguin Random House group of companies
whose addresses can be found at global.penguinrandomhouse.com

First published by Michael Joseph 2018
Published in Penguin Books 2018
001

Set in 12.15/14.45 pt Garamond MT
Typeset by Jouve (UK), Milton Keynes
Printed and bound in Great Britain by Clays Ltd, Elcograf S.p.A.

A CIP catalogue record for this book is available from the British Library

PAPERBACK ISBN: 978–1–405–92260–9

www.greenpenguin.co.uk

For my sister and brother,
Sarah and John Reardon,
with love.

'I am out with lanterns, looking for myself.'
– Emily Dickinson

PART ONE

In the hushed hours of deep night, the cove looks just as it did a few hundred years ago, when men gathered on its shore to lure unlucky ships on to the rocks. Some say if you're that way inclined, sensitive to the flimsiness of what separates then from now, you can still hear the groan of timber on rock, the pitiful cries from the decks. You can see the treacherous, bobbing lamps, and the surrender of white sails sinking beneath the waves.

The blackout has returned Breakheart Cove to the seventeenth century. The civilizing lights that usually shine from houses dotting the cliffs have been snuffed out by dense-woven fabric that takes an age to put up as dusk creeps in. At Penhallow Hall, thirty-three windows must be covered as the sun sets.

Further up the coast, the war is more in evidence. There are two new pillboxes along the cliff path beyond the village of Vennor – one disguised as a tiny cottage, complete with cheery curtains of blue gingham. Further on still, straining against its steel cables, is the bloated outline of a barrage balloon. But back at Breakheart Cove there are no rolls of barbed wire to keep out the enemy. This small breach of the coastline has been forgotten by the war machine swinging into action elsewhere.

Out at sea, a bell-topped buoy is caught by the rising swell and chimes mournfully. And, as if in reply, the church bell just around the headland at Vennor begins to toll. It hasn't been rung for nearly a year now, not since war was declared the previous September, and it's never been rung at night.

The sound comes to people first in their dreams, but it's too urgent to be absorbed into sleep for long. Along the coast and in the crooked, tightly packed lanes of Vennor, lights begin to go on. Teeth are put in, shoes are put on. Disbelief settles into fear. The invasion has begun. The Germans must be coming, they say to each other. The Germans must be here.

But wait. There's something strange on the beach at Breakheart Cove, where steep steps rise to the path above. As the storm clouds part briefly, the moon illuminates wax-pale limbs, awkwardly splayed. She doesn't move, not as the rain begins to fall on her open eyes, or as the sea foam creeps and spreads, darkening the sand as it edges closer. It pulls back with a reluctant sigh before it can reach her, but the next set of waves are more determined. The distant thunder rolls for a last time as the water finally lifts and takes her.

FIVE HOURS LATER

At dawn, in the deep silence of the boathouse, Rose is reading someone else's diary, her eyes moving fast across bold strokes that have bled into thick, creamy paper. The last entry was written yesterday, probably not long before the party guests began to arrive, forcing Penhallow out of its habitual solitude. The ink is only hours dry.

She closes the book with infinite care and stands on shaky legs. The last embers of her anger have been doused by clammy dread, like water filling the mouth of someone about to be sick.

'Oh, Diana,' she whispers. 'What have you done?' But she thinks she knows, even as she says the words.

Speaking aloud alters the weight of the air around her. The boathouse, silent again but for the creek water lapping beneath the floorboards, no longer feels empty. Her eyes flick to the armchair and, for an instant, she sees Diana curled there, safely asleep under one of the airmen's jackets. But when she blinks she's alone again, the charge gone out of the room.

She knows in her heart that Diana left last night, while the bomber's moon still silvered the garden and the wind beat the sea into mist against the rocks. After what had happened at the party, it wouldn't have taken much to lure Diana down to Breakheart Cove, she who can never resist the dark pull of danger.

I

SIX WEEKS EARLIER

Sunday, 9th June: Diana Devlin's diary

Starved as I am of any amusement, I begin this diary in desperation. I can think of nothing else to fill the endless hours. The quiet here is maddening. There is nothing but the sound of the sea hurling itself against the cliffs and the lonely cry of a gull. It makes one almost long for the air-raid siren.

I last kept a diary as a child, when time unwound as agonizingly slowly as it does here. I burnt that little book later, afraid someone would find it, but it was useful at the time. The accumulating words weighed me down when I felt I might float away or vanish into nothing. Perhaps they will have a similar effect here, where I increasingly find myself at the mirror, checking I haven't disappeared.

That I'm here at all is Mother's doing. Who else? I think a small part of her truly believes that exiling me to the

7

very ends of England will transform me into someone better, but most of her simply wanted me gone.

'For God's sake, why the bloody land girls?' I asked, when she first made the announcement. 'Anything but them, with their fawn breeches and chilblains. Can you honestly see me mucking out stables and yanking at udders? Aren't the Wrens rather more my speed?'

She smiled then, small eyes glittering, and I realized the old girl still had some fight left in her. The Women's Land Army was a stroke of genius; she'd signed me up for the only war work guaranteed to be posted outside London.

I believe she dreamt up the scheme from her darkened bedroom, a damp flannel pressed to her forehead as the sirens began to echo through the streets and people turned their faces apprehensively upward. I imagine she didn't even wait for the all-clear before she began the letter sealing my fate.

It was prescient timing, I'll say that for her. That same afternoon, Jack Beresford had persuaded me down into the cellar of his family's enormous, dust-sheeted house, which had been abandoned for the duration, the decent art and furniture dispatched to the country. Jack had looked so suave in his RAF uniform when he called, wings and signet ring glinting in the sun, that the subsequent fumbling and apologies among the wine and cobwebs were all the more dispiriting.

Jack's dead now, poor old thing, lost somewhere beneath the frigid waves of the North Sea. My first kiss, and he no longer exists. When I heard, I wished I'd been a little more generous – let him do what he wanted. He was better than most of them.

Mother turned scarlet when she caught me coming in

from seeing him that last time. She might be as blind as a bat but she has the nose of a bloodhound. She said I reeked of drink, but I think what she could really smell, what terrified her enough to send me packing, was Men with a capital M. Or perhaps Lust. Either will have terrified her.

Still, she's won this latest battle. Her last words, just before she slammed the door of the cab taking me to Paddington? 'Diana, you'll find that war, like death, is a great leveller.' I tried to reflect on this rare pearl of wisdom while waiting on the platform for my train, head held high while everyone else was kissed and wept over, but all I could think was that it would never have occurred to her to pack me some sandwiches.

So here I find myself, banished to deepest, dreariest Cornwall, home of mead and piskies, where the locals glare and mutter under their breath when you encounter them in the lanes, and a round of sea shanties in the Mermaid passes for entertainment.

My billet is no less strange, though admittedly more civilized. I appreciate I've got off lightly with Penhallow Hall. I might have been sent to some Cold Comfort Farm sunk in mud and misery, where dull-eyed farm boys would have tried to mount me in the woodshed. Instead, I take my meals among the polished rosewood and silver of the formal dining room and sleep on a feather bed. There's electricity and hot water. We don't have to rise at dawn to plough fields or catch rats. The work is mostly weeding, planting vegetables and pruning. Even I can manage that.

And yet . . . There's something of the subtle nightmare about this house – where everything seems in order but still you're compelled to dart from room to room, certain

9

that grief and menace lurk somewhere, if only you keep looking. Our troubled host, Eleanor Grenville, seems perpetually on the verge of tears. Even on the good days she has the ground-down air of someone smiling bravely through exquisite suffering. It's impossible to approach her without giving fright, however much throat-clearing one does.

The source of this internal horror may have something to do with her redoubtable mother, whose great age and confinement to an invalid's chair have not diminished her iron grip on the place. One of the things I'll remember about Penhallow is the unrelenting thud of her cane on the floor whenever she demands attendance. Some nights that sound reverberates along the hallways of my dreams, beating out a rhythm as I try to find my way out.

I do have some company. There's another girl here and room for one more. I say girl: Rose is hardly that at thirty-two. In truth, I haven't quite pinned her down yet. She fancies herself as something of an artist, with her sketchbook and wild hair, but in his photograph, her husband couldn't look more ordinary. Frank is somewhere in the Atlantic with the navy but before the war he managed Rose's father's shop. Yesterday, I asked her if she was looking forward to going back one day and she gave me such an odd look. I think she secretly dreams of staying in Cornwall, scraping together the rent on a tiny cottage by selling sweet little watercolours. Rose never has a bad word to say about anyone but I've seen her face in unguarded moments.

The gong has just sounded for dinner, so I must rouse myself to go down. The insistence on this tradition is laughable. It's as if we were carefree young things at a house party in 1928, dressed in our beaded finest and waving our crystal saucers at the butler for more Pol Roger. Instead, we have a scraping of butter to last a week and mud under our nails. At dinner, we have Eleanor trailing off in the middle of a sentence and Rose worrying whether she's holding her knife correctly.

The gong-basher is Payne, Penhallow's sepulchral retainer. A woman who makes Mrs Danvers seem jaunty. She appears both ancient and child-like (albeit a child in mourning), her poker-straight grey hair held back with a black velvet ribbon and her feet in house slippers, which allow her to creep silently about. The combination is disconcerting, to say the least.

She's been clutching her breast and dropping glasses ever since rumours began circulating about a Canadian airbase being built nearby. On the day she found out she was apoplectic, eyes bulging and hands trembling at the thought of all the brawling, drinking and pillaging that would ensue.

I can't think of anything better than a bit of life in this cut-off place. I'm under no illusion that a Canadian airman will sweep in and save me, or indeed be any more adept at seduction than poor Jack Beresford. I just like it when things are shaken up. One good thing about this dreary war is that it encourages people to break the rules. To do extraordinary things they would never dare contemplate ordinarily. I welcome the thought of that. When one is as hopelessly bored as I am, one relishes a bit of danger. It takes one's mind off oneself. And that's always a relief.

II

Rose shields her eyes against the lowering sun. Another perfect day – there's been no end to them lately. Below her, the sea is cobalt where the water is deep, and a brilliant, unlikely turquoise close to shore. Here and there, as the water shifts and the sun strikes it, the blue is shot through with blinding gold.

She stretches out her bare arms and allows the letter she's been reading to fall to the grass. A warm breeze makes the flimsy sheet turn over a couple of times but she doesn't try to retrieve it, her heart beating faster as it's teased closer to the cliff edge. Suddenly the cheap paper lifts and is caught, spiralling up and up before the inevitable, fluttering drop to the rocks below.

On the cliff path back towards Penhallow Hall, she can't help running like a girl half her age. She's not sure if she's running from something or to it. She passes the steep steps down to the cove where the letter will have landed, wondering if it's already been snatched by the incoming tide, the paper turning to pulp, the ink run into meaningless blotches.

She comes to a halt under the giant pine at the edge of the broad lawn sweeping around the front of Penhallow Hall. She always stops here after she's been for one of her weekend walks – it's become something of a routine since her arrival a month earlier.

The Hall behind her is a handsome, sprawling house of stuccoed stone, whose lines have been softened by winter storms and the sea salt carried in the air. It's Georgian for the most part, with the inevitable Victorian frills. Marooned by lush, moderately famous gardens, it is grand yet mellow, like a peer dozing in his slippers.

The view from the pine is spectacular. To the east, along the coast-path, is Breakheart Cove and, further on, the village of Vennor with its deep harbour. To the west is the narrow mouth of Blackbottle Creek. Two different Cornwalls, depending which way you look. Wild and sea-lashed in one direction, secret and tree-shadowed in the other, the overhanging boughs of glossy laurel concealing a twisting creek, whose water lies mirror-still. She loves both. She's loved this place since the summer she came here as a young girl.

'Oh, here you are.' The voice, now familiar, is low and languorous. 'I was beginning to wonder if you'd been bundled away by a German spy. According to Cook, they're lurking in nuns' habits behind every other rock.'

Rose shakes her head, unable to think of a witty rejoinder. She's often tongue-tied in front of Diana, who now stands before her, a vision in a poppy-coloured dress. Her platinum hair is held back with matching combs, all except the single, waving lock that always falls over one of her knowing eyes until she flicks it away. She's not wearing stockings but she doesn't need them, her legs smooth and bronzed from rolling up the corduroy breeches of the uniform she so despises, and changes out of the minute she's finished work for the day. Secretly, Rose is proud of hers, and what it signifies. Not only her contribution to the war but her independence – her new existence outside the house she and Frank share in the Midlands.

'What have you done with your drawing things?' Diana asks. She smiles indulgently, as if Rose were not the elder of the pair by more than a decade but a forgetful child. 'You had your sketchbook with you when you left, didn't you?'

Rose looks down at her empty hands. Diana always notices these things. 'Oh, how stupid. I've left them up on the cliff. I'll have to go back.'

'And your letter from Frank. Did you leave that too?' Diana smiles again, showing her very white teeth. They're not perfect, the incisors too pointed, but this small flaw only seems to heighten the rest of her beauty. 'Oh dear, I do hope it won't have blown away.'

Rose looks at her sharply. She's sure she was alone up there.

'Shall I come with you?' says Diana. The pale waves of her hair glint in the sun.

'No.' Rose shakes her head again. 'But thanks. It won't take me long, and you don't want to scuff your lovely shoes.'

She hurries away, conscious that Diana is watching her go. She wonders, as she has many times, if she has been found out and written about in Diana's diary. Sometimes, when they're curled up in the sitting room the Grenvilles have given over to their use, Diana reads out selected passages. Always entertaining, they're occasionally rather cruel: she has a knack for describing people with wincing accuracy. She's an excellent mimic, too, and Rose often finds herself helpless with laughter as Diana re-enacts an encounter with Blewett the gardener or dour-faced Payne. She knows that Diana decided they would be friends, rather than it having been a mutual cleaving towards each other, but she doesn't mind. It's flattering and, besides, Diana can be excellent company.

Rose's sketchbook is exactly where she left it on the grass. Though she doesn't run back as before, she can't help stopping at the pine again. There's no sign of Diana now. Across the mouth of the creek she can just make out the house she once stayed in, all those summers ago. Not even a quarter of the size of Penhallow Hall, it's a neat, four-square house built in the middle of the last century for a little-known landscape artist. It's hard to see from where she stands, but its carved wooden porch and window frames are painted a dark ivy-green – or, at least, they were when she was there.

She hadn't realized at first that she could see it from the Hall. It wasn't until her third day that she looked over and, spying it there, neat and white against its small sloping garden, felt her stomach pitch with long-buried recognition. It was Chyandour, 'house by the sea'. She hadn't realized it was so close to where she'd been billeted; she'd hardly ventured to the village yet, and they'd taken down all the road-signs, turning the narrow, high-hedged country lanes into a maze for those who didn't know them. Which was the idea, of course.

She was sixteen when she'd spent the summer holidays there. And then, just a few weeks after they'd returned home, everything had changed irrevocably. For months afterwards, she had fingered her mother's possessions – the green enamel brush and mirror, the cameo brooch, the old cotton pinny that always hung on the back of the kitchen door, soft and colourless from so many washes – shocked each time that she had really abandoned them. When, without warning, her father had finally cleared everything out, Rose didn't know which was worse: the previous sense that her mother might be in the next room, or her total erasure. When she had surfaced from the worst of her misery, she found that she had also lost that summer in Cornwall, which had slipped into a past as unreachable as it was golden.

Rose watches now as the sun slips a little further and is caught in the window glass of Chyandour, setting each one alight. She's too far away to see if tape crisscrosses the windows. Perhaps the place is empty and abandoned, with no one to care if the glass blows in once the Germans start bombing. Perhaps, she thinks, no one has set foot inside since she ran back in for one last look in 1924, her father calling after her that they'd miss their train.

'Oh, let her go, Bill,' she'd heard her mother say. 'She needs to say goodbye.'

'It's a house. What's she got to say goodbye to it for?'

So that the charwoman due later would think the Careys a nice, respectable family, her mother had scrubbed the house to within an inch of its life. The kitchen table, scoured and denuded of its clutter – newspapers, Rose's books and the fiddly bits from her brother Charlie's model plane kits – was cleaner than when they'd arrived a month earlier. Then it had been just a table, a kitchen, a house. Now it was a beloved place.

Rose had wished she had time to run her hand over every object and learn by heart the view from every window. But her mother had promised they'd come back the following year so the regret Rose had left with was bittersweet and delicious – next summer dazzling on the horizon to sustain her for the months in between. She truly hadn't any inkling that her family, still visibly intact, was about to shatter into pieces, or that the boy would never write. If she had sensed either, she would have barricaded herself inside Chyandour and refused to leave at all.

Now, under the feathery shadow of the pine, she turns away from that vanished summer and looks instead at her wartime billet. She's just deciding what colour the dying sun is turning the house's walls, and whether she'd be able to mix the exact shade using the paints she'd brought with her, when she sees movement at an upstairs window. The sash goes up and a head appears.

'It's only me,' calls Diana. Her colours are bright against the muted house. 'What are you looking at so intently?'

'Just the Hall. It looks so pretty in this light.'

'No, not the Hall, Rosie Wright. Before, when you were looking over there.'

Rose blushes, hoping she's far enough away for Diana not to notice. No one has called her Rosie in years. No one has called her Rosie since that summer. It rears up again, closer but still out of reach.

'Are you coming up, then, Dilly Dream?' Diana's persistent tone brings her back to the present, to the Hall and its emerald lawn, rolled smoothly under her feet. 'I've got Al Bowlly on.'

She ducks back under the sash. Rose can hear it now;

Diana must have turned the gramophone round so the horn is facing the window. She can't make out the words over the distant boom of the sea against the rocks, but it's something sentimental in a minor key. She can feel it tug at her, melancholy and regretful.

'Daddy sent me five new records, a ten-shilling note and a decent fruit cake.' Diana is back and leaning out dangerously. 'He's obviously still feeling guilty for letting Mother banish me here.' She flashes a brilliant smile at Rose, who does her best to return it, though she'd rather be alone with the memories that pull at her more and more insistently.

'Come *on*,' says Diana, plaintively. 'I'm fed up of being on my own. I thought we could have a little party up here. Dance around until we're exhausted, then tell each other our worst secrets.'

She finds Diana in the girls' sitting room. The larger room next door is now a dormitory of sorts, with three single beds, a cabinet for each, a couple of drying rails, a cluttered dressing-table and an enormous mahogany wardrobe. None of the furniture matches, gathered as it has been from rooms above and below stairs.

When Rose arrived, earlier than Diana, she had left the best bed, which was not only next to the window but a foot wider than the other two. Diana, when she turned up the next day, took in the room with a single glance and went straight over to claim it. 'Awfully good of you not to take this one,' she said. 'You don't mind if I do, do you?' She hadn't waited for Rose's reply, dropping her coat, hat and gas-mask to the floor and launching herself on to the bed with her shoes still on.

Both the dormitory and the sitting room are on the east side of the house, which faces the open sea and apparently gets the brunt of the wind and spray in winter. 'Oh, joy,' Diana said, when Blewett told them. 'We have all that to look forward to.' The window frames require attention every other year, apparently, the salt eating away first at the paint and then the tender wood underneath.

By now, Al Bowlly has given way to something faster and jazzier.

'Glenn Miller,' Diana announces, when she sees Rose at the door. 'I hope the Americans get a move on and join the war. They'll liven things up no end. By the way, did you see any sign of her?'

'Who?'

'A stranger is to be thrust into our midst.' She has turned back to the gramophone, where she's sorting through the new records.

'What sort of stranger?'

'Our third land girl, of course. I heard Cook talking but only caught the end of it.'

The new arrival comes late, just as they are getting ready for bed. She glances around without a smile, then strides over to the unoccupied bed, between Rose's and Diana's.

'I suppose this is mine.' Her voice is clipped and short, her mouth hardly opening as she speaks. Cut-glass, Rose's father would say admiringly of the new girl's accent. It's sharper than Diana's languid tones.

'You can always have mine if you'd prefer the window,' says Diana, going over.

The girl shakes her head, the ends of her black, unfashionably short hair flying into her eyes so that she has to tuck it behind her ears. She does it without fuss, with none of the feminine flicking Diana employs. She reminds Rose of a boy, or perhaps a dog, shaking itself off after a dip in the sea. 'No, thanks,' she says bluntly. 'This one will do.'

No one has exchanged names yet, so Rose goes forward, her hand out. 'I'm Rose Wright.'

The new girl shakes it briskly, without quite meeting her eye. 'Jane,' she says. 'How do you do?'

It occurs to Rose that she isn't being unfriendly. She's only shy and trying desperately not to show it. After Diana has introduced herself, an awkward silence descends. Rose wonders if this will pass, or if the status quo she and Diana have established will have to shift to accommodate the new girl.

Her gaze falls on Diana, who has turned off the lamp so she can perch on the sill with the window open and the blackout curtains pushed back. Her silk pyjamas ripple in the breeze and her cigarette smoke blows straight back into the room, making the new girl frown. It's a mild night but there's something about the way the moon carves a cold path towards them across the sea that makes Rose shiver with apprehension.

Diana catches her eye and winks. 'And then there were three,' she says.

* * *

Wednesday, 12th June

Spent an awful day removing stones the size of my head from the new beetroot bed. Every fingernail is now torn and jagged. I'm starving but Cook says that, according to the butcher's boy, there is no bacon to be had south of the Tamar. And, sure enough, it's horrid pilchards again tonight – the stink of them has been curling up the stairs and under the door for ages.

I bet the Germans aren't eating such dull fare as us. Is all this sacrifice really worth it? Perhaps an invasion wouldn't be so bad. They say Hitler admires the British spirit. I offered this up at dinner, hoping to raise a smile, but Eleanor was staring off into the middle distance, plate untouched, and Rose looked vaguely scandalized. Why I expected to find a kindred spirit in a Midlands shop girl is anyone's guess.

Still no letter from Mother. I can't pretend to be surprised but even Daddy managed to send those records and he was never much of a correspondent. I'm a fool for looking expectantly at the pile of post on the breakfast table every morning. It was just the same at school.

I keep forgetting: Italy has declared war on us. I suppose they had to declare it or we mightn't have noticed. Ha-ha. In other, more significant news, our small party of land girls has a new and final recruit: Jane Fox. Words have doubtless been had at the highest levels to get her here because she's Eleanor's niece. Presumably it would not have done for any Grenville relations to get their hands too dirty.

In fairness, Jane herself has clearly had no part in these machinations. In fact, she appears to be brooding because she hasn't been sent to some Yorkshire hill farm to *suffer*. She didn't even tell us who she was the first night, so I think she'd been hoping to keep it dark for a while. As it was, Blewett betrayed her immediately the next morning, beaming and tugging his forelock and calling her 'Miss Jane' when we went out after breakfast.

She reminds one of an ill-tempered boy. She has no shape to speak of and simply goes up and down like an ironing board. Her hair recalls Joan of Arc's: extremely short and apparently hacked off with a blunt broadsword. No doubt this is what she's actually done (though perhaps with scissors). Her aunt Eleanor is a true English rose: all faded blue eyes and hair the colour of weak tea. Next to her, Jane looks like an irritable gypsy. You would never suspect they were related in a thousand years.

I've moved to the dorm to continue this because of the racket from the wireless. Jane is in there with Rose, listening avidly. I was so intrigued to set eyes on our new girl it didn't occur to me that things might change now she's here, ensconced in the middle bed. In my opinion, little Miss Fox should have her own bedroom in the same part of the house as her grandmother and aunt. That she hasn't strikes me as odd, and not a little contrived. Do they want her here or not? And if they don't, then why pull the strings in the first place?

All I've managed to ascertain about Jane is that her

fingernails are bitten to the quick and she has twin sisters, younger than her; there's a framed picture of them on the piano downstairs. They're all blinding sunlight to Jane's shade – and with their flaxen hair and piercing blue eyes they put one in mind of the *Hitlerjugend*. I can easily imagine the pair of them singing lustily as they march through an Austrian meadow, a scowling Jane bringing up the rear. I tried to quiz her about them and the parents again today but she wouldn't be drawn. Said she needed to concentrate on her double-digging. Even if she wasn't a Fox she would be Blewett's pet. She works like a Trojan.

'She's shown you a thing or two already, ha'nt she, Miss Devlin?' he crowed today, amusing himself enormously.

I took revenge later by telling him the curse had arrived with a vengeance. He couldn't pack me off inside quick enough, face scarlet. It was then that I caught Eleanor acting oddly for the second time today. She was in one of the downstairs rooms that's been dust-sheeted for the war; she didn't see me. I only noticed her because of the dark colour of her dress against the white – another of the dated, ill-fitting frocks she seems to favour. I watched for a good minute, but she just stood there unmoving, as though some enchantment had turned her to stone.

The first time was this morning, when I sneaked inside for my cigarettes. She was hovering in the passage outside our room, where she has no business being. She cried out in shock when I came up behind her, then scurried off, muttering about lost dogs, a hunted look on her face. Awkward was the least of it. There is something melancholic about her that makes my skin prickle. Cook tells me she hasn't left the grounds in *years*.

III

Eleanor makes sure the girls are all outside at their work before she goes to their bedroom, her bull terrier Brick at her heels. She doesn't want anyone to catch her up here again.

Though they abandoned it for the garden hours ago, vestiges of the girls' various scents hang in the air, each as different as the girls themselves. The sweet bergamot and vanilla of Diana's perfume is strongest, fittingly, but Eleanor can also discern Rose's attar of roses, a family joke on her name that has become a tradition, apparently. It suits her, though: that blend of clean and sensuous.

She goes over to the dressing-table. It's strewn with creams and hairpins and rollers. She replaces the fan-shaped blue stopper on what must be Diana's bottle of Shalimar, then clicks open and shut an enamel compact shaped like a shell.

She wonders if any of the cosmetics or potions belong to Jane. She doesn't think so. Jane is years away from bothering with make-up and scent. Eleanor picks up a battered old hairbrush and pulls a couple of black hairs from its bristles. This must be Jane's. She feels a rush of love for the girl, who is not only becoming aware of her looks for the first time but is already dissatisfied with them. She lets the hairs fall and the sun, streaming in through the windows where the blackout curtains have been hastily pushed back, burns them rust-red as they drift down.

Though the day's light has been admitted, no one has opened the windows to air the room. The climbing sun has made it stuffy. She goes over to lift the first sash and stops, her hand frozen on the catch. Brick nudges her leg and she puts out a hand to stroke his warm, bulky head. She knows how this room can affect her, even after all this time. It's why she hardly ever comes here.

Though she's been trying to visit the room for a while, it now takes an effort of will not to leave it, banging the door shut behind her and retreating to another part of the house, where the memories don't whisper so loudly. She manages it, though, by counting aloud to fifty, then pushing up the sash, the rush of sea air steadying her. She forces herself to walk to the other window and do the same. It's just a room, she tells herself. But even as she repeats the words, she's recognizing every knot of wood showing through the window's paintwork, every join in the faded rosebud wallpaper, every warp in the glass that smears together the different blues of the sea beyond.

The water is peaceable today, a sheet of thick coloured glass. And she, somewhat unbelievably, is no longer a girl but a woman of thirty-four. She closes her eyes, trying to grasp hold of the years when she loved this room. When everything was before her and there was time enough for anything. But they are already trickling in, those other memories. The claustrophobia, the helplessness, the white-hot fury she felt – and still feels – for how things had to be. For how things still are.

'Of course you would try to blame me for your wilful-ness and lack of judgement,' her mother had said, from the faded patch of carpet that is still there, by the door. Her voice had shaken. 'Perhaps you might look to yourself, and to your late father for encouraging your hedonism and spoiling you so thoroughly, for allowing you to think that you could do what you liked, and hang the consequences. What a little fool you are, Eleanor. And now we must all pay the price for it.'

It was her mother who had found Gerald to marry her. He wasn't from Cornwall – he didn't know anyone in their part of the world, which was precisely why he'd been recruited for the job. And, to his credit, he didn't much care about the rumours when they'd eventually reached his ears. He was thirty-eight to her nineteen when they met; he'd lived her life twice over, a bachelor who had seen something of the world during his years in the army, mak-ing him relatively unshockable. He was kind to her and made her feel safer when she had been afraid for quite some time. Perhaps she doesn't love him in the all-consuming way she'd once assumed she would love a husband, but she respects and values and likes him a great deal. There is much to be said for that.

After they were married, Gerald suggested they go and live in Buckinghamshire, in the solid suburban house he had bought after he left the army and took up his White-hall post. It would have allowed her to escape her mother.

But in the end she couldn't leave Penhallow. The place is woven into her, just as she is bound to it. Fortunately, Gerald was happy to sell his house and take a flat in London, where he stays during the week. Where he stays almost all the time now, and has done since war broke out.

She tests herself most days, just as she promised Gerald she would: going to the coast-path gate and taking hold of the cold iron handle to lift the latch. But it's always the same until she turns back. The racing heart, the constriction of her lungs, the churning of her stomach. By tiny increments, her beloved home has become a cage. She doesn't even know precisely when the door was fastened shut.

Thinking about everything makes the dread stir inside her so she makes herself breathe slowly, as Gerald has taught her, not from the top of her lungs but deeper, from the diaphragm. When she feels steady again, she opens her eyes. If she can only train herself to feel inured to her old bedroom, she will have reclaimed a little more of the world.

The sound of laughter in the garden makes her turn back towards the window. It will probably be Diana, who is so ebullient and full of energy that Eleanor is quite cowed by her. She and Rose have breathed some life back into the house these past weeks, and although the lightened atmosphere reminds her painfully of the days before everything went wrong, it's a pain seamed with happiness on good days, when the full sun is shining on them. And there has been so much sunshine lately. It seems almost obscene, given what is going on across the water in France. Rose had said at dinner one night that the weather made the war almost impossible to believe in, and the words had resonated with Eleanor.

During the last months that this was still her room, she can hardly remember any sunshine, just the heave of a dishwater-grey sea as time slipped loose from its moorings. How she had longed for the return of summer then, when she would be able to go outside again. She dreamt of it some nights: soft, gold-lit afternoons, the treacly air alive with birdsong and bees; long shadows on velvet grass and a jewel-bright sea beyond. Waking was pure torture, when she would have to remember again all that was lost to her.

A noise in the hall outside brings Eleanor sharply back to the present. She's almost at the door when it's flung open to reveal Diana. Brick ambles over to greet her.

'Mrs Grenville, we meet again,' she says. Her green eyes sparkle. 'I do hope this is not a surprise dormitory inspection. My things are in a fearful mess.'

Eleanor flushes. 'Goodness, no. It's your room. I –' She realizes the girl is making light of her trespass and stops.

'Were you looking for something in particular?'

'No. I – It was Brick here. Do you remember, I was looking for him yesterday too? The naughty boy will keep wandering off.' She pats him and laughs, the sound horribly artificial. Flailing desperately for a topic of conversation, she gestures at the window. 'This was my room once, you know.'

Diana appraises her thoughtfully as she ties a headscarf around her pale hair. 'Is that so? Well, it must have been a jolly nice one. Lots of happy memories and all that. Thank you for giving it to us.'

'Oh, well, I haven't used it since I was young. I've hardly been inside since.' She smiles weakly.

Diana pauses, then returns the smile, which is one of her most dazzling. She seems to be able to switch them on like a lamp. 'Right, I must dash or Blewett will strangle me. I always forget something.'

After she's gone, Eleanor feels wrung out. She returns to her old station by the window, and her hands are unsteady as she presses them to the glass. Below her, the gate to the coast-path seems to mock her. She won't even try today; she knows now that there's no point. As the room around her lapses back into silence, the past sweeps over her again.

* * *

THIRTY-FIVE DAYS LEFT

Saturday, 15th June

A mildly interesting day in the end, after long, tedious hours of Jane showing up everyone else in the potato patch. She set about it like a thing possessed, while Rose tried desperately to keep up with her and I stood around smoking the cigarettes I'd cadged from the grocer's boy, who is so madly in love with me he can't speak in my presence, and only squeaks and mumbles until I wave him on.

A paltry dinner of pilchards AGAIN was hardly going

to improve matters but things looked up once I was able to have a cool bath, put on a clean dress and make for Vennor. It's hardly Positano, but we have to take what we can get here in the way of amusement. And for me, these days, that's seeing how long the butcher's queue is and trying to spot a Canadian airman.

En route to the village, however, there was a small diversion, in both senses of the word. I was passing above Breakheart Cove and it looked so tempting down there, the water clear and turquoise, that I thought I'd go down and see if it was safe for bathing.

When the tide's out, the small beach is shaped like a pail. I felt as if I was the first to disturb it in years. It's the sort of place where you feel anything could happen because no one would ever know, so high and enclosing are the walls of rock that shelter it. Once upon a time, I've no doubt it was just the spot for pirates fleeing the law or rivals duelling in the dawn mist. I was just imagining what I'd do if I was visited by the empty-eyed ghost of a ship-wrecked child when something moved over by the rocks and I almost screamed.

Fortunately, it was Jane and she looked corporeal enough. I was so relieved I didn't immediately absorb what she was doing, which was setting about a large rock with a piece of driftwood. As she brought it down, grunting with the effort, splinters of wood flew in all directions. She was so intent on her work that she didn't hear my approach and I hesitated then, wondering if I should simply slope off. I felt as if I'd caught her without any clothes on. But curiosity got the better of me, a sentiment that may end up carved on my gravestone.

'Preparing for the Nazi invader, are we?' I called, reasoning there was nothing I could do or say that wouldn't make her jump out of her skin.

She spun round, hair flying, the driftwood braced like a weapon. 'What are you doing here?' she cried, black eyes flashing. 'This is a private place.'

'Is it?' I said. 'Does it belong to the Hall, then?'

She floundered. 'Well, it did once, I think. But I didn't mean it like that.'

'You meant that it's your private place.'

She dropped the wood, cheeks scarlet. 'I suppose.'

'What are you so furious about anyway?'

That turned her belligerent again. 'None of your business.'

'Oh, go on, do tell,' I said, sidling closer. 'Perhaps I can help you. Surely you haven't fallen out with Blewett.'

'Not him.'

'Who, then?'

She eyed me warily, like a stray dog considering food in a stranger's hand. 'It's just my grandmother,' she said eventually.

'What about her?'

'It's nothing new. She simply wishes I'd never come.' She smiled bitterly.

I picked up the driftwood and scratched a big D in the sand. 'I'm sure that's not true,' I said casually. 'Is it?'

'You sound like Aunt Eleanor. She always says I'm mistaken, that Grandmother is just old and difficult, but I know she hates me. She always has. She whispered something to me once, when I was small, and I . . .' She tailed off, and when she looked at me, she seemed very young.

'What did she say?'

31

'It doesn't matter. I don't know why I said that.' She brushed herself down and turned to go. 'I'm going back to the Hall now,' she said stiffly. 'Goodbye.'

And off she went, her narrow back ramrod straight as she climbed the steps to the path.

I sat down to consider all this among the shells and sea-weed for a while, but the tide was still coming in and the wind was getting up, making a peculiar sound as it whistled around inside a narrow little cave I hadn't noticed before. It was enough to raise anyone's hackles and I was soon scrambling up the steps to the coast-path, breathing hard.

So that was a strange little interlude. I haven't been able to catch Jane's eye since. The only other thing of note I should probably set down for posterity is that Paris has fallen, with the rest of France certain to follow. This means that the Bore War ought to get considerably more interesting. Everyone has been droning on about it all day, quite as if it's the end of the world, which I suppose it might be. If Cook is to be believed, the Germans should be with us by teatime tomorrow.

I say let them come, if they're so determined. What difference will any of it make to me? I will still be stuck down here, squandering my golden youth digging onions. When Rose and Jane were listening to the Home Service earlier, faces pale and drawn, I desperately tried to muster some anxiety, but even imagining Nazi banners draped from the windows of Buckingham Palace left me curiously unmoved. London and the rest of the world feels like a distant dream in this sequestered place, and so does the war. As ever, I am on the wrong side of thick glass, looking in and trying to feel something.

IV

The bus to Fowey rattles along empty lanes. There's barely any traffic, people's cars covered and locked away since petrol was rationed at the outbreak of war. All the roads look the same to Rose, with hedgerows that rise up almost to the bus's roof, deserted crossroads, and occasional heart-lifting flashes of the sea. She moves to the left side of the bus to be nearer those glimpses of deep blue, unable to imagine how she's managed all those years in the land-locked Midlands. She doesn't know how she's breathed.

The sun warms the side of her face. The air in the bus smells of warm leatherette and stale sandwiches, and she stands to pull open a window, the breeze ruffling her hair as it streams in. She can smell the salt and the fields and the approaching summer. She wonders if he's out there, breathing the same air, feeling the same sun on his skin.

She cuts off the thought, aware she's been thinking about him more and more lately. Not Frank; she hardly ever thinks of her husband, though it makes her horribly guilty. It was the same with the letter she'd let the breeze carry over the cliff, and the way the words had sing-songed in her head as she ran back to Penhallow, her heart a little lighter. *I don't miss him. I don't miss him.*

No, it isn't Frank who's on her mind. It's him. The boy from sixteen summers ago. It's ridiculous, really, the way he's insinuated his way into her thoughts and dreams again. He's probably never given her a second thought. She shakes her head, and a little girl across the aisle regards her curiously.

She was at another billet before Penhallow and the small farm in the north of the county, on the lonely fringes of Bodmin Moor, could not have been more different. She'd arrived in February and most days couldn't see beyond the boundary of the field she was working in, so thick was the white mist that clung to the land. There were fleas in her mattress and no electricity in the room she and the other land girl shared.

When the regional officer came to do her first inspection, Rose was ready, intercepting her at the gate to ask if she might transfer. The officer, who was new to her post and still sympathetic to unhappy land girls, said she'd see what she could do. When Rose was summoned to the office in Truro to arrange an alternative, she caught sight of the name on a list of available places. Not Penhallow, which she didn't know, but Vennor, the nearest village. The upside-down V had jumped out at her, like a long-lost friend.

'What about that one?' she'd said, pointing, a catch in her voice.

The kind regional officer smiled conspiratorially, misunderstanding. 'Oh, yes, I can see why you'd fancy that.

Penhallow Hall. Sounds awfully cushy, doesn't it? Well, I don't see why not. They've put in for three girls altogether so you won't be on your own. You'll be by the sea, too. What a treat.'

I know, Rose managed not to say. *I spent my happiest summer there.*

It's not until the bus turns off towards Fowey that there are any proper signs of life. The crowds get thicker as the bus winds its way downhill towards the harbour, and Rose is so busy looking at them that she doesn't at first notice what they are looking at.

It's the mother of the little girl across the aisle who finally draws her attention to it.

'Will you look at that!' she says wonderingly.

Rose turns. It's an arresting sight. The harbour is in full view now and it's crammed with boats. Not in any normal way, such as you might see when there's a storm coming, but so astonishingly packed full of every size and type of vessel that you can't see any water between them. If you wanted, you could step from one to another without getting your feet wet.

A little further on, the street becomes so dense with people that the driver can't go any further, and Rose and her fellow passengers have to get off. The whole town has apparently turned out to see the spectacle unfolding in its own harbour.

'What are all those boats for?' she overhears a young boy ask his mother.

'They've brought the men home from France,' she replies, her eyes not leaving the harbour.

'Is my dad there?'

'No, love, he can't come back yet. He's got to stay out at sea for a while.' She catches Rose's eye and smiles sadly at her. Rose turns away and begins to walk, anxious that the woman may engage her in conversation and discover that she, too, has a husband at sea. She always feels a fraud when she talks about Frank these days, as though he lends her some status she doesn't deserve.

Closer to the harbour, she can see that some of the boats have already disgorged their loads. Men stand or sit in bedraggled groups, their faces and uniforms streaked with mud and oil. Some are looking up into the empty blue sky; others stare at their feet. She doesn't think she's ever seen such exhaustion. A band of WVS ladies have set up a canteen and are doling out soup and rough hunks of bread. The men who haven't already finished theirs are shovelling it into themselves, their eyes unfocused but their movements intent.

Most of them are grim-faced but one musters a smile as Rose passes. 'You're a sight for sore eyes,' he says. 'You're welcome to nurse me back to health, if you like, love.'

Embarrassed, but trying not to be, she smiles at him and his companion, but doesn't stop to talk. She's not sure what to say to these men who have been brought back from France. She's not sure whether she will offend them if she says she's glad they're back in one piece. Perhaps they won't want to be reminded that they've had to retreat and be rescued.

Further along the harbour wall, where the crowds begin to thin out, she stops for a moment to get her bearings.

A small fishing boat, having somehow navigated its way through the crush of other vessels, is mooring up just below her. The gangplank goes out and the men begin to file off. Most are in uniform, as dirty and unkempt as the rest, but one is wearing a soft blue shirt, his arms where he's rolled up his sleeves a smooth nut-brown.

The tumult around her slows, the noise falling in pitch. She puts her hand up to shade her eyes from the sun. It can't be him. It can't. But then she realizes it can. The boy from that summer. All this time she's been thinking of him as he was when she knew him: as much boy as man, his face soft and his shoulders still broadening. The man below is easier in his own body, inhabiting it fully now, just as the boy's fisherman father had done all those years ago when Rose glimpsed him once, hauling in his nets. But the fine-boned face and the thick, wavy brown hair that's longer than most men's and sun-tinged gold: they're all Sam's. She murmurs his name to herself: Sam Bligh.

He moves so he's directly below her, which means she can no longer see his face, and she holds her breath, caught between wanting him to look up and the urge to run. Because she has aged too, she knows. If he has ever thought of her, he will have pictured a slender girl with hair tied back in a heavy plait, colt-legged in an old tennis dress. She puts a hand to her hair. It's still long and thick but she'd found a single silver strand only the month before, tweaking it out and letting it fall to the floor before she could think too much about what it meant.

She turns so her back is to the sea and counts to twenty in her head. *He's here*, she reminds herself. *He's actually here, in the same place as me.* The words chime in her head, jubilant again, but her body is still afraid. Her legs have turned to jelly. She's dreamt of seeing him again for sixteen years, on and off, but now he's just feet away a significant part of her wishes she could be transported back to Penhallow Hall and do this another day.

She's known seeing him was a possibility, of course. On the couple of occasions she's ventured along the coast-path to Vennor, she's dressed with especial care precisely because there was a small chance she might see him on one of the village's winding lanes of white-washed cottages. But she wasn't expecting him in Fowey, and she wasn't expecting this assured-looking man, who is so calmly helping the worn-out soldiers come ashore.

She peers down again but he's gone. The men he was with are still there, but there's no sign of him now. She scours the crowd but the only person she recognizes is the woman with a husband in the navy. She checks a last time, heart still beating too hard, then walks determinedly away, further along the Esplanade until the crowds thin.

There's an empty bench with a view of the harbour and she sits down, trembling. It's cooler here, the breeze sharp on her slightly damp skin. On the far side of the estuary, a soft morning haze is still enveloping what she thinks must be Polruan. There are boats there too, but they are toy-sized from where she is and not nearly so many, the clear waters between them glittering under the sun as they might during any ordinary early-summer morning.

She doesn't know what she would have said to him, if he hadn't vanished. She knows that a stubborn, still-humiliated part of her may not have said anything. After all, he'd promised he would write, then hadn't bothered once, not even a single scrawled postcard. It was unfair and entirely illogical, she knew that even at the time, but a small part of her had hated him after things had gone so wrong at home. For not sensing how miserable and desperate she'd felt, he who had once told her, on a darkening beach in late summer, that she felt like the other half of himself.

She had seen him whenever he could escape from helping his father untangle the nets in the loft perched at one end of the harbour. He couldn't come up to the house in case her father saw him and she didn't know where he lived in Vennor – he'd made excuses not to show her – so they had relied on meeting each other at ten sharp each morning, by the steep steps leading down to Breakheart Cove.

Now, glancing back towards where she'd come from, she sees that people are drifting away. She's only there to run an errand for Blewett – picking up a small part for a roller from the ironmonger – and the thought of it is beginning to nag at her. She's also thirsty, and it's this that finally persuades her back into the throng.

The men who've disembarked are steadily processing up through the town, apparently to buses waiting to take them to the railway station. Their smell colours and thickens the air: a blend of sweat, damp khaki and heavy oil from the boats' motors.

After she's been to the ironmonger's, she goes into a tearoom, finding it almost deserted. At the counter, she goes to order a cup of tea, then asks for a glass of lemonade instead. The woman who serves her isn't inclined to chat and Rose is glad. She's still unsettled and doesn't want to make small-talk.

Eventually, the flow of soldiers runs dry and the streets regain some semblance of normality. When she steps back outside, Rose sees that a good number of the boats that were crammed into the harbour have gone too, though it still looks crowded. She's just wondering how long she'll have to wait for the bus when she spots it up ahead. The last person queuing has just boarded and Rose begins to run, suddenly wishing to be away from Fowey. The driver smiles at her as she rushes up the steps, slightly out of breath, and hands over her return ticket.

She finds a seat at the very back and takes a last look at the harbour, part of which is just visible beyond the King of Prussia pub. It's then that she sees him again, in the shade of the little lane leading along from it, his silhouette lean but strong against the sun-struck sea.

She goes completely still and, though a part of her wants to run back down the aisle and get off before the bus takes her from him, she finds she can't move. She looks desperately towards the front, where the driver is taking his time changing the destination board as he chats to someone in the front row. Glancing back out of the window, she sees that Sam is going to pass right by her. All he'll have to do is look up. He has to notice me, she thinks. She won't bang on the window. If he doesn't see her, it isn't meant to be. Just as it wasn't earlier, when she lost him in the crowd.

It's only because he lets a boy on a bicycle cross in front of him that he pauses and looks around. Until then, he had seemed quite intent on his thoughts, eyes cast down to the road. She had almost given up on him. But then, a smile for the boy still on his lips, he does. Just like that. Their eyes fasten on each other, just as they had the first time they'd met, on the coast-path. Neither looks away, as strangers would, or smiles as old acquaintances ought to – if the acquaintance didn't mean much.

'It's me, Rose.' She means to mouth silently through the glass, but she's whispering and it's loud enough for the woman sitting in front of her to turn round with a questioning look.

Smiling, his eyes bright, he shakes his head and cups his hand to his ear, just as the driver finally puts the bus into gear with a grinding shriek.

'Rose Carey,' she mouths, a laugh bubbling up and out of her as she gestures to herself, feeling ridiculous. Her maiden name comes to her lips automatically.

Outside, he begins to laugh. She's forgotten how openly he does it, not covering his mouth with his hand as Frank does because he doesn't like his teeth. The bus lurches into motion and starts to trundle down the road. She stands and yanks open the small high window above her seat. He is walking beside the bus now, his face turned up to hers.

'I'd have known you anywhere, Rosy,' he calls up. 'You didn't need to tell me twice.' He smiles again, and quickens his step to keep level with the bus, which is gathering pace.

'Do you live here now?' she says, embarrassed at the urgency of her tone. Other people on the bus are turning round.

He shakes his head. 'Still in Vennor.'

The bus is pulling away and he comes to a stop, letting it go. She turns to the back window.

'I'll find you,' she murmurs to herself, and puts her open palm flat on the glass. But somehow he's understood because he nods and raises his own hand.

The woman in front is still looking at Rose when she sits down. Though it's too warm for them, Rose delves in her handbag for her gloves and pulls them on, covering the ring on her left hand.

* * *

THIRTY-ONE DAYS LEFT

Wednesday, 19th June

I went to see my new friend in the village today. When I say friend, I am, of course, being ironic. It would be like claiming friendship with a wolf. It was only the second time I've been alone with him, though I've seen him around the village a few times. He always seems to be loitering by the harbour slipway looking threatening, while everyone else hurries past, desperate not to catch his eye. His cronies – a ragbag of cousins and brothers, some without teeth, others apparently deranged – always stare at me quite brazenly, while he hardly gives me a second glance. Admittedly this is what initially piqued my interest. And I knew he knew I was there because he went quite still, as if readying himself to pounce.

The first time we ended up alone was only for five

minutes. We bumped into each other on one of the narrow lanes that Vennor specializes in, too narrow for both cars and sunlight. The knowledge that someone might come upon us at any minute lent the whole thing a certain frisson. Equally, the thought that no one would and that we would be left to our own devices made me shiver in the shade.

After we'd stood there looking at each other, he leant in and said, 'I've never seen anyone look as good as you in my life.' He was so close I could smell him, all engine grease and hot skin, and the combination was oddly alluring, like maleness undiluted.

His name is Dew Bolitho. I had no idea that people living in the twentieth century were called such things, though Cornwall is generally a law unto itself. I laughed when he told me, but he didn't like that much, narrowing his eyes until they were slits. I don't think people ever laugh at Dew. He must be in his early thirties and is very handsome in a dangerous sort of way, with dark skin and curling black hair and eyes that really do flash with menace. He's the image of a pirate and I told him so. To this, he merely shrugged, as if to say, 'Well, I would be, wouldn't I?' Even compared to Daddy's most self-important friends, I've never seen such shameless swagger in a man. I can't help but admire it.

'I've heard you get things,' I ventured next. I thought I ought to be vague, in case Cook had misinformed me.

'Things?' he said, his lip curling into something distantly related to a smile.

'Yes. Stockings and powder and, well, anything, really. I've got money.'

'I bet you have.'

Then he told me to come and call on him at his 'net loft'

on the harbourside, which nearly made me laugh again. Wishing to regain the upper hand in that shadowy little alley, I said I might, then sashayed off without a goodbye. I knew then that I should never go back, that I should write a begging letter to Daddy instead (though I doubt even he would agree to send a nice bottle of something strong). But Dew Bolitho unnerved me. Precious few do that, these days.

When I found him in the net loft today, he was alone, and I didn't know whether to be pleased or not. It was gloomy inside and reeked of cigarettes. There was hardly any fishing paraphernalia, unless you counted a ragged old net strung across the beams of the roof, which looked as though it hadn't seen the open water in centuries. Everywhere boxes and crates and barrels were piled up as high as me. They towered over the desk Dew was sitting at, casting strange shadows across his face. He didn't say anything when he looked up, just handed me a filthy enamel mug and sloshed an inch of brandy into it.

He didn't join me in a drink, instead lighting a cigarette and smoking it so intently that it might have been his last. He watched while I swigged my brandy in three big gulps, then sauntered round from behind the desk to pour me more. I let him, my nerves jangling, caught between the urge to get out and the urge to drink until I didn't care.

'I suppose your ancestors used to smuggle this stuff,' I said, raising my mug and deciding it couldn't hurt if I stayed a little longer.

When I told him I was billeted up at the Hall, he seemed quite interested.

'The young girl's been allowed back, I've heard,' he said. 'First time in years.'

'Allowed, you say? That's an interesting way of putting it.'

He shrugged, and I knew I wouldn't get anything else out of him about that. Since I'd caught Jane at Breakheart Cove, and she'd hinted at the trouble between her and her grandmother, I had been on the lookout for other signs. This discord had instantly made me like her more.

'You been down to the cove by the Hall yet?' he said, which made me start because I'd just been thinking about it. Unease ran down my spine, like a cold fingertip pressed to the vertebrae.

'Why do you ask?'

He paused, eyeing me as he did, head on one side. 'I used to go there sometimes, when I was still a lad.'

'Looking for hidden treasure?'

He smiled wolfishly, showing his teeth, and I swallowed more brandy. 'You could call it that. The kind of treasure you mean hasn't been found there since my grandfather's time. It was for him and his gang that they named the place.'

It wasn't because they were incurable romantics, of course. Oh, no. 'Breakheart' is for the breakers that used to haunt the place, led by the infamous Jed Bolitho. I'd assumed I knew all about pirates and smugglers, but it turns out that the breakers were a breed apart: utterly cruel and remorseless.

Dew told me that their trick was to station themselves at the cove on nights when they knew a laden ship would be passing close to the rocks. Then they held up their lights, confusing the crew into thinking they were further out than they were. When the ship was inevitably scuttled and sunk, the breakers would not only plunder all the bounty in the hold, but drown any survivors who'd made it to the beach so they couldn't identify them to the revenue men.

Barbaric, but it gave me a shameful thrill to think that the man I was talking to was a direct descendant of such wickedness. I was alone with him and no one knew where I was.

After that chilling little history lesson we returned to the more mundane subject of the black market. Cook had told me that Dew Bolitho could get me Hitler's moustache clippings if I offered the right price, and certainly my order of face powder and three pairs of nylons seemed to present no difficulties. It was he who suggested the gin. I'd decided it would be too humiliating to ask but it was, again, as if he could read my mind. I pretended I didn't care either way but I think he saw straight through me.

'I'll have it all for you by Friday,' he said, with the ghost of a wink. 'Maybe Saturday.'

I opened my handbag. 'Shall I pay now?'

He smirked as he lit another cigarette. 'I think you're good for it. Anyway, I know where you live, don't I?'

'For God's sake, don't come to the Hall. You'll ruin my reputation. Someone like me isn't supposed to know someone like you.'

At that his smile vanished, and he held my eye until I looked away. I must say, he's even handsomer when he's angry. 'Oh, don't worry,' he said, after a long pause. 'I don't go up there. It's not for the likes of me.'

We stared at each other a while longer – me determined not to look away again, though I had to in the end. Those dark eyes of his seemed to be boring into the very depths of me and weighing up which parts he would take.

'Were you after anything else?' he said eventually, the smirk back.

To my great annoyance I found myself bustling out, cheeks aflame and shouting, 'Cheerio!'

I didn't enjoy the walk back to the Hall. There wasn't another soul on the path and the wind had completely died, making me feel as though I had wandered into the eye of a storm that would soon break over my head. There's a point, just before the steps to the cove, where the drop to the sea is sheer vertical rock. I always dare myself to look over the edge but I didn't want to today. With the air so still, the only sound to be heard was the rhythmic suck of the water. You hear of people jumping off cliffs because they're mesmerized by the churning sea below them, thinking it much closer than it is.

Remembering this made me sway and that was when I saw the figure out of the corner of my eye, standing at the top of the steps. I whirled round but there was no one. Whatever it was, it wasn't very tall. It definitely wasn't Jane. In another mood I'd have made myself go down there and look, set my mind at rest, but I couldn't face it today. Instead I ran all the way back here, heart thumping. This place is addling my mind.

V

Eleanor hesitates at the top of the cinder path that winds down to the creek. Looking round to check no one is watching, she sets off before she can change her mind. It's cool and quiet among the rhododendrons that crowd the path, the sound of the sea abruptly cut off in this part of the garden. It doesn't feel quite peaceful, though – not in the way she remembers it. Now it's expectant. *Here she is at last*, the trees seem to murmur to each other. *Here she is, come back to us.*

Something pale off to the side makes her startle, but it's only sunlight glancing off dark leaves. The blood fizzes in her legs but she forces herself to keep going, down towards the boathouse that juts out over the creek. Like her old bedroom, it's another place she has avoided because of its associations.

As she approaches the small building and sees what a sorry state it's been allowed to fall into, with peeling paint and missing tiles, her heart clutches with longing and regret, making her forget her fear. Cobwebs, like hanks of grey hair, hang from woodwork gone mossy, and dust smears the window that always reminded her of an old-fashioned galleon's.

One of the steps leading up to the room she isn't yet ready to enter has rotted right through. She creeps around for a proper look inside the watery cavity under the little building and sees that the boat is still tied up there. Her hands start to sweat when it seems to be moving, but it's just the slow roil of the creek water. Relief and something like disappointment flood through her. She can see now that the drift of dead leaves in the hull hasn't been disturbed for a long time.

Dizzy from the strain of being there, she goes to sit at the creek's edge, next to the weeping willow. The ghostly twin of its reflection is outlined in the water and, as she watches, it shimmers slightly. As a girl she'd pretended there was another world at the bottom of the creek, and that the darker, more mysterious version of herself who'd stared back at her was a lost sister. She doesn't crane over to look today, unconvinced that the face gazing back at her will be her own.

She breathes slowly, until her insides begin to unclench. She'd argued with her mother about Jane again this morning but, ironically, it was anger that had galvanized her into coming here. She'd left the house before it could ebb away, as it usually did, because the box inside the boathouse has been on her mind for a while.

When she plucks up the courage to go in, the air tastes green and mildewed. Goose pimples rise on her bare arms as she lifts the box down. The key, which is still waiting in the lock, turns easily. The photographs she's looking for are about halfway down the large pile inside. Although she hasn't seen them for so long, they act upon her as the view from the window of her old bedroom did a few days earlier: disturbing in their familiarity.

Some are of the Silver Moon balls and other celebrations, but others are less formal, many of them taken in the garden. The one she most wants to find is the one she kept under her pillow one summer, only shoving it into the box after everything had gone wrong.

Now, when she finds it, the sight of it is more painful than she has anticipated and she has to look away, blinking back tears that make her vision swim. She'd hoped they wouldn't come so easily. It's all so long ago.

She'd taken this particular photograph herself, which was unusual because it was generally Robin, the younger of her two older brothers, who was behind the camera. It was of him and his best friend from school, taken in 1914 when they were fifteen. Both boys are wearing sheepish smiles, navy fisherman's sweaters too big for them and the impractical white trousers they had decided completed their outfits that summer. Eleanor can vividly remember how proud Robin was of this get-up, their mother's caustic remarks having no effect whatsoever.

The pair had gone sailing up the creek that day, leaving the camera behind so it didn't end up falling into the water. She'd waved them off, wishing there was room for her too. Even if she hadn't remembered how bright the morning sunlight was, it's easy to tell from the way the boys are squinting. The first war had turned the picture into a cliché: two golden boys, handsome and privileged, smiling for the camera on a July day with everything still before them.

Despite their identical clothes, the boys are opposites: the friend as dark as Robin was fair. There are no names on the back of the photograph but Eleanor doesn't need them. She remembers his name as well as her brother's. Of course she does: Sébastien, the accent on the first *e* for the Spanish half of his family. She traces a thumb over his face.

The last time he came to Penhallow was also the first that he came without Robin. It was years after the war; she had thought never to see him again. She hadn't even known whether he'd survived the trenches that had swallowed her brother in 1918, though she had always wondered. But then he came out of the blue, two days before the ball they held every summer, and her mother had insisted he stay for it – a last frail thread leading back to Robin, Eleanor always supposed. Of the three of them – Hugo was the eldest – Robin had always been their mother's favourite. Eleanor had written an invitation for Sébastien herself, though she'd felt too self-conscious to deliver it, turning it into a keepsake instead.

It was part of Fox family lore that it never rained for the Penhallow Silver Moon Ball – and never would. They all believed it, even her pessimistic mother, and somehow the enchantment had always held. On the day of the last ball, there was no hint that tradition was about to be broken, no cold prickle of impending disaster. Perhaps the sea had tried to warn her, but she was too distracted to listen.

Her head snaps up at a whisper beneath the heavy silence of the room. She holds her breath and listens, her hand reaching out for something to hold on to as the familiar dizziness comes over her.

'Is that you?' she whispers. From beneath the floor-boards, in the shadowy void where Robin's beloved old boat drifts and bobs, comes a soft creaking sound. The boathouse had been his place. If she couldn't find him in the house, he would be down here, stretched out in the hull with a book and a cushion stolen from the house under his head. He'd pull up the bottle of lemonade that was cooling in the dark creek waters and they'd drink it together.

She hears another noise, and this time she's too disturbed to stay still. She shoves the photographs into the box, turns the key and bangs out of the door. As she runs towards the path, she doesn't dare glance back at the boat.

The return journey seems longer. Her breath hitches in her chest as she remembers she's left the box out of place on the desk, the key still in the lock, but she can't face going back. When she emerges from the gloom of the rhododendrons, the sun blinding on the lawn, the trill of a bicycle bell brings her violently back to the present, setting off her dizziness again.

It must be the butcher's boy – she needs to catch him because it's Cook's day off. Still, she can't resist looking back down the path now she's out in the reassuring sunshine. When she sees the flash of blue, too vivid to be natural, she is hardly even surprised.

She holds out her hands and sees that they're trembling. She makes a bargain with herself: if she manages to be sensible during the exchange with the butcher's boy, like any normal person could, then she's wrong about the garden. But even as she turns and walks towards the house in a pretence of purposefulness, she knows she's not imagining it. Something uncanny is down there by the creek; something has come back for her. And part of her hopes it has.

VI

Rose is still buoyant from her encounter in Fowey and feels no urgency to see Sam yet. It's enough to know he's there, just a mile down the coast-path in Vennor. It's enough to know he remembered her quite as easily as she remembered him. It would have been better – simpler, probably – if he'd looked blankly back at her, but he hadn't, and she wouldn't swap that for anything.

Diana, always as sharp as a tack, senses that something has changed. She has been glancing at Rose questioningly since she got back from Fowey, though she hasn't said anything. They're on their way down to dinner a couple of days later when she finally does. The three of them eat their evening meal in the dining room with Eleanor, and take turns to serve and clear the plates since the housemaid has left to go and work in a factory by Plymouth docks.

'So, are you going to tell me?' Diana pushes her long, lean arm through Rose's. Her bare skin feels smooth and cool. It strikes Rose that she always feels slightly pudgy and pale next to her.

'Tell you what?'

'You've been mooning around with this vacant look on your face since your little jaunt to Fowey. Why didn't you tell me you were picking something up for Blewett? I could have come with you. We might have made a day of it.'

Rose had deliberately not told Diana about it, seeing the errand as a chance to get away by herself, which she never can at Penhallow. Even in the deepest hours of night, the others are there, their little sighs, gurgles and murmurs not letting her forget they're just a few feet away. At home she was often alone for the entire day, turning on the wireless when the silence of the house began to seem oppressive. She'd forgotten that solitude could feel like a luxury, too.

'Rosie, are you even listening to me?' Diana breaks into her thoughts. 'I'd have liked to see all those little boats full of uniformed men. I'm still astonished something so dramatic could happen in Cornwall. Didn't you want me to come?'

Diana has a way of making you feel it's bad manners not to tell her everything, even your innermost secrets. Usually it seems well-meant, solicitous even, but in the last couple of days it's taken on an intrusive, relentless edge.

Rose smiles as blandly as she can, aware of Diana's eyes on her. 'I don't know why you're trying to make a mystery of it,' she says. 'I simply didn't think to ask you, that's all. I suppose it didn't occur to me that you would be so interested in going to the ironmonger's for Blewett.'

'Silly, of course I don't have the slightest interest in *ironmongery*. But anything for a change of scene. I'm sure even sleepy Fowey would seem like Piccadilly Circus after two months here.'

'Well, it wasn't sleepy that day.'

'See, you're beastly for leaving me out. I've got literally nothing to put in my blasted diary.'

Rose feels a spurt of irritation, which she tries to cover with a laugh. 'Diana, thousands of men have been rescued from France – from Brittany and Dunkirk before that. They've been landing all over the south coast. Paris has been bombed. France has just surrendered. Saying you've nothing to write about is absurd.'

'Oh, I know, I know. What extraordinary times we're living through, et cetera, et cetera.'

Rose laughs again, this time genuinely. 'But we are. You must see that when you're not being so wilfully uninterested in the enormous thing that's going on right this minute.'

'Rosie-dozy, I'm just so much more interested in you.' She pinches the tender flesh on the underside of Rose's arm. 'You've been distant since Fowey and I want to know why. I demand to know, in fact.'

'It's nothing,' Rose says, suddenly impatient. She disentangles herself from Diana as they walk into the dining room. 'It's just the war. It feels closer now.' Her cheeks burn with the lie. She's hardly given a thought to the war since seeing Sam. It's not just him, though. She'd received another letter from Frank this morning. He was even more insistent about his next leave in this one, making her dread the thought of the cheap hotel room he'd find for them near Paddington, and the sound of other couples through the thin walls after the light had been turned out.

In the dining room, the low sun is shining through the windows, mellow and soft. The rosewood table gleams, reflecting the glassware and cutlery and an enormous vase of freshly cut roses. Rose knows all this will be Eleanor's doing; she works far harder around the house than her mother must think proper. Cook has said that the old lady doesn't approve of her daughter's insistence that everyone call her by her first name. In truth, Rose struggles with it sometimes. It doesn't seem quite right, somehow, not to call her Mrs Grenville, however unassuming and meek Eleanor is.

Eleanor – Rose makes herself say it again in her head – is opening the French windows when she notices they've come in. She whirls round and gives them one of her sweet, uncertain smiles. 'Oh! Oh, it's you two. And there's Jane behind you. How lovely. Isn't it a beautiful evening? I do so love June. I always say it but I do. I think it's my favourite month. There's still so much of the summer left.' She stops, her eyes flicking between them, her narrow fingers worrying at her cardigan buttons. Rose smiles as encouragingly as she can.

'Are you quite certain it's warm enough to have the doors open, Eleanor?' The voice is one Rose has heard before only at a remove, from the other side of the house where she and Diana never go. She's never caught any of the words, but the tone, querulous and dissatisfied, travels clearly enough along Penhallow's corridors.

Mrs Fox has been wheeled in by her nurse-companion. 'No, not there, Payne,' she says now. 'Like this. Goodness, how you fumble.' Payne stands back from rearranging the travel rug on her mistress's lap, her cheeks stained with dull spots of colour.

'My mother is dining with us tonight,' says Eleanor, weakly. 'I'm not sure what the occasion is but I –'

'You don't need to sound so apologetic about it,' her mother interrupts. 'I was eating dinner in this room long before any of you were born. Heavens, that draught.'

'I – I can close the French windows if you prefer, Mother, but the air is very soft tonight.'

'Sea air is deceptive. My neck will be stiff by morning if I sit there.'

'Well, I must close them, then.'

'No, no. Please don't on my account. I won't hear of it. But perhaps I might move to the other end of the table.'

The next minutes are spent adjusting things so that Mrs Fox has her own crystal wine glass and napkin ring relocated to the other end of the table. When Eleanor drops a fork on a side plate with a clatter, she freezes for a moment and, though nothing is said, Rose sees Eleanor catch her mother's almost imperceptible shake of the head.

They've only just begun eating when Mrs Fox turns to Eleanor. 'What a great deal of food these girls have on their plates. I don't know how Cook manages.'

'Yes, she does a marvellous job,' says Eleanor. 'But . . . but of course all land girls are entitled to extra rations, to keep their strength up.' She glances down at her plate and swallows.

'Are they indeed? Well, they look very well on them. I still wonder if they wouldn't be more comfortable eating at the table in the kitchen, rather than with the family.'

'Well, I suppose one of our girls is family.' Eleanor smiles tightly at Jane.

Mrs Fox glances critically at her granddaughter. 'One forgets when she comes to the dinner table with soil under her fingernails.'

A deep flush creeps up Jane's throat. She tenses as though she's about to push back her chair and run from the room. Eleanor smiles valiantly, as if willing her niece to stay in her seat, but her hands are gripping her cutlery so tightly that her knuckles are white. 'Well, Mother,' she says shakily, 'I like to think I'm taking our example from the head of the Land Army herself, Lady Denman. I was reading only the other day how she's turned the whole of Balcombe Place into the WLA's headquarters.'

'How very patriotic of her,' remarks Mrs Fox. 'I wonder what her husband thinks about it.'

'I shouldn't think he minds, as it's part of the war effort. Apparently the place is simply full of typists, with stacks of uniforms up to the ceiling. Even the tennis courts have been given over to livestock.' She laughs timidly, and Rose hurriedly joins in.

'Gracious. I suppose you're trying to tell me we've got off lightly?'

'No. Only – well, I suppose it's just so pleasant to have people in the house.' She stops and looks down at her plate again.

'And I suppose your mother is not *people*,' says the old lady.

'Oh, no, I didn't mean it like that. Only that . . .'

'It's always the past with you, isn't it, Eleanor? I've never understood those who persist in looking back when one can only go forward. It's unhealthy to dwell, as I've always said.'

'I suppose you would rather brush everything under the carpet,' Eleanor says in a rush. Everyone turns to stare at her. The water in her glass, which she has picked up distractedly, slops about. 'Like you always do. I suppose you would like us to pretend that nothing you didn't like had ever happened. That none of us has feelings about anything at all.'

A strangled sound comes from her throat and Rose wonders if she's trying to stifle a sob. Mrs Fox lets out a desiccated bark of laughter, which makes Payne, hovering at her elbow with a wine decanter, jump. 'Eleanor, I rather think you've had too much to drink. What an example to set to these girls, to your young niece.'

Only Mrs Fox has drunk any wine, though no one points this out, even Eleanor, who is ashen-faced after her outburst. In fact, no one speaks at all for the rest of the meal. When it's finally over and they all file out, Rose feels giddy with relief.

Mrs Fox is like a tyrant queen, Eleanor one of her ladies whom she dislikes and distrusts. It's abundantly clear that there's no love lost between mother and daughter; the difference is that Eleanor had seemed exhausted by their exchange, while Mrs Fox was deriving some grim enjoyment from it.

They stand and watch as Payne pushes Mrs Fox's chair to the bottom of the stairs. The old servant is a large woman, not fat but tall and flat-chested, her sallow skin stretched tight over a brow made wider by her oddly youthful hairstyle. No one breaks the silence as she gathers up Mrs Fox with apparent ease and carries her up the stairs. There's something deeply unsettling about this spectacle, and Rose glances at Eleanor and Jane, who are standing together. The latter is frowning, obviously embarrassed by the whole performance, but Rose can't read Eleanor's expression. She's retreated into herself, her face a blank mask.

'Are you bringing the chair?' The disembodied voice from the floor above is imperious and Eleanor steps forward without hesitation, folding the wheelchair and carrying it up after them.

'Good heavens,' says Diana, taking Rose's arm again. 'Eleanor is positively saintly. Or she was until she let fly. I think she shocked herself as much as the rest of us. What a peculiar lot these Foxes and Grenvilles are.'

Rose nudges her. 'Keep your voice down. Jane will hear you.' In fact, Jane has already stumped off up the stairs.

'Don't worry about her,' says Diana. 'She'll be off to read the history of the seed drill or something equally dull. It makes you wonder, though, doesn't it, when you see them together?'

'Wonder what?'

'Oh, Rose, don't be so incurious. You're really not yourself, are you? I wonder what's happened between them, I mean, what Eleanor was referring to. It's obvious they despise each other.'

'Well, I wouldn't say despise . . .' Rose begins, though that's exactly how they behave.

'Oh, I would,' says Diana. 'Gosh, this place is thick with secrets. Now, when are you going to tell me yours?' She skips up the stairs, pulling Rose after her.

* * *

Saturday, 22ⁿᵈ June

Rose is still going about as though she's mildly concussed. Lord alone knows what's happened to her, though I've narrowed it down to her little foray to Fowey. I had been resisting pressing her because I wanted to see if she'd tell me herself, but she clearly isn't going to breathe a word, which I think pretty mean-spirited of her. I tell her everything.

Well, that's not strictly true. I haven't told her about Long John Bolitho for one thing, but that's only because she would give me one of her sorrowful looks. The ones that say, 'Oh dear, Diana, I do wish you'd have more care.' They always make me feel cross and oddly ashamed, coming from her. But she has no reason to keep things from me. There's nothing Rose could say that would shock me.

In the absence of anything else to amuse me, after we'd finished in the garden today I turned my attentions to the aged spectre in the east wing: Eleanor's mother. She caught my interest after dinner the other night, when she graced us with her presence for the first time and was so awful to Eleanor – a scene even I, with my vast experience of such things, found excruciating. I'd been wondering since if I dared go up to her room to say hello.

In part, I thought it would be fun to see if I was a match for her, but chiefly I wanted to get to the bottom of why she and Eleanor so dislike each other (not least to feel a little less hopeless about relations between me and my own mater). Also, Cook told me she is a prodigious drinker, signs of which I observed at dinner, when she drank all the wine by herself. My spirits order from Dew has been delayed so things on that front have been getting rather desperate. There are only so many cigarettes one can smoke in the long hours between dinner and bedtime, especially since this double summer-time lark has made the evenings go on for ever.

Old Ma Fox's room is enormous and lavish, and is obvi-ously the intended master bedroom of the house. Presumably she never moved out to make way for Eleanor and her husband Gerald (he of the undisclosed but critical war job that keeps him in London, lucky devil). The far end of the room is virtually all window and overlooks the rose gardens I spend half my life titivating. Today it reeked of the late-flowering Himalayan Musk (appalling that I now know that). It turns out you can barely hear the sea from that side of the house, let alone see it, but that's how Mrs F likes it, apparently.

'I've never understood this fondness people have for the sea,' she told me, mouth pursed, after she'd summarily dis-missed Payne. 'It's nothing but a nuisance. If people aren't drowning themselves in it, they're cavorting half naked on the beach and then bringing sand in on their shoes.'

'From our rooms we can't escape the sound of it, even if we wanted to,' I said.

'I haven't set foot in that part of the house since the twenties,' she replied darkly, fingering the cane that lay across her lap. 'I refuse to.'

'Goodness. Do you really hate the water that much?'

She gave me a mocking look. 'The reason I haven't been there, nor ever will again, has nothing to do with the sea.'

'How very Gothic,' I said, interest lighting like a match.

She considered me, and I think she was tempted to divulge more, but the moment passed and she wouldn't be further drawn, swivelling her eyes – a bright cold blue, like chips of ice – back to the roses below.

Such a heavy silence followed that I was ready to creep out, but then she waved me towards an alcove cupboard. To my delight, it was stacked with booze. I silently blessed Cook.

'A small Dubonnet will restore me, I think,' she said, quite as though I was a lady's maid of yore. Still, she didn't object when I also poured myself one, sloshing in a large measure while my mind turned over what might have gone wrong on our side of the house.

'So you are one of these land gels,' she said, adroitly changing the subject before knocking back her drink in one. 'You hardly seem the type to be grubbing around in the earth.'

'No, quite,' I agreed. 'I was made to join by my mother.'

'How curious.'

'Not really. She isn't the doting type. The Land Army offered the best chance of a posting far away from home in London.'

'Where in London?'

'Knightsbridge.'

'I don't know anyone there.'

'Nevertheless. I suppose the house will have to be closed up if the Germans start bombing in earnest.'

'I can't abide London. Dirty place. Too many different kinds of people all mixed up together.'

I must have smirked at this because she pounced: 'Are you laughing at me?'

'It's refreshing to hear someone say what they really think. That's all.'

She snorted. 'Eleanor's always been rather wearingly nice. She certainly doesn't get it from me. I don't think you've told me your name.'

'Diana Devlin.'

'I always think one has to be careful with alliteration when it comes to names. It can make a girl sound rather fast. Or like an actress, which amounts to the same thing.'

'Well, perhaps I am rather fast. May I ask what your name was, before you were Mrs Fox?'

'I was the Honourable Lavinia Lascelles.' She smiled at this, very pleased with her joke about alliteratively fast girls. 'And so, Miss Devlin, you must tell me what the other one is like. My daughter can scarcely bring herself to speak to me so I find I know nothing about anyone, even those under my own roof.'

'Rose? Well, I'm beginning to think she might be a bit of a dark horse. Her background is deeply ordinary, of course, but her artistic bent rather complicates the matter. She likes to go off sketching on fine evenings, cliffs and trees and suchlike. I don't think life at home in Solihull as a draper's wife nourishes her soul, put it that way. Perhaps the war has done her a favour – she certainly seems more attached to Cornwall than to the absent Frank. There is a third land girl, of course.'

She beetled her brows and I laughed. I knew she would

feign ignorance, just as she had at dinner. 'I refer to your granddaughter.'

She looked out of the window again. 'Oh, her. Didn't you know her indulgent aunt procured her those dreadful dungarees? She's not a proper land girl. If she's told you she is, then she's lying. I had hoped she'd lost the habit.'

This was a welcome turn-up for the books. 'Lying?' I repeated. 'Why would anyone pretend to be a land girl when they aren't?'

'Nothing is ever enough for her. She can't be a land girl because she's only fifteen years old. She should be spending the school holidays at home, like her sisters. But, no, she must come here and "do her bit".' She spat out the last words as though they were obscene. 'She was always a plain little thing,' continued the adoring grandmother, tetchily. 'Always to be found reading and scowling as a child.'

'I can well imagine,' I said obsequiously, though what I was actually thinking was, *Poor old Jane, she's not much better off than me.* Having come to find out why Mrs Fox didn't much care for her daughter, I was beginning to think it was the granddaughter who was despised more. 'Are Jane and her sisters your only grandchildren?'

'Yes, and the twins are quite another breed of child. Such outgoing, sunny girls, with the Lascelles blue eyes and blonde hair.' Her expression softened until it looked almost fond. 'Of course, they've been kept from me far too much. They've hardly spent a summer here.'

'Kept from you? But why?'

She gestured towards the drinks cupboard with the cane and I topped us both up. 'It doesn't matter now,' she said, after sucking down half the glass. 'It was how it had to be. Why things have been allowed to deviate this year, I can't imagine. Eleanor has promised Jane's father she will return to school in September but I have my doubts. The summer will end in uproar and grief, mark my words.'

I felt a shiver then, and the oddest sensation that the walls had inched a little closer. *They're all mad here*, I thought, *and I'm going to go the same way.*

As the silence yawned, I took the opportunity to study her properly. She would have been quite a beauty once. She has the cheekbones, you see, and so few have. She must have been thinking the same sort of thing because she crinkled her mouth into a chilly little smile.

'You remind me a little of myself. Of course, we wore rather more clothes in my day' – her glacial eyes raked over my bare calves – 'but there are similarities in colouring. Except for your green eyes, you might be a Lascelles.'

'I suppose Jane must take after the Fox side. Or her mother, perhaps.'

She didn't answer but fixed me with that gimlet eye again. I can entirely see why everyone quails under it.

There's something in all this Jane business I can't quite put my finger on. It's perfectly obvious that Mrs F approves of the twin sisters but not Jane. And yet it's Jane who's here, toiling with us in the garden. It seems perverse, as if the entire Fox family is intent on making each other as miserable as possible. Perhaps it really is as simple as that. Families can be brutal to each other, God knows. But what about Jane being a liar? I wouldn't have thought her capable of guile, but then I remember the expression on her face when I caught her at the cove. There was wildness there, evidence of the sort of damage I can always spot at ten paces.

From what little she's so far let slip about her parents, I sense that they're not terribly keen on her either. The only person who seems to like her is Eleanor, but then Eleanor's too nervy to be anything but nice to everyone. As for Jane still being a schoolgirl, I suppose it explains the lack of a bust.

It was Mrs Fox who broke the silence. 'But what about you, Miss Devlin?' she said. 'Have you been presented yet? You're the right sort of age. It was still Queen Victoria when I was a debutante, of course.'

I pulled a face. 'The less said about my short career as a deb, the better, I think. Besides, white was never my colour. It drains me.'

'Ah, yes, I remember now. Mrs Phelps wrote to me about you.' She raised a drawn-in eyebrow. 'You got yourself into rather a lot of trouble at school, didn't you? Expelled for all sorts of wickedness – although the specifics remain tantalizingly vague. According to Mrs Phelps, the experience has done little to reform your character since. Apparently your poor mother was at her wits' end before you came here. I was in two minds whether to let you come at all. I finally agreed on the condition that you passed a probationary period, the length of which is to be decided at my discretion.'

She laughed nastily while I reeled, the Dubonnet churning inside me. No one had thought to tell me any of this. Freda Phelps is something high up in the WLA, an odious busybody whose sister was housemistress at my old school. It was Mrs Phelps who found me such a respectable billet so quickly and so far from home.

'Well, it doesn't take much to reach the end of my mother's wits,' I eventually managed to quip, at which the old girl threw back her head and laughed.

'I rather like you,' she said. 'Despite your dubious reputation. You may come again and, in the meantime, I shall be keeping my beady eye on you.' She gestured to the window so I would know she meant it literally.

Payne was hovering in the passage when I took my leave, the expression on her large white face eager. No doubt she was hoping I hadn't come through unscathed. When, a moment later, the thud of the cane shook the floor beneath us, we both jumped. She pushed past me, her old-fashioned dress rustling stiffly, and I caught a whiff of camphor and milk on the turn. As she closed the door behind her, I heard the creak of Mrs Fox's laugh, lower now, and somehow malevolent.

VII

Eleanor has been drifting in and out of sleep for hours before she remembers that Gerald is due back today. She must have taken an extra sleeping tablet in the night, though she has no memory of doing so. One confused night, her dreams disorientating her sense of time, she fears she will take too many and not wake up at all. There was a time when the prospect wasn't as frightening as it should have been, but she feels wicked about that disregard for her own life now, when so many men have no choice in the matter. Besides, she would never leave Jane here alone with her mother.

After dreaming all night of her brother and Sébastien as boys, the urge to return to the boathouse this morning is almost overwhelming, but she doesn't know exactly when Gerald will arrive. His job at the Ministry of Information has him keeping such odd hours that he finds it difficult to sleep. Once or twice, he has driven down to Cornwall through the night, arriving grey and shaky with fatigue, his clothes smelling of a dusty office she'll never see. She knows instinctively that he won't approve of the boathouse. He won't say so, not to her face like her mother would, but he'll think it morbid. He won't understand that what is down there, waiting for her, is real, as real as the news from France.

In silent compromise to him, she decides to go outside only so that Brick can play with his ball. It's hardly her fault that the dog loves the part of the garden where the cinder path begins, where the lawn suddenly tips so steeply, allowing him to barrel down to where the rhododendrons thicken before banking round, joy flexing in his muscles. She throws the ball again and again but her eye barely leaves the distant point where she saw the flash of blue before, like a fallen piece of Heaven.

She doesn't realize she's talking aloud until a hand on her arm makes her cry out. It's Gerald, his face drawn and pale from the long drive. 'Darling, it's me,' he says gently. 'I've just got back. Who are you talking to?'

They make it through the rest of the day uneventfully enough. Gerald doesn't press her about her behaviour in the garden, or about the fact that, even as he led her back to the house, she couldn't help looking over her shoulder, desperate not to miss some sign.

Gerald's introduction to Diana and Rose over dinner goes surprisingly well. Jane and he get along well together too, the two of them chatting amiably about what's been done in the garden. The general sense of ease is mainly down to Diana, whose charm is a formidable weapon Eleanor would fear if she was in love with Gerald, or if she thought for a minute that Diana had any serious intent. As it is, she merely watches as her husband basks in the white heat of Diana's charisma, grateful not to be the centre of his attention for once. Thankfully her mother has stayed in her room.

After dinner, the girls back upstairs, Eleanor joins him in his study.

'Remarkable young woman, that Diana,' he says, with an inevitability that would make her smile if she wasn't taking such care to seem calm.

Gerald has taken his usual seat by the fire, which is lit even though the night is much too warm for it. He's tall but spare, and has always felt the cold since his time in Egypt with the army. The nights in the desert had been perishingly cold, the shock of them intensified by the searing days.

'Yes,' she agrees, as she pours them both a drink. 'She's a force to be reckoned with.'

'I'd say that a girl like her is capable of charming even your mother, but there are limits.'

An image of Robin, his hair as bright as Diana's in the sun, flares again in her mind, as it has periodically all day. She wonders whether she might feel less agitated if she told Gerald about the box of photographs she's unearthed, even though she mustn't say anything else. Perhaps it would be a small release of the pressure she can feel building inside her, making her toes and fingertips hum with sensation.

People think Gerald insensitive when they first meet him but he's not. He's surprisingly good at putting himself into other people's shoes. He knows everything about her past, of course. Well, almost everything. There is something she's never told him. And now there's the boathouse. She can't tell him about that either. Who could understand that but her? The room around her dims a shade and her eyes flick to the corners.

'The other girl seems nice enough, too,' he says, making her twitch back to attention. 'Rosemary, is it?'

'Just Rose. Yes, I like her a great deal. Her husband is in the navy.' She hears her voice, slightly too loud.

'Are you managing, darling? With these extra people to worry about?' He holds out his hand to her and she reaches forward to give it a brief squeeze, conscious he'll notice how cold her fingers are. She knows he's really asking about Jane.

'It's wonderful to have her back here. As Mother has reminded me, in no uncertain terms, the thing is to look ahead, not back.' She tries a wry smile, which doesn't come off.

He sips his drink. 'She doesn't seem quite as cross as I remember her. Jane, I mean.' He smiles to soften the words. 'God, how long ago was it?'

'Years ago. She was nine.'

He shakes his head. 'So long.'

'I haven't yet seen as much of her as I hoped,' Eleanor says, as brightly as she can, though, to her frustration, she can feel the warning prickle of tears. 'She's no doubt been sucked into Diana's orbit. The girl is irresistible to both sexes, it seems.'

Gerald raises his eyebrows at her. 'Come on, old thing, there's plenty of time. And it's good if she's got a friend near her own age. Hasn't she been a bit of a loner at school?'

The word stings. 'Only according to my brother. But, then, he and Olivia have never been terribly kind to her.'

Gerald reaches over to pat her knee. 'Well, I wasn't criticizing, you know that. I like Jane. Very much.'

'You barely know her. Neither do I.'

They sit in silence for a while, sipping the whisky that's beginning to take effect. She realizes she hasn't asked him anything about his work since he got back. It's like that at Penhallow, if you're not careful. The world shrinks so that even Vennor seems like a distant planet, unreachable and irrelevant.

'Have you managed to get out at all lately?'

It's as if he's heard that last thought. She hesitates, considers lying, not to deceive Gerald but just to know how it would feel to say, yes, she has been out, that only yesterday she ran some errands in the village.

But she's always found it difficult to lie outright. She shakes her head miserably. 'I just . . . can't. I have tried. I even opened the gate for a whole minute the other day, but somehow I couldn't persuade myself through it. Mother says it's no good and I should give it up.'

'Well, don't listen to her. You'll get there. I have every faith in you.'

She swallows another mouthful of whisky. She doesn't drink much when Gerald is away – the sharpened anxiety the following day isn't worth it. She's forgotten how becalmed it can make her feel in the moment; a temporary homecoming to her old self. Snug in the warm cradle of drink, part of her believes she might be able to leave Penhallow tomorrow. The possibility – the not-impossibility – glows in her mind.

'When will you have to go back to London?' she says. 'Not too soon, I hope.'

He sighs and shifts, and Brick, dozing on his feet, lets out a long groan in response. 'Probably tomorrow night. I shouldn't really be here at all, weekend or not. There's so much going on.'

'Oh.' The familiar dread coils around her stomach. She always forgets how much safer she feels with Gerald here, until he is back and about to go again.

'I would stay longer if I could.'

'I know.'

'I'll try to come again in a few weeks. Don't forget you've got Jane, though.'

'Yes, for now.'

'Why only for now?'

She finishes her drink in a gulp. 'Mother's watching me. She's already said I'm fussing over her too much. That I should keep my distance more. Even from her room I feel she's spying on me, checking I don't put a foot wrong – or, rather, willing me to, so that Jane can be sent back.'

'I presume it was your mother's idea to put her in with the others, on that side of the house?'

'She thought it would be best. "Most fitting", I think she said.' Eleanor smiles bitterly.

There's silence for a while and then he reaches across to take her hand. 'When I came back this morning, darling, you were talking to yourself.'

'Was I? I expect I was talking to Brick. Lots of people talk to their dogs, you know, not just the mad.' She tries to laugh.

He sighs. 'I don't think you're mad. But I don't think it was Brick you were talking to. Is it proving too much, do you think?'

She stands so abruptly that the dog wakes up and whines, his ears back. 'What do you mean by that?'

Gerald rubs his eyes. 'I know how much you've been looking forward to Jane coming since your brother said she could. But . . . Well, I must say I'm rather concerned now I've seen you. You seem . . . fragile, darling. And rather hectic.'

The shadows in the corners begin to shift and seethe. The room and everything in it seem suddenly unreal, a box of furniture and plaster and carpet floating through empty space. She wraps her arms around herself until the sensation subsides. 'There is nothing wrong with me,' she manages to say. 'You will not send her back to them. I am perfectly well.'

'If you say so.'

She kneels at his feet. 'Gerald, please. I will take care of myself. I'll be good, better than I've been. I'll try the gate again tomorrow. Just please don't send her back.'

He puts his hand up and strokes her hair, the expression in his eyes infinitely sad. 'I would never do anything to hurt you, darling, you must know that by now. I'm not like her.' He raises his eyes to the ceiling.

'Do you promise?'

He nods. 'Yes, though I shouldn't need to. You should be sure already.'

She leans back against his knees, her hand reaching out for Brick's hot flank. She tries to match her breaths to the dog's slow, steady ones.

'Eleanor,' Gerald says after a while. 'Can I come to you tonight?'

The whisky and the fire and the relief of his promise

were finally making her sleepy but her name wakes her up. That and what he's asking for. In her mind, Sébastien stands before her in the shadowy gloom of the garden, wearing a suit borrowed from her dead brother. She blinks and he's gone. She looks over at her kind husband, gaunt and exhausted in the firelight, and nods, mainly for him but also because if she doesn't, she fears Gerald might change his mind about Jane.

VIII

'Rosie?' Diana's voice sing-songs stridently, breaking the peaceful air. She and Diana are walking through an unfamiliar part of the garden, where the ground falls steeply away to the creek. It's astonishingly quiet here, away from the pounding of the waves.

'Hush a minute,' says Rose, holding up a hand.

She wishes Diana wouldn't call her Rosie. That had been Sam's name for her, though he'd spelt it 'Rosy', like pink cheeks. She can still picture him writing it in pencil, self-conscious that he was left-handed and had to curl his wrist around so he didn't smudge. Perhaps he'd never written because he'd lost her address, the scrap of paper working its way out of his pocket as he climbed the lanes towards home. But perhaps he'd let it go, as she had let Frank's letter be taken by the wind.

'What are we listening to?' Diana interrupts again. 'I can't hear a thing.'

'Exactly. It's completely quiet. You can barely even hear the sea. It's so tranquil.'

Diana laughs perplexedly. 'Noise means life, things happening. Why would anyone prefer this? You're so peculiar these days, darling. Is it something to do with that last letter from Frank? I don't think you've mentioned him in *ages*.'

Fortunately they have reached Jane, who is already hard at work. She straightens up and blows her fringe off her face. The sun is already hot.

'Sorry for the wait,' says Rose. She nods in Diana's direction. 'Unavoidable delay.'

She picks up a spade and holds it out to Diana but the girl's hand is at her side.

'Oh, damn, I've forgotten my gas mask.' Her mouth, brightly lipsticked in defiance of Blewett, pouts prettily. 'It's such a bore, but I'll have to go back for it. Don't tell the Führer when he arrives.'

After she's gone, Rose tries to push the letter out of her mind. She doesn't want to think about her husband; she wants to think about Sam. She wishes she could go back to bed and do nothing else. But now that Diana has reminded her of Frank, other realities start to trickle in unpleasantly. That Sam might have a wife. That he might have children, too. Her stomach turns over coldly. There is something sobering about the thought of children. The spectre of them seems to cordon him off from her in a way that feels final.

She's just started digging when Diana sidles up again. Her gas mask swings on its string at her hip and she's covered her hair with a violet scarf that makes her eyes startlingly green.

'Share a cig with me?' she wheedles, one hand playing with the ends of Rose's hair as she lights up with the other.

Diana is always touching her. She's so close now that Rose can smell her rather heavy perfume. It isn't fresh. Diana always dabs a few drops behind each ear at bedtime, and it mingles with the cigarette smoke and the warm scent of her skin. Rose resists the urge to pull away. She's not used to it. She and Frank have never been tactile.

Diana narrows her eyes appraisingly, head on one side. 'I don't know, Rosie, mooning around, lost in thought, no appetite, moaning in your sleep. You do realize you're showing all the symptoms of acute lovesickness?' She covers Rose's hand where it clasps the spade. 'But if I'm right, I don't think it can be for poor Frank. Not from the way you stuffed that letter in your bedside cabinet. You haven't got another man back in Solihull, have you?' Her eyes sparkle.

Rose tuts primly, feeling herself colour. 'You do talk rot, honestly.'

She tries to pull her hand away but Diana holds her fast. 'Oh, Lord, I'm right, aren't I?' She lets out a peal of delighted laughter. 'I was only teasing, but I've hit the proverbial nail on the head. Who is he? You must tell me immediately. Look, even Jane's intrigued.'

Jane has straightened up again, a sharp line between her brows as she squints at Rose in the bright sunlight.

'There's no one. This is ridiculous.'

'What about in Fowey, then?' Diana persists. 'You've been in a dream since you went there. Did you meet one of those poor defeated soldiers and fall in love at first sight? Is that why you keep staring that way?' She gestures along the coast. 'Westward to Fowey where you've left him?'

Rose's temples prickle with sweat. 'It's nothing to do

with any man. If I've been looking over there, it's because I know the place. I stayed here before, when I was young.'

'Stayed where? Not Penhallow?' Diana glances over at Jane. 'Don't tell me you're a relation, too? The Solihull branch of the Foxes.' She smirks.

'No, of course not to Penhallow,' says Rose. She doesn't know why she's said anything at all, except that she feels like she might burst if she doesn't allude to Sam and that summer in some way soon. 'It was a family holiday we had nearby, that's all. We stayed in that house over there.' She points it out.

'So that's what you've been staring at,' says Diana. 'How sweet. How old were you?'

'Sixteen.'

'Oh, I bet Rosie at sixteen was a lovely thing, perfectly ripe and ready for love. Like a pretty peach.' She reaches out to pinch Rose's waist. 'I'm *positive* there was a boy, too. Wasn't there? No one looks so soulful over a house. Was he your first love? Did you let him —'

'We're not all like you,' Rose cuts in, before she can stop herself. She hears Jane's intake of breath.

Some unidentifiable emotion crosses Diana's face, though it's quickly smoothed away. A lock of her blonde hair twists as a surprise wind buffets the three of them. 'No, you're not like me,' she says, her voice gone cold. 'Neither of you are, more's the pity. Things round here would be a good deal more fun if you were.'

It's then that Rose hears a sound, a low note, different in pitch from the sea. Jane has heard it too, her foot pausing on the head of her spade; she scans the horizon, then points. 'There.'

It's the only blot in the empty blue, black as ink until its wing catches the sun. It passes over them at some great height Rose can't begin to estimate. She puts her hand up against the sky and fits the plane inside her fingertip and thumb, no more than a quarter of an inch apart.

'German reconnaissance,' says Jane. 'It must be, at that altitude.'

They watch until it's too small to see. After the noise of it has also faded into nothing, they remain quiet, going back to their work without another word.

Rose realizes that the unknown German high above has inadvertently diverted their attention from the conflict with Diana. He has also, for half a minute or so, brought the war down among their heads. The future, which had stretched out as languorous as a cat in the sun, feels suddenly concertinaed; time drastically shortened. She makes up her mind. She will find Sam today.

Later, when she finishes work, she tells herself she won't make an unusual amount of effort with her appearance. There isn't time if she's to get back before she's missed, and she doesn't want to arouse the eagle-eyed Diana's interest further. Still, she can't help but take a little extra care, dabbing on a bit of lipstick and powder once she's safely out of sight on the coast-path. *Look at you, a married woman*, a tight little voice says in her head, as she eyes herself in the mirror of her compact. Snapping it shut, she shoves it to the bottom of her handbag.

The streets of Vennor are busier than she's seen them, everyone reluctant to close their doors on the glorious evening. The village's tangled lanes are in shade by this time, so people have gravitated towards the water, some of them sitting on the seats cut into the harbour wall.

Her eye is caught by one woman of about her own age, sitting in a sunny spot, her eyes closed against the dropping sun. Next to her is a pram, the hood down and a small fist just visible above its swaddling of lemon-coloured blankets. The woman might have been Rose, if things had gone differently with Frank. If he gets his own way, she might still be. Her nerves jangle. She's never told anyone this, but every time her monthlies arrive, she feels a spike of relief.

Frank is what people call a man's man. After she and Frank had got married and found themselves alone in a house of their own, she had been shocked by how silent he was with her. She wasn't prepared for that, not after the years he'd been coming round to the Careys' house for dinner, garrulous with stories from the shop.

Perhaps it was true what they said, that it had all been about the chase for Frank. Once he had her, it was as if he didn't know what to do with her – or the vast plains of routine and intimacy he found himself navigating. A small, cynical part of her suspects he married her for the shop. Though her father hasn't said so explicitly, she knows he will leave the drapery to them jointly one day.

A frenzy of barking shakes her back into the present. Outside the bakery, a bird-like old lady is trying to pull her large dog away from a crust someone has dropped in the gutter. The animal is tangled in its lead and Rose hurries over to help free it.

'Oh, thank you, dear,' says the lady, who is tiny, her hands clutching the lead no larger than a child's. 'He's too strong for me to manage, really, but I said I'd look after him for my Johnny. He's away with the navy.' She smiles proudly. 'A second lieutenant.'

'So is my husband,' says Rose, immediately wishing she hadn't. 'Well, he's not a second lieutenant, but he is away with the navy.'

The old lady pats her arm. 'With any luck it'll be over soon. Then they can all come home,' she says. 'Thank you for helping me with Pip here. I'm Mrs Browning. Jean Browning.'

'Oh, it was no trouble at all.'

'You're a new face to me,' she says. 'So many people far from home. What is it that brings you to Vennor, dear? Visiting relations?'

'No, I'm with the Women's Land Army. There are three of us up at Penhallow Hall, growing vegetables.'

'Looking after those wonderful flowers, too, I hope.'

'Yes, those as well.' She hesitates. The same urge that had come over her in the garden earlier is back. She gives in to it. 'Mrs Browning, I don't know if you can help but there's an old friend I was thinking of looking up. Someone I knew when I was a child, when I came here on holiday.' She's aware this is not quite true; she hadn't been a child, not in the way she'd thought about Sam.

'Oh, yes?' Mrs Browning smiles at the prospect of being helpful. 'What was her name?'

Rose lets out a nervous laugh. 'Actually it was a him. Sam Bligh. But it doesn't matter. I don't suppose you know him anyway.'

She sees the old lady's momentary confusion as she tries to put it all together: the reasonably well-spoken woman asking after the fisherman's son. She realizes she's twisting her wedding ring round and round and makes herself stop, just as Mrs Browning's face clears.

'Of course I know Sam. Everyone knows everyone round here. Sam's the lighthouse keeper, out there.' She points in the direction of the horizon. Beyond the harbour walls, the sea is like a sheet of gently buffed metal, blue turning to dull orange as the sun sinks slowly towards it. The lighthouse, silhouetted against the sky, rises up out of dark grey rocks that, close up, are marbled with purple and cream. Rose knows this because she and Sam clambered over there once at low tide, slipping in their shoes because the rocks were too sharp to go barefoot.

'I thought he'd be a fisherman, like his father,' she says softly, but she can picture him in the lighthouse, a solitary figure at his post, a watchful gaze on the dark sea as the light blinks on and off, again and again, right through the night. It's perfect for him.

She feels Mrs Browning studying her face. 'That's right, dear,' she says slowly. 'But I don't think Sam ever went out on the boats. I suppose he followed his own path. Of course since the blackout the lamp isn't lit every night – only when our own ships need it.'

Rose tries not to betray her excitement. That he is known, that he has a job – all this makes him more substantial in the world. A tiny, irrational part of her has been frightened that she imagined the scene at Fowey.

'You might find him at home, if you're planning to call in,' continues Mrs Browning. 'And even if he's not there, you'll probably catch Morwenna.'

'Morwenna?' Her voice falters.

'His wife. She was a Bolitho, you know. Still is, to all

intents and purposes. Her brother is Dew Bolitho.' She raises her eyebrows and shakes her head disapprovingly, though the name means nothing to Rose.

'Morwenna,' she repeats quietly to herself. Just as Sam himself hadn't been quite real, neither had the prospect of any wife. When Mrs Browning said he was the lighthouse keeper, she'd seen him up there so clearly it had felt like the whole truth of him.

'So we're both grown-up and married now,' she says, dredging up a smile for Mrs Browning, who gazes back at her with frank curiosity.

'How funny,' she says, once she's given Rose directions. 'Here we are and I don't even know your name.'

'Diana,' she replies, and the lie rolls easily off her tongue, before she's even thought about it. 'Diana Devlin.'

The air is chillier once she's in the shade of the cottages built so close together, and she rubs her cold arms. She thinks of turning round and going back to the Hall but Diana and her sharp eyes are waiting there for her. When eventually she finds the place, part of her wishes she hadn't. It looks a little worse than its neighbours: more cramped, the whitewash dingier. There are no lights on inside and all she can make out through the tape on the window is the rectangle of another window at the back of the house, a drooping line of washing just visible through it. The downstairs seems to consist of a single room. She thinks back to the proud boy she knew, and is certain he won't want her seeing this.

She hurries away, and it takes some effort not to break into a run as she nears the harbour. The heart of the village is still busy with people reluctant to give up the day. Gulls circle and swoop above her and, through an open window, she can hear a wireless. Not music but the news, the voice low and serious. When she gets to the harbour wall, she stops to gather her thoughts, her hand gripping the stone to steady her. She gulps air, which is fresher here than among the lanes, and then she sees him. Sees the pair of them. Not Sam and Morwenna. Sam and a young boy.

The two of them are ambling slowly in her direction. She turns and runs back towards the bakery, which has now closed, tucking herself into its shady doorway. As they pass her, just a few feet away, Sam's hand pats the boy's shoulder. The child looks up adoringly, his little face rapt. They are nothing alike, the boy's skin paler, his hair a colourless ash where Sam's is rich. He must take after his mother.

A mean-spirited thought creeps into Rose's head. There's something appealing about the boy's expression but he isn't a beautiful child, and if he takes after Morwenna then . . . She pushes the thought away, ashamed. She has no claim on Sam any more, if she ever had. Who is she to judge the looks of his wife, let alone those of a small boy?

She watches them until they climb out of sight and then, suddenly desperate to leave the village behind, hurries towards the sloping lane that will take her back to the coast-path. There, the finality of him having both wife and child makes her cry, the path ahead of her blurring.

It would have been bad enough if he'd only been married, but she knows very well that people make mistakes when it comes to that. Sometimes there isn't much to break apart. But a child can't be a mistake. As Penhallow's chimneys rise up at her out of the deepening dusk, she makes up her mind. She won't go and see him now, not even as an old friend. No one knows her in Vennor except Mrs Browning, and even she doesn't know her real name. If Rose doesn't seek Sam out, she knows he won't find her.

Miserably, she fishes out the powder compact she'd looked into less than an hour earlier. It's not just that her eyes are bloodshot and watery, the light has gone out of them too.

* * *

TWENTY-TWO DAYS LEFT

Friday, 28ᵗʰ June

It's a quarter to three in the morning and I'm writing this under the eiderdown using a torch. I've tried to go back to sleep but it's impossible, my heart juddering too hard in my chest. Once you start noticing your pulse it starts leaping and stuttering horribly, convincing you you're about to drop dead. A stiff drink might help but the gin has gone and I'm far too jittery to search the pitch-dark house for other supplies.

The first I knew of it was when I woke with a start about half an hour ago. I sat up, senses as alert as if there'd been an enormous bang, but Jane and Rose hadn't stirred. Then I heard a voice – or, rather, two voices – in the passage outside our room. One was low, monotonous, like a chant, the other agitated and high-pitched.

I crept to the door and put my ear to it but I still couldn't make out any words. As soundlessly as I could, I turned the handle and stepped out into the passage. A dim light was burning further up, in the direction of the stairs. I was tiptoeing towards it when the agitated voice cried out again, much more clearly now I was so close.

'Take your hands off me, Payne! I know he's in there – I know what they're doing together. Let me go!'

Mrs Fox's voice – for it was hers – rose in a screech and there were sounds of a scuffle. I crept closer until I could see them. Payne was holding her mistress by the shoulders and trying to manoeuvre her into the wheelchair. I didn't know the old lady could walk at all, but it appears she can, albeit unsteadily. Even as I watched, she staggered backwards towards the head of the stairs and there was a suspended moment when I thought she was going to topple over the edge. But then Payne wrenched her back from the brink and at last manhandled her into the chair.

'Oh, madam, my poor madam,' she crooned, as she knelt in front of her. 'And we'd been doing so well. You haven't come in months. You know you're not up to this side of the house. Let's get you back now. You'll have forgotten in the morning, like you always do, nothing but a bad dream.'

'I tell you, they are in that room together,' Mrs Fox shrilled over her, bony hands gripping the arms of her chair as she tried to lever herself up again. 'Why will no one listen to me?'

Suddenly spent, she slumped to the side, her mouth slack. Payne hastily checked her pulse but then the old lady began to keen, and though it wasn't very loud, it was the most dreadful, unearthly sound I have ever heard: a corrosive blend of regret and fury.

It was at that moment that Payne swung round and saw me. My mind had me scuttling back in here and slamming the door, but my feet were rooted to the spot.

She strode over and pushed her face right into mine. She was breathing hard through her mouth and I held my own breath so I couldn't smell the sourness of hers. I thought she'd tell me off for spying, or perhaps swear me to secrecy about what I'd witnessed, but she didn't say anything at all. Instead she began to hiss, tiny droplets of spit hitting my face. I ran then into the dorm, jumped into bed and hid under the covers, trying to summon some of that old childish conviction that if you can't see them, they can't see you.

Payne has cracked open a memory I generally keep locked up. It came upon me so vividly that Penhallow disappeared and I was transported back to Flete, breathing in the foetid air of a sick-room. I was the only one in there at the time. I'd been made to go and sit by the bed and hold the occupant's hand, which had gone the queerest purple, the nails ridged and yellow. While I sat there, eyes fixed on the mustard-striped wallpaper so I didn't have to look at the figure propped up on pillows in the bed, his hand suddenly gripped mine, the other clawing at the bedsheets. He muttered my name a couple of times and, not too long after, the awful death-rattle began. I had the clear thought that I should call for the nurse but found I couldn't speak, my hands shaking.

I was only fourteen. That room, his hands, my hands, that dreadful noise – all of it came to me in my dreams for months. Still does, occasionally.

IX

The three land girls have been in their sitting room since dinner. Rose is trying to read but her thoughts keep wheeling back to her disastrous visit to Vennor. She finally gives up on the book, tossing it to the floor, and watches Diana as she twirls around to a record she's put on. She hasn't stopped moving today. Rose feels tired just watching her.

'Do you think we can we have the wireless on after that song?' says Jane, who is sitting in an old wing chair by the window, her legs crossed and an enormous, dry-looking volume entitled *On the Efficient Cultivation of Land* spread open on her lap. 'I'd rather like to listen to the news.'

To Rose's surprise, Diana twirls straight over to the gramophone and lifts the needle, cutting off the song mid-chorus. Then she turns on the temperamental wireless Eleanor had installed for them when the news started getting really dismal.

They listen in silence to the reports about Pétain's Vichy government, de Gaulle's Free French, and finally the attacks on merchant shipping by U-boats in the Atlantic.

Rose finds herself imagining the German submarines down there in the dark, freezing waters, circling beneath the waves like sharks. Frank's somewhere on that same body of water. The thought makes her queasy with guilt. She can't bear to think about him as well.

She concentrates on their own sea, its soft churning just discernible beneath the newsreader's voice. It's an oddly comforting background to such serious words, perhaps because the movement of the tide goes on regardless, and will continue to, whatever Hitler has in store for them.

When the news ends, Diana turns off the wireless and throws the end of her cigarette out of the window. Seeing Rose catch her at it, she mouths an apology. Rose has told her a hundred times not to do it; they only have to pick them up the next day, once Blewett has spotted them on the lawn below the window.

As sinuous as a cat, Diana comes and sits at Rose's feet. She tenses, waiting for Diana to ask her again why her eyes were bloodshot yesterday, but she doesn't say anything, simply leaning against Rose's legs and looking, for once, rather wrung-out.

'I feel we haven't talked properly for ages, Rosie,' she says, too softly for Jane, who has resumed reading, to hear. 'I'm still your friend, aren't I?'

Rose hesitates, then lays her hand on Diana's hair. It's a soft pearlescent colour in the low light of the room. She begins to stroke its silky lengths. 'Of course you are, silly,' she murmurs.

'I know I've been getting on your nerves and I'm sorry, Rosie-Rose. It's only because this place puts me out of sorts. I spend half my time bored and the other half looking over my shoulder.'

'I know it's hard for you here.'

They lapse into silence, Rose leaning back in her seat, Diana's head warm against her legs. Over in the opposite corner, Jane's eyelids are drooping, her head now resting on her hand. Feeling Rose's gaze on her, she blinks, shuts the book and gets to her feet. 'I keep reading the same paragraph over and over. I think I'll turn in.' She yawns and stretches.

Rose smiles. 'Goodnight, then.'

'Shall we have a little drink?' says Diana, once they're alone. 'I thought I'd wait till our Girl Guide went to bed. I want to tell you something. I've been saving it up.'

'What is it?' It's a relief to know she's not Diana's only source of interest.

Diana smiles in a show of glee that doesn't quite reach her eyes. 'A few things, some of which I discovered when I went on my charm offensive to Mrs Fox's room the other day. First, the easy one. Jane is only fifteen!'

'Really? I thought she must be at least seventeen. She's tall for her age.'

'Yes, I just thought she was a greenhorn.'

'Surely she hasn't lied to join the Land Army.'

'No, we just assumed she'd joined – and that her proper uniform was delayed. You know they're always short.'

Rose shakes her head. 'She's less than half my age. Fifteen. That makes me feel very old.'

'Well, at least we're old enough for a drink. Please say you'll join me for one before we go off to Bedfordshire. Just a teeny one.'

'I don't know. I don't think I'll need any help tonight.'

'Oh, go on, Rosie, it's ages since we talked properly, just the two of us. And I've been craving a drink all day to calm me down. Besides, I haven't told you the rest yet.'

She goes over to the sofa and pulls it out from the wall a few inches. From behind it, she extracts a dust-rimed bottle of what looks like port.

Rose rolls her eyes in amusement. 'Where did you get that?'

'Pinched it today from the study. Eleanor's Gerald is never here to miss it. There's only half a bottle left anyway so we may as well finish it off. Sorry I've no decent glasses. A lamentable oversight, I know.'

'Well, one simply can't get the staff these days,' says Rose, allowing herself to give in to Diana's charm.

Diana smiles and it looks genuine this time. 'Oh, Rose! I was beginning to think you'd gone off me entirely.'

They clink tooth-mugs and sip the sweet ruby-coloured liquid.

'Gosh, it's quite good actually,' says Diana. 'Though, I must say, port always reminds me horribly of Christmas visits to Great Uncle Theobald's. That man had the most appallingly wandering hands.' She waggles her fingers at Rose. 'Mother never wanted to hear anything about it, of course. He's dead now, thank God.'

Diana tops them up and Rose begins to feel pleasantly woozy in the warm room. Diana is throwing it down as though it's water. Jane had closed the windows and secured the blackout on her way out and the sound of the sea has been reduced to a distant hush. Only a single light is burning, a standard lamp with a fussy fringed shade, the pool of its light soft and warm.

Diana pulls the other armchair right up to Rose's so the two seats face each other, almost touching. She sits down and stretches out her long legs, bare feet nestling under Rose. She reaches for her tooth-mug, which she's filled again. The inside of her lips is stained a deep burgundy.

'You don't do anything by halves, do you?' says Rose.

'No. I've never seen the point of half-measures, quite literally in this case.' She raises her glass. 'Chin-chin.'

'Do you suppose it's the war?' says Rose. 'Thinking that you may as well do something you wouldn't normally because who knows what tomorrow will bring?'

The alcohol is making her think of Sam again, but not in the way she had been since she'd seen his son, which had felt like a kind of mourning. Now he's back to being someone out there waiting, only a mile or so down the coast-path. The news from France always seems to stir her, these days, just as the German plane had.

'Oh, but I've always been horribly reckless,' Diana is saying. 'I've always known that we're dead a long time. *Carpe diem* and all that. Now, listen to this. When I went to see Mrs Fox, she let it slip that she hasn't set foot in this part of the house since the twenties. But then in the middle of the night, I woke up to find her in the hallway outside our room, raving about someone being inside. Payne had to *restrain* her.'

Diana opens her mouth as if to say something further, then shuts it again. Instead she smiles, much more uncertainly than usual. 'It was horribly Gothic, like something out of M. R. James.'

'Perhaps you dreamt the whole thing,' says Rose.

Diana frowns. 'I did not, but let's not talk about it any

more. It gives me goose-flesh talking about it in the gloom. Anyway, I wanted to say something to you.' She looks down, a lock of hair falling across her face. 'I wanted to say sorry properly for making you so cross in the garden. When I was teasing you.'

'I don't remember being cross.'

'Well, you were. It was just before that German plane went right over us. Oh, look, you've gone inside yourself again now, like you always do these days. Something did happen that summer, though, didn't it? I think there *was* a boy. Do tell me – it's such a tiny little secret. It'll take my mind off everything. The thing is, those old bats scuffling in the hallway last night gave me a bit of a fright.'

Rose doesn't answer immediately. The port is heavy and warm in her blood, and wonderfully loosening. Diana wouldn't even blink at the notion of a married woman thinking about another man. To her, it will probably seem perfectly natural. She considers the girl opposite her. The drink is calming her too; she's looking drowsy and young. Just as beautiful, of course, but everything that can be brittle and challenging seems to have ebbed away for now.

'Yes, all right,' Rose says softly. 'Something did happen.'

She sees the flash of Diana's teeth as she smiles. 'I knew it. Although I'm beginning to think there's a bit more to it than a silly boy now. You look so terribly serious.'

Rose swirls the dark liquid around her tooth-mug. She thinks of what she doesn't want to tell anyone, like what happened with her mother, and what she is willing to offer up to Diana tonight. In truth, part of her is desperate to speak about Sam again. What does it matter now anyway? She's not going to see him.

'No, you were right the first time,' she says slowly. 'There was a boy.'

Diana sits up straighter, the light falling on her face. Her eyes, dark in the low light, glitter. Rose wonders if this is going to be a mistake.

'I knew it, you minx!' she says. 'Oh, how delicious. Was he your first love? I want to know everything.' She shares out the rest of the port, ignoring Rose's feeble protestations. 'Oh, come on. If you think you're going to bed now, you've got another think coming.'

'What about you?' says Rose, stalling because she's suddenly afraid she'll say too much, that she'll mix up the past with the present. 'Who was your first love?'

Diana shakes her head. 'Never been in love. Not even close. I despise them all. They're only good for one thing, as any honest woman will tell you. And too many of them are complete duffers at that, too. Now, don't you dare try to distract me, deflecting my questions. We're talking about you, about Rosie's romantic adventures in the halcyon summer of . . . God, when would it have been? I'm too blotto for sums.'

Rose sighs resignedly. 'It was 1924. Centuries ago to you, I'm sure.'

'Oh, hardly. You're not that ancient.'

'You were what, four years old? Five?'

'You're deflecting again! Now, indulge me, please. Start with how you met.'

Rose knows the alcohol is scattering her inhibitions but, as she finishes the port, she can feel the desire to confide crowd out caution again. The peaceful, dimly lit room is like a cocoon. It'll be such a relief to give up some of what she's been carrying around.

So she tells Diana about the toffee colour of his skin and how much paler her arm had looked next to his, even by the end of the summer. She even tells her how the heat of him against her made her insides feel watery, making her pull away, embarrassed. How they swam together at the cove on the hottest days, the shock of his bare legs slipping against hers making it hard to breathe, though she had blamed the chill of the water. How he had kissed her so intently once, near the end of their days together, the evening air around them completely still, that it felt as if they were locked up in their own private room together.

'Did you only kiss?' It's Diana's first interruption and Rose is surprised by the intensity in her face. She's not even drinking any more, her half-empty mug forgotten by the side of the armchair.

Rose is glad her cheeks are hot already. 'Well, I suppose it went a little further than that, but we were pretty innocent, really. We were both horribly furtive when we had our last kiss. It was in the village because I was late to meet him at our usual spot – my father had said I must pack first. It was pure luck I saw him in Vennor but we were surrounded by people and unsure how to be with each other, both of us knowing full well that it was the last time and that it ought to be special. I remember wishing I hadn't gone at all – that we'd said goodbye in private the day before.'

Diana makes an impatient noise, half snort, half sigh. 'Sixteen-year-old boys generally want more than a kiss.'

'Perhaps. And he was a little older, actually. More like

seventeen. But he was a gentleman.' She sounds prissy to her own ears and it isn't quite true, anyway. She isn't willing to explain how their kisses in the privacy of Breakheart Cove had gone on and on, and how perfectly their bodies had seemed to fit. She remembers the first time they fell back so they were lying pressed together on the cooling sand but she can't possibly explain to Diana how that evening, and all the ones that followed, had contained the most intimate moments of her life – all of them more meaningful and transporting than anything she had done subsequently in her marriage bed with Frank.

Before Diana can extract anything more personal from her, Rose resumes and there are no more interruptions until she mentions Sam's reluctance to show her where he lived.

'Hang on, so he was a local boy?' says Diana.

Rose nods. 'What did you think?'

'I don't know, really. I suppose I assumed he was on holiday with his people, like you.'

'Oh, no. His family have – had – been in the village for generations. His father was a fisherman. That's part of what made it so special, you see. He knew it so well. He took me to places I would never have found on my own. There were days when we wouldn't see another soul, even though it was midsummer.'

Diana laughs. It sounds sharp to Rose. 'Golly, a fisherman's boy. I had no idea he was so ordinary, the way you've been speaking about him.'

The words sting and she wishes she could take the story back. 'He was anything but ordinary. And, besides, if you're such a dreadful snob you'd better stop talking to me. I'm ordinary too.'

'Don't get prickly, Rosie. You're not one of those horrid socialists, are you? Is that why you're looking so furious with me?'

Rose lets her head fall back against the armchair. 'It didn't matter to me that his father was a fisherman. I couldn't have cared less.'

'But I bet it mattered to him. I bet he was ashamed that he lived in one of those postage-stamp-sized houses in the village. Did he meet your parents?'

Rose sighs. 'No.'

'Why not?'

'Because of my father. My mother wouldn't have minded.'

'But your father wouldn't have approved.'

'Why are you picking holes in this, Diana? Why does it matter what my father would have thought?'

Diana's face is flushed as she picks up her drink and drains it in one. Perhaps it's the port that has so abruptly turned her mood. 'So, anyway,' she says, 'what happened to him? This fisher-boy of yours.'

Rose hesitates. She's wary now. The conversation has transmuted into something harder. 'The summer came to an end,' she says, 'and that was that. I went back to my own life.'

'But surely you must have written to one another. Or couldn't he?'

'Of course he could write. He went to school. But he chose not to, I suppose. I waited, but there was nothing.'

'And you didn't write to him?'

'I'd given him my address. He was to write first. And when he didn't, I didn't have his. I don't think I'd have tried that anyway. Too proud.'

Diana pulls a face. 'Oh, no, that can't be the end.'

'Sadly, it was.' She shifts in her seat. 'We both grew up and got married.'

'How do you know he's married?'

The port has made Rose's thoughts fuggy. She can't think quite clearly now what she can say and what she can't.

'You haven't seen him, have you?' Diana's face sharpens, and even as Rose flails around for the right answer, she sees something in Diana's expression that she can't quite identify, something more than a simple hunger for secrets.

After a pause, she shakes her head. 'Of course not. I expect he's away, fighting.'

'Isn't fishing a reserved occupation?'

'He's not a fisher– What I mean is, he always said he didn't want to follow his father. It's such a hard life, and so dangerous.'

Diana looks at her unblinkingly and Rose struggles not to glance away. Still without breaking eye-contact, Diana stretches out her arms and digs her feet further under Rose, wiggling her long toes. Rose flinches as a nail digs into her flesh.

'Tell me his name and I'll ask around for you. I've got a friend in Vennor who knows simply everyone. Everyone's a second cousin in a place like this.'

Rose's laugh rings out falsely. 'Oh, goodness, it hardly matters now. It's all so long ago. I'm sure he wouldn't even remember me.'

Diana smirks. 'Oh, I'm certain he would. And wouldn't it be lovely if you could be reunited? Perhaps you could go to tea with him and his wife. It's always fascinating meeting the wife or intended of the men one has had a dalliance with, don't you think?'

'I wouldn't know.'

'Come on, Rosie, give up his name. I'll be the soul of discretion about it, perfectly subtle.'

Rose swallows, the beginnings of panic sluicing away the alcohol. 'No, but you see the only reason I remember him so fondly is because of what happened afterwards.' Her voice sounds shrill, desperate even, but she can't bear the thought of Diana digging around in the village for information about Sam. Telling her she's already seen him would be a bad error, she knows that in her bones. Something has shifted between her and Diana in the last few minutes, though she can't grasp what. The room doesn't feel like a cocoon now. Now she can't wait to leave it.

Diana folds her hands over her stomach, a smile playing at the corners of her mouth. 'So? Don't stop there. What happened afterwards?'

'My mother.'

'What about her?'

Rose takes in a sharp little breath. 'She died.'

Diana's head snaps up. 'Died?'

'Not long after we got back. I think that's why that summer has always been so important to me. It sounds like a terrible cliché but things weren't the same afterwards.'

'Oh, darling, that must have been awful for you.' Something like genuine sympathy wars on Diana's face with satisfaction at discovering something so valuable. 'Assuming you liked her, of course.'

Rose winces at the flippancy of the words.

'I'm sorry, Rosie.' Diana sits up properly and takes Rose's hands in her own. 'I shouldn't make light. I always make light of everything, beastly creature that I am. It's a horrible habit. Will you forgive me?'

Rose nods. She feels slightly sick. She desperately wants to go and wash her face with cold water and go to bed.

'What did she die of?' Diana says quietly, after a respectable pause.

Rose pauses. She doesn't want to talk about this. But then she starts to speak anyway.

'There were times when she was ill, when she went to bed for a week or two and we had to be quiet around the house. It's why we were in Cornwall, actually. Recuperation, it was supposed to be. She'd been here as a girl and loved it. I thought she was feeling better by the time we left, but as soon as we got home she seemed to decline again.'

Rose has never really spoken to anyone about her mother before – not even Frank, who staunchly disapproves of any mental frailty. He thinks she feels the same. He would never understand that she can be angry and sad and miss her mother terribly all at the same time. She did try to talk to him once, in the early days of them courting, but he'd stopped her mid-sentence, holding up his hand and saying, 'Least said, soonest mended, or so I reckon.' She hadn't known whether to laugh or cry. She'd never tried again.

Now she looks up at Diana, who is watching her carefully. She tries to read the younger girl's expression again but she's too exhausted. 'She committed suicide, you see. My brother and I found her, when we came in from school. She – she was in the bath.'

For once, Diana is silenced.

Rose gets to her feet, her head spinning. 'I've got to go to bed now,' she says. 'I feel awful. I'm not used to drinking.'

Diana stands and takes Rose's hands in hers, which feel amazingly warm and alive. 'Thank you for trusting me with this. You poor darling. You go on now,' she says gently, all her hardness melted away again. 'I'll tidy up in here.' Briefly, she pulls Rose to her and kisses her somewhere near her ear. It's Rose who steps away, patting Diana on the back as she does.

'Thank you. Please don't say anything about this to anyone, will you? Even that diary of yours.'

Diana shakes her head. 'Of course not. Cross my heart.'

When Rose glances back from the door, Diana hasn't moved. She's watching Rose, her face in shadow. As Rose walks to the bathroom, alone once more, the relief of her confession starts to feel more like vertigo, as though there was an edge she hadn't even known was there until she was over it, and falling through empty air.

* * *

TWENTY DAYS LEFT

Sunday, 30ᵗʰ June

I can't stop thinking about what Rose's mother did to herself. I can't get rid of it. It was the same all night too, an eternity passing before the blackout turned to grey. I couldn't close my eyes because every time I did I saw her as Rose must have found her: limp and unresponsive in cooling water stained pink. And when I think of that, my mind goes to the bathroom at home. The gleam of the black and white chequerboard tiles, steam swirling in the air and Daddy's cut-throat razor balanced on the rim of the bath. I remember how I got up to push the window open a crack because the water was too hot and the white spots flurried in front of my eyes and I slipped and banged my head on the tap. I didn't want to do it after that. I cried and cried until I was so exhausted that I thought I would fall asleep in the bath and drown, which would have been ironic, and thinking of that made me laugh and cry at the same time, and later I put Daddy's razor back and no one ever knew.

Rose was already asleep when I got to bed after tidying the sitting room, as though drained from her confession. I suppose a sentimental part of me had envied what I'd pictured as a humdrum sort of upbringing: parents the quiet, doting sort – him pottering contentedly in his shed and her turning out steak and kidney puddings in a floral housecoat. But I was wrong and it's hardly a comfort because I liked to think of Rose in that way. It was the sweet ordinariness of it all: Sunday lunch with the wireless on; rows of carefully planted marigolds; people calling each other 'lovey'.

She was chalk-white and shaking by the time she'd finished telling me. It was like hearing about something that had happened only weeks before, not sixteen years ago. She was still raw with it.

I had a letter from Daddy today. He's never had any talent for correspondence but almost outdid himself with this particular missive. It was no more than half a side, every sentence as dry as a bone. He might have been writing to the milkman to amend his order. He did at least include another ten-shilling note, which didn't really make up for it, but had to do. 'Your mother sends her love,' he put dutifully at the end, though she won't have sent anything of the sort. That woman doesn't have any love to impart, least of all to her only child. I can't help thinking that she and Mrs Fox would get on famously.

Which leads me to wonder why on earth Jane would want to live with the disapproval of Grandmother Fox when she doesn't have to. I had no choice about living with Mother all those years. I can only think it must be even worse at home in London for the wretched girl. No doubt this is why Eleanor is so solicitous, though anyone can see it embarrasses Jane terribly. The girl is like a dog that's totally unaccustomed to being petted, flinching and freezing whenever Eleanor tries to snatch a kiss goodnight. That sinister episode with Payne in the hallway the other night was my warning to leave well alone, but I find I can't. Jane, for all her gauche awkwardness, is no different from me. Neither of us fits.

Later. The village was unnerving tonight when I went just before dark, the place utterly deserted, the full moon casting it in a chill, ghostly light. The wind had strengthened by the time I got there, keening mournfully in the rigging of the harbour's boats. The outer walls were being slapped steadily by a sea that seemed to be working itself up, very slowly, into a temper.

Dew had company in his net loft: one of his lieutenants, who was not introduced but I assumed was a younger brother or cousin. He looked like a skinny and squashed-face version of Dew, with none of the latter's brains and charm. I can't decide if I'm relieved or not to have had this unlikely chaperon in attendance. I think Dew himself was undecided; he seemed irritated by the chap's presence but didn't dismiss him either. Perhaps he wanted to show me off.

Still, even with the other man standing there staring at me, I could feel the frisson between me and Dew like electricity crackling through the tobacco-fugged air. If anything, the addition of a third person only heightened the tension.

'You'll come back, won't you, when you want more?' he said, when he handed over my package of goodies, his fingers brushing the sensitive inside of my wrist and a slow smile turning up one side of his mouth. The air lit up again, and I knew he meant me to return when he might be alone.

Thoughts of that made me unable to settle when I got back, my whole body tingling, so I popped in on Mrs Fox, hoping to cadge a little something that would help me sleep.

She was bright-eyed and full of nasty vigour at first, asking after the port I pilfered (no flies on her) but I said she should look to Cook. I told her I'd caught the old boiler tippling in the kitchen the other day, though of course she's a staunch Methodist and never touches the stuff. That'll serve her right for telling the ARP man I've been showing a light when I have my bedtime cig. I know it was her.

'You haven't told me why you don't go to the other side of the house yet,' I put in, after ten minutes of carefully innocuous conversation about nothing much: the war and so on. I'm not sure I'd have had the nerve if Payne had been there, but I was feeling emboldened after braving the net loft. 'Did something dreadful happen there in 1924? A guest dropping dead, perhaps, or a haunting?'

She gave me dreadful daggers and gripped her cane more tightly. 'You are by some distance wide of the mark,' she said eventually, in a low, dangerous tone that would have impressed Dew.

A less foolhardy person would have left it there, but discretion has never been my forte, and I wanted to think about something other than Rose's mother. 'I suppose I could ask Eleanor,' I said. 'She would have been there at the time.'

She looked at me balefully, twilit shadows creeping into every crevice of her face, and I thought again of her wailing on the landing. 'You will say nothing to Eleanor.'

'But it was so long ago. What harm can it possibly do?'

In reply, she rapped the arm of my chair with the head of the cane. The crack on the wood was so loud and abrupt that I reared back in my seat. She missed my fingers by half an inch.

'That's enough from you, madam,' she said, and thumped this time on the floor, hard enough to make the window glass shiver. Payne answered the summons so quickly that she must have been at the keyhole. As she crossed the room to her mistress, she gave me one of her blood-freezing looks.

'You've made me tired, Miss Devlin,' Mrs Fox said, and her voice had changed again, this time to a petulant child's. Her blue eyes had gone blank and her body rigid; she looked for all the world like an ancient doll. 'Go down and tell Cook I won't take my usual cocoa tonight. I am too weak for it. Payne, you will carry me to bed.'

And so I was abruptly dispatched, hardly the wiser but rather more intimidated. Clearly I have underestimated her and will have to tread much more carefully if I am to be allowed back. Anyone with an ounce of sense would heed the warning clear in Payne's eyes, but the flames of my interest have only been fanned. They say that what we recoil from in others is what we are secretly ashamed of in ourselves. Perhaps that's why my nose is so attuned to the scent of other people's horrors. I'm thinking not just of Mrs Fox but Rose, too.

X

Rose is the first to wake on Sunday. She knows there's no point in trying to doze; her mind is too agitated. It's probably only the physical work in the garden that is allowing her to get any decent sleep at all. Not wanting to wake the others, she tiptoes out to dress in the shared bathroom.

The air in the small, white-tiled room is still chilly, the sun not yet high enough over the house to have warmed the floor beneath her feet. Not that it ever gets very warm in here; the room is an afterthought, facing inward on a small, shady courtyard where Cook smokes a single cigarette at five each afternoon.

Last night had been awkward, once a restless Diana had got back from wherever she'd been and joined Jane and Rose in the sitting room. It had been a peaceful evening until then, the wireless chuntering on in the background, Jane reading and Rose doing her best to rescue her last good pair of stockings. Diana broke into the scene as a whirl of noise and fizzing energy that bordered on the hysterical; she was babbling something about spies on the coast-path and ghosts in the Hall as she kicked off her shoes, her sudden movements scenting the air with alcohol.

Rose hadn't asked her about any of it and neither had an uncomfortable-looking Jane. There is something about Diana that makes you seek her approval or at least not invite her scorn, even when you're angry with her. Perhaps this is what people mean by charisma.

Rose knows that she's really more furious with herself. Remembering how easily she'd confided in Diana about Sam and then her mother makes her feel sick now, as though she'd put out her most precious possessions with the rubbish. She'd had far too much to drink. She's so trusting and open when she does, which is why she hardly ever indulges. Frank doesn't like women drinking anyway, has always said it's coarse. Still, she can't help feeling resentment towards Diana, who had poured her drink after drink and extracted everything from her with such ease.

She hadn't wanted anyone to know in this place that is from the time before her mother died. The way Diana had looked at her yesterday reminds her of returning to school after the funeral and understanding that, despite what they'd been told by the teachers, the other girls all knew the truth. Even the kind ones, who didn't fall silent when she walked into a room, couldn't help their eyes straying to her wrists, as though what her mother had done might have left scars on her, too.

Rose straightens the waistband of her skirt and slips her feet into her shoes, deciding not to bother with stockings. At least she hadn't let Diana leach everything out of her, particularly the fact that she'd seen Sam twice. A wave of emotion eddies through her at the thought: an acute blend of yearning and frustration that there can't be a third occasion.

Outside, the early sky is the colour of lemon rinds. The air is still cool with dew but warming all the time. Penhallow is quiet, the blackout still shuttering all the windows except one small one on the top floor. Perhaps Payne is already up and dressed.

The view out to sea from the lawn always takes her breath away. She can't imagine getting used to it, even if she stayed for ever. Of course that's impossible; as soon as the war ends, she'll be expected to return to Solihull, to take up her role as Frank's wife again, as far away from the sea as it's possible to be in England. The thought – repeated often to herself, like a punishment – settles on her, heavy and sullen: a hint of November dampening the sparkling morning. With an effort she pushes it away, breathing in lungfuls of sweet Cornish air.

She knows it's self-indulgent to turn towards Chyandour and deliberately stir up her memories again, even as she's doing it. It's disorientating how familiar this stretch of the path seems, lodged in some dusty crevice of her memory all along, only misplaced rather than lost all these years. The strange thing about the walk, now that she's doing it, is its very ordinariness.

That summer has shimmered, perfect and elusive, for so long it has attained mythical status. Now, shoes kicking up dust from the dry path, a hand out to brush the sea campion and silkweed, she remembers how real and normal it was, and the thought makes her calmer than she's been in days. *Sam is a mortal like her*, she reminds herself. *He's just a man.*

She reaches a bench, which brings her up short. For a moment, the susurration of the sea grows louder in her ears and she glimpses the ghost of her younger self, kissing Sam. The gouge he'd made with his penknife is still there on the wooden seat; not a heart – they were too self-conscious for anything so obvious – just a curving point, like a wave about to break.

She turns to see if Penhallow would have been visible back then, if she'd been able to take in anything other than him. And there it is: a corner of roof, pale stone and dark grey tiles, a couple of upper windows. Without the distraction of Sam Bligh, it would have intrigued her sixteen-year-old self. It strikes her that Eleanor was almost certainly in the house at the time. Poor troubled Eleanor, hardly more than a girl herself, might have watched them from one of those windows.

She remembers something else, another fragment of memory hidden until now. An evening when she had slipped out to see Sam after dinner. It was dusk, the two of them at the top of the steps down to the cove, neither wanting to part. She had perched on the rail that went down the flight as a banister. He was standing facing her, and when he leant down to kiss her, she remembers her hands clamping around the rail's cold metal. They'd both heard the music at the same time, lifting their heads to catch the strains over the sound of the waves below.

'Where's it coming from?' she'd murmured, as his face came closer again, but he hadn't answered then. Afterwards, when she really did have to go, and the breeze had thrown the music briefly closer, he had gestured behind him.

'There's a big house up there. They'll be having their annual ball.'

As she'd run back to Chyandour, her hands smelling of iron and her blood thrumming, the music, carried faintly on the air, stayed with her all the way. It had even crept like sea mist through her open window as she slept, seeping into her dreams.

She's still thinking about this when she reaches the bridge over Blackbottle Creek. Her mind elsewhere and her eyes on her feet, she is only dimly aware of an approaching figure – just conscious enough of someone's approach to smooth down her hair, which has been blowing about in the breeze, and to move slightly to the left of the path so he or she can pass.

But the other figure doesn't move aside and go on. He comes to a halt in front of her. She looks up and sees that it's him. They stare at each other for a long moment and the only coherent thought she has is that, later, afterwards, she will treasure this coincidence as a sign. She will be glad of such an intense, dumbfounded pause, because it's so far from the polite, meaningless chitchat anyone else would have launched into by now.

She had seen him just the other day, with the boy, but on the coast-path she thinks of as theirs he feels new to her again, so much more real than the figure in the village and on the other side of a dusty, finger-smeared pane of glass.

'Hello,' she manages eventually, breaking the silence that looks to go on and on. She smiles and he mirrors her, just as he had when she smiled at him from the bus. She remembers then that it had always been this way between them, that he had always waited to see what she did and said when they'd met each day, so that she'd had to be brave first.

Now, she makes herself look him in the eye. 'I hoped . . . I mean, I wondered if I would see you. Not today, not here, but in Vennor.'

She can't quite believe he's there in front of her, not when she deliberately chose to go in the opposite direction from the village where he lives.

'I always come this way,' he says, the colour on his cheeks high, visible even in his tanned face. 'I walk the path most mornings.'

'I saw you the other day,' she blurts, wanting to confess straight away. 'With your boy.' She looks at her feet.

'Jimmy, you mean? He's a good lad. Turned eleven last month. I can't remember what it was like in the house before he came along.' He smiles fondly to himself.

'I suppose it was a good deal quieter,' she says.

'Yes, something like that.'

They fall silent and Rose casts around for something to say. She doesn't know how to be with him now he comes with others: a wife and a child that are completely apart from her.

'He must take after his mother,' she says eventually. 'In looks.'

Sam frowns in confusion. 'Oh, well, I don't know, really. He might do.'

'He doesn't look much like you, I mean.' Rose blushes, realizing this might be offensive, but Sam's face clears.

'Oh, Jimmy's not mine. He's an evacuee. I don't have any of my own. I was late to get to the church hall and only him and another boy were left. He looked like he needed a good meal and a kind word. I had to take him.'

She doesn't trust herself to speak. The colours in the scene around her are suddenly brighter, as though daubed in fresh paint. Eventually she says, 'I haven't any either. Children, I mean.'

His gaze rests for a moment on her wedding ring. It's as good as saying it aloud. *But you've got a husband. And I've got a wife.*

But the boy is not yours, she thinks.

As if he can hear her, he looks back up from her ring to her face. 'How long's it been, Rosy?' he says softly. 'Sixteen years, isn't it?'

'Yes. Half our lives.'

'Seeing you here, it feels like it was only last summer. Last month, even.'

'Yes.' She nods. 'And a hundred years ago at the same time.'

'You never came back,' he says, and above the rueful smile, his eyes betray the old hurt. 'You said you'd be back the next summer.'

She resists the urge to take his hands in hers. 'I wanted to. You've no idea how much. It was my father, you see – he didn't want us to come again. But what about you?' She doesn't even try to hide her own hurt. 'I waited and waited for your letter.'

He frowns. 'I wrote to you the day after you left.' He glances out to sea, embarrassed remembering it. 'It was a daft sort of letter, really, and I wondered if that was why you didn't write back.'

'But I didn't get it. It must have got lost in the post. Didn't you . . . I mean, was it only . . .'

'Do you mean did I try again?' He looks her in the eye. 'I sent you another half-dozen. More, probably.'

Rose shakes her head. 'When did you stop?'

'When the next summer came around.' His voice hardens. 'You didn't come back to Chyandour, and I couldn't remember any more why I'd done it for so long.'

Rose can't think of any reply. This is her father's doing, she knows it. She wonders if he threw them away, or burnt them in the fire when she was out – or whether they're hidden away, unopened in some drawer, crisping and yellowing with age. She's suddenly furious: about what might have been, about all the years she's wasted being unhappy. She glimpses another version of herself, if her father hadn't interfered, and it makes her want to cry.

'I didn't get any of them,' she says quietly. She checks to see if his expression softens, if he believes her. 'I was heartbroken when nothing came. I waited and waited and then, after the third week, I couldn't convince myself any more that a letter would come. That was when my mother . . . Well, I didn't expect anything after that. It must have been my father who took them. He wouldn't have approved. He'd have thought it was romantic nonsense when we lived so far apart.' She can hear the bitterness in her voice.

In reply, he reaches out and, for a moment, she thinks he's going to stroke her cheek. He had always cupped her cheek in his hand before he kissed her. She steps towards him just as he steps back, his head turned towards the sea again. 'He approve of your husband better, does he?'

'Oh, yes, he adores Frank.' As soon as the name is out, she wishes she could take it back. A horrible, jealous part of her has said it because she's had to live with the name 'Morwenna' for days.

'Frank,' he repeats.

It hovers in the air between them.

'I don't –' She stops. 'He's away. With the navy. I haven't seen him in months.'

Sam considers this. 'So why are you here and not at home? I couldn't work it out.'

He's thought about her since Fowey. It makes her glow.

'I'm a land girl.' She shrugs, embarrassed, when he smiles. 'I know I'm older than most of them but I didn't want to stay at home and mind the shop, or work in a factory. I wanted to get away.'

'And you came back to Vennor.' His smile widens.

'I saw it on the list. It jumped out at me.'

'Like a sign.'

She swallows as she realizes he's moved towards her again. They're standing closer to each other than people generally do. She can see where the skin inside the collar of his shirt gets lighter. She lifts her hair so the breeze can cool her hot neck.

'So are you at one of the farms?' He's watching her and she shifts about under his gaze.

'No, I'm just up there, at Penhallow Hall.'

'Not a bad billet.'

'No.'

The conversation until now has been conducted at exactly the same pitch as their exchanges in the past: every word and look absolutely significant, and stored away even as it was spoken, to be pored over later, alone and wakeful in their respective single beds. She doesn't want it to slip into everyday chatter.

'Sam, I never forgot about you.' The words come out so softly that he has to lean towards her as the boom of a wave against rock snatches the words away.

'And I never forgot you either,' he says. 'My sisters got at me, mooning about for you so long.'

'I'm sorry. When I see my father, I'll –'

'No, no. He was just being your dad. Protecting his only girl.'

She shakes her head. Her father was anything but protective when it came to Frank. Standing there on the path with Sam, she can't think how she came to marry someone she has always felt so indifferent about, someone she has nothing to say to. It was as if she'd sleepwalked through the last decade and a half.

'You missing him?' Sam breaks into her thoughts.

She colours because it's so far from the truth. 'I shouldn't say it, I know, but I don't. We . . . We're not . . .' She stops.

Sam nods, not quite meeting her eye, and she can't tell if he's glad or disapproving. He doesn't offer anything in return about his wife and the silence makes Rose feel worse.

'I suppose I ought to be going back now,' she says, suddenly miserable. It was like this too, sometimes, she recalls, her moods swooping up and down from one moment to the next. She wills him to know this, and when he does, or seems to, and smiles again, the glorious morning comes back into focus: the glinting sun, the bright birdsong and the stirring scent of deepening summer.

'I'm going back that way,' he says. 'I'll walk you to the Hall, if you like.'

'Yes.'

They don't talk as they walk and she wonders if he's thinking the same things as she is. She feels happily sure for now that she'll see him again, and soon, the certainty of it is spreading through her warmly. The path narrows in some places, where the gorse has grown unchecked, and a couple of times she brushes against Sam by accident. Each time it happens, she feels it as a jolt, leaving her a little bit more alert and alive each time, as though he's giving off tiny electric shocks. She has the fleeting urge to push their bare forearms together as they did years ago, and marvel again at how dark his skin is against hers. Perhaps she will. Next time.

Too soon they reach Penhallow's gate.

'Here we are then,' he says. 'Delivered safely to your door, or almost.'

'Thank you. It's been . . . well, it's been so lovely to see you –'

'How do you find it here, then?' he interrupts, glancing away with the embarrassment of keeping the conversation going so obviously and clumsily.

'Oh.' She blushes. 'Well, I like it. Mrs Grenville is very kind to us and we have good food and comfortable beds and a sitting room of our own. I suppose I've fallen on my feet.'

'There more than one of you, then?'

Something primal in her is reluctant to mention Diana. 'Oh, yes, younger than me but nice, easy to get along with.'

'I hope I'll see you soon, Rosy,' he says, after a pause.

She's just turning, her hand on the gate's latch, but he's suddenly standing right behind her, so close she can feel the heat coming off him.

Still with her back to him, she has, for a wild, terrifying instant, the sense that he's going to brush her hair away from the tender spot between her neck and shoulder and kiss her there. Perhaps he almost does; she thinks she feels his breath minutely moving her hair. But when she turns he's already stepped away, and is looking off down the path that will take him back to the village.

'Do you think we will?' she says.

'I do. Well, I hope so. Come and see me in the light-house, if you want. There's ships coming through for the next week at least. I'll need to light the lamp for them.'

She's smiling as he turns and walks away with his easy, long-legged stride. If he'd invited her to take tea with him, Morwenna and the little evacuee boy, she might have cried. But he hadn't, and she knew, really, that he wouldn't. That isn't how things are between them already, and she thinks he knows that too.

Closing the gate behind her, she lingers for a while. It's cool and green on the grass, in the shade from a laurel bush, the rasp of the sea more distant now it's on the other side of the gate. She can feel the encounter with Sam already spooling away from her – an episode wrapped carefully in tissue paper. Though the dew on the long grass underfoot is beginning to soak into her shoes, she isn't ready to go back inside and up the stairs yet, to where the others are surely beginning to rouse themselves and wonder where she's got to.

'Who were you talking to?'

Rose looks up from her feet so fast she cricks her neck, the hot pain of it making her shut her eyes. When she opens them again, Diana has drawn a little closer. While

Rose is in shade, Diana is lit by the sun, her edges blazing. She's wearing a full-skirted dress the colour of buttercups with a narrow black belt and Rose thinks, as she has so many times, that there is something unreal about her beauty. Even after the nights she drinks too much, and there seem to be more of those lately, there is never any sign of it in her face.

'I wasn't talking to anyone,' Rose says, smoothing her hair back. Her hands are trembling slightly and she fights the urge to put them behind her back, like a naughty child caught stealing.

'I heard you. Come on, do tell.'

'It was just a man I met on the path. He was going on to the village.'

'So why not say, if that was all it was?'

Rose's mind is blank. All she can think of is her and Diana's conversation the other night and the feeling that she had tumbled over some unnamed brink. She can feel the danger of it again now, despite the benign air of the garden. She casts about for something to say, knowing that the longer it takes her to answer, the odder it will seem.

Diana puts her head on one side, her mouth curling into a smile. 'You look terribly flustered, darling. Who was this man to bring such high colour to your cheeks? It wasn't your fisherman, was it?' She laughs and then, when Rose still stands dumbly, widens her eyes. 'Oh, Lord, it was, wasn't it?'

Rose swallows, considers shaking her head, then realizes she could never pull off such a lie, not with Diana. She can still salvage this, though. She doesn't need to tell Diana about Fowey or how he still makes her feel or how she's planning to see him again.

'Actually, yes,' she says, too brightly. 'He walks the path every morning, apparently.'

She waits for Diana to clap her hand over her mouth in excitement, or rush forward and press her for more details, but she doesn't move. They are still too far apart for two people having an intimate conversation. Rose takes a few steps towards Diana, the sun as she steps into it surprisingly strong. She feels as if she's been awake for hours.

Still Diana says nothing. Her green eyes have narrowed and Rose doesn't know if it's only because the light is so bright.

'It was nice to see him again,' Rose hurries on, when the silence yawns, her voice faltering. 'He was telling me about his wife, and the little evacuee boy they've taken in.'

'How saintly of him. Well, I did think he'd still be here. His sort always stay put, don't they?' She appraises Rose anew, her head on one side. 'I must say, though, it does all sound rather rum.'

'What do you mean?'

'Well, it's strange that you were only telling me about this chap the other night, and then – who'd have thought? – you're miraculously reunited with him, just outside our gate. Do you know, I can't help thinking it's a little too strange. Were you fibbing the other night, Rosie? Was the reason you didn't want me asking around after him because you had already found him? You haven't spared two words for me since our talk. Were you scared you'd give the rest of it away?'

Cold unease washes through Rose. 'Well, even if I had

already seen him, which I hadn't, I don't know why you'd be so put out. What's it to you anyway? And I didn't look for him because I'm a married woman, in case you'd forgotten.' She means to sound nothing more than mildly exasperated, but her voice shakes. 'I suppose I knew I might see him one day, but I didn't go looking for him. Why would I have done? He's just a boy I was friends with for a few weeks when I was young. It was nothing.' It physically hurts her to say the last words.

Diana is looking off to the side with her arms folded, red lips curled and petulant. She doesn't seem to be listening, her expression closed.

'It all makes sense now. I suppose you saw him in Fowey that day and that's why you came back all pleased and secretive. And, wait a minute, was it him you were meeting when you went off to Vennor all dolled up?'

'I wasn't dolled up.'

Diana looks her over. 'Compared to today you were. You're as pale as milk now. Why's that?'

'Why are you so cross with me?'

'I'm not cross. If I'm anything, I'm a little disappointed.'

'Disappointed?'

'That you felt you couldn't tell me, of course. I thought we were friends.'

'We are. But, Diana, listen, there was nothing to tell. I just met him —'

Diana holds up a hand. 'I don't really care. I feel suddenly quite bored of it, in fact. Let's just forget about it, shall we?'

She gives Rose a chilly little smile and walks away without another word. Rose remains standing on the grass, going over the exchange in her head and trying to work out what has just happened. Instead she recalls her very first impression of Diana, formed the moment Eleanor introduced them. *I would hate to make an enemy of that one,* she'd thought. In the intense embrace of Diana's friendship over the following weeks she'd forgotten that. Now she understands at last the feeling of tumbling through air. The dazzle of Diana distracts from the damage underneath, but Rose can see it clearly for the first time: rocks beneath a placid sea.

* * *

NINETEEN DAYS LEFT

Monday, 1ˢᵗ July

I am full of hate and bile today. I dropped a tooth-mug out of the bathroom window earlier, just to watch it smash in the courtyard below. I was tempted to chuck Rose's wash-bag after it, but that would have been too obvious. I would wish myself away to another place but what settles around me coldly is that I have nowhere else to go.

I thought Rose and I were getting somewhere the other evening, when she told me all about her mother. *This is what it must be like to have a bosom friend*, I thought stupidly. I'd even decided I would tell her properly about what happened to me. But she is still full of secrets and plans, and it's obvious I play no part in them. I would rather die than chase anyone for attention and affection. I swore I would never do that again.

Mother always says you can't be comfortable with those from a different background and perhaps, for once, she's right. I've decided to pal up with Jane instead. I blubbed a bit this morning after Rose, fool that I am, though it was mostly out of anger – not hurt. It's just that when she came through the gate and I saw her face, all open and happy and glad, I wanted to slap it.

Jane found me in another part of the garden later, wiping my eyes idiotically. If she'd asked what was wrong, I'd have packed her off but she simply passed me her handkerchief.

'You don't remember me, do you?' she said, after a while. She had joined me on the grass and was gazing at the sea, which was glittering unfeelingly. 'Of course not, why would you? I wasn't going to say anything about it. I don't really know why I am now.'

I looked at her: the ridiculous hair, flat on one side from where she'd slept on it; the elfin face; the freckles that stood out like points on her sunburnt cheeks.

'Remember you?' I said, relieved to think about something else. 'Whatever do you mean?'

She smiled shyly. 'You went to Hambledon College, didn't you? Well, so did I.'

I searched her face again but not even a faint bell rang.

'I wouldn't have expected someone like you to remember the likes of me. I was in a lower form than you. I expect girls like me simply got under your feet in the corridor. I remember when you got . . . well, you leaving.'

I snorted. 'When I was expelled, you mean? It's hardly a state secret.'

Old Hambles was a second-rate sort of establishment, set in a sprawling high-Victorian house just outside Godalming. I was made to go there because Mother did. It was run – and probably still is – by a Miss Ophelia Flack. Children's books had always given me to believe that headmistresses were either plump and kindly, or cruel and rake-thin, but Awfully Fat was both large and nasty. That was the first of many discrepancies between what I had expected of school and what I got. I had thought I might enjoy it, that things might go more smoothly than they ever had at home. I was wrong.

The school hadn't the slightest academic ambition, instead celebrating those who excelled at games and were popular. I don't suppose someone like Jane ever mastered either. I imagine she was one of the sensible ones, though: the type who didn't suffer unduly from either mistresses or bullies because she implicitly understood that she should take the insults without comment or tears. It was those who wept in the dorm, or sneaked to a mistress, or wrote home about their cruel treatment for whom it carried on for ever.

As for me, I didn't bother much with games but I did take care to ensure my place at the top of the social order. It wasn't very difficult. I never had an awkward stage, or any spots. Lots of the girls had pashes on me – I was forever finding sweaty little scraps of paper pushed under my study door, emblazoned with hearts and drenched in cheap scent.

I heard after I left that the suspected reasons for my

expulsion were legion and colourful. The whole school was speculating for months, apparently, which only added to my vast, carefully cultivated glamour. It was a shame I wasn't there to see it, like not being around for one's funeral speeches. Some thought I'd been caught smoking and drinking behind the wall at the far end of the lacrosse pitch. Others were certain I'd climbed down the ivy that covered Plantagenet House and gone into town to meet a boy. Others still thought I'd got myself with child. All wrong, of course.

'Well, this is a turn-up,' I said to Jane, even as I wondered what she might have on me, what she might have heard on the school's jungle drums, and why she'd kept the coincidence to herself this long. 'I'm sorry I don't remember you but school seems like a thousand years ago.'

Jane blushed. 'Of course it must. It feels rather horribly close at hand for me. I've only just escaped.'

I studied her carefully, still puzzling about what she might be after. 'I suppose you've got to go back in September. Oh, I know you're only fifteen,' I said, when her face fell, glad that it was she who was wrong-footed now. 'I'm afraid your grandmother gave the game away.'

She coloured again and I felt a bit sorry for her. It's been years for me and I still don't feel I've entirely shaken off Hambles. The ghost of its smell still creeps into my dreams occasionally: boiled vegetables, disinfectant and unhappiness, the combination of which always hung over the place like a rank old blanket. Sometimes it gets mixed up with my memories of Flete and I wake up positively saturated in hopelessness.

'The last time I voluntarily saw seven o'clock in the

morning I hadn't been to bed,' I said, through a pretend yawn. I didn't want to prolong the conversation about school, the thought of Jane knowing some of the more lurid Hambles hearsay making me feel precarious.

'Oh, I always wake up early when I'm here,' Jane said wistfully. 'I don't want to miss any of it.'

By now, we had got to our feet and were wandering towards the vegetable patch we'd been digging when the German plane had gone over.

'Is there anything down there?' I said idly, pointing at a narrow footpath that snaked through thick foliage. I had seen Eleanor coming up it a few days ago, looking tearful. Just visible, I could see what had to be the creek, its waters a deep oily green, quite unlike the blue of the sea.

'The boathouse, you mean? I don't think anyone goes there any more. It's never been used since I've known it. It was my uncle's in the old days. I mean, it sort of became his, before he died. His little boat is still there, I should think.'

It seemed as good a way as any of taking my mind off Rose, and Jane's off school. Plastering on a mischievous smile, I turned to her. 'Shall we go and have a peep inside?'

She hesitated. 'I'm not sure. It's probably locked up.'

I reached out for one of her hands, which made her flinch, and set me wondering if she'd ever nursed a crush on me too. 'I've got something I want to say to you,' I said, watching wariness creep into her eyes and turn them jet-black. 'There's no need to look so horrified. I only want to say that I wish we were better friends. I think we could be such bosom pals. A case of opposites attracting, perhaps. One dark, one fair. One good and one . . . well, one rather less good. Won't it be fun? And let's be honest,' I dropped my voice, 'we've more in common than we can ever have with Rose.'

She gave me a sharp look. 'Oh, you know I adore Rose,' I said quickly. 'But it's not just our backgrounds you and I share. We're both from London. We're closer in age. We have simply heaps in common.'

We started down the hill and I felt her give me a side-long glance. I knew I'd got her then; that if she'd had any ulterior motive, she was now simply smug that Diana Devlin of the upper fifth was walking next to her, having asked if they might be friends.

We reached the boathouse, a weeping willow casting it into a deep, watery shade. The air was cooler here, like the interior of a cave. I heard her take a hurried little breath.

'All right then,' she said, looking down, too shy to meet my eye. She added a shrug, as jerky as a marionette's. 'We can be friends. If you like.'

I clapped my hands in a show of delight and cried something like 'Oh, this is capital, I'm so pleased!' before reaching out and brushing that dreadful fringe back off her forehead. 'I think we'll get on famously. Do you know who you remind me of?'

She shook her head with trepidation.

'Jo March from *Little Women*. The one who sells her hair.'

She grimaced but I swooped in again: 'I don't mean because of your hair, only that you're so clever and book-ish, and when you're cross or pleased it's written all over your face in the most endearing way.'

I pulled her up the sagging steps of the old boathouse,

and she started again at the unfamiliar contact. 'Of course, you'd look completely different if you grew your hair out. Just a bit. You've got such pretty little ears and if your hair was longer, you could pin it back and show them off.'

She cleared her throat, her cheeks burning. 'I . . . Well, yes. It's just that I've had it short for so long.'

'And you don't want people to notice and think you've changed and are making some enormous feminine effort now, you mean?'

She nodded. It was exactly what she'd meant, of course. I put my hand on the doorknob of the boathouse and paused. 'So, are we agreed then? I'll be your coiffeuse and confidante and you, in return, can guide me morally. You'll be dreadfully good for me because, you see, while you're Jo, I'm just spoilt, vain little Amy. You'll teach me to be good, won't you, Jane? Do say you will.' I think part of me even meant it.

She agreed with a dazed nod and followed me into the boathouse, which wasn't locked after all. Inside it was mildewy, the air almost frigid. I'd expected it to be empty but there was a desk, an armchair and some other pieces of battered furniture. Stacked against the far wall were half a dozen tea chests and a couple of scuffed suitcases. Most intriguing was a box on the desk, the key left helpfully in the lock.

'Perhaps we shouldn't . . .' Jane began, but I'd already gone over and lifted the lid. Inside, it was stacked to the top with old photographs and letters.

'Secrets!' I cried, and she couldn't help but smile back. Though I'd mostly been feigning interest until then, to win Jane over, I wasn't pretending any longer.

I plucked a thick, creamy envelope out of the pile and lifted the flap. Inside was an invitation. It was a lovely thing: bevel-edged and embossed in silver – the sort of quality that costs a small fortune at Smythson's. In an old-fashioned copperplate, it was addressed to some foreign fellow, a Sébastien. The date on it jumped out at me like a frightened cat: 1924.

'The Penhallow Silver Moon Ball,' I said, running my finger over the raised letters. 'Sounds just my sort of bash.'

'I think they had them every summer,' said Jane. 'I've never heard of any Sébastien, though.'

I ran my finger over the letters. '1924 again,' I said aloud, more to myself than to her.

'That was the last of them,' Jane said. 'That's probably why they kept it.'

'The last ball?' I said, holding up the invitation. 1924 was the same year Mrs F stopped visiting our side of the house. She'd told me so the first time I went to see her. 'Are you sure? Perhaps it's just a coincidence. A lot can happen in a year.'

Jane frowned. 'I don't know about any coincidence, but the last ball was definitely in 1924.' She shrugged. 'I know that because it was the year my grandfather died. No one thought it right to carry them on after he'd gone.'

This makes sense, of course – eminent sense – but I always know when a plot is thickening nicely, like a sauce after one's chucked in a handful of flour. Besides, if they didn't stop the balls when Jane's uncle Robin died in the Great War, why halt the tradition when old Mr Fox, who'd no doubt had a good innings and so forth, shuffled off?

After that, I could tell Jane wanted to go. It was partly

that she felt we were trespassing on family business, but I think it was also because the boathouse has an atmosphere you could cut with a knife. Even I was beginning to get that prickling feeling I always have on the coast-path these days, as though someone is watching me, perpetually just out of sight. Jane is too sensible to admit to such things, but I felt it in that funny little place all right. The walls weren't just damp; something else was leaching out of them too. Something like melancholy.

Outside in the sunshine, as we walked back towards the Hall, I blew away the ghosts with funny stories about Blewett, and whether we might be able to sneak off for a swim later, and generally showered Jane with friendliness, which she gulped down like a man in a desert oasis. She looks quite different when she lights up and by then she was positively beaming.

I knew what she was thinking. It was as if I had opened up her head as I did that box. An unfamiliar feeling was stealing through her, and it must have dawned on her that this, at last, was the sensation of being wanted, of feeling sought out. And not by someone who was related to her: not kind Aunt Eleanor, or even Jane's twin sisters, when they were still small and reasonably likeable. Someone else. Someone who didn't need any friends, or have to like her at all. Someone like me. It was really very easy.

XI

After Gerald returned to London, it was easier for Eleanor to resume her visits to the boathouse. They have swiftly become the focal point of her day, so that she wonders what she was doing with her time before. The place and its contents exert a pull on her that feels physical, tangible, as though the past itself is tugging like a magnet on the iron in her blood, drawing her out of the house and down to the creek.

She's calmer there than anywhere else now, no longer frightened by the noises she hears in the watery cavity below her feet, or the way Brick stands alert by the door, tensed for the stranger about to enter. Because, of course, it's not a stranger who's there with them, she's sure of that. The lapping of the creek water as it's displaced by weight in the boat; the rustle of movement in the rhododendrons; and, yesterday, a milky blue marble dropped by the steps. All these signs are intensely comforting to her.

She's been through all the tea chests now – full to their brims not only with more old photographs and invitations but sketches of the house, a notebook of not-very-good poems and a hundred other little souvenirs of girlhood, from train tickets to peacock feathers and tangled strings of beads. One small package she'd lifted out to inspect yesterday had fallen out of its tissue-paper wrapping and into her lap. The silver was tarnished and the paste stones dull, but it made her breath catch all the same. It was the diamanté headband she'd sent for in the same week Sébastien had arrived at their door.

Now she begins to clean it, having brought the tin of polish and a cloth from the house for the purpose. She hadn't considered taking the headband back with her, to clean it where there was a sink to rinse it afterwards. It was as if all her old things are from another place and must be kept inside the boathouse or an enchantment will be broken. Her mother would say it was superstitious non-sense, but she hasn't removed a single thing, even to rescue it from the damp that inches greenly up the walls. This is because, in the boathouse at least, the past is still alive. It runs alongside the present, a darkling mirror image, like the world she used to pretend lay at the bottom of the creek. For the moment, it remains just out of view but it's strengthening every day. It has begun to creep, like ivy, up the cinder path towards the house.

It is the war that is in retreat now, as remote to her as a child's history lesson on a sunny day, when everyone else is playing outside. A government leaflet Gerald had told her about arrived soon after he left for London. It gave instruc-tions on what to do if the 'invader' came. Its words had briefly made her fluttery inside, similar to the sensation she experienced when she tried to leave Penhallow and walk to the village, but then she'd come to the boathouse and the apocalyptic words had drifted away. Even the news that Falmouth docks had been bombed for the first time hadn't really penetrated.

Her eye is caught by the box on the desk and Falmouth fades into nothing. It's where she left it but it looks wrong. It takes her a moment to realize that the key is no longer in the lock. She puts down the headband and looks over the side of the desk. The key has fallen into the dust and she picks it up, wiping it off with the polishing cloth. She knows she left it in the lock, turning it hurriedly before rushing out, still afraid of the boathouse then.

'Did you knock it out?' she says to Brick, who looks back at her with solemn brown eyes, his tail thumping against the blanket she has spread out for him.

When she lifts the lid and finds Sébastien's invitation at the top of the pile, she knows someone else has been there. She remembers tucking it in towards the bottom because the sight of it had made her feel nauseous. Someone has been going through her things, and she knows innately that it's someone in the present, someone from the house. *Diana*, she thinks. There's a hunger in the girl Eleanor hadn't noticed at first, distracted by the extraordinary looks and careless manner she had envied from the start. But it's there, and she can see it now that everything else is becoming so clear: the gnawing emptiness that needs other people to feed it.

Her cheeks are hot, though there's nothing incriminating or even very embarrassing here. Still, she feels as though someone has walked in and caught her undressing. She leafs through the contents of the box, trying to see them as a stranger might, and is slightly mollified.

There are no clues to tell anyone anything of that night, let alone what happened in its aftermath. None at all. She closes the lid smartly and turns the key, this time hiding it in an old jewellery case inside one of the tea chests.

Picking up the headband again, her thoughts are already pulling her back to the date stamped on the invitation she's just locked away. The past blooms around her again, like the damp marks encroaching over the walls.

Though it had ended so differently, that last Penhallow ball had begun just as all the others had, with the clatter of preparation deep inside the house. The slow transformation of the garden had followed, as lanterns were threaded through bushes and trees, and snow-white cloths were spread on tables that would later hold salvers of food and saucers of champagne.

As the rosy dusk deepened, she had leant out of her bedroom window and heard the hum of the guests as they made their way towards the house along the coast-path, their motor-cars left behind in Vennor, neatly lined along the harbour wall. They had sounded to her in that moment like an approaching swarm, though she'd dismissed the thought as silly. Another warning ignored, like the sea that seethed in the cove below.

She remembers how her mother had always complained that expecting half their guests to walk up the coast-path was lamentably bohemian, not to mention inconvenient, but everyone else adored it. It was part of the experience, they said, to approach the house at walking pace, as you would a fairy kingdom that can only be entered when the stars align. It served to build their anticipation. They would sniff the twilit air for mown grass and Penhallow's famous flowers. They would see if anyone could catch a glimpse of the house's lights reflected on the sea as they rounded the last bend. Sometimes, if the wind had died, you could see them out there on the water, shimmering dreamily, like a great ocean liner sinking beneath the waves.

It was another of the occasion's rituals, along with the dress code inspired by cool moonlight: white tie for men and girlish, debutante white, with silver sashes and trimmings, for the women, even the old matrons.

Eleanor sighs, the boathouse coming back into focus. Strange to think that final ball would have been cancelled had her father not insisted it went ahead; one last enchanted evening before he went. He had been dying for months and, by the time July came around, all the flesh had melted from his bones, leaving him astonishingly, distressingly thin in his evening dress. It was new, hurriedly ordered from an outfitter's in Truro because the old one hung off him so absurdly. Still, in the short time between being measured for it and its delivery, he'd shrunk again.

He'd worn it only twice: at the ball and again when he was buried in it, on a bitter November day the same year. As Eleanor stood with her mother in the small, undulating churchyard above Vennor's east cliff, eyes red and streaming from grief, exhaustion and the wind, she worried aloud that he wouldn't be warm enough in the thin stuff of the suit. 'He can't feel anything now,' her mother had replied. It seemed to sum her up.

Afterwards, everyone assumed that the tradition of the ball had been allowed to die with her father. Which was convenient, really, when it had had nothing to do with him, and everything to do with Eleanor and what she'd done that night, after the sky cracked open and the rain began to fall. She had been caught out, and it was her own fault for not listening to what she was being told. She won't make the same mistake again. She's listening now.

She stands and checks again that the box is locked. Closing the door behind her, she finds she isn't quite ready to leave. It'll be fiercely hot in the upper reaches of the garden but here, next to the creek, where a soft breeze soughs in the willow leaves and the kingfishers dart, blue as Robin's favourite jersey, it will be pleasant to sit awhile. She allows herself a quick look inside the boat as she passes it and her heart skips when she sees that the dead leaves that had littered the bottom have gone.

She turns to the bank, jubilant at this unassailable proof she could show Gerald if he was here. But then she sees what's in the water, and the sight of it makes her knees buckle.

A huge arc of the green water has gone, replaced by the silvery skin and scales of dead fish. There must be hundreds of them. She is drawn closer, despite her horror and the panic surging wildly through her, and sees that not all of them are dead. Some, beached in the reeds and mud close to the bank, are flapping weakly, their rainbow sheen dulling. Last night, she'd been jolted out of her drugged sleep by a sound that wasn't a sound. No one else had woken; when she'd opened her bedroom door, the house was silent and dark, and they confirmed over breakfast they'd heard nothing. The aftershock of it reverberates around her head again, as she begins to run back towards

138

the Hall, heart galloping and hands clamped over her mouth to stop the scream that's spilling out anyway.

* * *

SEVENTEEN DAYS LEFT

Wednesday, 3rd July

The war has reached us here at last. Eleanor has been put to bed in shock after discovering that all the fish in the creek have been either stunned or killed by a mine that exploded in the night, set off by who-knows-what. Just think: if I'd gone for the midnight swim I'm always promising myself, I might have been obliterated, scattered across a mile of water. Apparently the whole coast is mined; a black-spiked necklace keeping us in and the Germans out. It's not just Eleanor; the idea that they're under there has unsettled everyone.

That said, I didn't quite believe the outlandish tale until I went down to the creek myself. A lot of the fish had been collected by this time, the locals coming in little boats to scoop them up and take them home for supper, but even so there were enough left for the smell to be pretty unbearable in the sultry heat of afternoon. As I stood there, a hot wind buffeted around the boathouse, ruffling my hair and making the willow leaves flutter, like the fish as they died. I got the shivers then, and had to hurry back to the house.

Eleanor, who rarely wakes because of the Veronal she takes, had heard or, rather, felt the mine go off under water, just after one in the morning. The rest of us slept right through, which is disquieting in itself. A small, twisted part of my mind immediately thought of Mother's reaction to the telegram if I had been killed. I tried hard to picture her collapsing to the floor, prostrate with grief and regret, but it lacked the aura of truth. When it comes to blaming me for things that couldn't possibly be my fault, the old girl has form, and I can well imagine her deciding that getting myself blown up was just another means of calling attention to myself.

Talking of betrayals, Rose and I are barely speaking, after she took huge offence at a harmless comment I made. I had gone to fetch something from the dorm after dinner and walked in on her parading about in front of the mirror with her hair done differently. She was horribly embarrassed.

'I daresay you're trying out styles for when you go and see your fisherman,' I said, before I could stop myself. 'What a lucky fellow. Or is all this effort in preparation for Frank's next leave?'

She blushed scarlet at that, which spoke volumes.

'I must say, I would never have suspected you of something like this. It just goes to show.'

'Something like what?' she said stonily.

'Well, you know, *adultery*.' I whispered it stagily.

She threw me a filthy look.

'Aren't you even going to deny it?' I pressed, but she didn't reply, instead going over to the bed to fold and refold the same blouse. Her hands were trembling.

'Oh, I see, so you're not going to speak to me any more. Well, fine. If that's what you want. I'm hardly going to end it all because you've decided to ignore me.'

Her face went white and then blotchy and I realized what I'd said. 'Oh, listen, I didn't . . .'

'No, don't,' she said. 'Just don't. You'll only be hateful.'

Not half an hour later, I caught her whispering with Eleanor on the stairs. As soon as they spotted me, they shut up. I fully expected Eleanor to smile then, and try to dispel the awkwardness with her usual nervous babble, but she didn't. She stared at me balefully, while Rose gazed steadfastly at the wall. I couldn't bear to pass them, so turned and fled back to the dorm, no doubt leaving them to laugh at me. Since then I've had that precarious feeling again, as though I'm balanced on a crumbling ledge that is about to fall away into the sea. It strikes me, not for the first time, that we are little more than strangers here, our enforced proximity masking the fact that none of us really knows the other; none of us knows what the other might be capable of if put under enough strain. Strangers, breathing each other's air, but never our worst secrets.

I even had a minor contretemps with Jane yesterday, after quizzing her in the garden. I don't know why I did it, possibly because I could. Possibly because she isn't Rose. She ended up going off in high dudgeon, tears leaking from her gypsy eyes. The heavier the armour, the easier the flesh inside is to puncture, or so I've always found.

I'd persuaded Blewett to let the pair of us work in the rose garden, thinking it would be more civilized than the usual digging. In fact, the damned thorns were drawing blood every five seconds and I gave it up before my hands were entirely cut to ribbons. I found a sunny spot by the fountain where I thought we could sit down and have a cigarette, though Jane still flatly refuses to smoke. So, that irritated me, and then she asked if I was planning to do any work at all today, which really riled me and is probably why I started on her.

It wasn't much. It's that I'd remembered the time I saw her so livid at the cove.

'Darling, I've been meaning to ask,' I began. 'Are you having any more luck with Grandmother Fox?'

She turned with an eyebrow raised, a pricked and bleeding finger stuck in her mouth. 'Why do you ask?' she mumbled.

'Well, I was thinking about the time, before we really knew each other, when you were giving that rock such a thrashing at Breakheart. I hate to think of her still upsetting you so much.'

'Is that why you're always going to visit her?' she replied, with more pluck than I would have expected. The surprise made me bristle.

'Oh, come on, Jane. You must know I only go for the free drink.'

'If that's the case, then what is it you're getting from me?'

'I'm actually beginning to ask myself the same question,' I shot back, before I could stop myself. 'It's certainly not your sense of humour.'

She brandished her pruning shears at me. 'Grandmother has already summoned me for one of her warnings today,' she cried, her eyes filling ominously. 'And now you're being beastly too. I thought you were my friend.'

'Tell me what the horrid old battleaxe said,' I said more gently, going forward to put my arm round her.

She shook me off. 'No, don't. Just don't.' Then off she stormed, presumably for a good old cry.

It was then that a noise from above made me look up. Payne's ugly head was poking out of one of Mrs Fox's windows, like an eavesdropping gargoyle. Triumph lit her pallid features.

'Do you always listen in to other people's conversations?' I called weakly but she had already withdrawn, the window closing noiselessly.

I remembered then something Rose had said to me, when I'd been particularly cutting: 'One day, Diana, you're going to find you've pushed so many people away that there's no one left.' If I'd rolled my eyes any harder at the time, they'd have fallen out of their sockets. How priggish I'd thought her, with her knowing, sorrowful expression. But now . . . Well, I worry about people seeing Jane's puffy puppy eyes. And I worry what Payne has said to Mrs F.

Anyway, that little melodrama was yesterday. Today I managed to do not a single stroke of work. Blewett, I knew, had gone off to Liskeard in his beloved Morris Eight van to collect the roller that broke last week. He hates to use up any of his precious petrol coupons but Eleanor managed to dissuade him from trying to lug the thing back on the bus. I know from the day he picked me up at the station that he drives slower than a glacier moves so I felt I could take off most of the day with impunity.

It was turning into another scorcher but I didn't want to

burn my nose so I went in to see Mrs Fox, ignoring the silly shiver of apprehension as I approached her room. I'd been meaning to go since Jane's and my discoveries in the boathouse and then, after yesterday, I wanted to see if Payne had told tales. Clearly she hadn't, and the old gal must have missed me because her eyes lit up like two tiny gas flames when she saw who it was. Payne, thank goodness, was nowhere to be seen.

'Shirking again, Miss Devlin?' she said, but I don't think she minded. She knows the work's beneath me.

'Do my old eyes deceive me or have you taken up with my granddaughter?' she continued.

I glanced towards the window. 'Oh, yes, we're firm friends now,' I said carefully, wondering if I'd been wrong about Payne keeping her powder dry.

'Promise me you'll do something about that hair of hers,' she continued. 'She looks like she's in Rouen, ready to be burnt at the stake. Oddly, I thought I saw her flouncing away yesterday, looking most put-out.'

I tensed. 'A storm in a teacup,' I said, as breezily as I could. 'I was teasing her and she got cross. I had to grovel later.'

She raised an eyebrow but said nothing else.

'Tell me more about Jane,' I dared to ask later, after I'd lightened the mood by telling tales on Cook, who, I've discovered, buys cigars from Blewett. 'What was she like when she was growing up?'

Mrs Fox sniffed. 'She was hardly here.'

'Oh? But she was born here, wasn't she?'

'How do you know that?'

'She said so herself. Said she had an affinity with the place and was glad she was Cornish.'

'It was only so my daughter-in-law could be looked after during a difficult confinement. They went back to London when Jane was a few months old.'

'But she always came to stay in the holidays, didn't she?'

'Only when she was young.'

'Why did she stop coming?'

She looked out of the window. 'My eldest son, Hugo – Jane's father – didn't think the place was doing her any good.'

'With all its beaches and fresh air and gardens to run about in?' I lowered my eyes as she gave me a pointed stare.

'The girl was becoming too attached,' she replied eventually, her mouth pursing and puckering. For half a moment I could see the skull behind the skin. I got up and poured us both a drink without asking.

'Too attached to Penhallow?' I said, once I was fortified, my throat burning from gulping the stuff so fast. 'Why didn't Jane's father inherit this pile anyway? Why's Eleanor got it?'

'The London house is more than sufficient for Hugo's needs. He never much cared for Cornwall. Finds it backward. Penhallow was entailed to him too, of course, but he made it over to Eleanor as recompense after –' She broke off.

'After what?'

She jabbed a ring-crowded finger in my direction. 'Goodness, how you pry. Didn't anyone ever tell you that curiosity killed the cat?' Her blue eyes had darkened and I suddenly felt cold.

It took some effort, but I gave her my best guileless smile. 'I hope I've still got a few lives left. Besides, there's nothing else for a sociable girl to do here.'

'What about what we pay you to do outside?' she

returned, but I realized that the danger had veered away again for the moment.

I laughed, relieved. 'A guinea a week isn't pay, it's a pittance. An insult.'

She snorted as she does when she finds me amusing, in spite of herself. 'Incorrigible gel.'

If I can be sure Payne isn't gawping from the window, I may go back to the boathouse to poke around some more on my own. There are those tea chests and suitcases Jane and I didn't even begin on, and I'd like to look more closely at the photographs too. Jane told me they were probably taken by Eleanor's older brother Robin.

One of my earlier theories about 1924, now reluctantly dismissed, is that Jane was accidentally swapped at birth in the local cottage hospital. Though I was quite taken with the notion of some poor girl, with Mrs F's eyes and cheekbones, gutting fish in Vennor, I've since come up with something more plausible. It's safest to keep it dark for now, though, until other things crystallize. Anyone could read this book, after all. Both Jane and Rose know where I keep it. I'm considering hiding it in the boathouse, where no one would think to look.

XII

Last night Rose had found that if she stood on a chair by the far window in the dormitory, she could just glimpse the lighthouse around the headland. It was a chance discovery, made when the top of the blackout came down as she was getting ready for bed, Diana and Jane still next door, playing a last hand of rummy. She'd clambered up with a shoe in lieu of a hammer and seen it there in the distance, the powerful beam flashing on and off, briefly lighting up the dark water and the sky.

She'd always found the sight of it snapping on and off, momentarily banishing the blackout, reassuring, soothing even. *We're still here*, it seemed to say. Now she couldn't help feeling he was signalling just to her, telling her to come. *Tomorrow*, she'd whispered. It might be too late otherwise.

Tomorrow is now today, but it's well past nine when Rose escapes, the evening moving swiftly into the arms of night. She pauses on the other side of the garden gate, once she's safely out of sight from any windows. Her breath is coming fast and shallow and she makes herself exhale slowly through her mouth. She doesn't think anyone saw or heard her leave on stockinged feet.

Though it isn't yet dark, the journey back will be, if she's gone for an hour or so. An hour with him. She can't yet imagine it. When she's tried she always finds herself remembering occasions from when they were young. It might be different now, in all sorts of ways. She sets off down the path before she loses her nerve.

The sight of the village, as she approaches it, is eerie enough to distract her. Though she's perfectly aware of the blackout, it's still a shock to see the place so shrouded in darkness, as though it's been abruptly deserted, the inhabitants spirited away by Barbary pirates.

Among the lanes, sounds reassure her that Vennor hasn't become a ghost village after all, that there's life behind the shuttered windows and curtained doors. The Mermaid sounds as it always does, the low rumble of male voices interrupted by the occasional shout of laughter. The smell of tobacco and spilt beer has found its way past the heavy blackout fabric that's drawn across the door and the bottle-glass bow windows.

She crosses the bridge and takes one of the crooked lanes that threads upwards and along the other side of the village. A picture of Frank steals into her thoughts and makes her falter, but then she hears the rattle of a latch just behind her and hurries on, not wanting to be seen by someone who would wonder where an outsider was heading so late.

As the going gets steeper, the cottages thin out. To her right, as the path follows the curve of the headland and leaves the harbour behind, the dark, shifting mass of the sea spreads out to fill the view. Just then a cloud is blown clear of the waxing moon, lighting the scene more clearly. She glances behind her and is struck by how ancient it all looks: the silhouettes of the lightless cottages, the moon's reflection netted by the still harbour waters and, behind the village, the hill that rears up like a huge, earthbound wave. It would have looked the same to a smuggler two centuries earlier, as he glanced over his shoulder to check no revenue man lurked in the shadows.

She hastens on, nervous again, and finds the fork in the path she hoped she remembered. This way is much less trodden. Only he comes this way, she thinks, and the thought comforts and excites her as the spikes of gorse prick at her stockings from both sides.

When she gets to it and looks up, the tapering, conical shape of the lighthouse is so exaggerated from this angle, the wisps of cloud overhead speeding so fast, that she sways where she stands. She puts a hand out to the thick granite to steady herself and tries again. There, close to the top of the tower, a light shines out from an oblong gash in the stone. He's here. She turns the huge iron handle of the door and steps inside.

The air inside the lighthouse is cool, a whole day's warmth unable to penetrate stone walls that are four feet thick and windowless at ground level, built to withstand all the fury of a winter storm. Above her an iron staircase winds, a spiral uncoiling up into the darkness, like the spine of some ancient creature.

She begins to climb, the soles of her shoes clanging softly against the metal. As the staircase goes round and she gets higher, she wonders if she should call out, but then she hears a voice above her.

'Rosy?'

She stops, gripping the rail so she doesn't lose her balance. He's there, just above her, framed in an open doorway, even more handsome than she remembered.

'I thought I was imagining things,' he says.

'You said I might come.' Her voice trembles.

'But then you didn't, and I began to think you wouldn't at all.'

'Well, I did. I hope you don't mind. I can always go if –' She gestures downwards.

'No. Please. I'm so glad you did. Come up. I'll make some tea.'

She hauls herself up the last steps, less out of breath from the climb than the thrill of what she's doing, and follows him into a curious little room, brightly lit and much warmer than it was on the stairs. It's shaped like a segment of orange, with a rough table and two mismatched chairs against the flat part of the wall. Further along she sees a deep sink that needs a good scour, a grubby sliver of soap hanging next to it from a length of twine. Pushed awkwardly against the curving wall, under the window, there is a cupboard full of tinned food. The only other item is a small stove. It's a deeply masculine room, with nothing pretty or comfortable in it except a faded old rug.

'There's not much about it,' he says gruffly, and she wonders fleetingly what she thinks she's doing here with this man she hardly knows now.

'Have you got anything apart from tea?' she asks, her voice still unsteady. 'I never feel much like it in summer.'

He turns and smiles and she knows in a rush that it will be all right.

'There's an old bottle of brandy,' he says. 'It's supposed to be for the coldest nights, but perhaps we can make an exception.'

He pours a generous slug into two mugs and hands her the least chipped one. 'No one but me and the reserve keeper ever comes here. Having you here makes me see that it's a bit . . .'

'Spartan?' She laughs and takes a gulp of the brandy, pausing so she doesn't cough. 'Why wouldn't you even bring a cushion to sit on if you're here so much?'

He pulls out one of the chairs to reveal a limp square of dark green fabric that might once have been a cushion. 'Like this one?'

They smile and drink simultaneously from their mugs, which makes them smile at each other again. In that moment, she doesn't care about Frank or Morwenna, or if anyone saw her come. All she cares about is in that bare little room.

'Do you want to come and see the light?' he says.

She's perfectly happy where she is but sees the enthusiasm in his eyes and nods. The stairs up to the very top of the lighthouse are cut slightly narrower as they go, the walls closing steadily in. Being careful not to look down, she follows Sam slowly upwards.

'John Smeaton worked out how to build them like this,' he says, over his shoulder. 'Before him, whatever they built was swept away by the sea almost as soon as it was finished. Do you see how the stones are dovetailed? When a wave smashes against them, some of its power is taken away by the way the walls taper.' He stops and waits for her to catch up. 'Go steady now. There's no hurry.'

At first, when she reaches the top, it's a relief just to stop climbing. Then she looks around her and sees why he wanted to show her. In place of stone walls a dozen or more panes of glass surround them. It feels as though they are flying high over the land, closer to the stars that are beginning to show, one by one, than they are to the earth that lies at their feet, a dark bulk whose jagged edges she can only just make out.

In the far west, beyond Land's End and the point where she imagines the Channel and the Atlantic to meet in a clash of currents, the last blush of sunset glows like a distant fire. Closer to them there is nothing but darkness; she can't see a single light showing in the village and along the coast towards Penhallow. Everyone, it seems – even Diana – is obeying the blackout tonight.

She is just about to joke that he could do the ARP warden's job for them in no time at all, when the huge lamp suddenly flashes on, making her gasp and stumble backwards into him.

'I should've warned you,' he murmurs close to her ear, as they are plunged back into darkness, his grip tight on her shoulders, and her eyes full of stars. 'It comes on every ten seconds. If you visit again when it's still light outside, I'll show you the workings properly. It weighs two tons but floats in a bath of mercury. You could move it with your little finger.'

He leads her over to the nearest pane of glass. Directly below them, she glimpses the curving line of the harbour wall before the lamp temporarily blinds her again. It looks small and vulnerable from their great height, like something built of sand by a child on the beach.

'In the old days, when the first lighthouses were going up, the local people didn't want them,' he says. 'For years they blocked them being built.' He is standing so close that she can feel the warmth of his breath on her skin, as she thought she had by Penhallow's gate.

'Why would they have done that?'

'Well, the smugglers didn't want them there, but nor did the villagers who profited from the same trade one way or another. I don't think they cared much about the wrecks. It wasn't them in the ships that broke up among the Shackles.'

'The Shackles?' She looks down at the dark sea and shuts her eyes as the lamp flashes on again.

'The rocks out there, just under the surface. Once a ship's among them, it's hard to get her out. The sea'll dash her against the rocks until she's all smashed up. They're why the light was put here, though that wasn't until the worst of the smuggling had been stopped anyway. Plenty of ships had gone down by then, all hands lost.'

He falls silent and she stares out in the direction he's pointed to. When her eyes adjust, there is no sign of any treacherous rocks, only heaving water.

'Sometimes I think I can feel it move,' he says after a time.

'What?'

'This place. The lighthouse. When a gale's blowing through. Not much – just a few inches – but it feels like it sways.'

She laughs and half shudders at the same time. 'I wouldn't like that. I'd be frightened here on my own at night. I'd start thinking about all those people who'd been drowned out there. I'd be listening on the wind for their voices.' She looks down, embarrassed, but he steps closer, his hands reaching tentatively to her waist but then rising to her shoulders.

'You're all right,' he says softly, as the light flashes on again, illuminating the planes of his face. 'I've got you.'

When it's dark again, she takes a breath and moves closer to him, standing on tiptoe so her face comes closer to his.

'I know it's not right . . .' he begins, but she surprises herself by laying a finger against his lips.

'Don't,' she says. And then she kisses him.

She doesn't remember the journey back to the Hall, though she must have made it through the dark. It seems no more than seconds from the moment she leaves Sam at the lighthouse to the point she lets herself back into Penhallow's garden. Later that night, she wonders if she sensed that something had changed in the time she had been absent, if there was something to be read in the way the moonlight stripped the garden of its colour. But there was no sign, only coincidence. Awful coincidence.

'Oh, Rose, we've been looking everywhere for you.' Eleanor is pale under the hall's pendant lamp. She's clutching a piece of paper. 'There was some confusion with the telegraph boy – oh, it doesn't matter now. He brought it just after nine, with apologies.' She hands over the paper, which Rose now sees is a telegram.

She pushes it back towards Eleanor, her heart skittering. 'I can't. Will you open it for me?'

Eleanor looks as though she wants to refuse but takes it all the same, ripping it open with trembling fingers.

'He's dead, isn't he?' Rose says woodenly.

Eleanor is reading fast, her eyes scanning back and forth. Then she looks up. 'No, he's not. But you'll have to be brave because he is missing. Missing in action, it says.'

In bed, the brandy Eleanor fetched her still hot in her throat, the others asleep at last, Rose asks herself if she would still have gone to Sam had the telegram arrived when it was supposed to. But she can't bear to think about the answer to that, just as she couldn't face the questions she'd seen in Diana's eyes just now, as she'd turned out the lamp without a word.

* * *

FOURTEEN DAYS LEFT

Saturday, 6th July

First the mine going off in the creek and now Rose's Frank, who is missing at sea. A telegram turned up last night, after the telegraph boy had had a mishap on his bicycle involving a loose cow and a ditch, or some such parochial nonsense that threatened to make me laugh, quite inappropriately.

Obviously Rose wasn't here when the hapless boy finally rang the bell – she'd sneaked out, clutching her shoes, just after nine (I saw her from the window where I was smoking and keeping guard – I simply knew she'd go). So, of course, when a whey-faced Eleanor came up with the fateful telegram, Rose was nowhere to be found. I felt almost smug that, for once, it wasn't me who'd gone AWOL. I was all for opening the telegram because the suspense was absolutely killing, but Eleanor said we mustn't. I couldn't take my eyes off it as we waited, though. Such an innocuous object to herald the possible end of a life.

I wasn't on the scene when Rose finally reappeared from her 'walk on the coast-path' (ha!), nor did I see her face the moment she received the bad news, but I did see her just after and, let me tell you, something about her reaction wasn't quite right. Jane says it was the shock, but I remain unconvinced. 'Furtive' was the word that popped into my head as I watched her gulp Eleanor's brandy, as though forty things had happened to her all at once and she didn't know which to feel first. Jane didn't want to admit it because she's so good, but I don't mind stating the truth: Rose was not quite as distraught at the contents of that telegram as she ought to have been.

I'm going to sneak out myself after dinner (rabbit pie, apparently. Blewett's been shooting them in the garden. Poor old bunnies but, heavens, they smell delicious). I can't spend another evening listening to the dreary Home Service. It makes me grind my teeth. Unlike Rose, I know where Eleanor keeps a torch. I'm telling myself I'm just going for a little twilight stroll, but the bad part of me is planning to pay a call on the dastardly Mr Bolitho. In my defence, I'm running low on provisions.

Who knows? If I'm nice to him, he might even stand

me a gin in the saloon of the Mermaid. It's been centuries since a man bought me a drink. I thought I might ask him about this friend of Rose's, see if we can work out who he is. Though it wouldn't occur to little Jane in a thousand years, it's obvious to me that Rose went to meet the fisherman last night. I can read her like a book with very large print.

Later. I'm writing this in the sitting room so I don't wake the others. The pen keeps skittering all over the paper because my hand is shaking. I've just checked the hall clock and it's almost midnight; I was much longer than I thought. I shall tell this in order, as rather a lot happened and I feel it's going to be important that I set it all down, without forgetting any of the details. I sense it may be crucial later.

As I'd expected (and, I suppose, hoped), Dew was ensconced in the Mermaid, a ring of rough-looking toadies around him. As I made my entrance, the place fell silent and I almost lost my nerve. I felt as though I had boarded a ship whose crew hadn't laid eyes on a woman in months. I was about to turn and exit when Dew finally stood and gestured for me to go through to the slightly more salubrious saloon. He might've done it sooner but I think he was enjoying the whole room's concentrated envy, not to mention my reliance on him for my virtue.

It was cosy in there, with the black-beamed ceiling virtually around our ears, tobacco-stained walls and a hundred knick-knacks cluttering the place rather appealingly. You know the sort of thing: horse brasses and pewter tankards and pictures of grisly shipwrecks. I had two gins in quick succession and felt my cheeks begin to warm up.

I can't remember much of what we talked of at first, only his suggestive eyes (jet-black, with arrestingly long lashes) and the way he commanded the room, apparently effortlessly. Every so often, a shifty-looking chap would come in and whisper in his ear and he would give brief instructions, then dismiss him with a nod.

There is something about the power he wields so non-chalantly that is as frightening as it is seductive. It puts me in mind of Herr Hitler and mad Unity Mitford; was it these qualities in the man that had bewitched her to the degree that she put a gun to her head? Of course Dew is about eight hundred times easier on the eye than the Führer.

The conversation spiralled out of my control after I brought it round to Rose. Now, sober again, I know it was a grave error to tell Dew anything. He's as sharp as the knife I later discovered he carries in his back pocket.

I was halfway down my third drink when I asked him if he knew of a fisherman's son who'd taken in an evacuee boy.

'Sam Bligh?' he said immediately, and I laughed.

'Good Lord, there really are only about half a dozen people in this place, aren't there?'

His face darkened. 'What do you want to know about him for?' he growled, and I realized with a sinking sensation that he might be jealous.

'He's just a friend of someone I know,' I said quickly.

He sat back and surveyed me. 'Who's that, then?'

'Oh, it doesn't matter, really. She just mentioned him in passing, that's all.'

'A "she", is it? First I've heard of Sam Bligh having any woman friends and I'd know – my sister's married to him. She look anything like you, does she?' He grinned nastily.

I flashed him one of my best smiles. 'Hardly. And, look, don't lose your rag. Forget I said anything. Tell me the story of Old Glassjaw Bolitho again. I liked that one.'

It would have been the easiest thing in the world to tell Dew that Rose and his brother-in-law had met up already. I've no doubt he would have made short work of telling his sister, which would soon have put the tin lid on it for Rose. But something stopped me. Some silly residual protectiveness towards her, I suppose.

But he didn't fall for my ruse anyway. 'No, you tell me more about this friend of yours at the Hall who's somehow come to know the lighthouse keeper.'

'Lighthouse keeper? How adorable.'

He softened slightly at this. 'If you didn't know that, then perhaps this friend isn't you after all.'

My stomach lurched. 'Gracious, no. I can assure you I've never laid eyes on your sister's husband.'

'Good. What about the Fox girl, then? Is it her?'

'Jane?' I scoffed. 'She's a mere child.'

'Fifteen is old enough for most things.'

'How would you know how old Jane is? I've only just found out myself and we share a room.'

'Oh, I know the Fox family of old,' he said, looking up from his glass with a bitter smile.

'Do you?'

He let out a mirthless laugh. 'I wasn't always like this, you know. When the master was still alive . . .' He tailed off.

'The master?' I repeated. 'I would never have dreamt you'd call anyone that.'

He was about to reply when the door banged back and

three Canadian airmen came in, one so tall he had to duck. I looked back at Dew, curious and rather fearful for his reaction, and watched his face go completely blank.

I hoped they wouldn't notice me in the corner but naturally they did, nudging each other, then calling over to ask if I needed another drink, which I tactfully refused without a smile, only too aware of a glowering Dew beside me.

I realized then that every Cornishman in the pub had stopped talking to stare at the strangers. In the tense silence, the barman served the airmen their beer sullenly, not even giving thanks as he took their money. There was an unoccupied table next to us and I willed those boys to go through to the other bar with all my might, but they didn't, of course. They'd barely sat down when Dew addressed them.

'That table is taken.'

'Yeah?' said the tall one. 'Who by?'

'Me,' said Dew.

'Look, we just want to have a quiet drink,' one of the others said.

'Have it outside, then.' Dew stood and, a beat later, the tall one followed suit. He was bigger than Dew by a head.

'We don't feel like going outside,' he said.

'I won't ask again. You're outsiders so you'll go outside.'

'What about her?' The airman gestured at me. 'You're not telling me she's from this place, looking like that. Why don't you come with us, honey? You're way too good to be in here with him.'

Dew moved so quickly I didn't see it happen. The next thing I knew, the airman had stumbled backwards into his stool, blood pouring from his nose, his beer spilt and frothing over the table. One of Dew's henchmen materialized out of the shadows and held open the door for the airmen. In under a minute, it was as though they'd never come in at all, conversations resuming and broken glass unobtrusively swept away.

'Shall we go?' Dew said, though it wasn't really a question, and I found myself getting obediently to my feet, heart hammering uncomfortably.

The net loft has only a single bare lightbulb, high in the rafters, creating plenty of dark corners. None of his cronies had followed – unlike last time, we were very much alone. I'd thought he might launch himself at me immediately, but I was wrong-footed because he did nothing of the kind. Instead, he sat down at his desk and produced an orange. A real, mouthwatering orange. I haven't seen one in months. Then he got out his knife and proceeded to peel it in one long strip, looking at me with those velvet eyes all the while.

'Come here,' he said, when he'd finished, and I went. The incident with the airmen, mixed up with all the gin, had done something to me. I was half appalled, half excited.

We stood very close as he fed me the first piece, which was easily the best thing I have ever tasted, like sunshine on the tongue.

Then he kissed me and he did it so well that, after a while, I began to feel as if I was made of something more liquid than flesh and bone. I could have gone on like that for ever but then he backed me up against the desk, his hands clamping around my hips, and suddenly I was eleven

161

years old again, dressed in pale blue taffeta and wishing I could be anywhere else but the room I was in.

I'd been staying at Great Uncle Theobald's house. He'd cornered me in his boot room, which had a cobwebby old lavatory just off it, if you didn't mind wading through a forest of rubber boots and empty shell cases jammed with canes and broken umbrellas. He must have seen me go in and thought it would be a jape to barge in on a young girl when she had her knickers round her ankles. Fortunately I had finished my business and was just pulling the chain by the time he blundered through the door, purple-cheeked and breathing raggedly.

Strange that it should have been I who later saw him turn up his toes. Poetic justice, perhaps. It probably did me good to witness the moment he left this world for the next. When Mother came in afterwards she said, in her meaningless way, that he was at peace now. I replied to the effect that if God was doing his job then that was highly unlikely, which naturally caused a fearful row.

Anyway, this onslaught of memory rather ruined the mood. I pushed Dew away and raced for the door.

'You'll regret this, you little cock-tease,' he called after me, but I didn't stay to explain.

I cried all the way back here, so blinded by my own ridiculous tears that I nearly stumbled off the cliff at the highest point. The wind was loud up there, and I took the opportunity to scream into it until I was hoarse, hating everything and everyone but most especially myself.

XIII

Rose stops work to rest, pushing the damp hair from her forehead with the back of her hand. She's been out in the garden since half past eight and the sun has given her a blinding headache. She's been trying to think about Frank, about where he might be at this precise moment, but she can't seem to grasp the likely reality: that he is at the bottom of the sea. Her mind keeps sliding off and back to Sam, which only makes her despise herself more.

Because of the telegram, everyone is treating her as if she's made of glass. That, and the routine of her work in the garden, makes the fact that she was up there at the top of the lighthouse, the huge lamp going on and off, like someone throwing a switch on the world, quite unreal.

'You'll have to come back when the mist rolls in,' he'd said to her before she left, when neither of them had wanted to be the one to end the visit. 'It feels like you're up in the clouds. That's when I have to put the fog horn on.'

She realized then that she had heard it once, in her second week at Penhallow, before the weather eased into tranquil summer. It had echoed strangely through the swirling white air, lonely and mournful, though it must have sounded like deliverance to anyone aboard a lost ship.

In the garden, she massages her temples, wishing they could have just one overcast day so she might stop squinting. Her skin is sticky with sweat. All of them feel grubby after ten minutes of work in this heat.

'Why don't you go on in?' says Blewett, coming over and taking her spade from her.

His usual gruffness has given way to an awkward, rusty sort of kindness. Eleanor has clearly told him the news.

She goes to protest but then nods. 'I think I will, if you don't mind.' She's aware that Diana is looking at her. 'I'm afraid I didn't get much sleep.'

'Go on, then,' says Blewett. 'Back to your bed. You can join us tomorrow. Miss Devlin here can pull her weight for once.'

She intends to go to sleep; she is genuinely exhausted. But it's a nervous kind of fatigue that makes her afraid to lie still with her eyes closed. So when she goes into the dormitory after a cool wash, she changes out of her uniform into the first dress that comes to hand without really thinking about it.

Even in her distracted state, vanity makes her glance in the mirror on her way out. Shadows smudge under her eyes, but otherwise she looks much better than she should. Her skin is dewy and her loose hair shines. She looks away, shame making her stomach roil.

All the way to Vennor, she tells herself that if he isn't at the lighthouse she won't come again. She'll return to Penhallow and worry about her missing husband, like any decent wife would. But he is there.

He gets to his feet when he sees her in the doorway of the little orange-segment room and, even in her anxiety, she can't help noticing how handsome he is, with his sun-streaked hair and easy grace.

'What is it, Rosy?' he says.

'It's Frank. He's missing.' The last word rises as a sob. 'I don't know what to do. I feel as though I made it happen, coming to you.'

He goes to her, taking her face in his hands. 'No, you didn't. It had happened already. You just didn't know it yet.'

'But I feel . . . I feel as though . . .'

'You're being punished?'

She bows her head, allowing him to pull her close. There are only the two hard chairs so he draws her down to sit on the faded rug, which is lying in a patch of sun.

'It's war,' he says softly. 'It's a terrible thing but people all over are getting hurt, getting killed. It's got nothing to do with you and me.'

'But it's still wrong, isn't it?' She sits back against the cold stone wall. 'It's still a horrible thing to do, to be with someone else when your husband is out there injured or . . .' She can't say it. She knows that if he's dead she's released from their marriage, even if Sam isn't from his. She's sick with shame at the part of her that's bargained Frank's life away in her daydreams for weeks.

So that she doesn't think about that any more, she leans over and kisses Sam, near but not quite on his mouth. To her humiliation, he jerks away slightly.

'I wasn't expecting that,' he says, smiling, his fingers to the place her lips had touched.

In other circumstances, she might have laughed it off

but she can't manage it today, saying nothing and not meeting his eye. Perhaps, in trying so hard to recapture the past, she's got him wrong after all.

'What's your wife like?' she says, to spite herself. She looks out of the narrow window opposite, through which she can see an oblong of deep blue sky.

'Why do you want to bring Menna up?' he says quietly.

The diminutive makes her wince. 'I suppose I just want to know.'

'That doesn't sound like you, Rosy.'

He's right, it doesn't. She sounds combative, brittle, like Diana does these days. She pushes on anyway, and it's not all contrariness; part of her really does want to know. She's thought about going down to Vennor to try to glimpse this 'Menna' who's married to the man she's never stopped thinking of as her own.

'Just tell me what she looks like,' she says now, battling to keep her voice light. 'I can't imagine her at all.'

He shifts position away from her slightly. 'What does it matter?'

'It matters to me now. I don't know why.'

He looks at her, then seems to relent. 'Well, she's dark, darker than you. Black eyes and hair.'

Rose manages a small laugh. 'Men are always hopeless at describing looks. What's her hair like, apart from being black?'

'Different from yours. Long to the waist and straight as a poker.'

'That's better. And what about her shape? Is she taller than me?'

'An inch or two smaller. Bit thinner. Now, can we talk about something else?'

166

'How much thinner?' She hates Morwenna in that moment, with her skein of dark hair and tiny waist.

Sam takes a deep breath and reaches out to Rose's nearest leg. When she doesn't push him off, he begins stroking her, down to the knee and up again. She can feel the heat of his fingers through the thin cotton of the skirt she'd pulled down modestly. She's not wearing any stockings under it, the day much too warm for them.

'She's as skinny as she was at twelve, Menna is,' he says into her hair. He kisses her just behind her ear, then further down her neck. 'No flesh on her.'

'Not like me,' she says, but she's only pretending to be cross now, all her irritability evaporating with his touch. She sits up and takes his hands. 'Look, I'm sorry for asking you about her. I was only being jealous. Will you tell me about your evacuee boy instead? Jimmy, is it?'

Sam's face softens. 'He came to us from London last year. His whole school came from Bermondsey. I think he was glad to get away, though, not like the others. Most of them went back at Christmas, after the bombing raids never happened, but not Jimmy.'

'Didn't his parents want him back?'

'He's only got a dad, and he's a drunk. He's violent, too, and I think Jimmy was getting the brunt of it because his older brother had left.' He drops his head.

'Tell me,' says Rose, stroking the silky hair at the nape of his neck.

'It's him and Menna,' Sam says, in a low voice. 'They don't get on. She doesn't get on with him, I should say.'

He tells her how Jimmy had come to the lighthouse tear-streaked and shaking when he'd only been in Vennor for a couple of months. He hadn't said a word but Sam knew Menna had hit him. He'd told the boy to take off his shirt to see if she'd done any damage and what the boy revealed, silently, his face closed by shame and his shirt balled in his fists, was a series of scars that his dad must have made with a belt, some of them white and ridged, other still pink and raw. Menna's own handprint, where she'd obviously just slapped him, was right between the boy's thin shoulder-blades.

'Jimmy didn't want me to say anything because he's frightened of her and the rest of her lot, but I went straight home and told her she wasn't to touch him ever again, even if he wet the bed every night. That's why she'd lost her temper, you see. I don't think she does hit him any more, but she still calls him names sometimes. I've heard her at it. It's beyond me how someone can hear a child cry out for his dead mother in his sleep, then call him a Cockney rat the next day.' He shakes his head.

Rose feels foolish for making him compare her to Morwenna. It seems so childish after what he's just told her. 'I'm sorry,' she says, leaning down to put her cheek against his. 'But at least he's got you.'

'Come here,' he murmurs, his voice thick – just like it had been when they were so young. He turns his face so their mouths meet and it strikes her that she's an adult now. They don't have to stop like they used to. She decides to let everything go – Morwenna, Frank and even poor little Jimmy. All of it floats away until there's nothing left but Sam moving over her, the sun casting tiny rainbows in the dark depths of his hair and the hard stone beneath her body.

*

That night she lies awake for a long time, the rhythm of the sea in the almost total dark creating the illusion that her bed is floating, the water causing it to tilt and roll very slightly. She knows that, down in Vennor, Sam will be lying beside his wife. For an instant, she imagines him getting home and feeling like she does, his every nerve-end aflame and wanting more, so taking it out on a lithe and naked Morwenna, her dark hair splayed out on the pillow. With an effort, she pushes the image away.

'I don't love her any more,' Sam had said to her, as she'd left him at the lighthouse. 'I don't know if I ever really did.' She repeats the words to herself until she falls asleep. She refuses to think about anything else.

It's only a couple of days later that she finally sees Morwenna for herself. She's in the village on an errand for Eleanor, her whole body tensed in anticipation of bumping into Sam. It's Jimmy she sees first, and for a split second her heart lifts, assuming him to be with Sam, as he was before. But he isn't. He's with a woman, her black hair tied back tightly. Despite the heat, Rose's arms goose-pimple.

There is a vestige of beauty behind Morwenna's hard expression and Rose thinks she might have been lovely as a girl, with her cheeks rounder and her hair loose. Sam had told the truth about her figure; she's made entirely of angles – the sort who looks better in clothes than out of them. Her face, caught as she says something to Jimmy, is unhappy, a caustic blend of impatience and discontent that makes her look older than she must be.

Rose watches as they cross the cobbles, the boy dropping back, his eyes on his feet. 'Stop lagging behind,'

Morwenna cries, voice echoing, as she grabs the boy's arm and pulls him after her. He loses his footing on the uneven ground and stumbles to his knees. 'Oh, for God's sake,' Rose hears her say, as she yanks him to his feet and begins brushing him down so roughly that he wobbles again.

Rose is about to turn away, not wishing to see more – she can't do anything about it – when Morwenna straightens and looks right at her, narrow eyes sharpening. Rose stops breathing, suddenly convinced that the woman must know who she is and what she has done with her husband. She feels certain that the enormous secret must be written in her face. But then Morwenna walks on, Jimmy trailing behind her, leaving Rose to catch her breath.

* * *

ELEVEN DAYS LEFT

Tuesday, 9th July

After dinner tonight, I set off for the village, though those journeys increasingly feel like running the gauntlet, every gorse bush bristling with menace as I hurry past. Still, I'd thought it would be better than sticking around the Hall, with everyone's hypocritical disapproval making me want to scream, and Jane's hungry eyes following my every move.

I also wanted to make things up with Dew who, from the safe distance of the Hall, always seems so tempting. I admit that the bottle of Gordon's I left behind last time also played a role in my decision. I didn't notice Rose slip out after she and I had done the dishes in deadly silence, but I realize now that she must have set off just before me.

I entered the twilit village at a brisk trot so I didn't lose my nerve about Dew, who really was very angry last time, but was brought up short when I spotted a couple in the shadows cast by the harbour wall. They were so entirely welded together that I couldn't make out any identifying features, and was about to tiptoe past so my heels didn't alert them when the woman pulled back to get her breath and I saw she was wearing Rose's shoes.

For an idiotic moment, I actually thought some village hussy had stolen Rose's favourite courts, but of course it was her and I'll admit the shock of it made me queasy. It was foolish, really, because I already knew how the land lay. Perhaps it was simply the surprise of seeing someone you know behaving like a stranger that gave me the urge to push her into the oily harbour water. Instead, I lurked in a doorway until they finally disentangled themselves. I wanted to get a good look at this lighthouse chap once and for all.

The biggest shock was how good-looking he is. I think I was expecting a Cornish version of Frank: miles away from ugly but distinctly average nonetheless. In fact, Sam Bligh is undeniably dishy, with broad shoulders and long legs.

I was so thrown by all this that I forgot about Dew and even the gin. As soon as they started kissing again, I made a run for it, and didn't stop until I reached Penhallow's gate, my calf muscles in agony because I hadn't paused to take off my heels, and my undigested dinner churning inside me. The path survived and the gate safely closed behind me, I felt all my upset and nerves twist into cold fury. For how dare she? How dare she pass judgement on me when she was out there in the night, betraying a husband who has (probably) only been dead mere days? I remember her in the garden that time, her expression so pious and condescending, saying, 'We're not all like you,' as though I was the cheap, promiscuous one.

And someone has been going through my things again. I'm certain it's Jane, hunting for souvenirs to add to the silver bracelet of mine I found tucked in her pillow case yesterday. I left it there, thinking it quite endearing at the time, but tonight I find the idea of it oppressive and slightly sinister. I wonder if she's stooped to going through this diary. I really must move it. Perhaps you're reading this now, Jane. If so, you'll have discovered the hard way that eavesdroppers never hear good of themselves.

I feel tonight as though all these Penhallow women are against me, and I'm reminded that it's always been like this with my own sex. Men are generally quite simple to please, while women are reliably hateful and jealous, desperate to bring me down – even my own mother. Now Payne creeps around after me, watching and biding her time until she can go to her mistress with an exhaustive and punishable list of sins. What with her, and now Rose and Eleanor in cahoots, I'm certain it won't be long until they all come together to decide I am such a poisonous presence, especially in regard to naive, impressionable little Jane, that I must be sent away immediately.

XIV

Rose is afraid all the time now: of getting confirmation that Frank is dead, that the invasion is happening, that she and Sam will be found out. But her biggest fear – the one that has crept up on her in the last couple of days, like a slow-building wave – is that Sam will change his mind and tell her not to come to him any more. She knows it's utterly selfish when Frank is missing, and when there's a war on, with so many people hurt or grieving. But she is in love, she supposes, and it's as absorbing and terrifying as it is glorious.

Given this, she worries how much strain Sam is under at home – unlike her, he has to face the object of his betrayal every day. She never dares ask him how he bears it; she's afraid of putting the idea into his head.

After a long day of lifting beetroot, her hands sore from pushing the spade into the hard-baked ground, it's finally evening and she is on her way to the cove. The lighthouse hasn't needed to be lit for a couple of days now and there's been no opportunity for them to meet anywhere else, Sam saying he had too much on. She hadn't pushed him to explain exactly what – at the time she hadn't felt she needed to know, his hand in hers, or stroking her hair. It was only afterwards that she wondered, the fear of losing him edging stealthily in again. Walking along now, anticipation firing inside her, she thinks that if they hadn't been able to arrange tonight she'd have gone mad.

They have all got used to the wonderful weather, those flawless skies and benign breezes, taking it for granted. Tonight, though, for the first time in ages, it feels as if it could turn quite easily, if the mood took it. The wind has got up, and even down on the sand in the sheltered cove, it buffets disconsolately around her, making her wish she'd worn something with sleeves. She sits on a flat rock and stares at the sea, which is choppy and bad-tempered beneath a mackerel sky the colours of smoke and flame.

She's been waiting there for almost an hour, or so she estimates, cursing herself again for never wearing a watch, when Sam finally appears. For some time, she's been watching the steps instead of the sea, and when she sees him she springs up and runs towards him, wrapping her arms tightly around his neck.

'Oh, God, I thought you weren't coming.'

He pulls back, gently disentangling himself from her. 'I nearly didn't. I – I couldn't get away. And look, Rose, I can't stay. I just came to tell you that. I didn't want to think of you here, waiting.'

'But you've only just got here. You can't go already.'

Sam looks down at the sand. 'I have to. I shouldn't have come at all probably, but I knew you'd be waiting. I need to get back now, though.'

'Back where? To the lighthouse? I'll come. I'll follow, once it's darker.'

He puts a hand through his hair and glances behind him at the steps. She feels it suddenly in the very pit of her stomach: he doesn't want to be here. He wants to get away as soon as he can.

'Sam?' she says. 'What's going on? Has someone said something?'

He looks at her, then shakes his head. 'I've got to go. I'm sorry.' He leans in and swiftly kisses her, catching her near but not on her mouth. Then he turns and strides towards the steps.

She runs after him. 'Wait! You can't just go without telling me what's wrong. Have you changed your mind? Is that it?' She feels as if she might be sick, right there in the sand.

'No!' he shouts, and she steps back with the force of it. He's never raised his voice to her before. She tries to read his face but she can't. 'I haven't changed my mind. For God's sake, give me some credit.'

'What, then?' She makes herself say it softly, so she doesn't scare him off. She can't bear him to go like this.

He rumples his hair again. 'I think her brother might know something.'

'Whose brother? Morwenna's? How would he know anything?'

Sam shakes his head. 'He just would. He knows everything and we've been careless. We shouldn't have met at the harbour. And anyone could have seen you going back and forth to the lighthouse.'

Fear clutches at her. He's working up to saying it's too dangerous. 'Has he actually said anything?'

'He came round last night saying he hadn't seen much of me lately. He said the last time he called in and Menna said I was working, the lamp wasn't even lit. Something about Jory, too, seeing me by the harbour the other evening.'

Rose doesn't know these men yet they are part of Sam's life – the other part, which doesn't include her. He's tethered to Cornwall and always has been. She'd liked it when she was sixteen; she'd envied how woven into the place he was, how entirely he belonged, as she never felt she had in her own home town. But she sees now how tight the ties that bind him are, and how powerless she would be to break them.

She lets him go, then. She knows she'll make it worse if she runs after him – she'll make herself feel worse later, too. Long minutes after he's left, kissing her only distractedly on the cheek, she remains standing where he left her, going over his words and how he'd looked when he said them. 'Trapped' is the word that comes into her head. He'd looked trapped.

He was kind, Sam, soft-hearted – she doesn't think he'd be able to tell her straight if they had to stop. He'd probably grow more and more distant, in the hope that she would end it for him. As she argues with herself, she begins to shake from worry. She doesn't notice the tide creeping towards her until a finger of freezing water wraps itself around her ankles, making her cry out in shock. She looks around her and, for the first time, the cove seems an unfriendly place, full of foreboding.

When she gets to the top of the steps she lingers on the path until she understands two things: that she's hoping

Sam will come back, and that he isn't going to. The clouds have made it dark earlier than usual and she shivers at the intimation of what autumn might be like here: not only the lash of the wind off the sea and the endless hours of blackout but the emptiness if Sam has gone. She's hated autumn since her mother's death.

She begins to run, and doesn't stop until she's closed the Penhallow gate behind her. It's much warmer in the garden, out of the wind. It feels like summer again, the heavy scent of the flowers that haven't yet closed for the night stealing round her. She tells herself he hasn't gone, that he loves her still, but she also knows that something changed between them tonight.

She's almost at the bathroom door when Diana comes out of the sitting room further up the passage. Her cat's eyes widen when she spots Rose.

'Ah, here she is, Penhallow's very own escapologist.'

'Not now, Diana,' she says sharply. 'Please. I'm not in the mood.'

Diana walks towards her. 'Oh, really, and why's that? I must say, you seem to have lost some of your shine tonight. Did you and lover-boy have a row?'

Rose tries to go into the bathroom but Diana steps in front of the door. 'Well, did you?' she says. 'It's no good pretending with me, like you do with everyone else.' She reaches out and runs her finger down the thin blue cotton of Rose's dress, following the line of her hip.

'Just getting the sand off.' She smirks as Rose pulls away. 'I would have thought scarlet a better colour for you, darling.'

'Keep your voice down,' Rose hisses. 'Jane will hear you.'

Diana smiles coldly and Rose remembers what Jane had said in the garden this morning. *Diana's been strange the last few days. Have you noticed? I'm afraid of saying the wrong thing in case she bites.*

'So, what happened on the beach?' Diana's smile has gone. 'Did he try to push things on too fast? Or have you already let him do it? You probably let him ages ago, didn't you?'

'No, I have not,' she says, hoping the passage is dim enough to hide the lie in her eyes. She tries to push past Diana but the taller girl is easily stronger, for all her indolence in the garden, holding Rose off with one long-fingered hand spread across her midriff.

'You know, Rose, you've just reminded me of something Mrs Fox once said. I think she was talking about Eleanor, but the cap fits you better. She said that it's the quiet ones you have to watch.'

* * *

NINE DAYS LEFT

Thursday, 11ᵗʰ July

The damned Sickly Creepers have come upon me, as I suppose they've been threatening to for a couple of days. It's maddening that they've decided to descend now, when I've been doing so very well to keep my bad thoughts at bay.

The 'Sickly Creepers' is a term I invented as a child and still use for days like today, when all the colour and texture of life leaches away and everything is left tainted and grubby. They settled around me for the first time at Great Uncle Theobald's Sussex house, when I was eight years old. In my head, I always called him GUT for short, in ironic homage to *Ballet Shoes* and the Fossil girls' sainted Great Uncle Matthew – or GUM, as he was affectionately known. GUT's house, Flete, was a beautiful place and my infant memories of it are vague and magical, gold-hazed: a sprawling red-brick house of inglenooks and polished flags encircled by lawns whose velvet perfection had only required about three hundred years of careful rolling.

None of this changed materially in the subsequent years, only its owner's interest in the prettiest of his great-nieces, but this was enough to ruin the place for me. To everyone's bewilderment (except perhaps my mother's) he left the whole kit and caboodle to me in his will and, do you know, I'm still not sure whether he intended it as apology or revenge.

I woke just before three this morning and couldn't go back to sleep. At home, I would have taken one of my bromides but I ran out weeks ago and have heard nothing from home about another prescription from Dr Brookner. If it had been light I would finally have gone for the bathe I'm always promising myself – for some reason cold water helps when I feel like this, leaving me oddly calm and serene afterwards, a state I'm not otherwise familiar with. Whenever I have a bad spell in London, I always go to the ponds on

Hampstead Heath and thrash up and down until my lips turn blue. Getting in is awful, especially in winter, but afterwards I always feel sluiced out and squeaky-clean; made new again, somehow, and free of the damned old Creepers.

But this morning felt too dark and forbidding to risk swimming. I couldn't quite summon the nerve, though I got as far as the steps to the cove, where I looked down and could make out little more than white foam because the moon was swaddled in cloud. It was so dark I became afraid that I wouldn't see anyone approaching until they were virtually on top of me. The thought sent me scurrying back to the house.

The sense that someone is watching me from the shadows has not diminished with the passing days. Quite the opposite. I've had it half a dozen times now, not only on the coast-path, where I thought I saw the child, but in the garden too. Yesterday I caught myself thinking Mother must have sent someone to spy on me and that frightened me. I haven't had such a peculiar thought in a long time.

'You'll go to Flete,' was a refrain she liked to use when I was being disobedient as a girl. 'You'll go to Flete if you insist on being so entirely unmanageable.' She was left at a loss once GUT was dead and the threat evaporated with him. It's possibly no coincidence that I was expelled from Hambles two months after his funeral. There was no longer any punishment I was genuinely afraid of.

Though she threatened it all the time, she only sent me there alone once, though there were plenty of visits *en famille* at Easter and Christmas and the rest. I was thirteen and reaching the age when my appeal to the old man was waning. I had recently got the curse and my breasts were budding. When I arrived, he came out to greet the car and, while Townsend took in my case, he folded his arms and looked me over critically.

'You're swelling up,' he said irritably. 'Too much milk and butter.'

He was angry with me for the whole fortnight I was kept there, as though I had chosen to grow up just to spite him. But, then, everything was always refracted through his viewpoint. A rich man with good servants and no wife is a monstrously self-centred creature.

I had enjoyed a moment of optimism out there on the drive, a wild hope that my growing up would act like a fairy's protective cloak, rendering me invisible or at least uninteresting to him. That wasn't how things went. In fact, it was rather worse than it had been because at least before he had been in a good temper with me.

I didn't intend to put down any of that. It hasn't had the same cathartic effect as the swimming, although it's better than nothing. Goodness, how the quiet of the country turns the mind inward. Why people are sent to places like this to convalesce from mental breakdown I can't imagine.

I have drifted spectacularly off the subject. I meant only to write about my Silver Moon Ball idea. I thought of it in the small hours, when still wakefully wandering the house, trying to trick my mind into distraction. Penhallow always feels stuck in time but at night it's truly the preserve of its past inhabitants. It's the same at home in London; a family of four boys lived in our house before Daddy bought it and as a little girl I always imagined them creeping out at night to slide on the banisters like Peter Pan and his Lost Boys, even though in real life they were probably all balding, with dull jobs in the City. I suppose I don't think you have to be dead to be a ghost – for aren't our old, lost and better selves also capable of haunting us?

Anyway, around half past four, by which time I was sitting cross-legged on the grand piano smoking my seventeenth cigarette, the clouds parted and the most brilliant, and indeed silver, moon lit the garden. It was both unearthly and arresting, as though the world had been dipped in mercury. And that was when I thought that the resurrection of the Silver Moon Ball might be just the ticket. Not only as distraction for my unquiet mind but also to do my faithful Jane a good turn, even if she does sneak looks at me while I'm getting undressed. If anyone really is plotting to get rid of me, at least I'll go out with a bang, having done something for someone else for once. I was never the sort to whimper.

XV

It takes Eleanor more than a week to work up the nerve to leave the house after the incident at the creek. When she finally decides she can't bear to stay inside a minute longer, she goes first to Gerald's study for a drink. He always refers to his early-evening whisky as his sharpener but spirits have always had the opposite effect on Eleanor, making her feel detached and foggy, which is exactly what she needs today.

Then she takes the familiar, heart-sinking way to the coast-path gate, because she feels guilty she hasn't fulfilled her promise to Gerald for a while. Taking hold of the cold iron handle, she breathes slowly out. This close to the gate, she can see what's on the other side through tiny gaps in the wood – or at least a striated version of what is just beyond reach, picked out in different colours: the brown earth path, the green of the bushes, the myriad blues of sea and sky.

The alcohol she'd gulped down is seeping into her bloodstream, making her limbs heavy. She watches her hand twist the handle as though it's not part of herself. The latch lifts and the sea breeze pushes the gate towards her, just a couple of inches. 'When, one day, it feels important enough, you'll do it,' Gerald had said once. She allows the gate to swing open a little more, the creak as it does making her heart skitter.

'Eleanor?'

She whirls around, slamming the gate shut as she does so, her other hand on her chest, where the beat misses its cue, thumping hard to make up for it. Miss and thump. Miss and thump.

'Oh, Diana,' she manages to say. 'You frightened me.' The girl before her shimmers in an apple-coloured dress, like a woman in a painting, a dizzying blur of green and gold that's not quite real.

'You're surely not going out?' Diana says, coming closer. Her heady perfume, stronger than usual, makes Eleanor's head reel. She blinks at the younger woman, wondering if she's trying to suppress a laugh at her ridiculous behaviour.

'No, I'm not going out,' she murmurs. 'I'm not going anywhere.' She pushes past before Diana can ask any more questions and hurries across the lawn, the house to her right seeming to bend and loom towards her as though it's begun to slide very slowly down the hill. She trips halfway along the cinder path, stumbling over and tearing a hole in her stockings. A single drop of blood wells to the surface of her shin and she wipes it off. She puts the finger in her mouth and the metallic tang seems to cut through some of the confusion in her head, so she sits there, head resting on her drawn-up knees, until she feels almost normal.

The creek lies dark and unmoving when she gets there,

with no sign of the horror of before. Everything else is quite as it should be too. The explanation comes to her then, and the relief is indescribable. *Of course* it wasn't Robin who'd sent the fish as a sign. He would never have frightened her, the little sister with whom he had always been so gentle. It must have been something else playing tricks, some other, more malign spirit that had also been attracted to this liminal place where time could circle back on itself.

But today it's Robin's place again, the soft air a caress on her cheek. A flash of brightness inside the boathouse makes her rush up the steps, part of her reasoning it could be sunlight catching in the warped old glass of the window, but the rest of her believing he's welcoming her back.

Inside, her eye falls on the suitcases. She hasn't gone through them yet. There's something especially forlorn about old clothes that she hasn't yet wanted to face. Perhaps it's because they're worn next to the skin, making the memories associated with them more intimate and oddly painful than the things you think would be: the letters, the photographs, the battered old diaries.

She finds the dress almost immediately. It's horribly creased but miraculously untouched by moths, though it's made of pure silk. She hesitates, then undoes her blouse, glancing over her shoulder to the door as she slips it off. When she lets the dress slide over her head and down to bunch at her hips, she shivers, the fabric as cold as a stream. She looks at her bare arms, and remembers how lean and smoothly unmarked they'd been when she wore it last. Strange to think that girl no longer exists, not really.

She remembers that first kiss on the night of the ball: long and loosening, and so unexpectedly good it had stopped her caring about anything else. She supposes, in a way, that it wasn't just that other girl's first kiss, it was also her last.

Thinking of her own lost youth and beauty, it's not much of a leap to recall the image of Diana by the gate just now. She is only a couple of years older than Eleanor was when she last wore the white silk dress. She pictures again Diana's green dress and smells her heavy scent. Where can the girl be going looking like that in the middle of the afternoon? What secrets is she keeping? Could it have been her uninvited presence that so disturbed the creek's serenity the other day?

And then she thinks of how Jane looks at her glamorous new friend – that combination of wonder and fear, as though she's already braced for hurt. Eleanor knows exactly how that feels, and it makes her want to return to the gate and padlock it against Diana so she can't do any more damage.

XVI

Rose is in the dormitory, her shoes kicked off so she doesn't make the eiderdown dusty. She still has an hour before dinner and it's peaceful in here, with the windows pushed up and no one else around.

Her day in the garden had seemed to drag on interminably. Blewett had been in a foul mood because of an imminent visit from the regional inspector, who couldn't know about the pruning and so forth they'd been doing for Mrs Fox. He'd berated them for half an hour for not digging a big enough vegetable patch on the top lawn, though he had specified the dimensions himself.

Diana's unexplained absence after lunch hadn't helped his mood; there seemed to be nothing he could say or do to keep her at her work. For a man who had run a team of under-gardeners and boys for more than a decade, this was humiliating, and humiliation had turned him nasty. Poor Brick had been slapped and chased off with a rake when he was caught eating peas off the stalk and

Payne – who'd come to nag on Mrs Fox's behalf – was given short shrift at high volume.

Ironically, Diana would have enjoyed it all immensely if she'd only bothered turning up. Rose was glad when she didn't, though, the aftertaste of last night's unpleasant exchange outside the bathroom still sour in her mouth. Diana hadn't said a word to her this morning and, although Jane was behaving normally, it had given Rose the disconcerting sense she had turned invisible.

She arranges her pillow so it cushions her back against the iron bed-frame and picks up her book, hoping it will distract her. She misses Sam every second she isn't with him but his lack is particularly gnawing at her today. She had thought she loved him the first time round, but at least then she had been able to enjoy herself when she wasn't with him. Then, it had been enough to know he was out there somewhere, still hers even though they weren't within touching distance. Today she's miserable in his absence, and even before that her moods have lifted and swooped alarmingly. It's disturbing that something so wonderful has made her so unhappy, and so quickly too.

She's only managed a page of her novel when the creak of the door makes her look up. She's expecting to see Jane but it's Diana. She looks strange, glittery somehow: a peculiar blend of anxious and excitable. Her hair is slightly dishevelled, which it never is, one comb stuffed clumsily into it much lower than the other, giving her a lopsided, girlish look, like a child wrenched out of an absorbing game. Her mouth, bright with fresh lipstick as always, is twisting as though she's trying not to laugh, or perhaps cry – Rose can't tell.

'Diana. Are you all right?' The girl looks so odd that she forgets they aren't friends.

With what seems like a supreme effort, Diana stills, her expression regaining its usual wry nonchalance, her high colour evening out as Rose watches, transfixed. Diana turns to the dressing-table and tips the mirror so she can inspect herself in the glass. Taking up a comb, she deftly repairs her hair. Rose watches her reflection and realizes she can also see herself, just visible behind Diana, little more than a pale oval face and a dark tangle of hair.

She's about to get up and leave – not only because she's remembered what happened last night but because she doesn't feel quite safe – when Diana turns and walks over to the bed, perching on the end like she used to before relations had cooled between them.

'Hello, old thing,' she says, as if Rose hadn't spoken before. 'What are you doing in here on your own?'

Rose is ashamed at how relieved she is. Diana is mercurial; perhaps she's forgotten what passed between them last night; perhaps she just wants to make friends. And Rose is so afraid about Sam today that it feels too hard to turn down any kindness, even from the person who could bring everything down around her.

'I – Well, I'm not doing anything really,' she says carefully. 'I was just reading.'

Diana looks at her without saying anything, her expression inscrutable now. Whatever emotion Rose had seen when she came in has been entirely pulled back inside her.

'What is it?' Rose says, alarmed by the silence. 'Has something happened?' Her voice cracks on the last word as anxiety floods her. Is this why Diana is suddenly speaking to her? Has a telegram arrived downstairs about Frank?

Diana smooths her green dress over her bare legs. 'No one's hurt. It's nothing like that. I do have something to tell you, though, Rosie, and you'll have to be brave.'

Rose feels her stomach heave itself over with a slap. 'What is it? What do you mean?' She sits up straighter, her book falling to the floor.

'It's about your friend, Sam,' says Diana.

'Oh, God, is he all right? Tell me quickly.'

'Yes. Yes, I said no one was hurt,' Diana says, a note of impatience briefly hardening her voice. 'It's just that I know how much he means to you.'

Rose opens her mouth to deny it, but no words will come. She thinks she'll be sick if Diana doesn't tell her whatever it is immediately.

Diana sighs. 'I heard some rumours about him today.'

'From who?'

She waves her hand about vaguely. 'A friend of mine in the village.' She glances up. 'They say he's likely cheating on his wife again and I thought –'

'Again?' Rose cuts across her.

Diana pauses, then blinks a couple of times. 'Oh dear, I do hope you won't shoot the messenger. I just wanted to warn you. I mean, I know you won't have done anything serious, despite my teasing last night. I know that the two of you are only old pals from childhood and someone's got the wrong end of the stick, but I thought you should know. Those villagers are poisonous and, really, you don't want to cross the Bolithos. They're awfully rough sorts.'

'The Bolithos?'

'Morwenna's family.'

'How do you know about her?' Her voice is high and panicked.

'Oh, I don't. Only her brother, Dew, he's an . . . acquaintance of sorts. He gets me things, nylons and so forth. I don't ask too many questions, if you know what I mean. Anyway, he was furious about something when I saw him in Vennor today and I prodded and pressed him – you know how I do – and in the end he admitted it was to do with his brother-in-law.'

'You said "again" before,' Rose says, faintly. 'That he was cheating again.'

'Apparently he has form. I'm not surprised, really, given those looks of his. I don't suppose you get too many like him to the pound, not in these parts.'

'How do you know what he looks like?'

Diana pulls at a lock of her blonde hair, eyes cast down to Rose's eiderdown. 'Well, you told me, didn't you? Skin the colour of toffee, wasn't it? The point is, I'm sure he's still delicious and I would never blame you for wanting him, Rosie. We're only animals, really, and there is a war on. And Frank –'

'Sam's just a friend,' she says woodenly.

Diana edges up the bed and takes Rose's hands. Her skin feels hot and dry, almost feverish, and Rose fights the urge to pull away. 'Oh, I know you would never cheat on Frank. I told Dew that and I think he believed me. He seems to think it's all Sam's fault. He's done it to his wife a few times, apparently, though he always comes crawling back, begging forgiveness and saying she's the only one he's ever really loved.'

She pauses and Rose holds herself completely still so she doesn't give anything away. Her hands have gone cold and clammy in Diana's, she knows.

'Dew said he doesn't know how he does it,' Diana continues relentlessly, 'not when he seems like such a quiet sort. What was it he said? Oh, yes. "Sam Bligh has always had the women eating out of his hands."'

She squeezes Rose's fingers until her wedding ring cuts painfully into the flesh around it. 'Anyway, darling, I thought about it all the way back and my theory is that someone must've seen you and him walking on the coast-path together that time. Or perhaps at the cove – or by the harbour? Either way, they've put two and two together and made fifty. This is precisely why I could never live in a place like this. Such spite and small-mindedness. They haven't anything interesting going on in their own lives so they have to make up horrid lies about other people's.'

'Truly, he's just a friend,' Rose says again.

'Oh, I know that. It's everyone else I'm worried about.' She frowns prettily.

'Was I mentioned by name?'

'No, but Dew knew you were from the Hall.'

Rose's mind is racing. She thinks of that grotesque country custom of centuries ago, the effigies of adulterous couples paraded through the streets by the whole village, the shame and ruin of it. She's coming to see that a place like Vennor is raw and pitiless under its twentieth-century skin. She's sensed it once or twice in the lanes. With the beating sun and threat of invasion making everyone edgy, it wouldn't take much for it to turn, the civilized years falling away.

'And you told him nothing was going on, that I was married?' she says in a rush.

'Of course I did. I said so,' Diana murmurs, in a soothing tone. She pats Rose's hand and sits back. 'It'll be all right. I can't see that Eleanor will even hear about it up here. She never leaves Penhallow, you know that. And old Mrs F can't, with her legs.'

Eleanor. Rose hasn't even thought about her. She seems so gentle, so kind, but would that change if she heard rumours? The rumours, Rose reminds herself, that, if Diana has got it right, aren't even as bad as the truth. Perhaps she will be dismissed, or thrown out of the WLA altogether. Perhaps the Bolithos will come for her first, taking her down to the village to exact justice. She takes a shaky breath.

'That's it, darling. Deep breaths now,' says Diana. 'I told you, it'll be all right. All you've got to do is stay here, away from the village and all that vile gossip. And him, of course. Not that you'll want to see him again, I'm sure, not if he's angling for you to be his next conquest. You'll be safe here. And if anyone says anything, they'll have me to deal with. Look, shall I fetch us a drink? I think we both need it after all that.'

She's gone before Rose can answer, the door left ajar. Rose hears her humming as she goes along the passage and into the sitting room to fetch whatever she's hidden in the cavity of the sofa this week.

Ten minutes after she's returned and handed Rose a

193

bottle of cooking sherry with an apologetic moue, Diana falls abruptly asleep on the next bed, her brow smooth, her cheeks flushed pink. Through her shock, Rose is grateful to her, not just for being there next to her but for being her friend at all.

The dusty, sour-tasting sherry she's just gulped down begins to work inside her, blurring things and distancing her from all she's just heard. She hides the bottle under the bed and makes herself picture Sam. Still, she does it tentatively, as someone would step out with bare, tender feet on sharp stones.

What Diana has told her bears no relation to the man she knows, or thinks she knows. There's nothing smooth or oily about the way he's been with her. She simply doesn't recognize the Lothario figure Diana has painted. But perhaps that's where his success lies: in that touching awkwardness when he's shy, and in his rare combination of beauty without vanity, as though he's never bothered to look in a mirror and see what he is. Perhaps that is what's so devastating – to others, as well as her. She can't deny how strange he'd looked at the cove, and how he'd left her there on her own, even though she'd begged him not to.

She thinks of his skin, softest where the sun has never scorched it, deep brown and calloused on his hands. Toffee-coloured, as Diana had remembered. There's a scar on his right thumb, where he'd cut it on broken glass when he was nineteen and profoundly drunk for the first time in his life. He'd woken the next morning to find a pale flap of skin hanging by a thread. It had healed with a raised scar that goes pink when he's hot, and is shaped like a small *r*.

He'd told her one night that he always thought of it as standing for her, for Rosy. She had kissed it then, secretly minding that he'd had these experiences without her. She'd felt irrationally jealous of whoever had been drinking with him that night; she had been jealous even of the shard of glass that had got under his skin while she was more than two hundred miles away.

Silently, because Diana is next to her, she begins to weep. For him as well as herself. For the scar that supposedly stands for her name. She shifts down the bed until she's lying flat, and pulls the eiderdown over herself. The tears run down her temples and into her hair. She's such a fool. To think she'd believed him when he said he'd never forgotten her. When he said he'd written her letter after letter. Her father hadn't stolen them; they were likely never sent. As a single shuddering sob escapes her, she glances across at Diana. She isn't ready to show anyone how distraught she is. As far as everyone else is concerned, he can't be anything more than a fragment of her past, a coincidence that's briefly distracted her.

She thinks of going to him after dark to confront him, to beat her fists on his chest and ask him why he's lied to her. But perhaps he hasn't lied, or has done so only by omission. He'd never said there were no others besides Morwenna and she'd never thought to ask, assuming him to be as hopelessly romantic as herself. Besides, she knows that going to the lighthouse would only be an excuse to be with him again. She knows a desperate, pitiable part of her doesn't care what he's done with anyone else. Without the alcohol's deadening fug, she couldn't have framed the sentences at all, but she makes herself repeat them in her mind, inuring herself to the pain. You won't see him again. He's gone now. He never really existed.

* * *

SEVEN DAYS LEFT

Saturday, 13th July

After some pretty ghastly days, the Sickly Creepers have almost slunk away. Now, I feel about three stone lighter, though I suppose they might still be hovering somewhere over my head, ready to pluck at my hair. It's devilishly hard to remember what it is to feel normal when one is held fast in their dank grip but perhaps it will help next time that I'm writing about it now. I can refer to this entry when I inevitably dip: a line of defence against the next bout of hopelessness.

That I am back in Rose's favour, and she in mine, has helped. The truth is that Jane doesn't soothe my soul like Rose. Lately I've felt as though I'm stranded in the middle of a frozen lake, cracks and fissures radiating out around me. Rose has, for the moment, made the ground feel a little more solid. And I'd been having the most awful nightmares about GUT before, some of them so potent and suffocating that they were spilling over into the whole day. Last night I slept like the dead.

I do feel rather badly for Rose but it's not as though I had any choice. I keep forgetting she's deep in the Slough of Despond over Mr Lighthouse and rush up to tell her something amusing, only to see that she's been crying again. Her poor eyes are permanently pink. She's still pretending nothing happened between them, of course, but I can understand that. A girl has her pride.

Still, things couldn't have continued as they were. I had little choice but to tell her a few fibs about Sam, as well as people in the village having their suspicions, which I'm sure they do. She still hasn't grasped the way a place like Vennor works, with everyone tied by blood, marriage and centuries-old resentments. It's not like London, or even blessed Solihull; people keep watch here. They notice everything, especially if they're like the Bolithos. She's lucky I got to her first.

I must say again that Sam Bligh isn't what I expected. Not just his rather wonderful face up close, but his evident devotion to Rose. I certainly had no thoughts of seducing him – it's just that I've become accustomed to captivating men in a single glance. I'm not boasting; it's simple fact and they are simple creatures. He wasn't remotely interested, though, and, in a peculiar way, I'm quite glad he didn't fall for the old Devlin charm. I'm getting sentimental in my old age.

In between rescuing Rose from herself, I haven't forgotten my idea to raise the Silver Moon Ball from the ashes. I believe that once you start a thing you have to push on and see it through. Conviction is the thing.

Later. 'If only we had more dances to go to,' I said, in a wistful tone, to old girl Fox tonight, having gone up to see her after dinner, determined to quell the doubts that had begun to mutter in my ear. 'There was one in April, in a church hall in St Austell, but it was frightfully limp.'

She held out her sherry glass for another tot. 'I suppose they might hold one in the Baptist hall,' she said, penny not yet dropping. 'That's where the WI meet, and have their jumble sales.'

'Lord, how humdrum,' I replied. 'I can barely contain myself. I expect, if they really push the boat out, we'll get some bunting and a glass of lemon barley each. It's fanciful of me, I suppose, but I was imagining something more sophisticated, more memorable. Something that will get everyone talking. But how? And where?' I trailed off but she only looked at me beadily.

'I suppose Penhallow hosted some wonderful occasions in that lovely ballroom with the enormous windows,' I continued doggedly, when it became clear she wasn't going to take the bait.

'It's not a ballroom, it's an orangery,' she said severely.

'Well, whatever its official function, it's a wonderful room.'

For once, I wasn't lying or exaggerating for some nefarious purpose. It's not a huge room – Penhallow is not a huge house – but there are windows on two sides that reach to the ceiling and are curved like half-moons at the top. Criminally, the floor is covered with vomit-coloured lino but I peeled back a corner one slow afternoon (I was malingering inside after telling an appalled Blewett I had women's troubles again), and beneath is a wonderful marquetry floor. So, orangery my foot, though there are a few dusty ferns in the corners. Mainly, it's being used to store camp beds and blankets, these days – some do-gooding favour to the WVS on Eleanor's part, in lieu of anything that would actually require her to leave the house.

When I glanced back at Mrs F, she was obviously miles away. I caught another glimpse of her as she would've been when she was young, a few centuries ago.

'It was a ballroom sometimes,' she said, so quietly that I had to drag my chair closer to hers by the window. Outside, the evening sky throbbed a deep orange that stained the room sepia.

'Oh, yes?'

'Not for many years now, of course, but we used to hold an annual celebration in summer. Once it got too dark to be in the garden, everyone went into the orangery to carry on the dancing. We'd open the doors so it was cool and the scent of the late roses would drift in. When the band stopped playing between songs, you could hear the sea.'

As I listened to her, actually quite agog, it struck me that Rose would love to hear about it. Ghosts of balls past and all the rest of it are precisely her cup of tea. She's a terrific one for looking back and I'd never understood it till then, but I suddenly realized there was something rather spellbinding about the idea of what had gone before and can't be fetched back. Especially when it involved a first-rate party absolutely swimming in booze. I thought about the dresses and the music and the servants – not Cook and lugubrious Payne, but handsome footmen in tails gliding by carrying trays stacked with delicious morsels. Now look at us. Holes in our stockings and a single measly egg a week unless Eleanor's ancient, disobliging hens can trouble themselves to lay any extra.

Thinking about food made my stomach give an indecorous gurgle, which jolted Mrs F out of her reverie.

'Who was it who said that one can never be too thin?' she said reprovingly.

'Or too rich. Wallis Simpson, wasn't it?'

'Well, about that, if nothing else, I'm inclined to agree with her.' She sniffed.

'Oh, absolutely,' I nodded, 'especially the rich part, but one doesn't want to lose all one's curves. Anyway, let's not talk about it. It makes me even more ravenous. I want to hear more about these Silver Moon Balls.'

Her blue eyes bored coldly into me as I realized too late my slip. 'Who told you what they were called?' she said, the words fired at me like hailstones.

'Eleanor,' I gabbled. It's sort of true.

She harrumphed nastily. 'She doesn't learn. The foolish girl never learns.'

'Why did they stop in 1924?' I said bravely, reasoning that I'd got this far.

She stared at me for so long that I began to wriggle.

'My husband died,' she said finally, in a wrung-out tone. 'The tradition went with him.'

For once, she was unable to meet my eye. A seasoned liar myself, I knew she wasn't being truthful.

'Well, with all due respect to the late Mr Fox,' I said, 'I wonder if now might be the perfect time to revive such a gorgeous ritual. It's just what everyone needs to take their minds off this awful war. One night of loveliness with you presiding over it, Mrs F. A chance to get your diamonds out of the bank. Wouldn't that show the village busybodies a thing or two?'

She shook her head stonily. 'It's out of the question.'

'Oh, no, but why?'

'Never mind why.'

'So there's another reason they stopped, then?'

'I didn't say that.'

'Well, then, as I see it, there's simply no excuse not to hold a dance here – and soon, while the weather holds. Cock a snook at Hitler by reliving the past. I know it'll hardly be the same as before, what with rationing and a gaggle of Johnny-foreigner airmen as guests, but it would still be enormous fun. A last hurrah before Göring's jack-boots descend, what?'

She glared at me and I knew I'd overdone it. Her hands were gripping the arms of her chair tightly, knuckles bone-white. 'I don't wish to discuss this further,' she said. 'There will be no ball this summer. You will stop interfering and let the past rest.'

The silence lengthened, and when she held out her glass for another drink, her hand trembled more than usual. In the house beyond, a clock began to chime and a faint rustle close by told me that Payne was listening outside the door again.

'I was talking to an old acquaintance of yours the other day,' I said eventually.

Mrs Fox had been lost in her thoughts, but her eyes swam into focus again. 'Oh, yes?' She sounded suspicious, no doubt wondering if I was going to try to bring up 1924 again.

'Yes, he spoke very fondly of your husband. The master, he called him, most deferentially. I suppose he must have worked for you once.'

She smiled thinly, her hands loosening their grip.

'Gracious, what mixed company you must keep. I can't think your mother would approve. Who was this man?'

'I'm sure you would remember him. He's the sort one does. His name is Dew Bolitho.'

She started so violently that her drink, which she was just reaching for, slopped on the floor.

'Yes, he does rather have that effect,' I said, getting up and casting about for something to mop up the spill.

'That man has no right to speak about this house and this family.' Her voice, guttural with fury, made me freeze. 'Tell me what he said to you!'

'Not much,' I squeaked. Always fierce, she looked murderous now, her cheeks mottled and her blue eyes popping. 'Only that he knew the family. Look, if I've spoken out of turn –'

'He's broken his promise,' she said, apparently to herself. 'I knew he would. I knew that bad blood like his would eventually out. It always does. Well, he won't get another penny from me.'

'You're paying him?' I said, too surprised to hold my tongue.

She jerked her head up, her eyes widening. She'd forgotten I was there.

'You!' she cried. 'You put on such airs but you're only better than him by name. Do you know what else Mrs Phelps said about you in her letter? That you were disturbed. That behind that pretty face something was damaged. And she was right, wasn't she? I see it now. You're nothing but soiled goods.'

I stepped backwards and almost tripped over a rug. Mrs Fox screeched for Payne, who flung back the door with a crash, as ferocious as I've ever seen her.

'What have you done?' she spat in my direction, as she rushed over to the old lady, her eyes blazing coldly. 'There, there,' she crooned, stroking her mistress's hand while staring fixedly at me. 'Payne's here now, madam. Payne's here.' Her voice sounded odd and I realized it was an approximation of baby-talk, such as a nanny might use to a child.

Mrs Fox had gone limp, her eyes closed, the lids quivering. In one swift movement, Payne picked her up, as she had after dinner that time, and carried her over to the bed, propping her up against the pillows. A memory of the sickroom at Flete flashed on and off in my mind, like a warning beacon.

'Look here, I'm very sorry if I've said the wrong thing,' I began. I don't know why when she'd been so awful to me.

But Mrs Fox's eyes didn't open and Payne didn't reply. It was as if I was no longer there. Payne was humming tunelessly, her lips almost touching the old lady's cheek.

My mother once said something similar to me in her bedroom. It came back to me then, with all the force of a physical blow. She turned to me from her dressing-table, where she was taking off her garnets, and looked me up and down as she might have an unsatisfactory servant. I remember it was pouring outside, the wind hurling the rain against the glass. 'You know, Diana, you bring it on yourself,' she said impassively. 'There's something in you that other girls don't have, something impure. That's what men sense.'

XVII

Eleanor is dreaming about Jane as a tiny child when the knock comes. Turning over, she tries to return to sleep: to the beetle shine of Jane's hair and her small hands, sticky with strawberry jam, reaching out to be picked up. But then there's another knock and this time she sits up, knowing the dream is lost.

'Who is it?' she calls, wondering if Gerald has come back earlier than expected, driving through the early hours to make good time. He'd telephoned last night to say he could be spared at the ministry for a day or two.

But it's Payne who comes in, her features severe even in the gloom cast by the blackout.

'Madam's woken and says she wants you,' she says. 'Straight away.'

Eleanor finds her mother sitting up in bed, an untouched breakfast tray by her side. Her hands, crammed with her ugly Victorian rings as always, are loosely clasped on the sheet. Her eyes are very blue in the clear morning light.

'Not yet dressed?' she says in greeting.

'Payne said I was to come straight away. I thought you must be ill.' *You're not dressed either*, she thinks, but doesn't say.

'That girl made me ill last night. I feel terribly weak this morning. Quite wrung out.'

'Girl? What girl?'

'The Devlin girl, of course.'

Eleanor feels her shoulders drop slightly. Not Jane, then. 'What has Diana done?'

'Ah, so she hasn't been to you yet. I expect she will. She's pushy enough to try it, having had no luck with me.'

'I don't understand –'

Her mother cuts her off. 'If you listen, I will tell you. She came to see me last night with some idea about resurrecting the Silver Moon Ball.'

Eleanor feels her skin prickle. To hear those words after all this time, from her mother's mouth, is shocking. They belong to another life.

'And so I asked myself,' her mother continues, 'how would this girl – this virtual stranger – know anything about those balls? At first, the answer seemed obvious. I thought it must be Jane.'

Eleanor thinks about the invitation she'd found at the top of the box in the boathouse. She pictures Diana rooting through her things with her elegant, tapering fingers. Could Jane have been with her? She does nothing but follow Diana about, these days. Eleanor has barely seen her. Anger swells inside her.

'I'm sure it wasn't Jane,' she manages to say.

Her mother gives her a withering look. 'I knew you'd

say that. You have always defended her, tried to protect her, as though that could make up for anything.'

The words are like a slap.

'It was a mistake to let her come back this summer,' she says relentlessly. 'I knew it would be and I've been vindicated. Well, it's a mistake I will rectify now.'

'What do you mean?' Her tone is uncharacteristically sharp and her mother shakes her head.

'Listen to yourself. You would never have spoken to me like that before *she* came back. You've lost your head, Eleanor – just as you did then. I knew it would be too much for you. Look at the way you're trembling now. I'll telephone Hugo and tell him she'll have to go back to London. He won't like it but she's not our responsibility and I won't have her digging things up with that Devlin girl, I simply won't.' Her voice rises and Payne comes rushing in.

'But Jane is our responsibility,' cries Eleanor, unable to keep the emotion out of her voice, not caring about Payne. 'She is mine, at least. If only you would let her be.' She stops and watches her mother's face turn to marble. She has always had the ability to retreat and shut out her daughter. It had made Eleanor feel desperate as a child, as though however carefully she cupped her hands, the water always leaked away. 'Please, Mother. Please let her stay. I've missed so much.'

A sly little smile plays on her mother's lips. 'You could always go back to London with her.'

Eleanor hangs her head, knitting her hands together to try to stop them shaking. 'You know I can't.'

'Well, it's your choice. As I view it, if she was that important to you, you'd find the strength to leave.'

'That's a cruel thing to say,' Eleanor murmurs.

'Someone must tell you the truth occasionally. I know Gerald doesn't. He's as indulgent of your frailties and fancies as your father was. There's something else,' she continues coldly. 'Something else that little troublemaker has found out. I wouldn't be surprised if she's working up to blackmailing me.' Her voice shakes with fresh outrage and Payne, at her shoulder, wrings her hands.

'What is it?' Eleanor says dully.

'It seems she's been talking to Dew Bolitho.'

Eleanor flinches. More words that are never uttered aloud. She plants her feet so she doesn't simply run out.

Her mother is also disturbed, her hands clutching at the sheet. 'It's all starting again. I can feel it. She and Jane are going to expose us. I won't have it. If they're gone, they won't be able to rake up the past.' Her head falls back against her pillow and Payne rushes forward to tend her.

Eleanor begins to run as soon as she is over the threshold of her mother's room. She avoids the creaking stairs just as she did in childhood, praying she won't meet anyone. She's halfway across the garden before she remembers that she's still wearing her dressing-gown and slippers. Her breathing has turned into great shuddering gasps, and she can't think how she manages it so effortlessly the rest of the time. Safe inside the boathouse, she bends over, her hands on her knees, and forces herself to breathe out slowly. Her chest is straining to do the opposite, to pull in air in quick, desperate sucks, but she keeps blowing out until her heart slows a little.

She's wanted to tell Jane the truth for so long, but now the thought of it all coming out is terrifying. Not because of the shame, which she doesn't much care about, but because Jane may not forgive her. She is still so young, with a young person's uncompromising sense of justice, everything either right or irretrievably wrong. She sees herself for a moment as Jane would if she knew: weak, selfish and horribly cowardly. No kind of mother at all.

It's Diana who has done this, Diana, forever bored and in need of stimulation, who has come here and gone through her things, who has been teasing the truth out of Dew, as if the events that have shaped Eleanor's entire life are just a game to while away the time. To think that she had ever felt sorry for the girl, sensing for a while now that all was not well behind her glossy exterior.

But her instinct in the boathouse, when she had found the fallen key, and then again by the gate, had been right. Perhaps it is even worse, and there is nothing inside Diana at all: a beautiful husk of a person who will keep on until those around her are as empty as she is. She thinks of Jane, miserable on the journey back to London, back to her uncle's cold, loveless house, where she's always been made to feel like the odd one out she really is, and her anger stirs again.

She goes over to the battered old armchair that Robin and Sébastien had dragged down from the house all those years ago, and picks up a cushion whose needlepoint cover she had made, a badly proportioned boat picked out in blue thread. The sharp end of a feather is poking through and she pulls it out, letting it drift to the floor. There's another on the other side and she pulls that out too, then another and another. When there are no more to pull, she wrenches the cushion apart at the seams, tearing at the old fabric until it bursts open, feathers flying out to swirl around the room, a silent explosion of her own frustration.

* * *

SIX DAYS LEFT

Sunday, 14th July

I don't mind admitting it was a shock, what that old bitch Fox said to me about being soiled goods. Afterwards I got into bed and simply shook, my hands and feet like ice, though the room was still sweltering from the day's heat. The memories of Mother and GUT and visits to Flete came thick and fast, like memories do when you open the door to one, the rest tumbling in behind, each clamouring for their turn. When Rose came in later and asked what was wrong I told her to get out.

But this morning, after the letter that came for me, I felt hardened again, like I'd grown a new hide overnight. I'd fool-ishly hoped for post from home, but instead got it from Flete. The daily woman, Mrs Potts, had written to tell me that the tenants have moved out, worried about the house's proximity to the south coast, and the Luftwaffe, which will soon be droning over their heads, en route to bomb London.

She's no fool, Mrs Potts, and a throwaway line, between a remark about a leaking drainpipe and news of a new mouser for the barns, got me thinking. 'There's nothing of him left,' she put in casually, and I imagined then what the place might be like if GUT really had left it without stain, if Flete had miraculously returned to the peaceful, gold-steeped dream I remember from the time before I drew his attentions. Perhaps I could be happy there, I thought. It would be mine alone. It would ask nothing of me, and that might be enough.

Eleanor's Gerald got back late this afternoon. We'd not long finished in the garden and were upstairs changing out of our uniforms when I heard voices on the lawn. He was there on a deckchair chatting to Cook, who had brought him what looked like a large gin and tonic.

By the time I got out there, having made myself presentable, the sun was still strong but the long shadow of the pine tree had reached the deckchair. He'd dozed off, his drink forgotten on the grass. I picked it up and took a fortifying swig. The sea was murmuring somewhere below us, and it sounded like encouragement.

I lit a cigarette and let the smoke drift in his direction until it woke him up.

'Oh, it's you,' he said. 'Diana, isn't it? I must have fallen asleep.'

'Hello again,' I said, offering him my packet. 'Have you just got here?'

He smoothed down his rather sparse hair and I knew he was embarrassed I'd caught him unawares.

'Well, about half an hour ago. I don't suppose you've seen my wife?'

I shook my head. 'Not since yesterday. She wasn't at breakfast again so perhaps she's not feeling well.'

Gerald frowned. 'Perhaps. She's not in her room.'

Kicking off my shoes, I sat down on the grass next to the deckchair and saw his eyes flick over my bare feet. 'I'm glad you're back,' I said, with one of my best smiles.

'Oh, yes?' he said. 'And why's that?'

'Well, I've had the most wonderful idea, you see. For a party. I just need you to give me the nod and I'll take care of the rest. Eleanor needn't do anything at all.'

I didn't really expect him to say yes. I think the whole plan had been little more than a silent dare to myself. But when he called my bluff out there on the lawn, the shadow-fingers of the pine reaching for my feet, I felt a bit of courage was called for. For a shining minute, it felt like one magical night might just be the cure for everything that's gone wrong here since the last one. Of course, there was also the thought of Mrs Fox's face when she found out I'd got my way, after all.

So it might have been a rather good day, all in all, but then I went inside and told Cook about my triumph and her silly yokel's face turned all pinched and doomy. 'I know your sort, Miss Devlin,' she said, her fingernail sharp as she poked me in the chest. 'You get a taste for trouble and then you can't stop until you've drawn blood. Well, I just wonder whose it'll be.'

XVIII

Every time Sam sidles up in her mind, Rose makes herself think about something safe and ordinary. How she ought to file her nails or darn those stockings, or write a letter to the WLA to say that her six-month service armband has still not arrived in the post. These mundane tasks seem to shore up the numbness she's felt since Diana came back from the village and told her what she'd heard.

She has also been dimly grateful for her work outside, which is sufficiently physical to send her straight to sleep most nights, her sore muscles generally overruling her thoughts. Sleep and routine aren't making her feel better, but they are making time pass, and she hopes this will eventually heal her. It is a sort of grief, after all. She's in mourning for Sam and herself, and all she thought they had; the shameful irony that she's done no such thing for Frank, who might really be dead, doesn't escape her. There's been no further news of him.

Diana, in contrast, has barely left her alone. While Rose is grateful, she also finds her exhausting. The Diana who reminded her of an arch and languid cat seems to have disappeared entirely, replaced by someone almost frenzied. It's been worse since Gerald Grenville gave her permission to throw a welcome dance for the Canadian airmen. She talks of little else in the garden, and doesn't seem to have noticed how pale Eleanor is at breakfast when she turns up, how her hands tremble when she lifts her teacup to her lips.

'Are you all right?' Rose says to her this morning, after the others have left the table. 'Are you worried about Mr Grenville?' He'd had to go back to London after only twenty-four hours.

Eleanor shakes her head. 'Not really. There still hasn't been a single bomb dropped in London, thank goodness. And there's a shelter in the basement of the ministry. He's promised me he'll go down as soon as the siren sounds when there's a raid.' She attempts a smile but it only makes her look more overwrought.

Rose hesitates before covering Eleanor's hand with her own. It's ice cold. 'It's this dance of Diana's, isn't it?'

Eleanor flinches and tries to cover it by pulling her hand away and brushing some crumbs off the tablecloth. 'It's a lovely idea. I'm being quite ridiculous.'

'But this is your home. I can understand why you wouldn't want it to be invaded by a lot of strangers.'

'You're kind to say so but it's a large house that usually stands half empty. Really, letting Diana welcome the airmen here for a single night is the least I can do. Other people have had their houses requisitioned. All I've had to do is give you girls your bed and board.' She turns to the garden. When she looks back at Rose, her eyes are unfocused and feverish. 'Penhallow once made the most wonderful place for a party.'

'I can imagine,' says Rose. 'Diana said that your mother told her all about the balls that were held here.'

Eleanor blinks. 'I doubt that.'

That evening, as they go upstairs after dinner, Diana catches hold of Rose's arm and pulls her into the dormitory.

'In here,' she says, 'so Jane doesn't hear.'

'What is it?'

Diana's eyes blaze in the half-light. 'I found something out. I wanted to tell you but you've been so miserable about you-know-who that I didn't want to bother you with it.'

'Is it to do with the dance?' says Rose. 'Because you know Eleanor is very anxious about it. I talked to her this morning. She was trying to put a brave face on it, because it's for the airmen and she wants to do her bit, but it's an awful strain on her. No one ever comes here, unless it's a delivery van. Haven't you noticed? I expect it was difficult enough when we arrived. And she didn't seem right today, when we talked. I came away feeling even more worried about her.'

Diana rolls her eyes. 'Of course I've noticed how she is. Gerald was worried too, when I suggested it. But I'm going to do everything, with help from you and Jane, of course.' She winks. 'Eleanor needn't lift a finger.'

'I don't think that's what worries her.'

'It will do her good, I know it will. I have an idea to make everything all right here. That's what I was going to tell you about but I don't think I will now. You'll only disapprove. Everyone is so frightened of telling the truth, as though keeping secrets is a good idea.'

Rose feels herself flush.

'Oh, I don't mean you, darling, not at all. Listen, how are you feeling about all that? Still rotten?' She reaches out to stroke Rose's hair, winding a curl round one long finger.

Rose looks down so Diana can't see the tears that well up so easily these days.

'Do you know what would make you feel better?' Diana says gently.

'I don't want a drink.'

'No, not that. I was thinking you should write him a letter. Sam.'

Rose's stomach lurches at his name. 'Write to him?'

'It might draw the matter to a close for you. I think you might feel better if you wrote it all down. You don't even have to send it. I used to write pages and pages to Mother when I was at school, then burn them in the incinerator behind the kitchens. It was wonderfully cathartic.'

She agrees to please Diana and, if she's honest, to be left alone for half an hour. But once she begins, she can't stop. The tears fall as she writes, sometimes on the paper, but it doesn't matter because she's never going to post it. She writes about how she'd felt about him – how she still feels about him – then rips it up and starts again. The next version is more measured, the words chilly with pride. She's stopped crying now. She tells him how disappointed she is in him, how she wants never to see him again.

'How are you getting on?' Diana has appeared in the doorway.

Rose smiles for the first time in what feels like years. 'Yes, it was a good idea. I think it has helped, a bit.'

Diana claps her hands. 'Shall I put it out for the post?' She raises her eyebrows dramatically.

Rose shakes her head. 'No fear. This was for my benefit only.' She tucks the letter into a book and puts it away in her bedside table.

'Let's go next door then,' says Diana. 'I said I'd teach Jane to dance and I'm in desperate need of reinforcements.'

Rose stands. She knows that if she was to go over to the blackout and peel a corner back, there's a chance she'll be able to see the beam of the lighthouse. She knows it will feel like a summons, like a sign she should forget the cold, dismissive words she's set down, and just go to him. Instead she crosses to the door, where Diana is waiting for her.

* * *

TWO DAYS LEFT

Thursday, 18th July

I've been liaising with the WVS ladies today about the last details for the party on Saturday. Those old girls are so efficient they ought to be running the whole war. Everyone seems awfully keen on the idea, including the dashing Canadians; a hand-picked band of twenty officers are due to attend. If they don't bring cigarettes and gum, I'll personally turn them away. I must say, the thought of everyone coming here is a like a blast of fresh air whistling through my mind.

Rose is worried about Eleanor's nerves but I think it's just what she needs: to be taken outside her own head for once. And I should know about that. It will also do her good to see that Penhallow does not have to run according to Mrs Fox's iron rule. As for her, she's apparently incandescent, the idea of which fills me with a jittery glee. It didn't occur to her that I might ask Gerald for permission and, of course, once I'd mooted the idea to the WVS and the rest (which I did almost immediately), there was nothing she could do for fear of looking horribly unpatriotic.

I've done the right thing for Rose, too, by posting that letter of hers to Sam Lighthouse. There comes a point when decisiveness is called for. I didn't tell her this, but there was one letter I did keep for Mother to read. It wasn't long before I came here. Jack Beresford wasn't the only reason she wanted rid of me. It was a good letter, and it comes back to me verbatim. I have been reciting it to myself all day, when the doubts look like raising their ugly heads, along with the Sickly Creepers, who continue to lurk, waiting for me to stop for a single moment. Which is why I've been keeping myself busy, busy, busy, without letting up for a second.

I have thought a great deal about what you did, or rather didn't do, and I cannot find a way to forgive you for it. No doubt you had your reasons, and you will reiterate them to yourself as you read this letter, so that you might dismiss it and me. Still, I think you know the truth: that you have committed the greatest of betrayals.

A little dramatic, perhaps, but no less accurate for it. Things between us were different afterwards; she'd long viewed me as a foe but suddenly I was an equal one. The scales were finally balanced. We both know that her banishing me to Cornwall is the last gasp of her reign. As soon as I turn twenty-one, I'll be able to shake her off. And shake her off I will, without qualm.

Another confession, now, which I'll keep brief. I've done a foolish thing, even for me. I went to see Dew at the net loft last night because I found I couldn't sit still or stay inside. When I feel like this at home, I go up on the roof. It's a secret hideaway of mine, got to by clambering out of a skylight in the attics. There's a parapet up there, among the chimneys, and if I stand on tiptoe I can just spot the Serpentine on a clear day. It's horribly dangerous and Daddy would have a coronary if he knew, but it's soothing up there, with no one to bother me except the odd pigeon. I've done it since childhood and, let me tell you, it was quite an undertaking when I was eight years old and only four feet tall.

Dew was frosty at first, his ego still smarting from our last encounter, but he couldn't keep it up for long. I was too persuasive, even letting him have a kiss. In the heat of the moment, a new bottle of gin already tucked into my largest handbag, I said he should come on Saturday. I thought he'd refuse with derision but I caught a flicker of genuine pride in his eyes before he managed to stifle it.

'You want me to come up to the Hall?' he said slowly, his dark eyes unreadable again.

'Well, only if you want to. Half of Vennor are coming. Well, the nicer half, at least. And the Canadian chaps, of course. It'll be enormous fun.'

'I might,' he said, with a too-careless shrug. 'She know, does she? That you've invited me.'

'Who, Mrs Fox? Not likely. She'd have a fit. She's already livid that it's being held at all, quite honestly.'

A strange look came upon his face. 'I wasn't talking about her.'

'Oh, Eleanor, then? Well, no, she doesn't know either. She's to be disturbed as little as possible by the arrangements. I agreed that with Mr Grenville. She's very fragile, you see.'

He scowled and I saw that his hands had curled into fists. I leant in to kiss him again but he turned his face away, which made me feel like a fool.

'You can buy something decent to wear with the money you get from that old harridan,' I threw out, for pride's sake. 'I don't suppose you're often called upon to wear a suit.'

He grabbed my wrist and shoved me up against the wall, hard enough that my head banged against the bare brick. 'What did you say?'

'Nothing,' I stammered. 'Really, it's none of my business.'

'That's right, it's not.' His face was so close to mine that I could see his pupils dilate. 'You think you can play games with me, don't you? I'm not like other men.'

Then he began to kiss me hard and it hurt, his stubble rubbing my lips raw. The horror was rising coldly in me when he pulled back.

'Go, now. Back you go to the Hall. And keep that pretty mouth of yours shut or I'll shut it for you.'

So I went and, as if I wasn't shaken up enough, I definitely heard footsteps behind me as I left the village. I kept glancing back but, of course, there was nobody. I wonder now if it was one of Dew's cronies, sent to follow me. Anyway, by the time I got as far as the cove, I'd taken my shoes off so I could run.

I have no idea if Dew will come or not. At the very least, it'll be horribly awkward if he does. Mrs Fox will sniff out his bad Bolitho blood from fifty feet. The WVS ladies, too. And what will Jane make of my village friend? Every time I think about Saturday night, my heart trips over itself. I don't know if it's nerves, excitement or a flash of intuition. Whichever it is, it's too late to stop it now.

XIX

There are just two days to go before the dance, and Eleanor wants nothing more than to peel off her skin and step out of it. She's come to the boathouse in the hope that it will transport her from the present, but even here there's no comfort to be had. The little room is still strewn with feathers after her last visit and she picks them up methodically one by one, hoping the mundanity of the task will halt the mounting agitation she feels here today. Back outside when she's finished, she's certain she can smell rotting fish on the air.

Disgusted by her own weakness, she goes to Robin's boat and looks inside. Still nothing there. She hadn't imagined that, at least. She pictures herself getting in and pushing off with one of the oars. It would take only ten minutes to follow the looping curves of the creek out into the open sea, where the breeze would lift her hair and whip colour into her cheeks. She could be gone – her mother, the dance, all of it left behind – before the clocks at the Hall strike eleven.

Of course it's impossible. So she returns to the house, and picks up the telephone. After she's put through, and tells Gerald how agitated she's feeling, he doesn't immediately reply and she wonders, as she has so many times, if he's finally growing impatient of her cowardice.

'I know I'm being silly,' she hurries on. 'You did absolutely the right thing in saying yes to Diana. You're not cross that I was upset when you told me, are you?'

'No, darling,' he says quietly, then lapses into silence again.

She scrapes at the Bakelite with her nail, worried the allotted three minutes will run out before he's made her feel calmer. In the quiet between them, she hears the fizz and burble of other people's conversations. She would have dismissed them as crossed wires at the exchange a few weeks ago; now she knows better. Though she can't quite catch the words, she's certain she's listening to voices from the past. The ivy has crept up the cinder path to reach the house, she thinks. Persistent green tendrils will soon be pushing across the polished tiles to curl around her ankles. Just in time for Saturday night.

'What was that?' she says, aware that Gerald has spoken again.

'It's just that I can't help thinking I should have refused her,' he says, with a sigh. 'Persuasive or not. But, darling, look, she promised faithfully that she would arrange everything herself, without bothering you. And at least this way you don't have to worry about leaving the house. I thought that would make all the difference.'

She hesitates. They will be cut off at any second. And, truly, she knows she's on her own now. 'You're right, it has,' she says, with tinny brightness. 'I feel right as rain now I've talked to you. How silly of me to have worked myself up.'

'Well, if you're sure, then I am. And if that Devlin girl has anything to do with it, I'm sure it'll be a tremendous success. I'm looking forward to it, my love.' Relief floods his voice.

As the pips sound, they say their goodbyes and Eleanor replaces the receiver. She glances across the hall, to the door that leads to the garden, and is surprised to see that the ivy hasn't crossed the threshold, not yet. It's coming for her, though: the past. She can feel it gathering strength, a noiseless hum in her chest.

That night, she lies sleepless, despite taking two of her pills. Some time after three, she gives in and fetches Brick from the kitchen, allowing him up on to the bed with her. He falls back to sleep immediately and the warm, deep-breathing bulk of him, even his snoring once it starts, offers some comfort.

She wakes late the next morning from a dream about Sébastien. In it, a muddled version of the final Silver Moon Ball, she was both inside herself and watching proceedings from afar. As she opens her eyes and feels the ache of its loss, she also wishes she had known how lovely she was at the real ball, with her bare, gleaming shoulders and her first grown-up hairstyle. Eighteen years old and teetering on the cusp of womanhood.

Unwilling to start the day yet, Brick still fast asleep beside her, she pulls the sheet up under her chin and remembers how, on that night, Sébastien had appeared at her side, bending down to whisper in her ear, his long fringe of black hair tickling her cheek.

'Is that you, Ellie?' he'd said, teasing but only gently. 'I hardly recognized you.'

Ellie. That was new.

He'd danced the first three with her, their bodies pushed closer together than they had ever been before. At the end of the third dance, her mother had cut in, murmuring that Eleanor really ought to pay some attention to their other guests, but whenever she had looked for Sébastien after that, he seemed to be waiting to catch her eye, even as he led some other girl around the dance floor.

Soon, she'd thought. Soon we'll be able to slip away into the garden. And then he'll kiss me. She wasn't even surprised when, just after eleven, she saw him step outside with a drink in his hand. Checking her mother wasn't watching her, she straightened the hem of her dress and followed.

After the stuffiness of the orangery, the windows misted with condensation, the garden felt like stepping into cool, clear water. As the strains of the music receded, the hushing of the sea grew louder. Every so often, a particularly powerful wave hitting the rocks below sounded like a small clap of thunder. It wasn't cold but she shivered in her sheath of slippery white silk, glad of the gloves – bold black, to her mother's disapproval – which came up above her elbows.

As she wound her way between the roses, their perfume seemed to ebb and flow in strength, like pockets of warm water in a cold sea. The foliage around her was dark but the pale gravel that crunched pleasantly under her new

T-strap shoes was picked out by the lights from the house. She looked up to see the moon and watched a thick blanket of cloud begin to encircle it.

She saw his shirt first, the sharp lines of his collar luminous against his olive skin. He was sitting on the edge of the fountain, staring at the sea through a sightline cut into the bushes. When he looked round at her approach, she saw his surprise and stopped, confused. She'd been so sure she was supposed to follow, that he'd intended the night to unfold in this way, just as she had.

'I'm sorry, did you want to be alone?' she said. 'I thought . . .'

After a beat, he smiled. 'No, no. Come and sit with me. I was just thinking about Robin.'

'I thought of him earlier. You wear the same cologne as he did.'

'Yes.'

'Is that why you wear it?'

He nodded. 'Unfortunately it reminds me of myself now. I should have been more sparing with it.'

'Perhaps, if you only use it occasionally, it will become him again.'

He smiled again, sincerely this time. 'Perhaps.'

She sat down next to him and the stone through her dress was surprisingly warm. The sun had dropped into the sea a few hours ago, but the ghost of its heat was still there, lingering in the wide brim of the fountain.

'I pretend he's still here sometimes,' she said. 'By the boathouse especially.' She peeled off her gloves and gripped the stone on either side of her, to feel the warmth with her bare hands. 'I try to tell myself that I don't need to see him to know he's in some way still here.'

Sébastien didn't reply, his gaze fixed somewhere on the point where the horizon must be, though the muffled sky had merged with the dark water to obscure it. She let her head fall against his shoulder and realized that her usual nerves around him had receded. It was happening just as she had dreamt it would. Far in the distance, she thought she heard a low growl of thunder.

She turned her head to look up at him. 'I think Robin would be glad that it's you.'

He seemed baffled. 'What's me?'

'The first person I've fallen in love with.'

Eleanor forces herself out of the memory and pushes the covers back determinedly. Thinking of him still makes her ache. But picturing her younger self, so unaware of the consequences that would ripple out from that night, hurts more. She could weep for that girl-woman who had no idea how profoundly her life was about to change. It wasn't until she'd torn apart the cushion that she'd understood how much anger there was inside her. She had believed herself so full of fear that there wasn't room for anything else.

The girls will have been up for hours by now. All three – Jane rather reluctantly – have been given the day off from their duties to help decorate the orangery and the rose garden just outside it. She had hoped she'd be able to help them rip up the lino and dust the old Boston ferns that have somehow thrived, despite their neglect.

But now she feels the familiar panic move up inside her, like a fast-rising tide. She'll have to make an excuse, say she's got a splitting headache. There's something much more important she needs to do. The dream has given her

her instructions; they're her last chance to rescue tomorrow night.

She pushes back the covers and lets Brick out to patter downstairs and beg his breakfast from Cook. She hasn't time to see to him herself. She needs to get down to the boathouse and find the dress. And not just the dress but the rest of it too – even the headband she'd cleaned so carefully.

Blewett will be doing the heavy lifting in the orangery all day, where the girls must also be by now. He won't even realize she's set a new bonfire in the scrubby, forgotten corner of the garden he always uses, where the earth won't look any more scorched and bare for her destroying everything from that night, as she should have done so long ago.

But when she gets to the boathouse, the place is quiet and not in the right way – the expectant way that signals to her that Robin is close, that he is looking after her. Until the last couple of days, the silence here has been shimmering with the almost-sounds of her brother's presence. Now the place feels emptied.

She rushes up the steps and begins tearing clothes out of the suitcases, first the one she thought the things were in – and then another, growing more frantic as these and then the tea chests yield none of the items she needs. Eventually she sits, spent and desolate, surrounded by the wreckage of her girlhood. What she needs to make things safe has gone, and she knows for certain now that something terrible will happen tomorrow tonight.

* * *

Friday, 19th July

I've grown quite fond of the boathouse, and almost accustomed to its peculiar noises and atmospheres. At least no one can get at me here. It's also the only place I can hide my diary properly. I've been on my guard since Jane took the bracelet. And there's no privacy in the dorm whatsoever.

This is actually my second visit of the day; I came down with Jane straight after breakfast to have another look at the photographs of the Silver Moon Balls. Admittedly it was also to delay work on the orangery floor, but it turned out to be genuinely inspiring too. I also thought it might take Jane's mind off worrying about Eleanor. She didn't come down to breakfast again today.

'This will all end badly,' said Payne, on her way upstairs with Mrs F's tray. 'You'll wish you'd heeded Madam and me then, Miss Devlin.' She gave me a death's head smile that made my skin crawl.

Jane and I had to hunt for the key to the box, which took ages but was worth it because I discovered a lovely portrait photograph of Eleanor I hadn't seen before. She looked as fresh as a new tulip in a pale sheath dress. I turned it over and wasn't surprised to see that someone had written 1924 on the back. That year will keep popping up.

I turned to Jane. 'I've just had an idea.'

'Another one?'

'Ha-ha. This one's to do with you.'

She immediately looked wary. 'Me?'

'You've got years to fill out, darling, so please don't take this as criticism, but your boyish figure is much more suited to the fashions of the twenties. You would have made a wonderful flapper. Such a shame you were born too late to enjoy it. The good news is that, for one night, you can.'

I hadn't taken much notice of the suitcases propped up against the wall, noting only that they were full of damp old clothes. Going through them, I saw that many would have been very lovely once, though most are hopelessly out of date now. I found what I was looking for in the second case, pulling it out with a cry of triumph. It was so cool and slippery that it made me shiver. It was as though a ghost had slithered out instead of an old dress.

Obviously it's yellowed with the years but Jane's dark colouring suits it marvellously. When I held it up next to her face, it turned from dingy white into a lovely rich cream.

'I don't know,' said Jane, doubtfully, when in triumph I found the long black gloves Eleanor was also wearing in the photograph. 'Won't it be somehow in poor taste?'

'Why?' I said. 'I think Eleanor will be thrilled to see you dressed up in all her old finery. It'll be a wonderful surprise.'

Once we found the silver and diamanté headband right under our noses in a tea chest, nestled in tissue paper and looking as though it had just been cleaned for the job, Jane grudgingly admitted it might be fun. Later, back in the dorm, I finally convinced her by getting her to try the dress on. Even as crumpled as it was, and without the right shoes, she was a revelation in the glass. I really do have an eye.

'I look . . . I look . . .' She blinked dumbly at her own reflection.

'You look, as the Yanks say, like the cat's pyjamas. Like a different person altogether and at least two years older.'

'Do you really think so?'

'Yes, sweet Jane, I do.'

Notwithstanding the bracelet incident, I've grown really quite fond of her. I want her to know the truth. I feel she deserves it. And if that dress doesn't give Eleanor the excuse she's so clearly been looking for, I don't know what will. That the odious Mrs F might also get her comeuppance is only a small part of it, though I admit it's a part that gives me some pleasure in the anticipation. Mrs Fox and my mother are truly one of a kind. They both chose their reputations over their daughters, which seems like the worst kind of cowardice to me.

Or almost the worst. My mother had another surprise lying in wait for me. I discovered it quite by accident one heavy-skied day in April, not long before I left London to come here. It was this revelation that galvanized me into writing my bridge-burning letter. I'd drafted so many versions of it in my head over the years that it had almost become a hobby, but what I found out killed off the last of my restraint. I suppose I had always hoped she would prove me wrong, that she would say one day, 'I've been a pretty poor show as a mother, haven't I?' Once upon a time, I'd have tripped over myself to forgive her. For who in the world wants to admit that their mother simply despises them?

It came out over a game of gin rummy, of all things.

Mother had woken with one of her heads and cancelled her usual bridge four but was feeling better by the afternoon. She never much liked her own company, understandably, so had persuaded me to perch on the end of her bed and play a couple of hands. The conversation started almost congenially.

'Have you thought any more about the Innes-Cooper boy?' she said, as she picked up a club.

'I haven't thought about him at all,' I replied. 'He's unforgivably wet.'

'He'll inherit half of Aberdeenshire one day.'

'You say that as though it's a good thing. You know I can't stand all that tartan and shooting-party nonsense. Damp castles and picnics in the driving rain.'

'You'd be lucky to catch someone like him. You shouldn't turn your nose up.'

I threw one of my hearts down on the eiderdown. 'Don't you want me to be happy and in love when I marry, Mother?'

She knew I was being sarcastic, of course, but chose to ignore it. 'If you don't want him, then you shouldn't give him hope.'

'I haven't.'

'You don't even know you're doing it, do you?' She pursed her lips into a pious little smile. 'You've never really understood men, have you, Diana?'

'Oh, I don't know. I think I have a fair idea about them.'

Perhaps she was right about that part, though. Little does anyone know that, apart from a couple of inebriated kisses, I am as innocent in the ways of men as Jane.

Part of me quite appreciates the gargantuan irony of my mother banishing me here, to another houseful of women, despite what happened at school. I don't know if it was all GUT's fault. Sometimes I think it must have been – the dried spittle at the corners of his mouth, the false teeth that shifted about because he was too mean to buy a set that fitted, the damp palms and bony, searching fingers, the yellow, sulphurous breath, all of it combining to put me off the opposite sex pretty thoroughly.

It was strange when school changed from being the most awful bore to a place of refuge and affection. It's a shame, because what happened in the fifth might have gone differently at another school. Some boy cousins of mine experimented very happily at Charterhouse, quite certain it meant little and that they would grow up perfectly normal. At Hambles, though, it was not done. There was an almost palpable horror of it among the mistresses, led by the odious Awfully Fat, who was, I imagine, disgusted by the idea of any kind of intimacy at all. I think that was why she ate so excessively, her extra flesh a barrier between her and anyone who might try to touch her.

When she expelled me, and Mother and Daddy were summoned to take me away, she said nothing to them about what she had earlier termed my 'abhorrent Sapphic tendencies'. Perhaps she thought she was being merciful, not telling them the real reason I was finally being sent away. 'A wild nature that exerts a bad influence' was what she came up with, and I suppose it's possible to read between the lines of that, should you wish to. The other girl involved was in the sixth and, despite me being in a lower form, it was she who was allowed to stay. I was the pernicious one, apparently.

She looked a little like Rose. I see that now, though it's

taken me an age to admit it. She had the same artistic pre-
tensions and soulful eyes, and not dissimilarly unruly hair.
Her name was Belinda, which didn't suit her. I called her
Bee. She smelt of lavender water and pencil shavings. She's
dead now, of tuberculosis. She didn't go to the sort of Swiss
sanatorium I would have been bundled off to because her
people in Woking had no money. She was a scholarship
girl, which is why I was glad, really, that she stayed on and
finished. Anyway, perhaps Bee established a pattern in
me: a weakness for dreamy, bourgeois girls from boring
little towns, who could see the small amount of good in me.

But I digress. Back to the game of gin rummy in
Mother's bedroom, and me claiming to know something
of the ways of men, when all I really knew was GUT.

'What you've never grasped,' said Mother, with great
condescension, 'is that men are helpless when it comes to
their urges. They are animals in a way that we women are
not. The responsibility lies with us. And that's why you must
take care never to encourage them, Diana. It's a subtle skill
and one, I must point out, that you have never learnt.'

I should have stalked out then – gone on the roof and
had a cigarette – but my ire was up. 'And I suppose it was
my responsibility to fend off an old man when I was still
virtually in the nursery?' I said.

Her face darkened. She never could stand to talk about
him. 'I don't know why you had to make such a terrific
fuss about it,' she said eventually.

'A fuss? I was only a child.' To my shame, my voice
broke on the last word and her head snapped up.

'For God's sake, Diana,' she said, throwing down her
cards. And then she said it. 'Sometimes one has to put up

233

and shut up. I always understood that without being told. Why couldn't you?'

The wall behind her head seemed to rush towards me. 'He did it to you first?'

The muscles in her jaw were working, and it struck me that she wasn't distressed, only furious. There was no remorse in her eyes, just long-suppressed rage. 'Oh, don't fear,' she spat. 'He never liked me as much as he liked you. His will was ample proof of that.'

I let out a strangled noise that was half-laugh, half-sob. 'So, wait a minute, Mother. Let's see if I've got this right. Not only did you not stop him doing to me what he had done to you, but you were jealous that he liked me better?'

'I always loved that house,' she cried. 'Even with him in it. It should have been mine.'

I ran out then and was sick in the lavatory, the porcelain cold against my cheek once I was empty.

We didn't speak of it again, but I wrote my letter to her the following week, to which she responded by signing me up to the WLA. I don't know if I can ever go back there, whatever Mrs Potts assures me. I know Daddy wouldn't go against Mother if he had to choose; anything for a quiet life. Whenever we fought when I was growing up, he would go into hiding at his club. Women, to him, are like exotic pets: valuable but skittish, to be approached with great caution.

I suppose Penhallow is the closest thing I've got to a home now. On the walk down here tonight I thought I could smell smoke on the air, and I don't think it was one of Blewett's bonfires. I think it might have been my last bridge beginning to smoulder.

PART TWO

It's early evening when the steel cable anchoring the barrage balloon to the ground snaps. Like a whale piloting the deep, it makes almost no sound as it moves slowly but purposefully away. A southerly wind takes it out over the sea, beyond anyone's grasp, and here the east wind catches it, chivvying it along the coast towards Vennor.

There it drifts inland, the long tail of its cable scoring a line in the sand at Breakheart Cove before it reaches Penhallow, the first uninvited guest to arrive for the evening's festivities. But the garden is deserted, the preparations that have been going on all day abandoned for time being, as the people inside wash and brush and meet their reflections in the glass. Only one person notices the airborne leviathan, drawn to the window as its huge, bulbous shadow darkens the lawn.

She doesn't usually give credence to anything as silly as signs and portents but the balloon is such an arresting sight that her chest tightens with misgiving. She watches until it is out of sight, strangely reluctant to let anyone else know it's there. 'I don't like that sea,' Blewett had said earlier, and she'd dismissed it with a tut and a roll of the eyes, used to his bleak pronouncements about the weather that never come to anything, every day as blandly sunny as the last.

But now she sees that the sea has changed. It has begun to shift and churn in all directions, the blue crested with dirty white. From the rocks below she can hear its rhythmic boom, and it makes her think of a battering ram being heaved against a barred door. She glances up. Though the sky is still a clear quartz pink above the house, a mountain of cloud has appeared at the horizon. She goes to look again after she's finished dressing and, though the dark mass hasn't moved any closer, she's certain it's grown larger.

She considers what she has put in motion tonight. Mrs Fox, seething in her room while Payne stands sentry at the window. Jane, luminous in an old dress that once belonged to her mother. The guests who may already be on the coast-path, fingers of wind pulling at their hair and curiosity sharpening their laughter.

There's no stopping it now, whatever it is. For a brief moment, before she lights a reviving cigarette and turns her mind to the matter of which shoes to wear, she wishes she was the loosed barrage balloon, leaving herself behind.

XX

Diana stands back, her head to one side, and assesses Rose critically. Then she picks up the vivid crimson lipstick she always wears, the bullet short and stubby now that supplies are drying up. Rose shakes her head. 'I draw the line at red,' she says. 'I can't carry it off like you.'

Diana relents and hands her a soft shade of pink just as the door opens.

'Here she is!' Diana exclaims, slightly too loudly. 'Come in, Jane, so we can have a proper look at you.'

Jane had gone to change in the bathroom, too self-conscious to do so in front of them. Now she shivers, though her cheeks are flushed, and crosses her arms over herself. 'It feels like cold water on my skin,' she says.

Diana deftly fastens the last few buttons that Jane hasn't been able to reach, then angles the wardrobe door so she can see herself in the full-length glass. Rose takes the photograph Diana triumphantly holds out to her. It's Eleanor in what looks like the same dress.

She's never noticed it before but there is a likeness in

their features. It's only the difference in colouring that obscures the resemblance. Jane had once pointed out the photograph of her blonde sisters downstairs. 'You see, I really am the black sheep of the family,' she'd said, with a smile that hadn't quite come off.

Rose tries to catch Diana's eye but she's busy helping Jane put on a pair of long gloves. Her eye falls on the photograph again. 'Was this Eleanor's idea?'

Diana pauses. 'No, it was mine. And don't say anything because she doesn't know. It's to be a surprise.'

Rose opens her mouth, then shuts it again. Diana has been sharp-tongued and frantic all day, and she doesn't feel equal to a confrontation with her. Tonight she's as beautiful as Rose has ever seen her, despite the hectic look in her eyes. Her dress is made of midnight blue silk with a swirling skirt that draws the eye to her long legs. She's loosely waved her hair, which shines paler than ever against her dark dress. She's parted it low on the left, a pearl slide holding the other side back – all except a single lock, which falls coquettishly over her right eye.

Rose studies herself in the mirror. She's grown brown from being outside all the time but her eyes are shadowed from lack of sleep. If she could get out of this evening, she would. It's not just the letter she hasn't opened yet. The thought of the party fills her with inexplicable dread. She's had that song stuck in her head all day, as though she's going into battle: 'Wish Me Luck As You Wave Me Goodbye'. The sense persists that something is coming for her, that in just a few hours everything will have altered out of recognition.

She opens her evening bag and looks at the envelope she's pushed to the bottom without saying a word to anyone about it. It's stamped 'Maritime Mail' in red as usual, but the handwriting isn't Frank's. She has a good idea of what it will say, but she doesn't want to know for certain, not yet. She's not ready for it.

In the last few days, the old orangery has been transformed. It's now dressed for the occasion, just as they are. Though Diana never works hard in the garden if she can help it, she has thrown herself into preparations for this evening, and Rose can see that she's clever at things like that. The lino has gone, the floor beneath polished to a soft sheen the colour of new conkers. A wonderful old chandelier has been cleaned and rehung by Blewett who, grumbling, lost a whole day in the gardens to do it.

Though the sunset is hours off, the chandelier has already been lit, Rose sneaking a look at it before going upstairs to change. Its blaze of pale gold light had crowned the newly revived room.

'Ready to go down?' Diana says now. Rose nods reluctantly. Jane, she notices, has gone pale.

At the top of the stairs, Diana turns, her eyes glittering. 'Jane, you wait here. Rose and I will go first and find Eleanor. Don't move!' She rushes downstairs.

'It'll be all right, won't it?' Jane says quietly.

Rose squeezes her hand. 'Of course it will. You look lovely.'

When she gets to the bottom of the stairs, instinct tempts her to keep going, perhaps to find herself a drink. But she waits as Diana instructed, for the same reason she said nothing upstairs.

Eventually she hears Diana and Eleanor's mingled voices. Gerald, in black tie, is just behind them – he'd got back that afternoon.

'Right then, Jane,' calls Diana. 'We're here, so down you come.'

Rose looks up. As Jane takes the first step, carefully so she doesn't lose her footing, the light catches in the folds of the pale fabric, making it shimmer like crushed pearls. Rose glances at Eleanor and knows that her unease was justified. Eleanor's face has turned chalky and her hand is fumbling for Gerald's. He whispers something in her ear, his expression as baffled as it is concerned.

'Oh!' she cries. 'Oh!'

Rose glances at Diana and sees that, whatever this is, it isn't simple trouble-making. The expression on her face as she takes in Eleanor's is much more complicated than that.

Jane is hurrying down the stairs now, ungainly in the heels she's never worn before.

'Eleanor, what is it? Is it the dress? I said we shouldn't. I told her.' She gestures at Diana, who takes a step backwards.

'No one forced you,' she begins to say, but Eleanor is speaking too.

'Why have you done this?' she says to Diana, her voice ragged. Her chest is heaving. 'Is it a joke to you?'

'Eleanor,' says Gerald in a warning tone. 'Not now.'

Jane looks from one face to another in miserable confusion.

'It's one of her attacks,' says Gerald, his arm going round Eleanor to support her. 'She needs some peace and quiet. I did wonder whether this evening would be too much for her.' He looks pointedly at Diana, then leads Eleanor away.

Diana's face darkens. 'I don't know why everyone wants to blame her nerves on me.' She sounds petulant but her hand, which flutters at the loose lock of her hair, trembles.

'I don't understand,' says Jane, her voice high and panicky. 'Why is she so upset? Diana, what have you done?'

'Oh, for God's sake, haven't you worked it out yet?' Diana snaps.

'Diana,' says Rose, stepping towards her. She reaches out to lay a steadying hand on the girl's arm but is shaken off.

'Family secrets never did anyone any good, and I should know,' she half shouts, but she's not angry, Rose suddenly understands. She's frightened. She's on the defensive.

The three of them stand there in silence. Rose can almost feel the waves of emotion coming off the other two. Both are close to tears.

Then Diana pulls herself up to her full height. 'This is absurd. I'm going to find a drink. Why don't you join me, Jane? It'll make you feel better.'

The other girl shakes her head. 'No, I need to change.'

Rose knows she will go upstairs and cry. 'Do you want me to come with you?' she says, after Diana has stalked away without another word.

Jane sighs. 'No, but thank you. Do you know what they meant?'

Rose hesitates. She has an idea, the truth creeping in like the tide, but it's not her place to say anything about it to Jane, just as it wasn't Diana's. 'I don't know, but I do think your uncle was right. This is all too much for Eleanor.'

Jane nods gratefully. Rose can understand that the girl doesn't want it to be about her; it's much easier to think it's to do with whatever happened at some long-ago ball.

After that, Rose feels even more afraid of the evening ahead. The house around her is too quiet, too expectant, especially now that Jane, Eleanor and Gerald have retreated behind closed doors. She knows Mrs Fox and Payne will be upstairs too, listening for the first guests, Mrs Fox's patrician face sour with disapproval.

Wishing to shake off the oppressiveness of the house, and the letter rustling in her bag, Rose goes outside. It's not just what happened with Jane; she's harbouring an irrational fear that Morwenna will turn up tonight. It's ridiculous; someone like Morwenna would never have been invited. She and Sam belong to an entirely different set from the people who will be gathering in the old orangery and spilling out into the fragrant garden. The war might be throwing all sorts of people together but there are limits.

She wanders through the rose garden and under the shadowy pergola, where the clouds of Himalayan Musk are rampant, their scent almost overpowering. She crosses the lawn under their bedroom window and averts her eyes from the ghost of herself talking to Sam on the other side of the gate. Hearing approaching voices, she moves away, towards a more distant part of the lawn.

From here, she can no longer hear the gramophone that Diana must have put on, the sound of the sea rushing in to take its place. There's a menacing note to it tonight that Rose has never heard before, its assaults on the rocks more irritable, and more determined. It's strange because, here in the garden, the air is unnaturally still, like a room with the windows sealed, the temperature sultry enough to make her hair stick to the back of her neck.

Under the boom of the waves, she catches what sounds like a distant rumbling, right out at sea, and wonders if it might be approaching thunder. It comes again, slightly louder, and she doesn't know whether its arrival, if it reaches them, will be a relief or whether it will edge the evening towards something dangerous. Everyone has been saying all week that what they need is a good storm to clear the air. Now that it may be coming, she's not so sure.

On the far west lawn, the sky opens out in front of her, and she sees that the first flames of sunset are being smothered by a mass of towering clouds, the sea dulled to the colour of old pewter. The music is just discernible again as the breeze catches it and she recognizes the chorus, the tune rising and tumbling. *Wish me luck as you wave me goodbye. Cheerio, here I go, on my way.*

I hate this song, she thinks with clarity. Its false cheeriness makes her think of Frank and his navy pals. He's dead. She knows in her bones he is – the letter will be from someone who knew him, and witnessed his last moments – and she wishes she could find it in her heart to feel proper grief. She can't even remember what he really looks like, only the flat image of him that sits, ever-reproachfully, on her bedside table.

There's no Morwenna to be seen when she finally steels herself to go to the suddenly busy orangery, only a wash of cloudy blue uniforms and what must be the great and good of Vennor, Fowey and all the hamlets in between: a predictable collection of what look like retired generals, solicitors, doctors, magistrates and their wives. They have gravitated towards one side of the room, while the airmen are clustered around the table laden with sandwiches, slices of tongue, an enormous trifle and an even larger crystal bowl of punch. Next to it, stacked on the floor, are wooden crates full of bottled beer, presumably brought by the Canadians.

It's already stiflingly hot inside, the flung-open French windows to the garden making no difference; it's as warm without as within. Condensation is already beginning to blind the windows. She lifts her heavy, damp-swelled hair and wishes she'd put it up. Finishing her first glass of the sticky punch too quickly, she tells herself it's Dutch courage, though her fears about Morwenna have mostly ebbed away. The anxiety that lingers is more amorphous, but it's still enough to make her pour a second, more generous helping. Very swiftly, it seems, in the heat and the foreignness of the occasion, Rose is quite drunk.

She searches among the throng for Diana and sees that she's dancing with one of the airmen. He's matinée-idol handsome, with dark, brilliantined hair that gleams under the lights, but it's Diana who draws the eye. Her dark blue skirts billow and ripple as she's spun around, revealing inches of smooth thigh. Every man in the room is watching her and Rose suddenly understands how that hungry scrutiny might feel, and it's not as gratifying as she might have imagined.

She's still watching Diana when she feels a light touch on the shoulder. She turns, expecting Jane or perhaps a guest looking for the lavatory, and finds Sam there. In her shock, the first thing she registers is that he's wearing something she's never seen him in: a jacket and tie. He's hot and ill at ease in the formal clothes, running his finger round inside the stiff collar.

'What are you doing here?' she manages to say, blood thrumming in her ears. A bead of sweat runs down his neck and, even though she no longer trusts him, a base part of her wants to lick it off. The thought makes her feel desperate, and even hotter. 'What do you want?' she says, more haughtily this time, as she imagines Diana would do it.

He flushes and looks at his feet. 'I had to come. I couldn't help it.'

Without warning, her throat swells with the tears she's managed to hold back all day.

'I always cry when I just want to be cold,' she says furiously, swiping at her eyes.

He reaches out, perhaps to take her hand, but then pulls it back when he can't keep it steady. 'Please don't be cold,' he says. 'That's not you. Look, if you want to stop because of Frank, I understand that, I do. But I don't know why you're so angry with me.'

'Frank's not the reason I haven't come to see you,' she says. 'He should be, but he's not. And it's not because of what Morwenna's brother suspects, either.'

'What, then? I don't understand all this.'

In the lull between one song and another, they hear a low roll of thunder and both of them turn their faces up to the ceiling, as if they could see through the plaster to the sky above. Excitement eddies through the room, then again as another clap sounds in the distance, the loudest yet.

It's the chance Rose needs to get hold of her emotions. 'You must know the reason why,' she says. 'If you just stop and think for five minutes. But what about you? Why come tonight? Why not yesterday? Or the day before?'

He looks at her intently. 'Look, Rosy, did your friend put you up to writing that letter? Because it didn't feel like you.'

The room around her jolts. 'Letter?' she whispers. 'You got my letter?'

He nods, frowning with confusion. 'I had to come when I read it. It felt wrong, what you were saying. You sounded so hard and you're never hard.'

Rose turns slightly away from him to watch the dancers. She doesn't trust herself to look at him. 'You weren't supposed to get that letter. I only wrote it for myself. I didn't even sign it. Someone must have posted it for me.'

'I bet it was her, wasn't it?' He gestures towards the dance floor. 'Diana.'

She turns cold, then even hotter than before. 'You know Diana?' she says quietly.

'No. I mean, I've met her, but . . .' He tails off but his eye is still caught by her as she twirls into the arms of a new Canadian.

'I think you should go,' Rose hears herself saying, in a flat, remote voice. 'I can't talk to you here. I don't really know why you came.' Her mind whirs. How can he know Diana?

'Now, hang on a minute,' he says wildly. 'I don't understand any of this. What's she told you? Did she say something happened? Is that what you were getting at in the letter?'

She turns and walks to the back of the orangery, her shoulders braced as though anticipating a hard blow. She knows he'll be too worried about making a scene to follow her; he's uncomfortable enough here as it is.

She forces herself to study the room's strangers so she doesn't have to see him leave. It's growing more airless by the minute, the heat making the place feel unsteady, as though everything is about to come apart at the seams. Men mop their shining faces with handkerchiefs while their wives discreetly unstick damp dress fabric from their armpits. One older lady is sitting with her head between her legs, her husband crouching next to her with a glass of brandy.

Of everyone in the room, only Diana looks cool and unruffled as she turns and spins and laughs, as if the normal rules don't apply to her.

But they do, Rose thinks. They do.

XXI

Jimmy has only just got home when Menna bursts in behind him.

'Oh, good, you're here,' she snaps. 'Now, stay there and don't you dare move till I get back. I've got something to show you.'

The wild look in her eyes makes him obey her. He doesn't even sit down to wait. Menna turns so easily, especially when it comes to him. She's never liked him, not from the moment Sam brought him back from the church hall and the features of her small face pinched together with disgust. 'He's not stopping here,' she'd said, right in front of him. 'He'll have his hand in the tin as soon as I turn my back.'

Outside in the lane, visible through the window, Mrs Whitlow opposite's pot plants droop brown-edged in the heavy air. Earlier, his friend Tom had said a storm was coming and the words had made his stomach flutter with fear, like the feeling he gets when Dew is in the room. He can't think what Menna might want him to see, unless it's something to do with him being sent back to London.

Yesterday he'd lost the money she'd given him for the butcher's. He'd been so engrossed in his game of marbles on the cobbles of the harbourside that he'd forgotten all about it and then, when he did remember and checked his pockets, the coin had gone. She hadn't hit him this time but what she had said was much worse. She'd put her face right up to his, so close that her breath was hot on his face.

'I've had enough of you,' she'd said quietly, so Sam upstairs couldn't hear. 'You're going back to London and I don't care what he says. I'll put you on the train myself.'

He pushes his hand into his pocket and turns over the big green cat's eye he'd won yesterday, before Menna had said he had to go. A sudden gust of wind tears through the leaves outside and it strikes him that nothing seems like a lark today, even the war. It feels like there's a dark blot in the corner of all his thoughts now, the same blot he thinks he's seen approaching, like a warship from the horizon, when his eyes are half sun-blind from playing on the sand.

The invasion has already begun, some of them at school have been saying, the proof of it in a torn strip of what might be parachute silk found in a hedgerow near the Lostwithiel road. An advance party of spies is already here, apparently, hiding in the caves and creeks that the smugglers used two centuries earlier. But this is not the most frightening thing. What was it Menna had said? 'It's not my problem what your dad does to you when he's roaring drunk. You'd probably deserve it anyway.'

When the door finally crashes back on its hinges again, she is clutching a limp piece of paper. It doesn't look like a train ticket. 'You think your Sam is so perfect,' she says, brandishing it at him. 'You want to read this. That'll set you straight.'

Wisps of hair are damp around her face and she's shaking violently. It dawns on him for the first time that, although they're always arguing, Menna doesn't hate Sam after all. She loves him.

'Don't you want to know what it is?' she shouts, throwing the paper at him. 'I'll tell you, shall I? It's a letter from his fancy woman, which he hid in the lighthouse after it came in the post today. I knew he had something going on. Dew's been dropping hints but wouldn't give me a straight answer. Now I know what old Mrs Browning was on about in the butcher's, too.'

She goes to the stairs, half talking to herself as she climbs them. Jimmy stays where he is, though the urge to run out of the house – to go to Tom's or up the hill to Sam's mum – is almost overwhelming.

When she comes back down, she's changed into a red dress he's never seen before. It's slightly too short to be decent. Her hair is loose for once but it's lank and uncombed, a dent in it at the jaw where she's had it tied back all day. She smells of drink and Menna never drinks.

'You're coming with me,' she says. 'You'll have to do as you are.'

'Where are we going?'

'Where she lives, this friend of his. Up at the Hall. I want a word with her.'

Jimmy feels his insides turn over at the mention of the Hall. 'We can't go up there,' he says, as she steers him down the lane, her cold fingers pinching the flesh of his arm. 'Not tonight. They're having a party for the airmen. We're not invited.'

He'd seen the preparations when he'd crept into the garden earlier, though he'd only managed to catch a brief glimpse of the girl as she turned to go in, someone calling her name. *Diana.* He hadn't known it before but it suited her. It sounded rich, exotic. She had thrown away her cigarette as she went, and when the coast was clear, he'd darted out of his hiding place to pick up the smouldering end. It was dulled with her red lipstick and, just for a second, he'd put it to his own lips.

Now, as Menna hurries him along the harbour wall, he wonders who wrote the letter he had refused to read out of loyalty to Sam. He badly hopes it wasn't Diana. He hadn't been able to resist glancing at the bottom of the single sheet of paper, to see who'd signed it, but there was no name – not even an initial.

The idea of Menna blundering into the garden that has become his sanctuary makes him feel sick and desperate. He waits until they've reached the coast-path, then wrenches free of her. She grabs for him but he dodges away, breaking into a run.

'You'd better come back here,' she shrieks, but he suddenly realizes that she's used up all her threats. She's already told him he's going back to his dad as soon as she can swing it. If Sam is up at the Hall, Jimmy can warn him and maybe Sam will be able to intercept her before anyone else sees her.

When he gets there the garden feels different, just as everything else does today. It's no longer the serene, secret place he's come to think of, at least partly, as his own. He only found the place by chance – when he was alone on the path one day and noticed the gate standing ajar a few inches. He'd frozen when he'd seen the latch was lifted, apparently by someone standing on the other side, expecting them to come through and shoo him back towards the village. But no one did, and after a long minute, the gate was carefully closed.

There had been something spine-tingling about it: not only the strange silence of the unknown person on the other side, but the glimpse he'd caught of the garden beyond. He was used by now to the cool colours of the sea and the rocks and the beaches, the whitewash of the village cottages. But inside the garden of Penhallow – he'd later asked Tom the name – everything had been green, a hundred different shades, all of them lush and irresistible. Two days later, he'd stolen inside for the first time.

Even from the gate, he can hear the hum of people. The air is hot, sharp and sweet: nectar and newly cut grass; tobacco and women's scent. Faint music weaves through it all. There's not a breath of wind once the gate closes behind him, though he can hear how irritable the sea has become far below. He knows the geography of the garden quite well, and he'd seen where they were setting things up earlier. The guests will be in the rose garden and the room with the huge windows that go down almost to the ground. Instead of cutting across the lawn, he takes his own, now-habitual, route deeper into the garden, which he'd found to avoid detection by anyone who might be watching from the house.

It's longer this way but he doesn't want to meet anyone who might hold him up. Some of the Canadians know him by sight now. They'd given him chewing gum and cigarette cards and, once, 'a pair of nylons for your mother', which for some reason had made them laugh. He hadn't given them to Menna, of course; she didn't deserve them. He'd hidden them under a loose floorboard in his room, knowing he was secretly keeping them for *her*, waiting for some as yet unimaginable occasion when he could present them to her as a gift.

He's never been in the garden so late, at the tipping point of day and night, when the light is beginning to dissolve. It's larger and more forbidding in the gloom. He doesn't know if he'd have the nerve to go down to the creek as he usually does, where he likes to sit next to the tree that droops right into the water and watch the speckled sunlight dance on the surface. The soupy green air there is like swimming underwater.

It was at the creek that he'd seen Diana for the first time. She was coming out of a strange little building on stilts, an old boat rotting away in the shadows underneath. He could see she'd been crying and was angry about it, just as he always was with himself when he gave in to tears, swiping at her red eyes with her sleeve. Despite this, she was still beautiful in a way he'd never seen in a real person – only on the posters outside the Curzon.

After she'd gone, he'd crept up the steps and gone inside. The smell of damp was sharp but he could smell her too, a rich, heady scent that made him think of a place in a smart street in London he'd once glimpsed before the door was shut: red carpets and mirrored light. Beyond that, he'd heard the tinkle of laughter and music. He had breathed in the scent of her until the last of it had evaporated, the dank air closing in.

But he hasn't got time for the creek or the little boat he likes to float in tonight. He hurries on, a small shadow darting from bush to bush as the sky above him darkens another notch and thunder rumbles in the distance. He comes across them behind the tall hedge that separates the lawn from where the fountain is, marooned among thousands of flowers.

He sees her first because her hair, usually the colour of palest sunshine, glows shell-pink in the strange light. Then he sees that the person with her is Dew, strikingly dark in his snow-white shirt, and scuttles back behind a bush. This morning, when he'd picked up the cigarette end, part of him had wanted Diana to discover him. Menna's older brother is another matter entirely.

'I shouldn't have said anything,' Diana is saying, her voice piercing the syrupy air. 'It wasn't really my place to ask. And, really, it's just a load of dull old sticks in there who'll look down –'

She stops short because Dew has started to laugh. It's a horrible sound that Jimmy has heard before: grating and completely different from when Dew actually finds something funny.

'I thought as much,' he says. 'You're all the same, you posh girls. You like the idea of roughing it. It gets your type going. But only when it suits you, eh?'

'Look, it's not like that –'

Dew flicks away his cigarette. 'I saw you in there,' he interrupted, 'dancing with all the men, flashing your legs. I bet you think I'm in love with you, don't you, like all the rest? Well, you'd be wrong. I haven't loved anyone in a long time. I did think you were interesting, though, despite your accent. But you're not. You're just the same as them in there. And a little whore to boot.'

'Whore?' she says. 'How dare –'

'You thought you'd cause a stir if you walked in with me tonight,' he goes on, talking over her. 'That you'd shock the old bitch into her grave. But you've had cold feet, haven't you? Or is it Sammy's turn tonight? Will I find him in there if I have another look?' He gestures towards the house and Jimmy's stomach lurches queasily at the familiar name.

'Sammy?' Diana has begun to back away but Dew moves towards her, closing the gap again.

'Yeah, him. He's up to something and I wonder if it's you. I don't know if I believe in this *friend* of yours after all. Well, I haven't come all this way for nothing.'

Jimmy sees Diana glance sideways. He knows what she's doing from his own experiences with Menna, and his dad before that; she's looking for an escape route. But Dew is suddenly upon her, his mouth smashing against hers. Jimmy has to clamp his jaw shut so he doesn't cry out.

At first, she seems to surrender, allowing Dew to push her up against the hedge, which catches on the shiny stuff of her dress. But then she begins to struggle, her hands coming up to his chest to push him away.

'Oh, no, you're not doing this again,' Dew says, taking her wrists in one hand and pinning them above her head. 'I'm sick of you running hot and cold.'

Jimmy hovers in his hiding place, stifling the urge to whimper. Dew is hurting her now – he can tell from the way she's braced against the hedge. He watches Dew reach down for the hem of her dress and yank it up. The sight both sickens Jimmy and stirs him. But it's this that seems to give Diana renewed strength. She begins to writhe and twist, her voice forced out of her in short, breathless huffs. 'No. No. No.'

Dew loses his footing for a moment and she manages to dart to the side, almost falling as she scrambles into a run. She doesn't look back, the gravel scattering under her feet as she disappears from view. Way off towards the other side of the darkening sea, there's a low clatter of thunder.

'Fucking bitch,' Dew mutters, as he lights another cigarette. Jimmy crouches lower, holding his breath, but Dew doesn't come his way. He heads off in the direction Diana has just fled, towards the lit-up house.

XXII

When Rose returns to the orangery, having gone to the lavatory to compose herself, Sam is nowhere to be seen and she's as disappointed as she's relieved, until she sees that there's no sign of Diana either. Eleanor has made her arrival at last, Gerald's arm firmly around her. She doesn't look as though she's all there, glancing around distractedly even as people try to engage her in conversation.

Rose tries to focus her mind on Jane, whom Eleanor is presumably looking out for, and wonders whether she ought to go back up to the dormitory where she's probably hiding. But the distraction of other people's problems isn't working; she keeps coming back to the unbelievable fact that Diana posted her letter. There is no possibility it happened by accident; Rose had hidden it among her private things. It hadn't even been addressed. Diana has gone to quite a lot of trouble to do it behind her back. And Sam knows her. He'd recognized her and looked sheepish about it. Rose goes to pour herself more punch.

When she turns back with a full glass, Diana is there in

front of her. She looks as flustered as Rose has ever seen her. One of the straps of her dress has fallen down and her hair-slide has slipped. Rose reaches out and plucks a small leaf out of her pale hair, holding it out for her to see. Diana blushes deeply, adding to the unfamiliarity of her appearance.

'Where have you been?' Rose asks. *Who have you been with?*

Diana tries to laugh but it comes out as a choking gasp. She puts a hand to her breast and visibly tries to slow her breathing.

'Diana? Tell me.'

'Oh, Rose, you really don't want to know,' she says.

At the same time, Rose becomes aware of a disturbance by the door. A voice has been raised, a woman's voice. Her local accent is strong and people begin to crane to see who it is.

'Where is she, then?' the woman shouts again, clearer this time because the crowd has hushed and someone with a taste for spectacle has pulled the needle off the gramophone. One of the airmen shifts to the left, affording Rose a clear view.

'Oh, God, it's her,' she whispers. The room tips. Her irrational fear has come true.

'Where is she?' Morwenna cries again. 'I know she's here. I want to talk to her.'

Rose registers a few different things at once, even as her heart thuds and skips in her chest: a man stepping forward to get hold of Morwenna, their dark colouring so alike he must be some relation; Eleanor staring at the intruders, blue eyes wide, her expression stricken; Diana stiffening at her side.

'Get off me, Dew!' Morwenna shrieks. 'You here for her too, are you?'

He abruptly lets go or half pushes her; it's hard to tell. She stumbles but manages to right herself. As she lifts her head, she looks in Rose's direction.

'You!' she snarls, pushing through a huddle of old ladies. 'It's you I want to talk to.'

Rose is steeling herself to reply when Diana steps forward. 'Do I know you?' she says coolly. Only Rose is close enough to see that she's trembling.

'I've been hearing stories about you,' says Morwenna, coming to a stop a few feet away. Her words slur slightly. Rose wipes her slippery hands on her dress. Her brain feels as if it's stuffed with cotton wool. She's struggling to take in that Morwenna is addressing Diana instead of her.

'Golly, how intriguing,' says Diana. 'What sort of stories?'

Rose's mind is moving sluggishly against all the drink she's had, and the heat that's making her feel faint. *Oh, Rose, you really don't want to know.* Suddenly she remembers the way Diana's eyes had crackled with excitement the day she'd come back and told Rose about the village rumours. Of the way she'd tidied her hair in the mirror, smiling a secret smile as she did.

'You've been seen,' Morwenna is saying to Diana now. 'First with my brother and then with my husband. I'd know it was you anywhere. You fit the bill all right, looking like a tart but thinking you're better than everyone else. My cousin Lo saw you, leaving the lighthouse in a green dress, looking like the cat who'd got the cream.'

Rose feels as if she's swaying. What was it Diana had said about Sam, when she was wearing the dress that brought out her eyes? *I don't suppose you get too many like him to the pound.* As if she'd seen him herself. Seen and appreciated him. An image sneaks up on her then, of Diana and Sam entwined. She looks down at the leaf she's still holding.

'I've only just put it all together,' Morwenna continues. 'It was old Mrs Browning who gave me your name, said where you were. I saw her in the baker's. She comes up to me and she says, "That old friend of Sam's find you all right? Diana, she said her name was." I've seen this too.' She holds up a crumpled piece of paper Rose recognizes as her own.

Confusion wars in her head with a desperate hope. The letter is hers, and it was she who had lied to Mrs Browning about her name. Not Diana. She struggles to piece it all together but it's so airless inside the orangery now she can hardly catch her breath.

Morwenna jabs her finger towards Diana. 'Something's been up with him for a while. He's been lying to me about where he goes. Well, it's clear enough now. He's been with you – when you haven't been with my brother, that is. Dirty bitch.' She shakes her head in disgust.

'I don't know what you're talking about,' Diana says, but there's a tremor in her voice now. 'I don't know your husband and I barely know your brother. I tend not to mix much with your sort.'

She directs this over Morwenna's head, and Rose remembers that Dew is the name of Sam's volatile brother-in-law. He stares back at Diana unblinkingly, and even from across the room, Rose can sense his contained fury. One of the airmen, nudged by his friends, has begun to laugh silently at the scene, his shoulders shaking. It's not funny, though. Morwenna looks pathetic suddenly, her black eyes flicking from one hostile face to another, her cheap dress clinging to her limply.

'Where is Sam anyway?' she throws out desperately. 'I know he must have come up here to see you.'

'If he did, you could hardly blame the guy,' one of the airmen calls out. There are a few embarrassed titters.

Some new disturbance, this time at the other end of the room, makes everyone look round. It's Mrs Fox, Payne pushing her chair. They're a deeply macabre pair: Mrs Fox dressed in what looks like high Victorian mourning and Payne almost gurning with the effort of not smiling at the dramatic entrance they're making.

'What is going on here?' Mrs Fox begins, but then she sees the two strangers. Rose watches her face slacken, then twist in fury.

'You!' she shrieks at Dew, unwittingly repeating Morwenna. Her bony hand grips her cane and brings it down on the lovely floor, its silver tip gouging a hole in the wood. Her rings glitter in the light from the chandelier as she does it again. 'How is it that you are here, in my house?' In the single spat syllable of *you* are a dozen other words that everyone in the room hears, even the Canadians. 'I told you that you were never to set foot in this house again. How dare you defy me after all I've given you?'

'Mother.' Eleanor moves towards the wheelchair but Payne stands implacably in the way.

'No doubt this is your doing,' Mrs Fox continues, ignoring Eleanor. She has twisted round in her seat and is jabbing her cane towards Diana. 'You have blundered on with this idea of holding a dance, against my express wishes. You have forgotten that this is not your home, but mine.'

'Oh, I was under the impression it was Eleanor's,' returns Diana, and Rose cringes. 'Perhaps one day she'll crack and turn you out on the streets.'

Mrs Fox's eyes glow. 'Turn me out? It's you who will be turned out. I have already written to your mother and told her what you've been doing, the trouble you've been stirring up. I rather think it will be you who's out on the streets. From what I gleaned in the letter I received this morning, you have no home to return to. "Do what you will with my daughter," she wrote, "but please don't send her to me."' Mrs Fox lets out a terrible creaking laugh that makes Rose shudder. 'You're like a parcel nobody wants to claim.'

Diana stills, her face draining of colour. But then her hands curl into fists. 'I think the final piece of the puzzle has just fallen into place,' she says, and her voice is remarkably steady. 'Don't think you frighten me as you frighten Eleanor. You think you know all about me from some half-baked nonsense you've heard from Freda Phelps. Well, I know all about you. I worked out a while ago why you've been beating Eleanor into submission all these years, and why you dislike poor Jane so much. Really, it seems so obvious they're mother and daughter once you know.'

A murmur goes around the orangery and one of the airmen lets out a long, low whistle. Rose glances at Eleanor. She looks as if she might collapse.

'Diana,' Rose says, in a warning tone, but she takes no notice.

'What I couldn't understand,' she muses aloud, 'is why you were quite so enduringly furious with her. I mean, Eleanor shouldn't have opened her legs and all that, but these things happen. Why hadn't you simply ordered her and Sébastien to marry? No husband could be worse than a bastard in the family, surely. Even a Catholic one. But Sébastien was just a red herring, wasn't he? The real father was much worse than an inconvenient child might have been.'

'You shut that filthy mouth this instant!' Mrs Fox cries. But her composure is unravelling. Her cane jitters on the wooden floor as she begins to shake.

'The thought of Eleanor doing that with a Bolitho was more than you could bear, wasn't it?' Diana continues relentlessly. 'Pure Fox blood sullied by the lowest rogues in Cornwall.'

'Please, Diana, just stop it,' Eleanor says brokenly. 'Please.'

But Mrs Fox is shouting, drowning her words: 'They're all intruders!' she screeches. 'Trespassers! Get them out of here, Payne! Get them out. I won't have that Devlin girl here another night.' She begins to wail, a single plaintive note that makes goose-flesh rise on Rose's bare arms.

Payne wheels Mrs Fox away, and a rattled-looking Gerald gestures for someone to see to the gramophone. People start to talk among themselves again, believing the show to be over. Only Rose notices Jane sidle in through the French windows and come towards them. She's changed into her work clothes and it makes her look like a gardener's boy who's stumbled into the wrong room.

'Why can't you just tell her the truth?' Diana is saying to Eleanor, who has begun silently to weep. Neither of them has seen Jane approach. 'She deserves to know that she's yours. I've crossed your mother for you, so what's left to be afraid of? Don't you think you've been a feeble sort of parent for long enough?'

Gerald has just started to protest when a deep bass note, growing louder every second, makes everyone stop talking and look up. The gramophone needle is pulled off again.

'More thunder?' Rose hears someone say.

But it's not thunder.

One of the airmen appears at the French windows. 'Stukas!' he shouts. 'Coming this way.'

People rush outside. While thick clouds continue to threaten at the horizon, the rest of the sky glows hazily with the dregs of sunset. The bombers are flying towards them from the north and there must be a dozen in rigid formation, the throb of their engines vibrating and disrupting the syrupy air. They drone across the blood-orange sky like black-fly.

'Should we go down to the cellar?' someone behind Rose says.

'Is there a shelter here?' says another voice, more urgent.

'They're heading back to France,' one of the airmen says. It's the dark one who was dancing with Diana. 'They'll be empty now.'

But as he says it, one of the planes towards the back of the group drops something from its wing. It plummets through the air with a whine, a black full-stop that hits the water with an enormous splash. People scream as a hole appears in the sea, the water boiling around it. But the planes are moving away, the air returning to normal, engine notes altering as they move towards the horizon and are finally swallowed by the thunderheads.

Rose watches people as they file back inside, subdued now the hysteria has left them. There is still no sign of Sam and, in the absence of him, she needs to speak to Diana, force her to disentangle all the strands. She turns but Diana isn't there. Peering into the gloom of the garden, she catches a ripple of bright hair, moving towards the gate to the coast-path. It's then she realizes she's not the only one watching Diana go. Dew's dark gaze is fixed in the same direction and, from another part of the terrace, so is Eleanor's.

XXIII

Jimmy had heard the bombers coming before anyone else. He'd known they were German too – not from the illustrations in the identification books he can draw from memory, but from the noise of their engines. British planes sounded smoother. That deep, menacing throb could only be the enemy.

The Stuka reminds him of a vulture – a vulture that carries extra bombs on its bent wings, and is fitted with a siren that screams as it dives, to terrify those on the ground even more. The Trumpets of Jericho, they're called, because if you hear them you're probably about to die. Sometimes the wing bombs jam, and that's what must have happened to the one that unexpectedly drops. He holds his breath as it hurtles towards the sea.

He's barely recovered from the hair-bristling thrill of it when something pale in the dark of the garden catches his eye. It's her, and he follows without thinking, not even caring if someone sees him from the terrace where people are still lingering. When she pulls open the garden gate and steps through it, Jimmy has only a second to see she's turned left before it swings shuts again.

He counts to ten, then runs to the gate, slipping through it as surreptitiously as he can. He assumes she must be heading for Vennor and wonders if she knows where Sam is and if they've planned to meet. His stomach pitches again at the thought that she knows him.

But then she pauses at the steps that lead down to Breakheart Cove and turns round so suddenly that he hasn't time to hide.

'So my little shadow is real,' she says. He can't meet her eye so he watches her dress blow around her legs. 'You've been following me for weeks, haven't you? Little spy. I thought I was going mad.' She laughs and starts determinedly down the steps.

When he dares to peep over, cheeks hot with shame but unable to help himself, she's already on the sand. He watches as she goes towards the water, her shoes hooked over her finger. She doesn't so much as hesitate when the lightning flashes, illuminating the sea more brilliantly than the lamp from the lighthouse.

Close to the water's edge, she drops the shoes and takes off her dress in one graceful movement. Jimmy swallows and checks the path behind him, in case someone is watching him watch her. He goes down a couple of steps and crouches there, so he's harder to see.

The pale bits of her underwear are now on the sand, too, and he holds his breath as she pauses and seems to look up, right at him, her body as pale as milk against the wet sand. Her breasts are heavier than Menna's – he'd seen them once when she was dressing, which had earned him a stinging blow to his left ear when she caught him. Now he knows he wouldn't be able to look away for anything, even the Stukas reappearing in the sky. The helplessness of how he is around her makes him feel strange and awful: lightheaded and angry at the same time, itchy in his skin.

She swims for what seems like a long time, even as the guests begin to walk back towards the village on the path just above him. Far away, but perhaps a little nearer than before, the clouds crash together and a sudden thrust of air dries the sweat on his forehead. His mother used to say that thunder was the sound of God moving His furniture around, but tonight there's nothing so ordinary about it. It's ominous, as though something enormous is about to happen.

He watches her arms flash in and out of the water like blades. *Your sort*, she'd said to Dew and Menna back at the Hall, as he hid in the shadow of the open doors. As though they were dirt. He supposes she must think him dirt too, in that case, because he knows from Menna that he's lower still. It strikes him that everything has been spoilt in one blow: his uncomplicated love for Sam, his private game following Diana. Even the garden feels lost to him now. He'll be back in London soon and the thought winds him.

He thinks again of the strange feeling the girl has woken in him, which is so different from how he feels about Sam. It makes him want to own a little piece of her, to eat her up, to get inside her. He'd thought the gnawing hunger was what people called passion – the sort that made people write poems, and fight in the street. He wonders now if what he'd thought was a kind of love might actually be hate instead.

XXIV

After the bombers, the guests seem at a loss. Quite soon, once the first people have the courage to gather their belongings and announce they really must be going, though it's not yet eleven, more quickly follow suit. Soon only the airmen and a handful of others are left.

The humiliation of the earlier scene hasn't yet sunk in for Eleanor. Whatever Gerald gave her earlier, and again as the planes came over, had made her feel blessedly remote from everything. She floats through the dense heat of the garden, thinking about nothing much, not even the low thunder that dimly recalls another night out here, among the roses.

It's not until she sees Jane sitting on the edge of the fountain that the urgent present penetrates the gauze she's wrapped in.

'Darling,' she breathes, going to her.

'Is it really true, what she said?' The words come out as a sob. Tears course down her cheeks.

'Why don't we all go to my study?' says Gerald,

appearing out of the gloom. Eleanor peers at him for signs of anger but he looks the same as he always does: worried and kind. Dew was the one thing she had never told him about. It had just seemed easier to tell him it was Sébastien; that the reason they couldn't marry was his love for Eleanor's dead brother. She'd told him about it in a letter and when he'd replied the next day by telegram – *I received your letter. It changes nothing. Your loving Gerald* – she'd wished she'd trusted him with the whole truth.

Now, as Gerald quickly and unobtrusively takes control, even as her nerves jangle at the thought of the conversation she is finally about to have, she knows how glad she is that he is her husband. She notices for the first time how like Robin he is, not in appearance but in the way he makes her feel safe, or as close to safe as she ever feels.

They follow him meekly inside and he shepherds them into his study, efficiently fixing the blackout across the open window before turning on a couple of lamps. He pours Eleanor a whisky, then goes to the door. 'Unless you'd rather I stayed?'

Eleanor hesitates, then smiles at him tremulously. He won't be far away. 'We'll be all right,' she says. 'And, Gerald? Thank you.'

He gives her a quick, private smile and closes the door softly behind him.

Her daughter has curled into a huge leather wing chair and is still clutching the handkerchief Gerald handed her in the garden. Brick, who has followed them in, jumps up and burrows under her legs. Her hand goes to his head but her expression is numb, her dark eyes huge and unfocused. Eleanor wants to go to her but doesn't dare.

'You still haven't answered my question.' Jane's voice is flat now, as if she's withdrawn inside herself.

'How much did you hear?'

There's a long pause when, in order not to hurry her into speaking, Eleanor tries to tune into the rhythm of the sea behind the blackout, so she can match her breathing to its steady in and out. But it's too restive tonight to calm her, the waves crashing unevenly against the rocks. The thunder that rumbles every so often is closer now, though it's still unbearably warm.

'Not much I really understood,' Jane says eventually. 'I know you hated me wearing your dress, though. Will I have to go back to London now?' She stops to gulp down a sob. 'Please let me stay.'

'Oh, Jane.' She doesn't know how to begin. Even now, she can't help fearing the wrath of her mother. It will be a hard habit to break.

'It would have been disgraceful enough if you'd allowed Sébastien to do this to you,' she had said to Eleanor, when she finally admitted she was going to have a baby, on the evening of her father's funeral, when it was too late to do anything about it. Her mother's face had turned bloodless, her mouth hardening into a thin, unyielding line. 'At least we could have brought him back here and made him marry you. At least he would have been of our own class, even if he is a Catholic and a pansy. But that you could do such a thing with a creature like Dew Bolitho.'

Eleanor can still recall the visceral disgust on her mother's face. The memory of it has stayed with her for more than fifteen years. The difference is that she's no longer so ashamed. She's not quite so afraid, either. The old feelings are limping away in the face of her daughter's distress. *Jane*. Eleanor has been so frightened for so long, not only of her mother, but of Jane not forgiving her if she knew. Now, looking at her, tucked up with Brick, she's no longer sure that would be the case. She can even see the possibility that Jane might be glad.

'It's time I told you everything,' she says in a clear voice. 'I can't think now why I didn't before.'

She grips her whisky tightly. She won't skirt around her answers; Jane has a right to know who her father is. But there's no need to go into the details – though, even as she decides this, they rush towards her from sixteen summers ago, ghosts blown in from the sea, where they've been waiting all this time.

Eleanor left the garden by the gate she could see from her bedroom window. The whisper of the sea was much more insistent on the other side of it. Pulling it shut behind her, she tried to breathe slowly but the sobs kept rising, making her gasp. She put her hand over her mouth to stifle them, though there was no one to hear her. She knew she should go inside, tidy herself and return to the orangery, but she simply couldn't bear to. Not even the thought of her mother's exasperation – growing with every minute that Eleanor stayed away – could make her go back. She wondered if Sébastien was still in the garden, where she'd left him, or whether his good manners had forced him back inside.

She put her fingers to her eyes so she didn't cry again. To think that she had been so happy there with him, perched on the lip of the fountain, and yet now . . . It was probably less than twenty minutes since she had followed him outside. The fact of it seemed completely unbelievable. She wiped her eyes with the heels of her hands, cursing her white dress for not having anything so useful as a pocket where she could keep a handkerchief.

When her face was dry she set off along the path towards Vennor, anything to get away from Penhallow and the scene of her humiliation. The thunder was louder now, though the rain hadn't started yet. Far out at sea, sheet lightning lit the clouds. The rain would come soon, she knew. She could feel it gathering in the air high above her.

She couldn't see anything of Breakheart Cove from where she was, but she wondered if the village boys would be down there. They usually were on Saturday nights, if it wasn't wet or cold, and tonight the weather had remained sultry, even as the thunder grumbled on in the distance. She didn't care if they were there anyway; all she wanted was to get away. She quickened her pace as Sébastien's words came to her again and threatened to undo her resolve.

'I wish I could love you back,' he'd said, and she'd had just enough pride to shove his hand away from where he was cupping her cheek. She'd already made enough of a fool of herself.

'Oh, don't, Eleanor,' he'd said, his face stricken. 'Please don't hate me. I don't think I could bear it. You're all I have left of him.'

She'd known then, in a hot vertiginous rush, what he meant. Why he'd come all the way to Penhallow, as though he was making some sort of pilgrimage. Why he wore Robin's cologne.

By the time she reached the top of the steps down to the cove, the wind had picked up a little. Her face felt tight where the salt of her tears had dried and she wished she could wash it. She glanced back up the path but Sébastien hadn't come after her. A fortifying wave of fury that she had so little pride rushed through her, and stopped her turning back. Instead she went closer to the edge of the cliff and looked over.

It was hard to tell how many of them were down there, on the sand. They'd lit a bonfire but the flickering light wasn't much use, plunging the rest of the beach into deep shadow. From what she could hear of their voices, there were at least three or four, all male. She would know each one by name, just as they would know her, but she wasn't one of them. Her mother would be furious if she knew where her daughter was. She wondered if that was another reason she was here.

It was Dew Bolitho who called out to her first, as she descended the steps towards them. It usually was. He knew her a little from his job in the garden, and liked to draw attention to this in front of the gang. His gang, really.

'So what brings you down here then, m'lady,' he said. He always called her this if her parents weren't in earshot, as a mocking sort of joke. Whenever they crossed paths, which seemed to be more often lately, he bowed and scraped and tugged at an imaginary forelock to make her laugh. He was nicer when he was on his own, his eyes lingering on her more thoughtfully. He was very handsome, in an intimidating way. She'd always thought so.

'Aren't you going to say anything, then, m'lady?' he pressed as he got to his feet and wandered over to her.

She shrugged and stumbled, turning her ankle in a dip in the sand.

'Been drinking at the ball, have you, Cinderella?' one of the others called out.

Half obscured by the light of the fire, she could only make out Jory, Dew's cousin, and another boy she recognized but whose name she had forgotten. It looked like they had all been drinking, empty bottles upended in the sand.

Dew offered her a cigarette, which she took and puffed at inexpertly. It made her feel drunker and she sat down abruptly, just as the lightning flashed again. He joined her on the sand, his knees up and his voice low, so everyone else was excluded. 'We thought you were a ghost in that white dress, floating down the steps.' His mouth was close to her ear. She could feel the heat of his breath.

When he brushed the silk of her dress where it clung to her thigh, she wasn't sure if it was accidental. He passed her a bottle and she gulped down the liquid inside.

'Steady on, girl,' he said, with a smile, but it was only beer, warm from the fire and his hand gripping the glass. She wondered vaguely if it would matter if she lay back on the sand and went to sleep. Instead, she finished off the beer and asked for another cigarette. She thought about her father, who would be dead soon, and Robin, who had already abandoned her. She thought about Sébastien, who would be leaving tomorrow. She waited to feel pain but she didn't feel anything. Just a numbness that was not unpleasant, and was certainly better than the shame she'd felt in the garden when Sébastien pulled away from her kiss.

It began to rain then, and it was as if a switch had been thrown. It was dry and then it was wet: warm and soaking and intense.

The other boys shouted as the fire sizzled and went out, another clap of thunder drowning their voices.

'Come on,' said Dew, taking her hand and pulling her up. 'We'll wait it out in the cave.'

'But what about them?' she said, looking over her shoulder at the other boys as they ran, laughing and whooping, towards the steps.

'They're going home. You want to go back up to the Hall? I'll take you if you do.'

'No,' she said, shaking her head. 'I'll stay. I don't want to go back there.'

He grinned wolfishly, his teeth flashing white. He was smaller and broader across the shoulders than Sébastien but he had the same black hair and eyes, the same olive skin. In the gloom of the cave's mouth, he might have been Sébastien, but then the lightning flashed again, brighter, closer now. Thunder followed a couple of seconds later, making her jump. The crash made a chink of reason open up in her mind.

Go home, it said. *Go home now.*

Instead, she took Dew's outstretched hand and followed him deeper into the cave.

He turned back to her. 'I won't say nothing about this,' he said. 'I won't tell anyone.'

'What about the others?' she said.

'They won't either.'

He'd looked blurry and soft before, from all the beer he'd drunk. Now his eyes glittered with purpose. She didn't even know what she was agreeing to. All she knew was that he was making her feel better. And then he kissed her, and it wasn't what she expected. In as much as she'd

278

ever thought about it at all, she'd expected him to be clumsy, and as unpractised as she herself surely was. But he wasn't, not at all, and that undid the last of her.

He'd sent her two notes afterwards, both intercepted by her mother and burnt, and had even tried to visit her in person once, sneaking up to her bedroom to speak to her before her mother had burst in seconds later, shrieking with rage. She hadn't read what was in the notes and her mother had never told her, but she thought she could guess.

Dew had loved her for a time, or believed he had. And perhaps, if she was honest with herself, it had been stronger than that, more long-lived. On the morning of her wedding to Gerald, her stomach flat and empty again, she had received an enormous bouquet of white lilies without a card. They must have cost a great deal of money. She was almost certain it was Dew, who was by then making a lot more than he could ever have done as one of Penhallow's gardeners.

The funereal flowers had given Eleanor a fright; what she had always dismissed as childhood fondness must have twisted with time into something fierce and resentful. She supposed it was to do with briefly possessing something he hadn't known he could have, though she never flattered herself into thinking it was really her. What Dew had fallen for, even if he didn't realize it, was her good clean name. His was something grubby in their part of the world, despised for centuries by families like hers. He hated that.

She didn't know precisely when he'd decided to go the other way and embrace his heritage, to make the Bolithos wealthier and more feared than ever, but she's fairly sure it was after she was shut away in her bedroom so no one could guess what she had let him do with her.

It was her brother Hugo's idea that he and Olivia take the baby as soon as it was born. Her mother had been reluctant, wanting to cut all ties and have it adopted anonymously, but Hugo had had his way. Eleanor tried to make the best of it, believing it the only way she would ever see her child.

It had long been assumed that Olivia couldn't have children, so it was very difficult after the twins had come along, when Jane was four. Eleanor can still remember how bitter she had felt about that, her rather chilly sister-in-law with three girls, and her with none.

Her mother had long warned her she had to be sensible when Jane came to stay. She hadn't needed to voice the threat that always hung so heavily in the background of those visits: that they would cease altogether if she showed any sign of spilling the secret, of overstepping the mark. But then, when Jane was nine, there was an argument that changed everything.

It was supposed to be a wonderful summer because, for once, Jane was coming for six long weeks. Usually, Olivia took the girls to her parents in Sussex, perhaps allowing Jane to accompany her father to Cornwall for a week or two. She had never much cared for Cornwall – she thought the long journey a nuisance – and Eleanor suspected she was scared of her mother-in-law. But that summer Olivia's own parents were away on a cruise, and Eleanor's mother, wanting to see the twins, made it impossible for Olivia to refuse.

Eleanor had never spent such an extended period with

her brother's family and she couldn't believe how much and how obliviously they excluded Jane. Their contrasting looks seemed only to emphasize the gulf: the twins and Olivia so blonde and blue-eyed – Hugo had in looks married his and Eleanor's mother – and poor Jane with her tangled black mop and chocolate button eyes. 'She has only to look at the sun and she's as brown as a gypsy,' her grandmother had remarked acidly more than once.

After a week, she was so furious she could barely speak to Olivia. Of course she should have concentrated on Jane, gone off and done nice things as they always had, just the two of them, but every day brought Jane closer to when she would have to go back to London, where she wouldn't have anyone to take her part. Eleanor realized that the little girl had already endured years of being the odd one out, more tolerated than loved. And she, Eleanor, had done nothing to protect her except give her a couple of nice holidays.

She finally lost her temper over dinner one night. Olivia had been chattering about the twins for what seemed like hours, until Eleanor had asked her plainly whether she might manage to talk about Jane for a couple of minutes. Olivia had flushed with guilt; she wasn't a bad person, only a thoughtless one. But because she knew Eleanor was right, she overreacted. She said she would leave first thing the next morning if she wasn't welcome.

It would have been all right if Eleanor's mother hadn't been there, a sentiment she might have applied to so many occasions in her life. She would have apologized to Olivia and they would have got through the rest of the summer. Perhaps she would even have had time to gather the courage to make the move to London by September, to be closer to Jane, so that she knew all year round that she was wanted and loved. But Eleanor's mother was firm; she said Olivia should go, that it was high-time the visits ended, that coming to Cornwall was doing Jane more harm than good. The last argument had convinced Eleanor to leave it alone all these years.

When she gets to the end of her story, or a simplified version of it, she braces herself for the reaction. But Jane is dry-eyed, her brow knitted in thought rather than anger.

'So I am yours,' she says, pink staining her cheeks. 'And you are mine.'

Eleanor nods. 'Can you ever forgive me for lying all these years?'

'Yes, I can. I don't feel angry. I just feel . . . calm. It's strange.'

'If you want,' Eleanor begins, voice quavering, 'but only if you want to, of course, you can stay here with Gerald and me. I will sort everything out with your father, I promise.'

'I suppose he's my uncle. But what about Grandmother?'

'You leave her to me.'

Jane looks down at her hand on Brick's head. 'She said something to me once, you know. When I was small. She whispered it to me when you weren't there.'

'What did she say?' The quaver in Eleanor's voice has gone.

Jane takes a shaky breath. 'She said I was a changeling. I didn't know what that meant but then she said it was why I looked so different from my sisters, and then I understood. Another time she said I was a pirate child, that I'd been washed up at the cove and no one else wanted me. It seems stupid now, I suppose, but when she said it –'

She breaks off as tears stream down her cheeks.

Eleanor stands and goes over to the armchair, as she has wanted to from the beginning. She gathers Jane into her arms as best she can and rocks her gently, until Brick pushes his way into the embrace so determinedly that Jane laughs and blows her nose.

It's then that they hear something, the alien sound making both of them lift their heads. The dog's ears are already pricked.

'What's that?' says Jane.

Eleanor goes to the door, but the house beyond it is quiet. She turns off the lamps and moves to the window, pulling the blackout frame away.

She can hear it clearly now, strange and solemn on the air: a single doleful note. The thunder seems to have stopped and there's still hardly any wind to distort the sound. *As clear as a bell*, Eleanor thinks.

Gerald appears at the door, a reassuring silhouette against the brightly lit hallway. 'I feel like I must be hearing things,' he says. 'It can't be, can it?'

'It is,' Eleanor replies. 'Someone's ringing the bell at St Piran's.'

XXV

Rose is dreaming that she's swimming. She's in the sea and can't touch the bottom but she's not frightened. She's floating quite effortlessly, a gentle current carrying her along, in and out of pockets of water as warm as a bath. The sky above her is a deep, flawless blue, with no clouds in it or aeroplanes. Then the water gets rougher, so that her head goes under for a second. Beneath the surface she hears a sound, muffled and strange, its timbre summoning an image of a yellow hat with a veil that her mother used to wear to weddings and christenings.

She wakes, thinking of the cool of churches on summer days, to the distant but sonorous chime of a bell, echoing in through the flung-open windows. Putting on the lamp, she picks up her mother's watch and sees she's been asleep only twenty minutes. She glances around, her own shadow on the wall making her jump. There's no one else in the room; the other two still haven't come up. At the sight of Diana's bed, which she herself had made the previous morning, a little rush of anger and hurt flares inside her.

The bell continues to chime and she suddenly remembers the only circumstances in which church bells can be rung now they're at war. She hurries over to the window, peering behind the blackout, but there's nothing unusual to see. No shadowy hulks of surfaced U-boats out there on the water. No march of foreign boots echoing up the coast-path. Nothing but the bell, and even that stops as she withdraws from the window, its single note reverberating ominously in her head.

She puts on her dressing-gown and runs along the hall to the stairs. Eleanor is at the bottom. She looks exhausted but somehow lighter.

'I was just coming to check on you. Go into the study. Gerald's telephoning through to the police station in Fowey,' she says. 'I suppose I must go and see Mother.' Rose notes vaguely that she's still dressed.

In the study, peering through a crack in the blackout, she finds Jane. Mr Grenville is just replacing the telephone receiver with a clunk. He turns to them, a baffled expression on his face. 'Nothing,' he says. 'I got through and everything's quiet up there. No air raids, no sightings of anything out of the ordinary. Certainly no German boots on the ground. Someone's idea of a joke, perhaps? One of the Bolithos? Or what about the airmen? A few of them were pretty tight by the time they left. I think someone had put something in the punch. Had quite a kick to it.'

'Is Diana not down here?' says Rose. 'She's not upstairs.'

They shake their heads, Jane's expression hardening at the name. Rose had assumed Diana would go to Vennor when she left the garden, perhaps to find Sam. Now she wonders if her jealousy has blinded her to other, more likely, possibilities. 'All I want to do in this heat is jump in the sea,' Diana had said that afternoon, when they were adding the final touches to the orangery. 'It's the only thing that would make me feel cool and clean.'

Rose grasps the idea like a lifebelt. Diana has gone for a swim and after that, not wishing to face the wrath of the whole household, she has gone to sleep in the boathouse. Rose has never been there but she knows Diana and Jane found some old boxes and clothes, and that Diana has been there a few times alone, to be by herself. She is probably down there with her diary right now, writing about how ridiculous they all are.

Still, Rose sleeps only fitfully after Eleanor sends her back to bed. It's finally begun to rain, the parched earth swallowing it gratefully, the sea hissing as it's struck. Her dreams of drifting in the water under a perfect empty sky are replaced by strange sensations of Diana. She's saying things that Rose can't quite catch, the only clear parts of it the low, languid silk of her voice, and the laughter that catches between the words. Every so often Rose lifts her head to see if Diana has returned, but even after Jane comes to bed Diana's remains untouched, the sheets pulled straight and smooth and the pillow propped neatly at the foot because she can't bear to sleep with anything under her head. Outside, the rain continues to sheet down into a fretful sea.

XXVI

She seemed to take for ever to fall. As her arms wheeled backwards, there had been a look of utter shock on her face that might have been funny if it wasn't so terrible. Jimmy hadn't so much seen her land as heard it: the smack of bone meeting hard stone. A heavy sound with too much give in it, like an old ball thudding on sodden grass.

As he went down the steps, he tried telling himself that she would get up at any second, but he knew really that she wouldn't. He noticed the sound of the sea for the first time then; the greedy suck of it loud in his ears, like a living thing that could rise up and sweep him off the beach. Dew had told him about the wreckers once, though he hadn't wanted to know what they had done in league with that same sea, and he wondered if the cove was a haunted place, seething with ghosts the colour of fish eyes, their own sockets picked clean.

As he runs towards Vennor, he knows he'll never forget the racket of his shoes meeting the hard-baked earth of the coast-path. That and his breath, which is forced out of him each time he lands in short, shocked gasps. Inside his head, the same repeated words beat out the rhythm of his feet. *Go now. Run fast. And don't say a word. Go now. Run fast. And don't say a word.* Though they comfort him a little, he can't help crying out into the night at the highest point of the cliff: a strangled howl like an injured dog.

It's late now and the village, when he gets there, is silent. His footsteps echo hollowly on the cobbles and he wonders if there are more underground tunnels like the one Sam had shown him, the earth honeycombed like cinder toffee, with passages full of forgotten loot, and German parachutists, and the ghosts of smugglers who'd lost their way in the warren. The tunnel under the house – which Sam has sworn him to secrecy about – is where he'll go and hide now, just as they'd planned to when the invasion began. It'll be damp down there but he's got his pullover tied round his middle. He wishes she hadn't grabbed for the sleeves as she fell.

Thinking of that makes him want to sob so he hurries on towards the harbour. What light there is makes the water look like dusty black syrup. He pauses on the bridge and looks back, the air humming with a sound just too low to hear. Beyond the harbour walls, the dark mass of the sea heaves and swells. She'll still be down there, twisted and broken on the sand. She'll be dead for ever now, he thinks, and the finality of it makes him heave up his dinner, some of it splashing his shoes.

He'll hang if he tells, but he can't do nothing. He'll go to Hell otherwise. That reminds him of church, and he looks up towards the thick of the village, where he can just make out the bell-tower of St Piran's. He remembers what Sam had said could be done only in case of emergency.

He runs up the nearest lane, glad of the hill that's so steep it briefly stops him thinking about her face when she knew she couldn't save herself. When he gets there, panting and sweaty, the church door is unlocked, the latch heavy but well-greased and silent. It's cool inside, and perfectly quiet, the murmuring of the sea cut clean off.

It takes him a while to find the door to the bell-tower, and when he does, he trips twice going up the old wooden steps that are worn down in the middle. He rushes at the first rope he sees, before he can change his mind, swinging on it so it takes all his weight. He's afraid he won't do it at all unless he does it straight away, and then she'll haunt him, he knows she will. She'll come to him, her head at the wrong angle, until she drives him mad.

The bell is so heavy that the rope pulls him up with it. As he's lifted and the first huge clang floods the tower with sound, he lets go and falls in a heap to the dusty floor, hands over his ears. It rings a few more times, swinging with its own momentum, then falls silent. It's not enough. She'll still come to him unless he does it properly. He heaves on it again and again until it seems like he's already in Hell.

When he stops, exhausted, his ears are ringing so hard that he staggers. Somehow, he makes it back down the stairs and out of the door. People are already approaching the church – he can hear the nervous babble of their voices and the echo of their footsteps – but no one notices as he slips into the gloom of the churchyard and shins over the far wall, breaking into a run as soon as he lands on the other side. He doesn't realize it's started to rain until he sees his wet footprints on Menna's floor. Sinking to his knees, he begins to cry: rasping, violent sobs that leave him breathless and choking.

The wooden hatch leading down to the tunnel is so heavy that he thinks he'll never do it. In the end, he manages to jam a fistful of the rug under the lip so he can change the position of his fingers. From there, he can lift it just enough to wedge his foot into the gap, and eventually lever his whole body through.

It's pitch-black down there, after he lets the hatch thud back into place. It's not until his eyes have adjusted that he can make out a pencil-line of grey light marking out the hatch. He remembers the rug, left any-old-how. It will give him away immediately when Sam gets back. But when he tries to push the hatch back up to straighten it, not wanting to face anyone yet, he finds he's too weak, the shock of the fall and the effort in the bell-tower catching up with him, turning his muscles to water.

He sinks back down into the dark and hugs his knees to his chest, eyes screwed shut so he can't see the dark void of the tunnel ahead of him. He tries to pretend he's upstairs in his little room in the eaves but the sour smell of the tunnel makes it impossible. Instead, his thoughts steal irresistibly back towards the cove. He sees her on the sand again: a broken doll, hair splayed out around her head like weeds.

He hadn't meant to push her, not really. He had only wanted to stop her calling him those names, to stop her treating him like he was nothing – to *do something*, even though he was just a child and she was a grown-up, old enough to do as she liked with him.

XXVII

The sound of the rain has ceased by the time Rose wakes properly, the long night spent rolling in and out of disquieting dreams finally over. She hardly need look to know that Diana's bed is still empty. Padding over to one of the windows, she peers behind the blackout. The sky is a watercolour wash of palest grey but seems to brighten, even as she watches. The sea is becalmed again, though a broad brown ribbon of silt and flotsam proves that she didn't dream the previous night's weather.

The watch tells her it's almost half past five. Jane is fast asleep on her side, her knees brought up to her chest and the sheets clasped between her hands. Her eyelids flutter as she dreams. Rose carries her clothes silently to the bathroom so she doesn't wake her. When she's dressed, she finally opens the letter she's also brought with her. Her eyes trip down the page, reading so fast she can hardly make sense of the words. A good third of it is obscured by the censor's marks. It's from the captain of Frank's watch. *I'm sorry to tell you this but it's cruel to give people hope when there isn't any.*

She refolds the letter carefully and tucks it into her pocket, smoothing it down. Not wanting to face her own dry eyes in the mirror, she keeps her gaze lowered. For a moment, she makes herself picture it: the torpedo slamming into the hull of the ship, the familiar scene of the mess become fire and water; the little piece of home and order instantly obliterated. Men churned and broken and pulled down with the ship into the dark.

The sea. The same impassive sea is here too. She rushes downstairs and the lawn, when she steps out on it, is still wet. It shimmers, plumped and brilliant from the first long drink it's had in weeks. In the silence of the unbroken morning, she wonders what it may mean if Diana isn't inside the boathouse. She picks up speed, her bare feet damp in her shoes as she begins on the cinder path that will take her down to the creek.

When she pushes back the door and finds it empty, it seems horribly obvious that it would be. She looks around it anyway, though there is nowhere in the small space anyone could hide. The fear that's been swelling inside her starts to form itself into language. *Never came back. Missing all night. Nowhere to be found.* She's about to go – knowing she should run back to the house and wake Eleanor and say the same words to her, set in train a series of events that might lead somewhere awful – when her eye is caught by something pushed down the back of the armchair. It's a small leather book and she recognizes it immediately. Opening it to the first page only confirms it; she would know those irrepressible loops of dark red ink anywhere. It's Diana's diary.

Rose has always wanted to know what Diana writes. Now, a precipitous feeling of dread spreading through her, it's the last thing she wants to do. Not because of Sam; now that her thoughts are no longer skewed by drink and the oppressive atmosphere of the party, she can allow the possibility that the worst may not have happened: that Sam hasn't done anything with Diana or anyone else after all – that it was all mischief-making, and the love in his face last night was genuine. No, it's something else she's frightened of reading about.

She sits at the desk and turns the pages to find the last entry, but her mind has already gone to the darkest place she knows: to the day she got home from school and found her mother's note on the kitchen table; to the steam that billowed out when she wrenched open the bathroom door; to the livid smear of blood on porcelain. *I'm so sorry to do this to you, my darlings. I just couldn't bear not to any more. It's been so hard to carry on for as long as I have.*

She closes the diary and stands, her body vibrating with fear. 'Oh, Diana,' she whispers. 'What have you done?'

She knows she must go and check the cove. There's no reason Diana would still be down there if everything was all right, but she can't let herself think more about that for the moment or she'll be paralysed. What she thinks instead is that she should have gone down there hours and hours ago, before the rain began, before the bell started ringing. The memory of it now, its single baleful note in the dark, makes her shudder.

When she gets there, it's clear that the sea had sloshed right up inside the cove during the night. Fronds of sea-weed are drying out in curling clumps close to the lowest steps, their brown translucence like the glass of the Canadians' beer bottles.

She steps down on to the sand, her feet registering its firmness when usually it's so soft and powdery this far back that her feet sink into it. She rushes over to look inside the cold black mouth of the cave, but there's nothing inside.

She's about to leave, knowing she really must alert someone at the house, when she sees it. If she'd left it any later, she might have missed it – the strengthening sun beginning to throw shadows between the sand's undulations.

She bends to pick it up: a mother-of-pearl hair slide, curved to fit snugly against the skull. Caught in its teeth is a single hair, which gleams so brightly as the sunlight finally pierces the straggling clouds that Rose has to look away.

THREE DAYS LATER

On the Wednesday after the party, a body is found by retired oysterman Jolyon Nance, who had gone down to his usual fishing spot near the mouth of Blackbottle Creek.

Less than an hour later, the local constable, John Pascoe, and an Inspector Hector Grieves, called in from Truro, begin the steep walk to the first of several addresses they need to call on. They're hot by the time they get there, Pascoe removing his helmet to mop his forehead.

'What a day for it,' he remarks to Grieves, as he knocks on the door.

'I di'nt know she were there at first,' Jolyon says later, in the bar of the Mermaid, once he's got a pint or two down him. 'I must have been there an hour or more before I sees her hand poking up out of the water.'

What he doesn't share with the men gathered around him is that her hand was as white and coldly firm as a new candle, her dark hair like tangled seaweed, and that the thought of sitting there in ignorance of her all that time means he'll never go fishing at Blackbottle Creek again.

THE NIGHT OF THE PARTY, BEFORE THE BELL BEGAN TO RING

It was still dry when she left Breakheart Cove. By the time the Canadian airmen dropped her off at the station the rain was coming down hard. Finding themselves lost in the village lanes, they'd gladly picked her up in exchange for directions. As they drove away, tooting on the horn, she stood and let the cool rain soak into her salt-stiffened hair, only going inside when she began to shiver in the thin stuff of her dark blue dress.

'I don't suppose there are any more trains to London tonight?' she asked the man behind the counter, and at the sound of her voice, a naval officer returning to duty glanced up. He'd been waiting hours for his train – which was apparently stuck somewhere outside St Erth – and brightened at the sight of her. When it became clear she had no money to pay for her ticket, he leapt up and handed over the fare himself. She thanked him with a smile that left him temporarily dumbfounded.

As they sat down to wait for what would be the last

train of the night, he saw that she was shivering. 'Gosh, you're frozen to the bone,' he said. 'Here, take my jacket.' He placed it gently around her shoulders.

'That's better,' she said. 'Now, why don't we have a nice cigarette while we wait? I'll have to cadge one from you, though, I'm afraid. I seem to have left without any of my things.'

In the train, she pulled down the window as far as it would go. A cool breeze streamed into the carriage and in it he could smell the sea and the cooling earth of home.

'Do you think you'll ever return to Cornwall?' he asked hopefully. She was luminescent under the strange blue light of the blackout bulb, unearthly.

'Do you know, I think I might,' she said, after a pause. 'Once the dust has settled. There's a little place I've got my eye on for a friend, so I'm sure to visit her. I'm coming into some money, you see. And a house in Surrey. As of midnight, I'm twenty-one.'

He laughed and took out his hip-flask. 'It's probably undrinkably warm but we ought to have a toast if you've just come of age.' He checked his watch. 'It's five past twelve. You're free to do what you like in the world now.'

'*What I like*,' she repeated softly, her face thoughtful. And then she smiled again, and it was so dazzling that he forgot to ask her anything else.

He ran down the cove steps so fast that he nearly fell himself. At the bottom, she lay completely, awfully still. Under her head, her long hair seemed to be spreading and thickening across the sand and he couldn't work it out until he realized that it wasn't hair but blood. He stumbled back and sat down on the sand, breathing as hard as if he'd been running at full pelt.

When he looked up again, she was standing there, her dark dress sticking to her legs and her hair dripping over her shoulders. Not Menna. Diana. He'd forgotten she was even there but now he scrambled up.

'I didn't mean to,' he cried. 'Not like that. It's just that I couldn't . . . I couldn't . . .'

'You couldn't bear it any more,' she finished for him. 'I know.'

His teeth were chattering hard and she cupped his face with her hands. They were cool and smooth and smelt of the sea.

'Now listen to me carefully,' she said, her eyes looking

298

straight into his. 'You won't do any good telling anyone about this. You couldn't help it. People can't, you see, not when they're treated badly for so long and then they're given an opportunity to do something about it. A way to put an end to things, once and for all.'

'But I didn't mean to. It were an accident. I didn't . . .'

'Neither did I. I didn't go in there with any intention. But then he got hold of my hand and there was so much life still in it that I felt as though I'd never be rid of him. I knew he would get better and then it would all start again. It was easy, really, once I'd started pressing down with the pillow. He simply couldn't push me off.'

Jimmy shook his head, uncomprehending, and she met his eye again. 'Listen to me. You're going to go up those steps and then you're going to run home as fast as you can. You're my little spy, remember, and no one's seen you but me.'

He looked at her imploringly, tears starting, and she stroked his cheek, just once, as no one had since his mother. 'You had to do it,' she said. 'You couldn't help it. Just as I couldn't.' Gently, she pushed him towards the steps. Halfway up, he looked back and she nodded encouragingly.

'Go now,' she called, as the wind whipped her pale hair around her head. 'Run fast. And don't say a word.'

Acknowledgements

Huge thanks, as ever, to my wonderful husband, family, friends AND dogs. I don't know what I'd do without you. Thank you also to the fantastic Michael Joseph team, who are so supportive and lovely to work with. I am especially grateful for the expertise of Maxine Hitchcock, Hazel Orme, Clare Bowron, Claire Bush, Jenny Platt, Emma Henderson and most of all my brilliant editor Jillian Taylor, who helped me transform this book into something darker, sharper and generally *better*; a story much closer to what I'd originally set out to write. Thank you, Jill, for your unswerving conviction and buckets of reassurance. I also want to thank my amazing agent Rebecca Ritchie, who has already proved such an excellent advocate for my work and me.

I must mention Angie Butler, who kindly let me stay in her Cornish cottage for a weekend of research. A book she helped put together, *Digging for Memories, The Women's Land Army in Cornwall* (edited by Melissa Hardie and available to buy at westcountrygiants.co.uk) provided me with a great deal of insight into the women who spent the war on Cornish soil. I also had some help from Ian Neil at the shipping and mariners' charity Trinity House, to whom I directed daft questions about lighthouse operation. The usual caveat applies: any errors – whether to do with lighthouses, land girls or the war itself – are mine alone.

Lastly, I want to thank my writer friends, who have

been one of the nicest surprises of the whole publishing journey. I'm lucky enough to be part of several gangs now: two close to home, a couple more in London and one in Bristol – many of them found through Twitter. Thank you to all of you for your humour, wisdom and willingness to meet up for wine. There are a few I must mention by name: Susie Steiner, Katie Fforde, Amanda Reynolds, Hayley Hoskins, Vanessa Lafaye, Jenny Ashcroft and Emylia Hall. Brilliant women and writers all.

Also by
KATE RIORDAN

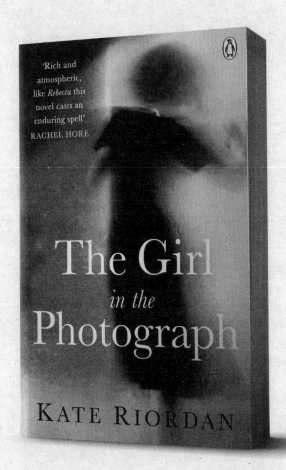

'Rich and
atmospheric,
like *Rebecca* this
novel casts an
enduring spell'
RACHEL HORE

The Girl
in the
Photograph

KATE RIORDAN

Read on for an extract . . .

Prologue: Alice

Midsummer, 1936

Fiercombe is a place of secrets. They fret among the uppermost branches of the beech trees and brood at the cold bottom of the stream that cleaves the valley in two. The past has seeped into the soil here, like spilt blood. If you listen closely enough you can almost hear what's gone before, particularly on the stillest days. Sometimes the very air seems to hum with anticipation. At other times it's as though a collective breath has been drawn in and held. It waits, or so it seems to me.

The word 'combe' means valley in some of England's south-westerly counties but the roots of 'fier' are more obscure. At first I thought it was a reference to a past inferno, or perhaps a hint of one to come. It seemed just the sort of place that would dramatically burn to the ground one night; I could imagine too easily the glow of it from the escarpment high above, smoke staining the air, the spit and pop of ancient, husk-dry timbers as the flames licked faster. But I was quite wrong: in Old English it means 'wooded hill', aptly describing the dense and disorderly ranks of hanging beech that leer and loom as you descend steeply towards the old manor house.

Things you would never accept in everyday life – strange happenings, presences and atmospheres, inexplicable lurches of time – are commonplace at Fiercombe. They have become commonplace to me. I have never grown accustomed to the darkness of night here, though. The blackness is total, like a suffocating blanket that steals over you the instant the light is turned out. When open eyes have nothing to focus on, no bar of light under the door, no chink of moonshine through heavy curtains, they strain to catch sight of something, anything. During those early nights here, my eyes would flick from where I knew the windows were to the door and back, until exhaustion turned the walls to a liquid that rose up me in oily waves.

Like a blind person, my other senses grew quickly acute for the lack of visual distraction. Even in the dead of night, when the house finally slept, I was convinced I could hear it breathe, somewhere at the very edges of my hearing, beneath the whisperings and scratchings I thought I could discern. Even in the day, when nothing looked out of the ordinary, I would still find my skin prickling with the vibrations of the place, something instinctive and animal in me knowing that things had been knocked out of balance, that something had gone awry.

I have been here a little over three years now, since the late spring of 1933. When I arrived from London I was not quite six months' pregnant by a man I wasn't married to. A man married to someone else. If it hadn't been for him and my own foolishness, and the subsequent horror and shame of my parents, then I would never have come to Fiercombe at all. What a strange thought that is now, after all that has happened.

When I think back to the time before I came here, it feels like someone else's life, read in a book. It's difficult for me to recapture how I truly felt about things then; how I went about my normal routine of working, the evening meal with my parents, going to the lido or the pictures with my friend Dora, and daydreaming about the man I thought I was in love with. I see now that I wasn't very grown-up.

I came just as spring was softening and deepening into languid summer. It was a beautiful summer – more beautiful than any I've known before or since – though I was still glad to put it behind me when autumn finally arrived. Too glad, perhaps. There were rifts in the valley that remained unhealed as the leaves began to turn but I was too busy forging my own new beginning to acknowledge them. The signs and clues were there; I simply chose not to heed them. I have let three years of contented life in the present chase away the unresolved past, just as the morning sun does the nightmare. Today's confession has changed all that and I can no longer turn away. They deserve better. They always did.

Alice

In the summer of 1932 I had never heard of a place called Fiercombe. I was still living an ordinary sort of life then. A life that someone else, looking in, would probably have thought rather dull. That was certainly how I viewed it, though I was reluctant to admit that at the time, even to myself. After all, admitting it also meant facing the likelihood that nothing more interesting awaited me on the horizon.

It wasn't until after I left school that I began to feel a creeping sort of restlessness. I had got a full scholarship to the local grammar and I had liked it there – not just for the solace of its rituals and order but for its pervading sense of purposeful preparation. Preparation for what was to come after: the tantalizing, unknowable future. What shape that would take I had no idea. Much of its allure lay in its very amorphousness, the vague sense of expectation that edges closest on those perfect summer evenings of which England never seems to have enough. Evenings gilded with twilight, the perfumed air brimming with promise. Yet the mornings after those evenings always seemed to go on in the normal way – the world shrunk to a familiar room again, consoling but uninspiring, the walls near enough to touch.

Quite suddenly, or so it felt, school was long behind

me and I was a woman of twenty-two. Still nothing of any note had happened to me. I remained at home with my parents, I had a job that I could have done perfectly adequately in my sleep, and there was no sense that whatever I had blithely expected to lift me clear of the mundane was any nearer. If anything, it seemed to have retreated.

My mother was no less frustrated by my lack of progress – though for rather different reasons. I was a good-looking girl, she told me somewhat grudgingly, so why did I never mention any gentlemen friends? Why was I not engaged, or even courting? After the milestone of my twenty-second birthday had passed, she aired those anxieties with ever-increasing frequency, her expression at once baleful and triumphant.

Triumphant, I suppose, because she had never really wanted me to go to the grammar school, believing that girls with too many brains were fatally unattractive to prospective husbands. Though the shortage of men after the Great War had been the crisis of an older generation, there lingered a sense of urgency for unmarried girls, at least in my mother's mind. She also professed not to see the point of school beyond the legal leaving age of fourteen. Anything after that was for boys, and girls with plain faces, she said. After all, no woman could keep her job after her wedding anyway.

For the time being, my own job – one I knew I was fortunate to have when so many had no work – contributed to the household budget, an aspect of it that even my mother couldn't criticize. Each morning I took a bus south to Finsbury Park, where I caught the Piccadilly line to Russell Square. Just off the square was the office where

I was the junior of two typists to a Mr Marshall, a minor publisher of weighty academic books. I had a smart suit I had saved to buy rather than make, and two handbags between which I transferred the gold-plated compact my aunt had bought me one Christmas.

On my first day I had felt rather sophisticated as I walked to the bus stop, the pinch of my new court shoes a grown-up and therefore pleasurable kind of discomfort. A few years on from that hopeful morning and I still occasionally felt a vestige of that early pride – it was just that sometimes, particularly during the afternoons, which were so quiet I could hear the ponderous tick of the clock mounted on the wall, I couldn't help wondering when my life – my real life – would begin.

I had never had any sort of serious attachment to a man. Perhaps the closest I'd come was a boy at school, whom I'd let kiss me a few times. At the grammar, some of the lessons were mixed and David had been in my French class. He'd thought he was in love with me during the last summer we spent there and, during those drowsy afternoons, when the high windows were opened and the smell of cut grass made us long for the bell, he would stare at me across the room. His gaze made my skin tingle warmly, and left me conscious of how I sat, how my hair was arranged, and what facial expression I wore. But the truth of it was not love, or probably even lust. What I liked was the way he felt about me, and I'm sure he was more in love with the sudden intensity of his feelings than he was with the girl in the next row.

Now many of my friends – David Gardiner too, in all probability – were married or engaged, or at the very least courting, yet I had failed to meet anyone. Dora, who was forever trying to persuade me out to meet a friend of whichever man she was currently interested in, teased me gently for being so fussy. My mother, being my mother, was rather more direct.

'You'll be left on the shelf if you don't get a move on,' she said one Saturday, when I had been made to accompany her shopping on our local high street in a north London suburb. 'I've said it before and no doubt I'll say it again, but if you spent less time reading and more time out and about in the fresh air or going to dances, you'd give yourself a better chance.'

I remember we were in the chemist's shop, which was hushed except for my mother's voice and the bell that trilled whenever the door opened. The air smelt of floral talc and carbolic soap, and faintly bitter from the medicines and tonics that were measured and weighed out of sight.

We had an argument then – about lipstick of all the ridiculous things: she wanted me to buy a brighter shade than I could imagine myself wearing. That led to other topics of discord and by the time we were walking home, past the new cafe that had just opened opposite Woolworths, we had returned to the subject of my job and her conviction that I would never meet anyone if I remained in it.

'Why don't you try for work in there?' she said, nodding towards a girl behind the cafe's plate glass, pert in her smart uniform with its starched white collar.

Shifting the bags I was carrying to my other hand, I couldn't rouse myself to reply.

'I know you're a typist in an office in town, and that's all very fancy,' my mother continued, 'but May Butler's daughter Lillian met her husband when she was waitressing and look at her now, with a house in Finchley and a little one on the way.'

Lillian had left school at fourteen and eventually got a job as a Nippy in a Lyons Corner House on the Strand. According to my mother, Lillian had been admired half a dozen times a day by her male customers, solitary men in suits who'd come in for a plate of chops or some tea and toast. Eventually, apparently without much ado, she had married one of them.

'I don't want to be a waitress,' I said wearily.

'You shouldn't turn your nose up at it – you don't earn much more than the ones in the nice places do.'

'Yes, but I –'

'Oh, I know you think you're meant for better things but it hasn't happened yet, has it? And it won't while you're stuck up there with old Mr Marshall.'

What she could not possibly have known was that only a week after that desultory wander around the shops I would at last meet a man I actually desired, someone who would bring the world to life for me, at least for a time. In fact, the circumstances that would throw us together were already in train: an appointment made, a crucial hour already approaching. For it was in Mr Marshall's office – the obscure, dusty office my mother believed had already sealed my spinsterhood – that everything was about to change for me.

As if to further dramatize this episode, to darken the line that marked before and after, he arrived towards the end of a particularly silent, stultifying day. I remember that he was a little out of breath after climbing the stairs to our small office. A late summer shower was flooding the pavements outside and he brought with him the smell of damp wool and cologne as he came noisily through the door. Mr Marshall heard it crash back on its hinges and came rushing out of his tiny room to greet the new arrival, whom he had obviously been expecting. They made a curious pair: Mr Marshall, an inch shorter than me and probably half a stone lighter, only came up to his visitor's chest.

'Who was that?' I said to Miss Cunningham, after they had gone out to lunch, Mr Marshall not having thought to introduce us. Miss Cunningham was the senior typist and didn't like me very much, perhaps because she knew I didn't aspire to her job.

'Mr Elton? He's too old and too married for you to concern yourself with,' she replied crisply.

After I had made her a cup of tea she relented, unable to resist demonstrating that she knew more than I did.

'He's the new accountant, if you must know. The old one's retired and now we've got him. Bit too sure of himself, if you ask me.' She sniffed and went back to her work.

They didn't return from lunch for two hours, and when they did, Mr Marshall was uncharacteristically flushed, eyes glazed behind his spectacles. Miss Cunningham got up and pointedly opened a window, though I couldn't smell any alcohol on them; only the rain and the new accountant's cologne.

While she was at the window he crossed the room towards me and I saw that his eyes were the same shade of deep brown as his hair. He didn't have a single feature that stood out as exceptional but they combined in such a way as to make him handsome.

'Pleased to meet you,' he said, his voice low and unhurried. 'I'm James Elton.' He shook my hand. His was warm and dry. 'I've met the lovely Miss Cunningham, of course, but you are?'

'Alice,' I said, more bluntly than I'd meant to because I was thinking about my hand being cold. I was forever cold in that office, regardless of the season. 'Alice Eveleigh.'

When I left work a couple of hours later he was waiting for me in the cafe that I had to pass to reach the Underground. I spotted him before he saw me: sitting up at the window on a stool that looked silly and feminine beneath him. If he hadn't glanced up from his paper at that moment, and raised his hand with a smile, I would certainly have walked on. It would never have occurred to me to tap on the window.

Of course, I didn't know then that he'd been waiting for me; he didn't tell me that until later. Instead, he smiled his easy smile and, when I hesitated, gestured for me to come in and join him. We had some tea and he tried to persuade me to order a slice of sponge cake. We talked about this and that: London, the weather, of course, and what I thought of my job in Mr Marshall's quiet office. I said, rather primly, that I was very grateful to have it and he grimaced, which made us both laugh.

That was the beginning. Shared pots of tea became habitual until one fog-bound autumn evening he appeared out of the shadows as I left the office for the day and suggested that we had dinner together. It was too filthy a night for a paltry cup of tea, he said. Perhaps we might try this little restaurant he had discovered down a nearby back-street.

Afterwards, on the way to the Underground, he stopped and pulled me towards him. I would like to say I resisted but I simply couldn't. In truth, my face was already tilted up towards him before his lips touched mine. You find that once something like that has happened, it's very hard to go back to how it was before.

He was almost fifteen years older than me. When I was eight or nine, a schoolgirl with pale brown hair cut to the jaw, he was a newly minted accountant. Each morning he took the Metropolitan line into the City, his briefcase un-scuffed, his newness such that he had not yet earned a regular seat on the carriage he always boarded.

His wife, when she came along, was a suitable, pretty girl called Marjorie. His domineering mother apparently approved; she and Marjorie's mother played bridge together, I think. He once mentioned in passing that Marjorie was an excellent tennis player, which I found both intimidating and fascinating.

When I met him he was thirty-six, already eleven un-imaginable years into his unhappy union. He once said that you would imagine time spent like that would crawl by – the inverse of it flying when you are enjoying yourself. But in fact those years, packed tight with obligation – the tennis doubles and dinner parties and whist drives – had been compressed.

Once, when I think he must have been rather drunk, he confided that Marjorie didn't like the physical side of marriage much. He was desperately unhappy, he told me, time and time again. They had made a terrible mistake when they got married; they had never really loved each other; the whole thing had been engineered by their mothers.

After that first kiss, I went around in a fug of guilt and excitement. I didn't confide in anyone, not even Dora. I knew that, despite all her casually knowledgeable talk of men, she had never gone beyond a certain point and would never dream of doing so with a married man. You simply didn't, and the boys we had grown up with knew it as well as we did.

When I wasn't with him I thought about him constantly, indulging myself in the delicious agony of it all and mooning about, like a girl in a sentimental song. Precisely like that, in fact: it was around that time that Dora bought a gramophone record of Noël Coward's new song, 'Mad About The Boy', and played it endlessly. Every day I felt queasy as I walked past the cafe on my way home from work – in case he was there, waiting, and in case he never was again.

He didn't appear for three weeks after the kiss and I felt eaten away by misery. When I finally saw him in the cafe one evening, head bent over his newspaper, it was as though the whole world – the sour breath of London's air, the hollow clip of women's heels and the rumble of the Piccadilly line's trains far below – ceased to be. I knew that nothing would have persuaded me to keep walking. I had been a nice, bookish sort of girl, and now I was someone different. I felt as though my life was out of my hands. It was like an attack of vertigo.

I only went to bed with him once, at a hotel. Of course,

that's all that's required, as anyone with their wits about them knows. Although it didn't occur to me then, I'm fairly sure I wasn't the first woman with whom he had been involved since his marriage. No doubt there had been dalliances, illicit kisses stolen, rooms booked for a couple of hours, even. He once took me to a nightclub tucked down an obscure lane behind Oxford Street that was so suitable for the job – with its shadowy corners, unobtrusive waiters and melancholy jazz music – that he must have discovered it in the course of some other liaison. I don't think I'd have minded that, though, even if I had realized it at the time. I think his attraction lay in his worldliness and how truly grown-up he seemed, so different from my own despised girlishness.

It was Dora who guessed the truth; I suppose I wasn't facing what was obvious at all. It was April by then and the weather had abruptly turned into something that felt like summer. One Sunday she rang the doorbell. I hadn't seen her in weeks, just as I hadn't seen James – who had disappeared without a word after our visit to the hotel. I stood at the top of the stairs and heard my mother asking her in. When she called me I went down reluctantly, knowing I looked pale and that my hair needed washing.

'Dora's come to see you,' said my mother. 'She thought you might go to the lido together.'

I smiled wanly at Dora. 'I don't think I will, if you don't mind. I don't feel very well.'

'You don't feel well because you're either at work in that office or cooped up in here,' retorted my mother. 'Go and get your things. Dora's come specially to see you. Where are your manners?'

I found I did feel a bit better out in the air. The lido was thronged with people; it was the first really warm day of the year and every last deckchair had been taken. Dora was lean in her bathing suit – mine felt tight and uncomfortable even though I'd been eating little. Before anyone could look at me I jumped into the unheated water, the shock of it dissolving the lead weight of my misery for a blissful few seconds.

After we'd swum, Dora wanted a drink. With our towels wrapped around ourselves we wandered into the relative gloom of the cafeteria. It was almost empty: everyone was sitting outside on the viewing terrace. I can't think why anyone would have wanted hot food on a day like that but they were frying something in the kitchen, the cloying smell of stale oil wafting through a hatch. I had hardly eaten that day but what little I'd had came up into my mouth. The thought of swallowing it made me retch again and I heaved into my cupped hands.

'Oh,' I said, and began to cry.

Dora took me to the ladies' lavatories and washed my face and hands for me, as if I was a child.

We looked at each other in the mirror. Her face was sharp and rosy; I was pallid and blurry-looking next to her, my brown hair lank on my shoulders.

'Please tell me you're not, Alice,' she said. 'Not you.'

'Not what?' I said, but, as I spoke, I knew.

'How long?' she said.

'I don't know it's that. I miss a month here and there. I always have.' My voice sounded desperate even to myself. 'Besides, it was only once.'

Dora simply stared at me. I tried to think of another

excuse but instead hung my head, the tears silently dripping off my nose and into the basin. A woman about my mother's age came out of the furthest cubicle and washed her hands next to me. In the mirror I saw her eyes flick over to my left hand, her lip curling with disapproval when she saw it was bare. She bustled out with her hands still wet.

'Will you get rid of it?' Dora said softly.

My stomach churned with fear at the decisions that had materialized from nowhere but now lay ahead, inescapable. 'It's against the law,' I whispered.

'I know that. People do, though.'

'I can't bear to think about it. I wish I could just lock myself in my room and never come out.'

'Why on earth did you let him?'

'He's getting a divorce. He said he wanted to marry me.'

'Oh, Alice.'

'What?' I said. 'What do you know of it? You're quite content to go to the pictures with a different man each week and you don't care about any of them. I suppose one day you'll just marry whichever of them happens to be taken with you at the time. I'm not like that. James and I love each other.'

Dora dried her hands on the roller towel. 'Have it your way, then. You obviously don't need my shoulder to cry on.'

She pulled open the door and looked back at me. 'I think you've been a perfect fool,' she said. 'I don't understand you, Alice, not any more.'

After she'd gone, I stood for a time, looking at myself in the mirror. I couldn't quite make myself believe what now seemed glaringly obvious.

When I got outside, Dora had gone, my clothes and shoes left in a neat pile. Feeling limp and dazed, I sat down and stayed there in the spring sunshine for an hour or more, watching the mothers and their children in the shallow end of the pool. The sound of the nearby fountain was soothing and I think I must have dozed for a while. When I woke, there was a wonderful second before I remembered the awful, incomprehensible fix I had got myself into. I sat up and tried to hug my knees close to myself, noticing with a shudder that it was now uncomfortable to do so. I stared down into the turquoise depths of the lido's perfectly oval pool until my vision swam with tears, which I blinked surreptitiously into my towel before any well-meaning person asked me what could be wrong on such a lovely day.

Of course, there was no conceivable way I could become a mother out of wedlock. Not just because I was woefully unprepared for it but because it would ruin my reputation. Needless to say, my parents would be mortified. I had been allowed to stay on at school because I had been good at my books. That would count for nothing now. I would lose my job and the wages that had made my parents' lives more comfortable. I had always been such a sensible girl. At the grammar, our teachers had told Dora's parents that I was an excellent influence on their more impetuous daughter, who hadn't got a scholarship like me and whose bank clerk father paid fees to keep her there.

Yet Dora would never have got herself into such a terrible mess. Impetuous she might have been, but she was never naïve. When she told me some of the romantic nonsense men had whispered to her, while sliding an arm around her shoulders at the Empire on a Saturday night, she always rolled her eyes. She knew what they were about while I, despite my cleverness, was as innocent as a child. I cast my mind back to all that James had said to me and understood why I had never told Dora about it. Somewhere in me, I had known she would laugh at me for being so easily taken in.

On my way home, while I still felt some semblance of resolve, I decided to do what I knew had to be done. I wasn't sure the pregnancy counted yet; I was barely three months gone and I hadn't felt a thing, apart from the sickness. There were medicines you could take but I didn't know exactly what or how much to ask for. If I went into a chemist's and asked for quinine or pennyroyal – both of them sounding like relics of evidence from a Victorian poisoning – wouldn't they guess what it was for?

In the end I bought a small bottle of cheap gin, telling the disinterested girl who took the money that it was for my father, and that evening ran myself a scalding bath. I was terrified my mother would smell the alcohol fumes on the steam so stuffed the gap under the door with a towel. As the water slowly cooled and the gin swirled into my blood I grew so dizzy and sleepy that I almost fainted. I couldn't even do that right, I thought, as I finally sat up and pulled out the plug. I'd nearly drowned myself instead of finishing what had scarcely begun inside me. I woke up the next morning with a nauseous, clamping headache, a furred mouth and a feeling of acute misery, but there was no blood.

I somehow endured a week at the office but the long, empty hours of the next Sunday undid me. Saying I was going out for some fresh air, I made the familiar journey to Dora's house.

'I'm sorry I called you a fool,' she said, once we were safely in her bedroom.

'No, you were right,' I said. 'I've been completely stupid.'

She sat up against her pillows. 'Have you thought about what you're going to do?'

I swallowed. 'I bought some gin but it didn't work. All I managed to do was nearly faint.'

'You do look awful,' she said, with her usual frankness. 'I'll have to tell Mother you've got a cold.'

'I was going to go to the chemist's,' I continued desperately, 'but I didn't know what to ask for. Then I thought of bumping myself down the stairs but I can't very well do that when my mother and father are in, can I?'

Dora stifled a giggle of hysteria. 'I'm sorry, Alice. I always laugh when I shouldn't, you know I do. The whole thing is just so awful. I can't really believe it yet.'

I sat down on the end of the bed and put my head in my hands.

'I've heard that Beecham's powders can work if you take enough of them,' she said. 'And washing soda, though I can't think how anyone would be able to force that down.'

'I think it's too late for all that. Perhaps if I'd done it weeks ago but now . . . I feel like it's taken hold, somehow. I don't think anything would work except . . .'

Dora sighed and covered my hand with hers. 'I think it's the only way. You can't possibly go ahead and have it.'

'No.'

We sat in silence for a few minutes until Dora spoke quietly. 'I know where you might go, I've been thinking about it. I heard Mother talking about someone once, when she thought I was upstairs. Remember she was a nurse before she married Father? Well, there was a midwife she knew then. They weren't friends or anything but she knew her. Anyway, it turns out that she does them in her kitchen. She lives in one of those streets the other side of the green, beyond the Empire. I know where it is because Mother said it was two doors up from the sweet shop on the corner. She said what a disgrace it was, all those innocent children walking past a house like that. We could easily go there one evening and no one would ever know. She charges two guineas – I'm sure that's what Mother said.'

'What do they do to it to get it out?' My voice was a whisper.

'I don't really know. I think they give you something to make it sort of come away, and then it's just like having your monthlies, only heavier.'

I nodded slowly because there was nothing else for it.

A few evenings later, Dora and I stood at a drab-coloured door. The woman who let us in was short and squat, her enormous, shelf-like bust emphasized by a dark apron.

'Don't just stand on the step, then,' she said, ushering us into a dingy hallway that smelt of boiled vegetables and something sharper.

After closing the door briskly, the evening sun shut out with a bang, she gestured for us to follow her towards the back of the house. Once in the kitchen, she looked at us enquiringly. When I didn't say anything, Dora spoke up.

'We've come ... Well, we've come for my friend,' she gestured at me, 'because she needs ...'

'I can guess why you're here,' said the woman, bluntly. 'I like to take payment first.'

'We were told it would be two guineas.' I could hear the tremor in Dora's voice.

The woman nodded. 'That's right.'

I took the money from my purse and put it into her outstretched hand. She transferred it deftly to the front pocket of her apron.

'Now then, lovey, how far gone are you?' she said, the endearment at odds with the situation.

'About three months,' I whispered.

'Not as late as some,' she replied. 'What have you tried already?'

I stared at her blankly and Dora broke in: 'She had some gin and a hot bath.'

'When it's taken, a bit of drink and warm water won't shift it,' the woman said. She pointed to a narrow table in the corner of the room. 'Take your underclothes off and get up on there. We'll soon have it done.'

I must have looked frightened because her face softened a shade. 'I've been a midwife for thirty years,' she said. 'I know what I'm about. You'll be right as rain in a few days. You've just got to think of it like we're bringing your monthlies on because they're late.'

I removed my shoes, stockings and knickers and folded them neatly on top of my handbag. I clambered up on to the table awkwardly, with Dora helping me, but kept my skirt pulled down and my legs together. Dora's hand on my arm was clammy.

I looked around the room, noticing a tray of congealed dripping on the side. Once I had, I thought I could smell it and it made my stomach turn. Through a smeary window I could see part of a yard, the door of an outhouse and a sagging line of washing.

Dora gave my arm a hesitant pat, then went to stand by the door. I knew how much she wanted to run back to her pretty bedroom, where she could lose herself in her magazines about Joan Crawford and Greta Garbo, the new vanishing cream and the latest permanent wave. I would have given anything to do that myself.

The woman unscrewed a jar, the contents of which she poked at with a spoon.

'What's in there?' said Dora.

'Slippery elm and a bit of pennyroyal,' she replied, without looking up.

'Do I drink it?' I said stupidly.

She laughed mirthlessly. 'You're an innocent one, that's for sure. Why would I have you undress for that? No, we put this up there to bring it on.'

I glanced at Dora but her gaze was fixed on the jar. 'Does it always work?' I said.

'It opens you up so I can have a proper look.' She unwrapped a metal knitting needle from a piece of cloth. 'You've nothing to worry about. I'll heat this up so it's sterilized.'

The needle was identical to those my mother had at home; I could picture a pair of them stuck in a ball of wool next to the wireless.

I scrambled down from the table and began dressing before I consciously decided to. Dora didn't move to stop me. The woman pulled out the needle she'd laid in the grate and clattered it down next to the dripping tray.

'Now then, don't get yourself all worked up. It'll be over before you know it. You don't want this baby, do you?'

I shook my head. 'But I don't want this either,' I said breathlessly. I felt as if I would collapse if I didn't leave that kitchen.

'Please yourself,' said the woman, crossing her arms across her chest as she watched me fumble with my shoes.

'Alice, are you sure?' said Dora. 'You can't afford anything else. A private doctor would be twenty times as much.'

'Let's go. Please, Dora.'

'Here,' said the woman, her hand in her apron pocket. 'I'll keep a guinea for my trouble, but you can have the rest back. God knows you're going to need it more than me in six months' time.'

The truth of the matter was not that I couldn't bear to have an abortion; it was that in the moment, I was more viscerally afraid of letting that woman put a dirty knitting needle inside me than I was of having a baby. Because, however hard I tried, I simply couldn't imagine that at all; the notion of it was as ungraspable as wet soap on porcelain.

When I got home, I caught sight of my face in the hall mirror. It was the colour of chalk. My mother was alone in the kitchen, washing the best china. She looked up when I came in, studying me for a moment before turning back to the sink. 'Are you going to tell me what's wrong with you?' she said, as she continued with the plates, the water steaming hot, her hands already puce. The clean china squeaked as she lifted each piece out of the bowl and placed it in the rack.

I leant against the cupboards, which hadn't altered since I was a baby, toddling around and getting under her feet. I got the biscuit barrel out for something to do and the action of easing off the stiff metal lid was so familiar that I nearly cried.

'What do you mean?' I said feebly.

Always sharp, she looked over her shoulder at me. 'Tell me the truth, Alice. I'm your mother. You've been acting peculiar for weeks now.'

The tears came then and I couldn't stop them, though I was at least silent about it, biting the inside of my cheek so that I didn't sob. They ran down my cheeks and began to soak into the collar of my blouse.

Without moving from the sink, she sighed. 'It's a man, isn't it?'

'Yes,' I managed to get out. 'But it's ended now.'

'So you've had your heart broken. Well, men will disappoint. Doesn't he want to marry you?'

'He can't.'

At that she turned. 'What do you mean he can't? I hope he doesn't think he's too good for you. Where does he live?'

I shook my head and she stared at me for a long moment.

'What, then?' she said but, as she did, I saw the possibility enter her mind. I watched her features seem to harden and narrow.

'Oh, so it's like that, is it?'

I looked down at the lino that was always sticky underfoot, however hard it was scrubbed.

'Answer me, girl! Is he married?'

'Yes, but he said –'

'He said what? That she was mad? That she had run away to sea? What nonsense did he have you believe?'

My voice was barely more than a whisper. 'He said that they had never been happy, that they would get a divorce.'

My mother tutted in disgust. 'And it never occurred to you that he would say that? I thought you were supposed to be the clever one.'

I wiped my face with the back of my hand.

'I did not bring you up to gad about with other people's husbands. You've never shown any interest in a man before – I was convinced you'd be a spinster all your life. And now this. The only thing to be thankful for is that he's thrown you over now, before things could get any worse.'

She dried her hands and leant back against the sink, arms crossed. 'I hope you've at least had the sense to keep this to yourself,' she continued, after a pause. 'That Dora's flighty enough to tell her mother. I can see *her* face now, pretending sympathy, when I next see her on the high street.'

'Dora won't say anything.'

My mother sniffed. 'We'll see.'

I took a breath. 'Mother, I won't be seeing him again but –'

'There should be no buts about it. You've had a narrow escape, by the sound of it. It's her I feel sorry for, the wife. Someone should tell her.'

My legs were trembling with the effort of not running

from the room. 'Mother, please listen. It was only once but I think . . . I feel awful every morning. My waistbands are tighter, though I haven't been eating much and –'

She went white with shock and put her hand back, blindly clutching at the sink's edge for support. 'You're not . . . ?'

I looked down, my heart beating wildly in my chest.

'Alice!' Her voice was jagged. 'Tell me. Are you pregnant?'

I swallowed, then forced myself to look up. 'I don't know.' I paused. 'Yes, I'm almost certain of it.'

'How long?' She was too horrified to shout.

'I – well, I –'

'Have you felt the quickening yet?'

I stared at her, confused.

'The quickening. That's when you know. You feel it inside, I can't explain it. You might be too early for it yet. It comes around three months.'

'I haven't felt anything like that. Just the sickness.'

'Some people think it doesn't count until you feel it. You must know how long it's been unless you're lying about it only happening the once.' She looked me straight in the eye.

'I'm not lying about that. It's three months,' I said quietly.

'Well, that's that, then. At three months it's taken. You can't do away with it that late and, besides, I've always thought that was a wicked thing to do. No, you'll go through with it now. And when it's born, you'll give it up.'

We stood in silence for a few minutes. I wondered what James was doing right at that moment to the north-west, where London seeped into the countryside. I wondered if he'd had dinner yet, cooked and served by his wife. I wondered whether I had crossed his mind at all.

'Go to your room now, Alice. I don't want to look at you. I need to think about this and to speak to your father.'

Little more was said until just over a week later. I spent the intervening days in a state of numbness, scarcely able to think coherently about the baby or what my mother would eventually say. In the end, my fate was announced after dinner, in the room with the display cabinet full of ugly china figurines and the gilt-framed print of Constable's *Hay Wain* above the mantelpiece. I suppose it was the only time the three of us were together.

'We've made up our minds, your father and I,' she began, after we'd eaten in near-silence. This was it, I thought. The next part of my life – perhaps all of it – would come down to this conversation.

As my mother began to speak, I glanced at my father but he was looking down at the tablecloth. His face was grey and thin with worry and shock, skin stretched too tautly over fine bones. She must have told him while I was out at work.

It was always stuffy in the front room. Next door, Mrs Davies was running a bath for her two young children. I could hear the water sluicing through the pipes in the walls. Unable to sit still, I picked with my nail at the faceted glass of the vinegar bottle until my mother pointedly moved it out of my reach.

'Now listen carefully, my girl,' she said. 'I wrote to Edith Jelphs last week. It's all arranged.'

'Edith Jelphs?' My mind cast around to place the name.

The memory came to me in a rush: an afternoon so bright that the curtains in my parents' bedroom had been pulled across and were lifting inwards on a soft breeze. My mother, mellowed by the weather, had let me look through her tin box of mementoes while she changed the sheets. I remembered being struck for the first time that she wasn't the sort of person who kept anything for its own sake and wondered why she had saved the contents of the tin.

'She's the girl in the photograph,' I said now.

'What photograph?'

'The one of you as a girl in Painswick.'

Though she seemed utterly at home in London, my mother had grown up in rural Gloucestershire. I had gone there with her as a child.

'Trust you to remember that,' she said. 'Yes, I'd forgotten I had that. She's housekeeper at Fiercombe, has been for years.'

'Fiercombe?'

'Have you not heard of it? And you, with your nose forever stuck in a book. It's an estate not far from Painswick. She went there as a maid when she was young and never left.'

'What's all this got to do with me, Mother?'

I think I knew then, but wanted to hear how she said it.

'It's all arranged,' she said again, her face implacable. 'You'll go when you start to really show. Edith was very good about it, wrote as soon as she could to say that you might, and to think we haven't spoken all these years. The family live abroad most of the year so you won't see them. She told them about your situation and it looks like someone's taken pity on you. You'll get bed and board in exchange for some light duties to pay your way. A bit of dusting, mending, that sort of thing.'

I remained silent. My father gazed absently out of the window. His foot was jiggling under the table; I could feel the movement through the floor. I knew he was desperate for the conversation to be over so he could go back out to his beloved garden and be wrapped in the undemanding cover of dusk. 'And what if I don't want to go?' I said, a childish stubbornness briefly surfacing.

'You'll go, all right. You've made your father ill with worry. Look at him.' She stood and reached over the table to grip my chin. 'I said, look at him. He's been so proud of you, doing well at the grammar and then getting your job, and this is what you do. No husband of your own so you get yourself into trouble with someone else's. Besides, what choice do you have? It's either Fiercombe or a mother-and-baby home in some godforsaken place. And who's going to pay for that, I'd like to know? No, you'll go to Gloucestershire until it's born.'

She sat down again and smoothed her skirt over her lap, a thoughtful expression on her face. 'I trust Edith Jelphs. I knew her as a child. This is for the best, and after all we've done for you, Alice, it's the least you can do.'

I glanced at my father and his eyes met mine briefly. They were full of sadness but there was something else there I had never seen. I suppose it was disappointment.

I swallowed the sob that rose in my throat as he got wearily to his feet and went out, closing the door quietly behind him.

My mother waited until his steps had died away. 'Alice, I know you think I'm too hard on you, that I've always been hard on you, but look what you've done – not just to yourself but to me and your father. There's many who would have disowned a daughter for this but we haven't so you'll do as we say. It's that or you'll be destitute.'

I knew she was right.

'You're best off at Fiercombe,' she continued. 'I've told Edith Jelphs that you were a newlywed who had only just found out she was expecting when her husband got himself killed. Knocked down by a motor-car on his way to work.'

Despite the roiling anxiety in my stomach, I almost laughed. 'You said what?'

'You heard me. She and the family would never have agreed to it if they'd known the truth. I said in my letter that you'd had a dreadful shock and that the doctor had said you must get away from London – for your own health, as well as the baby's. That your nerves might never recover unless you had some peace and quiet in a new place that had none of the old associations.'

She looked satisfied with the story she'd woven for me and I found myself almost admiring her inventiveness. I would arrive in Gloucestershire as a grieving widow rather than a fallen woman while she played the role of concerned mother from a distance – someone following doctor's orders for the good of her daughter's fragile health, not to mention her future grandchild's. It was perfect. She had even dug out my grandmother's narrow wedding band.

'Don't you lose that now,' she said, as I slipped it on, already feeling like a fraud. I shook my hand and found the ring fitted as though it had been made for me. 'You'll keep to that story if you know what's good for you,' she continued. 'This way, no one will talk behind your back or give you dirty looks for being in your condition and on your own – not like they would here, where they know there was never any husband, knocked over or otherwise. Your father couldn't have borne that sort of talk about you. You won't even have to do much around the house, by the sound of it. Edith said there was a maid who came in most mornings and that you could "recuperate properly" until the baby came.'

'When am I to go?' I felt unbelievably tired.

'Like I said, when you start to show. When you can't work any more. Another month or so, if you're like I was.'

'I'm not like you, though.'

'You're in no position to speak to me like that, young lady. I don't know if you realize the fix you've got yourself into. If you don't go, there's nowhere for you but the workhouse and let's see how far your grammar-school education gets you there. Don't think other girls like you haven't ended up there without a penny to their name. Sure as eggs, they have.'

She got up and reached for the cruet set. Her rings clinked against it as she picked it up, along with the butter dish and the teapot.

'Get the door for me, will you?' she said.

Mr Marshall, to my great surprise, seemed to notice me for the first time when I told him I had to leave my position in order to look after my sick mother. He wrote me an excellent reference and said my mother was lucky to have such a good daughter. It was more than I deserved or expected. I'm not sure if Miss Cunningham believed my story but, thankfully, she chose to remain silent on the matter. When I thought of all the lies my mother and I had crafted between us – her illness, my dead husband – I felt quite ill myself, but what other choice was there? None, as far as I could see.

The weeks leading to the day of my departure felt like an age. One afternoon during my last week at work I felt desperate enough to go and see James at his office, having dug out the address when Miss Cunningham went for lunch. I had the deluded idea that if I told him about the baby he would make everything all right. In the event, I knew from the moment I saw him that he would be horrified and left without saying a word about the pregnancy.

I finished work three weeks before I was due to leave; I was beginning to show too much to risk staying there any longer. After that, time dragged unbearably, with nothing to occupy my mind but my memories of James, the enormous mistake I had made and dread that I was soon to be exiled to a place where I knew no one. Dora came round when she could but her job at the local department store meant I was alone with my mother most of the time. I hadn't spent so many consecutive hours in her company for years, and the cloud of tight-lipped disapproval that seemed to hover around her turned the house into something like a prison. As if to rub salt in my wounds, I dreamt of James most nights – happy, serene dreams that were shattered on waking: contentment turned to misery. I became adept at crying silently into my pillow so my parents wouldn't hear.

On my last afternoon, I went to the local library in

order to escape the house. I hadn't been there since I was a schoolgirl, when Dora would have been in tow and protesting at the Goody Two Shoes worthiness of it. I had always liked the hushed atmosphere, though, and wished I'd visited more often.

It was almost empty by the time I got there, with nothing to be heard but the murmurings of an unseen conversation, the thud of books being stamped and the whispering of the trees that crowded at the tall Victorian windows.

I wandered around until I found myself in the history section. Idly scanning the names of kings, queens and fallen dynasties I hadn't thought of since studying for matriculation, my eye was snagged by a huge tome entitled *England's Manors and Mansion Houses*. I heaved it out and sat down on some steps abandoned by one of the librarians.

It had been printed in 1912 and had been taken out only half a dozen times since. Turning to the index at the back, I ran quickly through the lists of halls, abbeys and courts until I found it. There was only a single page reference, as if the author had felt it should be included but was unable to dredge up much about it. I leafed through the pages, missing the right one twice, until finally there it was: just a couple of paragraphs tacked on the end of a chapter about another, better known, house in the same part of the county.

Of course the English seat of the Fitzmorris family is not the only estate in the vicinity. Just a few miles to the west in the neighbouring valley, hidden to all but the most prying eyes, is the Fiercombe estate.

A place of uncertain origin and mixed fortunes, it has lately shunned attention, withdrawing quietly into the deepest recesses of the silent valley as if to blot out painful memories and to sink, gratefully, into a healing slumber. The trees that cloak and obscure the valley floor so well are a rare remnant of an ancient wood much reduced elsewhere but surviving here even as the people who own it come and go.

The estate's golden era ended as the last century dwindled away. It had enjoyed a brief flicker of local fame under the stewardship of the sixth baronet, Edward Stanton, and his wife Elizabeth, a renowned beauty, but those halcyon days turned out to be few indeed. Today, the springtime rambler is not encouraged to walk the paths that meander through the trees and bluebells towards a manor house completed when another Elizabeth was on the throne and now all but forgotten.

Elizabeth. That was the first time I saw her name. What did I think, if anything? I'm sure I traced the letters with my finger; perhaps I even whispered it under my breath, the hiss of the second syllable, the sigh of the last. But that was all. My interest in her and the estate's history was fleeting then – a faint glimmer of intrigue that glowed, then dimmed, though not before it had lodged itself at the back of my mind, ready to be brought out later. There, in the library close to home, close to everything that was familiar, she was not yet able to drown out the clamour of my own thoughts. It was later that she would come alive to me, when I was in the place that had once been hers.

I looked up from the book to see that it had started to rain outside, heavy gouts spattering the glass unevenly as the wind flung it about. My eyes went back to the stark black type on the page. Fiercombe. Tomorrow I would be there, among those ancient trees. I put my hand to my stomach and felt again the now-familiar jolt of disbelief and fear.

The day I was due to depart London for the west dawned mild and bright, a pink blush colouring the sky. I didn't need to leave for Paddington until after nine but I woke at five and was unable to get back to sleep, staring instead at the faded roses of my bedroom wallpaper, my insides tightly strung with nerves.

When it was finally time to go, my mother announced that I didn't need both of them to accompany me to the station and that she would stay behind. At the door, she pulled me back inside so none of the neighbours would hear her. 'Mind you don't get yourself into any more trouble,' she said, as she squeezed my arm. She was unwilling to show me any other sign of affection but her face was drawn and her eyes were puffy. 'You don't know how fortunate you are to be going there.'

She bent to straighten the hem of the light summer coat I had bought with the last of my wages, the generous cut almost successful in hiding my altered figure.

'Write and tell us how you find it,' she said. 'You know I won't be able to come until you're ready to have it, don't you? We can't possibly afford the expense of a visit before then.'

I tried to think about how things would be for me beyond the labour and the giving away of the baby in London's anonymous heart, but found I couldn't. It seemed as remote to me as hearing about something that would happen to someone else, many years from now.

Once we reached Paddington, I insisted that my father

didn't wait for the train to leave. He had said barely a word to me on the journey from home and I didn't think I could stand the tension between us a moment longer. The panic that for weeks had risen inside me whenever I thought about going away, nasty spurts of fear that only sleep could temporarily quell, had actually eased a little now I was on my way. I knew I would feel better still once I was alone.

'Please don't wait,' I said again, when he seemed reluctant to move. 'It won't go for almost half an hour yet.'

'Well, if you're sure,' he said, and considered me properly for the first time in weeks.

I glanced away because I thought I would cry if I didn't. My father had always made me feel quietly adored and I didn't seem to have ruined that entirely. He pulled me towards him briefly, then patted me awkwardly on the back. 'Take good care of yourself, won't you?' he said, and when I looked up from searching in my handbag for a handkerchief he had done as I asked, just as he always had, and vanished into the mêlée of the station concourse.

My hand was trembling as I pulled the door of the second-class carriage shut behind me and took a seat. After what seemed an age the whistle was blown, the last door was slammed and the train started to move off down the platform. I had unthinkingly chosen a seat facing backwards and, as we picked up speed and pulled away from the station's grimy bulk, I experienced the unnerving sensation of watching my hitherto life recede into nothing.

As we gathered speed across the metal tangle of tracks that erupted out of Paddington, I reflected on how strange it felt to be making a journey I had last done as a little girl. My mother had grown up just five miles north of the valley that shields Fiercombe Manor from the rest of the world, so this was a journey she had done many more times than I, clattering back towards the easy green fields of her girlhood.

She had left for London to work in service when she was sixteen. My father, a groundsman whom she had met a few years later, was a Londoner who didn't understand the appeal of the open countryside. On the contrary, he had found the silence and emptiness oppressive on his sole visit to meet my mother's family. It was too dark to sleep, he said, and never went again.

By the time I was born – a good way into the marriage – a pattern had already been established: my mother visited Painswick once each summer while my father stayed at home. In my earliest years I went with her, but at some point that had changed, my mother deciding there was no sense in taking a child on a long, stuffy train journey. After that I went to my father's sister in Archway instead.

My own memories of Gloucestershire soon narrowed to a few crystalline images: my grandmother's dresser with its ranks of blue willow-pattern plates; a morning when I was allowed to eat slice after slice of buttered toast because my mother wasn't there to say I was greedy; being wrenched through a late summer field by a dog that was stronger than me. After I had stopped going to stay, my Gloucestershire relatives seemed content enough with a new studio photograph of me every so often. There was apparently no thought of them coming to London. After my grandparents died, within months of each other when I was ten, we seemed to lose touch with the rest of them. Now I was returning, though I could never have predicted the reason for it.

The first leg of the journey passed quickly. I was hungry – I was always hungry by then – so I made my way to the buffet car and treated myself to a round of ham sandwiches, which I washed down with lemonade. I hadn't experienced any strange cravings, only the urge to eat lots of red meat and anything sugary. My mother had a sweet tooth and bought herself a weekly quarter of pear drops but I wasn't usually very partial. Now, however, I drank the glass bottle of lemonade as if it was water and went back to the counter to buy an iced bun. The man who took my money nodded his approval. 'I like to see a lady enjoy her food,' he said.

I smiled but put a defensive arm across my stomach, though I knew I didn't show much in my new coat.

I changed trains at Swindon and, though it was hardly the countryside, I fancied the air smelt different from the fresh-cut-grass scent of London's parks. It was earthier, with a hint of fresh manure that I found I quite liked. The branch-line train was rickety and slow, stopping so regularly that it never gathered any real pace. Unlike the deep cuttings of brick the Victorians had built to bury London's railway tracks from the terraces above, here we trundled through on high, the rails snaking along the ridges of lush valleys.

Finally we came to a jerky standstill at Stonehouse, where I'd been told to get off. The small platform soon cleared of people, with no one left looking for me, so I made my way out to the front of the station. A single, battered van idled there, its driver sound asleep, and a couple of boys were sitting on the kerb next to their bicycles, which they had flung down carelessly.

I had been wondering what on earth I was to do when a clopping sound made the boys look up. I followed their gaze. A horse pulling an open carriage was approaching in unhurried fashion. A weather-beaten man, wearing a flat cap low over his forehead, was holding the reins. As he turned into the station forecourt I realized with a start that he had come for me. The boys, also realizing this, grinned in my direction. I wondered bewilderedly what else awaited me.

The driver introduced himself simply as 'Ruck' before swinging my case into the footwell and helping me up on to the narrow seat. Behind us the carriage's seats were covered with sacking and strewn with an assortment of tools but it would have been quite grand when it was new.

We processed silently through a series of small villages, the iron-shod hoofs of the horse muffled by the earth road. The honey-coloured hamlets, where the cottages invariably cleaved towards an exquisite church, were even more picturesque than postcards and packets of fudge had given me to imagine – and much more so than I had noticed as a tiny girl. After Paddington's tired terraces, grubby streets and draughty terminus, it was almost obscenely pretty.

I knew nothing of the local topography then, still accustomed as I was to an orderly kind of nature, bound within the tidy perimeters of London's sprawling suburbs, the bright squares of lawn and plump hedges tended by office men after hours. I found out later that these villages, so sturdily set among the lanes and luxuriant pastures, are in fact balanced on a narrow ridge that runs between two deep valleys. This up-thrust of land marks the place where the Berkeley Vale meets the Cotswold escarpment. Beneath the rich, loamy soil two distinctly different types of bedrock have fused together; evidence of some ancient geological cataclysm of which there is no sign on the surface.

About an hour passed before we began our descent into the narrower and deeper of the two valleys, the very last of the Cotswolds' combes to the west. As the land fell away I reached for the handle of my case to stop it tumbling off into the dirt, and braced my knees against the front of the carriage. My other arm lay protectively across my lap. I saw Ruck's eyes flicker over me as I moved and wondered if there was a smirk on his weather-cracked lips.

'Won't be long now,' he said, his voice loud in air that had grown stiller yet. 'Though you won't find a deeper bottom in these parts.'

I blushed at the last words, feeling foolish for doing so. Later I discovered that he wasn't really making fun of me; that 'bottom', like 'combe', is a local word for valley. Or perhaps he was being sly, knowing I would be ignorant about such things and ill at ease in a strange place.

As we descended deeper, the light changed, turning ever more green and fractured as we passed beneath the thickening canopy of leaves.

'What trees are these?' I said a little shakily, to prove I wasn't bothered by the previous comment. He looked right at me then and, despite the diminished light, I could see the broken veins that fanned out across his cheeks from his nose.

'Beeches they is,' he said gruffly. 'There's bluebells here in spring, acres of 'em spread out through the trees as far as the eye can see. Like a carpet, they says. Folk come to look at 'em, folk from Stroud, sometimes Chelt'nham.

You've missed 'em this year. You're not too late for the glow-worms, though. You'll see them come dusk in July if you look hard enough. Some summers bring 'undreds of 'em to the loneliest corners of the Great Mead.'

I gripped the seat with my hand as we hit a deep rut in the lane, gritting my teeth as I imagined the baby being jostled about dangerously. Perhaps that would be no bad thing; I could go home to London if . . . I forced away the thought and glanced at Ruck to see if he'd noticed my discomfort. Perhaps he had because the pace slowed a little.

'There's not many that comes this way,' he said, as he pulled on the reins. 'It's the one public road in the valley but it's hard to find. There's folk who've lived round here all their lives what don't know about it or else don't bother with it. Too easy to get lost. Too many tracks off to the side that don't lead nowhere.

'O' course in the winter it's impassable. Or, rather, you can get down it easy enough – if it's icy, you'll be in the Great Mead wrong way up before you knows it – but you won't get out again. In high summer it cracks like a dried-up riverbed. Times in between it floods. Once you're down there, you stays.'

'Don't the family mind it?' I said. 'It must be terribly inconvenient.' I heard my voice, like a stranger's, in the unmoving air and it sounded shrill and affected. I felt the heat rise again in my cheeks.

'The Stantons? They's growed used to it, I s'pose,' he said. 'Or the maister has. Sir Charles. He were born to living in the country. Lady Stanton don't like it much, her think it too quiet. It's she what makes sure they're overseas most of the year now.'

'They don't ever spend the summers here?'

Ruck shook his head. 'Hardly the winters neither. It's France they goes to.' He drew out the *a* in France to a long 'aah'.

'Apart from a couple o' days last Christmas they haven't been back for nearly two year now. Down south to the French resorts they goes. Her was promised that by the maister, that when the younger boy were grown they didn't have to spend another summer here.'

'But why? I'm sure the winters can be hard but the summers must be glorious.'

He shook his head again. 'Her can't abide 'em since . . . Well, there were a bad summer here. Since then her's got notions about things. Sleeps bad. Flits around, she does, with this look on her face. The melan-cholic, they calls it. O' course, some of us are kept too busy to have it.'

He laughed then, a dry, creaking sound that made me shudder slightly, though it was harmless enough. By the time he'd recovered we were approaching a fork in the lane, no doubt one of the many that deceived the unwary.

'I'll take you the slow way down to the manor,' he said, his gruff manner resumed. 'You'll get a good look at it then.'

He pulled the horse off to the left, on to a path that was yet more pitted and overhung with beeches, their lowest limbs pressing in towards us as though they hadn't been cut back for a long time. It seemed as though dusk had already fallen under those heavy boughs, the light leached out of the day, although my wristwatch told me it was only half past two. I tapped the small circle of glass and the long hand jumped as though it had stopped some minutes back.

Instead of the steep path that had been leading us directly towards the valley floor, we now seemed to be weaving our way down a gently looping course. I allowed my legs to relax but kept hold of my case as the turns were sharp. The trees to our right soon grew sparser, the sunlight breaking through bravely to light up the brambles and tinge the ferns sepia.

'Keep your eye out,' said Ruck. 'Any second now you'll see 'er to your left.'

Slowing the horse as we turned another corner, he gestured off to the left, where the trees were thinner still. I sat up straighter as I caught the first glimpse, a flash of soft, sunlit gold among the dun-coloured bark of the beeches.

'Is that it?' I said softly, as if speaking too loudly would make it disappear altogether.

'That's the manor,' he replied, as triumphant as if it was his own. 'You'll get a better look if you hang on there. Keep looking now.'

He was right. At the next bend the trees had been cleared, presumably deliberately, to reveal and frame a three-gabled house made of the same stone as the cottages high up on the ridge. After the dim light of the wood it seemed even more golden than those more modest dwellings, its stone warmed by sunrays that had managed to reach over the steep valley walls and drench it.

The manor, I realized, was not very large. It made some of the grander houses I'd seen on postcards seem overblown by comparison. The glowering woods encroaching upon its north side made it look smaller still; a noble house in miniature. I was glad of this: where the wild valley was intimidating, the manor, reposing quietly in the sunshine, seemed welcoming.

Ruck looked over at me, clearly wanting some kind of response.

'It's a beautiful house,' I said truthfully. 'Much more beautiful than many of the more famous ones.'

He seemed satisfied with that. 'It's older than most of 'em too,' he said, as we negotiated another hairpin bend in the road. 'The gables were all built separate, you know. There's two hundred year between the eastern and western ends.'

'It's Elizabethan, isn't it?' I ventured, half remembering the small footnote I'd found in the library about it. 'The period it was completed in, I mean.'

'I don' know about that, miss. Five hundred year or more some of it's stood. That's all I know.'

When I think back to that memory, that first glimpse of Fiercombe Manor and the valley it seemed almost entombed in, I cannot recall any sense of unease. Beyond the mild embarrassment of being in close proximity to a stranger and the constant state of anxiety I was in about the baby, I felt almost grateful to be away from London and the chilly disapproval of my mother. I think I even felt a glimmer of something approaching enthusiasm at the thought of exploring the place, of it becoming known to me, its secret corners commonplace, and of seeing it as late spring eased into summer. It seems amazing in the light of what happened but I can't say I felt any foreboding about the valley at all. All the trepidation swirling around inside me was bound up in how convincingly I would be able to lie to Mrs Jelphs and what would happen to me after I returned to London, once the baby had been born and taken away, and I had to begin again.

After a time the ground began to level off: we had reached the valley floor.

'Not long now,' he said.

We rounded another corner and, quite suddenly, we were free of the woods and out into the sunshine. There wasn't a breath of wind so deep in the valley and I wondered vaguely if I would find it uncomfortable when I was bigger, and summer had come. It was as I was thinking this, absentmindedly stroking my stomach as I had taken to doing whenever I wasn't otherwise occupied, that I saw the graveyard and the tiny church in the far corner of it. Though I tried to cover it, the sight made me start.

Ruck nodded towards it. 'Only Mrs Jelphs ever uses the chapel now. There was a time when more came, when people was still here. They rang the bells then.'

'I assumed the nearest village was the one at the top of the valley,' I said. 'Stanwick, was it? Is there another?'

'Fiercombe had its own village of sorts. It weren't just the Stantons, you know. In the last century there was forty or more folk what worked the land or were in the house, or were family to those who did.'

I looked across the graveyard and the stones that punctuated the uneven ground, some of them listing dangerously, others sinking into the earth as though it were quicksand. He was right, of course: they couldn't all have been from one family. In the middle stood a tree, its slender trunk gnarled and twisted but its branches hidden by a profusion of pink blossom. Barely a petal littered the grass beneath, so undisturbed was the air.

'What happened to them all?' I asked.

He paused before answering. 'Fortunes come and go. When the big house went there wasn't any work to be had. Where they might have gone to Stroud or Painswick fifty year before, there was hardly no wool trade left to take 'em. In a few short years they was gone, as if they had never been here at all. The present family came here as the new century began but it were never the same. Now there's just a few of us what's left.'

'But where did they all live?' I pressed on. My glimpses of the place had not revealed any signs of a village, even an abandoned one. The valley felt entirely empty to me.

'You'll see if you go for a wander. There's a few cottages left, mostly tumbledown. A couple burnt to the ground. Others there's nothing left but the foundations and the weeds have hidden them well enough. Nettles high as your chest there now.'

We had by now passed the chapel and its lonely graveyard and I leant forward in expectation of my first proper look at the manor. Up close it was no less golden, the stone not only reflecting the late spring sunlight but apparently exuding a rich glow of its own. The age of the building and the hard winters it must have endured had softened every edge so that there was not a straight line to be seen. From timber to roof tile to window ledge, all was slightly askew, sloping, buckling or otherwise returning to the haphazard laws of Nature.

We came to a halt at the eastern end of the house. Ruck did not help me but he did take my case and wait for me while I clambered down awkwardly, clearing his throat and looking the other way in a manner that made me like him more. He led the way through a small but lovely kitchen garden that seemed very well tended. It was wonderfully fragrant, and even my city-deadened senses told me that mint, rosemary and sage all grew there. Behind tall ranks of hollyhocks, heavy ivy clung to the garden's walls and snaked up and around towards what I guessed was the intended front of the house. I decided that I would see it for myself, once I'd had a wash and changed my clothes. I lingered for a moment in the garden and, despite everything, felt something like anticipation swell in me. Behind the show-off perfume of the flowers you could smell something subtler: the first intimations of summer.

I looked back up at the valley walls, so steep that they might have been built for the very purpose of concealing my shame from the rest of the world. All this was to be my home for the coming months yet I had no idea what those months would bring. I wondered if I would be unhappy and lonely here, or whether Mrs Jelphs would guess what trouble I had really got myself into in London and send me back. A picture of James, as vivid as if he were standing in the little garden, flashed across my mind but, with all my strength, I pushed it away. Taking a shaky breath, I turned to the ancient door and pushed it open, telling myself it was going to be a single summer, that was all; a summer in limbo in the deepest countryside. I could never have imagined all that would happen in those few short months and how, by the end of them, my life would have altered irrevocably and for ever.

He just wanted a decent book to read ...

Not too much to ask, is it? It was in 1935 when Allen Lane, Managing Director of Bodley Head Publishers, stood on a platform at Exeter railway station looking for something good to read on his journey back to London. His choice was limited to popular magazines and poor-quality paperbacks – the same choice faced every day by the vast majority of readers, few of whom could afford hardbacks. Lane's disappointment and subsequent anger at the range of books generally available led him to found a company – and change the world.

'We believed in the existence in this country of a vast reading public for intelligent books at a low price, and staked everything on it'
Sir Allen Lane, 1902–1970, founder of Penguin Books

The quality paperback had arrived – and not just in bookshops. Lane was adamant that his Penguins should appear in chain stores and tobacconists, and should cost no more than a packet of cigarettes.

Reading habits (and cigarette prices) have changed since 1935, but Penguin still believes in publishing the best books for everybody to enjoy. We still believe that good design costs no more than bad design, and we still believe that quality books published passionately and responsibly make the world a better place.

So wherever you see the little bird – whether it's on a piece of prize-winning literary fiction or a celebrity autobiography, political tour de force or historical masterpiece, a serial-killer thriller, reference book, world classic or a piece of pure escapism – you can bet that it represents the very best that the genre has to offer.

Whatever you like to read – trust Penguin.